soybean
REVOLUTION

soybean
REVOLUTION

CHRIS BENTLEY

ISBN 979-8-9850664-4-9

Library of Congress Control Number: 2024908956

Cover and interior design by Tamara Cribley, The Deliberate Page

Printed in the United States of America

Email: Connect@ChrisBentleyInc.com

Visit www.ChrisBentleyInc.com

Facebook: @cbentley1160, Instagram: @christoph.w.bentley
& Twitter: @chris1bentley2

For my family with love

chapter 1

Gwen knew the moment wouldn't last, but still, she tried her best to hold on to it as long as she could. The problem was, though, the harder she tried to stay in the moment and feel the warming sunlight that was inching its way up her ragged denim jacket and the cool breeze that, without that sunlight, would make things too cold as she sat perched on her tree branch in a sickly oak tree by the industrial riverbank, the harder it was to stay in that moment.

Memories kept flooding back—the elevator ride, basement-level corridors, loss . . .

She shook the memory away, and only after the sun had blanketed her face with the early light did she let out a long sigh, allowing her lungs to deflate completely.

She reflected back to a year before when she'd lived in each moment—it came out of necessity. Now that she had bigger worries than where she would find food or a decent place to shelter each night, she had started to experience a problem with distractions for the first time.

"Hey Gwen!"

Talking about distractions. "Hey, Stan. What's up?"

"We're all gathered like you asked," Stan said with a smile that made the wrinkles around his eyes pop out, although his unusually youthful appearance meant that he could hide them pretty well otherwise. His average-sized frame was much more impressive with him standing on the hill at the start of the river's small beach and with the long morning shadows shooting off to his left side. Gwen had only known Stan for a couple of months. He was one of the first to sign up for their movement when asked by his best friend. Their mutual best friend.

"Great. I'll be right there," Gwen said as she looked for the best hand-hold for jumping off the sturdy branch she had been sitting on. "Wait a second. When you say all, do you really mean all, or is it more of a well, I told them all to come, so maybe they'll all be there eventually?"

Stan gave Gwen a grin that told her she didn't have to rush back to the abandoned warehouse she still used as her headquarters for their operations. She sprung down from the branch and landed on the gravel bank with practiced ease. She moved her cold legs toward the building where, by then, she hoped most of the people she needed would be assembled.

Gwen took one last look at the sun glinting off the cool gray of the river. But that cool gray was warming to deeper greens as the sun hit the massive marble monuments beyond the river, with ivy starting to weave its way into the cracks. Those monuments had been major tourist attractions of the city once called Washington D.C., she'd learned last year.

She'd learned a lot in the past year, actually, and not only about the history of the city she lived in. She'd learned that important people called senators probably drove in fancy cars to debate decisions for a country that was called the United States of America. A country she had never known, but for some reason, she was fighting to bring back. That was all Jefferson's fault.

Jefferson. So many thoughts and memories and pain and loss were now associated with that name. To say that he had been a friend or a mentor would hardly be a fair assessment of the relationship they had had before he was taken. Maybe a foster parent? Or was it more like a step-father? She shrugged. Since her parents had died when she was young, she didn't have a lot of practice when it came to family. But she had begun to experience family, she thought, in the sense of things being okay with the world because she was with someone who knew her, who cared about her separately from what she could bring to the table, somehow.

Jefferson's farm hadn't been just another place to sleep and to eat. It was as much of a home as anywhere she'd been in a very long time. Maybe for as long as she could remember. Being with Jefferson and trying to keep the things he had started alive and feeling the sense of connection from the crew members helped her to warm up to the idea of family, too. Maybe family had more to do with feeling safe and supported than with biology, because she was feeling similar home vibes about the crew she worked with and the warehouse that was their home base.

She held her breath for ten seconds, then slowly released it and ducked into the darkness of the warehouse. A group of shabbily dressed people, ranging from teenagers, with their mops of frizzy curls, to older members, with silver and white strands, shifted their legs absently either out of boredom or to try to fight the cold. Gwen pulled her jacket collar around her neck, realizing that it was nearly as cold in the warehouse as it was outside, where she definitely wished she could be at that moment. She cleared her throat and raised her hands, trying to get the group's attention.

The general murmur gradually subsided.

"Morning!" she said far too loudly and brightly.

The people closest to her winced.

"Sorry. I mean, good morning. Is that better?" She was rewarded with a few chuckles. *I'll take even sympathy laughs at this point.*

"I know a lot has changed in the last few months. You signed up to follow one person you knew and trusted, and now that person is gone, and I wouldn't blame any of you for wondering why you're still a part of any of this." Gwen fought the catch in her throat—and the thought that she was talking to a bunch of adults. *Keep it together!* "But you're still here. Maybe that's because you really like sleeping on lousy cots in cold, damp warehouses, drinking bad coffee, and eating military-style meals . . ."

"Hey! I'm cooking practically gourmet here!"

"Sorry, Stan. Of course you are," she said over the roar of laughter.

"Anyway, we all have our reasons for staying. For me, to be totally honest, it's mainly about continuing what we started because of who started it."

Gwen let the weight of the last statement sink in for a few breaths as a heaviness in her chest made it harder to breathe.

"Jefferson was a force of nature and a great leader. I'm certainly not that. I'm trying and learning and growing so much from working with you-all. And I promise I'm doing the best I can every day so he can be proud of what we've done when we get him back, hopefully very soon. So what do we need to do today?"

A few moments of awkward silence hung in the air, but thankfully, someone eventually spoke up.

"I'm determined to get our network systems back online today. I'm a bit ashamed of myself that it's taken me this many weeks to get things running."

Gwen nodded appreciatively, grateful for two reasons—for being saved from that awkward silence, but also because they really did need those networks connected. The whole reason they were in D.C. relied on tapping into the bank corporations' networks. So, without that, the whole group was basically just hanging out.

"Thanks, James. I know you'll get that done. Nice! Who's next?" She scanned the crowd with her arm, trying to bring up the energy in the room.

"I'll keep trying to figure out Jefferson's code signature that made it so easy for the slum lords to recognize him. I think I'm making some progress."

"Great. Thanks, Sam. That's really important. Our whole plan is built around corrupting their systems, and we don't want to underestimate them like last time."

Last time, she thought. Last time when Jefferson was in charge and back when she naively believed that everything had to work out because she believed so completely in Jefferson. Jefferson, who for all any of them knew, was still locked up with the contract enforcers.

The group slowly woke up, and several other task leads reported their goals for the day. By the end of the conversation, Gwen felt something close to hope, which she considered a definite win. "Thanks, everybody. Let's get after it!" I really need to work on that motivational speaker crap.

"Hey, Gwen, got an extra second?"

Gwen turned to the now-familiar voice.

"Sure thing, Stan. What's up?"

Stan smiled his warm smile that made Gwen smile right back despite the weight of everything on her shoulders. The morning sun was hitting Stan's mop of salt-and-pepper hair so that the white and silver streams showed through much more. Stan stood there, silent and smiling, for a few long seconds. Too many seconds for Gwen's anxious mind.

"You said you needed—"

"Yeah, but hold on," Stan said, cutting Gwen off.

"Come on, Stan, you know I have a lot to do today," Gwen said, looking past Stan to other people moving around racks of computer parts.

"How are you, Gwen?" Stan asked.

"What do you mean? I'm fine, I guess."

"No, I mean for real. How are you? Don't think we don't know how much weight you're carrying."

Gwen let the tension in her shoulders slowly drop, realizing that tension had been there all morning.

"Thanks for asking, Stan," she said, grateful for the way Stan always seemed to know when she needed a friendly check-in. "I'm doing okay, I think. All things considered. One day at a time, you know?"

"That's right. Good way to live. When Jefferson contacted me to ask for help taking down the big bad banks, you know what I thought?"

"What?" Gwen asked with true curiosity.

"There was no way in hell that it would actually work."

That was not what Gwen had expected, and her blank expression must have shown Stan that she didn't know how to respond.

"Don't get me wrong—Jefferson's plan was well-thought-out, like his generally are. And I hoped it would work out or that we'd be able to smack the banks around a bit, at least. To show them they aren't so smart."

Stan put hands on Gwen's shoulders and squeezed gently. Gwen was surprised to feel the warmth of his hands permeate through her jacket.

"What I'm trying to say is, all of us might have joined up for this venture for our own reasons, but I doubt many of us really thought we'd succeed triumphantly or anything like that."

"Great. So you're saying I'm working with a bunch of suicidal, misguided mental cases," Gwen said flippantly.

"Yes. AND"—Stan paused for dramatic effect—"you don't have to convince everybody every day that the plan that Jefferson had going or the one you're trying to salvage is a sure-fire thing. The people who've stayed will stick around for their own reasons. You're doing fine. That's all. Okay?"

Stan gave Gwen's shoulders one more friendly squeeze and smiled again.

"Thanks, Stan. I needed that, I think. I guess I have my own reasons for wanting Jefferson's plan to still work—that has nothing to do with the banks—too."

"Absolutely! Like the rest of us. And, on a separate topic, there's a slight problem. Not anything to worry about really, but I thought you'd probably want to know," Stan folded his arms across his chest and nervously rocked from his heels to his toes.

Gwen raised an eyebrow, feeling her shoulders inch back up to their former strained position.

"We have maybe a week's worth of food left."

"You call that something not to worry about, Stan? That is exactly the sort of thing to worry about. Are you sure we only have a week's worth left? Let's go over things together," Gwen frantically dashed in the direction of their food cache.

"Stop, Gwen. Wait. I promise that's all we have."

"Okay, then let's gather a group to go into the city to see what we can scrounge up. I used to be good at that. I could lead the group on raids like I did this spring—"

"Gwen, hold on. I think I have a good solution. That's why I said not to worry. I'll get it taken care of. Again, just thought you'd want to know," Stan said with a touch of false confidence.

Gwen slowly walked back toward Stan. "Well, yeah! Thanks for letting me know. What are we going to do about it?" Her mind was still racing to think of new sources of food they might be able to find quickly.

"We are going to let Stan figure it out. The role of head chef carries a heavy burden, but one I'm willing to carry bravely. And to the bitter end," Stan said, striking a dramatic soldier-at-attention pose.

"Great. So now you're mocking me and giving me something to worry about. Very kind of you, Stan," Gwen tried to fight a smile, realizing how serious of an issue this might be for their operations. People might have their own reasons for staying, but they wouldn't stay long if they didn't have food, at least occasionally. "So, what is this grand plan of yours?" She rubbed her neck, which was tightening by the moment.

"Members of our group have connections to some rather impressive farming operations that have been running off the grid for years."

"And by off-grid, do you mean shady? I'd say illegal, but that word doesn't really mean anything without police, right?"

"Right. Not illegal. Just not a part of the mainstream farmer's market supply chain. And these farms I'm talking about tend to help support operations like ours."

"So, you mean, then, that they are supporting people trying to disrupt the way things are now?"

"Precisely! Yes! It'll take some logistical maneuvering to coordinate with one of the farms, but we'll get things fixed up before we run out of everything."

Gwen thought back to where she used to live. Kansas. Part of the forgotten middle of the country. The part people got away from, if they could, after the Economic Wars and after the government safety nets were gone. Most of those who couldn't get away were dead by the time Gwen was barely getting by on leftover scraps—after the bank corporation abolished the world's governments and replaced them with a meritocracy.

"Have you ever thought about what a funny word meritocracy is?" Gwen asked more to herself than to Stan.

"I guess not. What makes it so funny? It doesn't strike me as being all that funny. Not now." Stan shrugged.

"Oh, yeah. Sorry. Thinking out loud, I guess. But the word is built around the word merit, which has such a perky, positive ring to it, doesn't it?"

Stan nodded with an acknowledging smile.

"Who'd ever think that so much mess would be caused by such a friendly term? That's all." Gwen ran her hands through her long dark-brown hair in thought. "Anyway, so we're good with the food situation? We're not all going to have to eat hope for breakfast?" Gwen asked with an uneasy smile, her mind still racing but a bit less fast, as hope and some confidence in Stan's ability counteracted some of her anxiety.

Stan grinned back. "Nice play on my words, my friend! Love it! Yes, we actually have a meeting with one of the larger independent farming operations set up this afternoon."

"Oh? That's great!"

"The jury's kind of still out on that one."

"The jury's out . . . I'm trying to catch up on old world-order phrases, but that's one I definitely don't know."

"Oh. Sorry, Gwen. It was a major part of the legal system. A jury used to be made up of a bunch of regular folks who heard arguments from lawyers, and they got to decide who won the case."

Gwen tried her best to understand. But the thought of having the sort of people she had interacted with in the wilds of Kansas determining the ruling of court cases seemed absolutely ridiculous.

"Which makes a lot more sense when you see it than when I try to describe it. Boy, hearing myself describe it makes it sound pretty . . . well . . . unbelievable. Anyway, the jury would leave the courtroom to discuss the case amongst themselves and make their verdict, so the phrase, the jury's still out means something isn't as clear as one might want it to be."

"Got it. Thanks. Sorry I asked, sort of." She shook her head. "But go on. Why isn't it a clear, wonderful thing that we're meeting with a group who can help us not starve?"

"Oh, we're not meeting with a group. We're meeting with Gerty."

"Gerty? Is that an acronym of some sort?"

"No. She's a woman. Gertrude. Completely a woman. But everybody calls her Gerty."

"I'm not even going to guess at what you mean by that, Stan," Gwen said, realizing that she was feeling a bit offended. Completely a woman.

"Let's say she's a bit of a firebrand. I'm sure she'll like you. She and I have a bit of a past." Stan scratched the back of his neck nervously.

"One of these days, you'll have to fill me in on what you mean, but lucky for you, I have a lot to do this morning. Question though—that past of yours won't kill the deal with Gerty, will it?" Gwen asked with a raised eyebrow.

"We'll have to wait and see."

"That's not encouraging, Stan—"

"I know. It might work to our advantage. At least we have some familiarity going in our favor."

"Let's hope so. No! You've got me hoping, too, now. It's a disease, I swear."

"Let's hope it's starting to spread, then," Stan said with a thoughtful nod.

Gwen nodded back, and with that, Stan walked off toward the make-shift kitchen area, which was little more than a sink and a couple of camp burners that somehow Stan had converted into a very functional kitchen where he worked miracles on practically every meal he made.

I sure hope it's spreading. Stan's eternal optimism helped. She pulled out a crumpled scrap of paper from her jacket pocket and ran through her to-do list.

1. *Give inspirational speech to rally the troops first thing in the morning.* Check. Well, she had said some words that might resemble a speech.

2. *Re-establish connection to the street kids.* Lots of steps buried inside that one. She still felt awful about the way she'd left things with that ragtag group. That one would be a work in progress, but she was definitely making some strides.

3. *Encourage the network team.* Gwen had no formal computer training, so she knew she wouldn't be any help with that, other than making sure the team had what they needed. So that's what she would do.

4. *Figure out what their next big push would be to attack the banks since their original plan fell on its face.* That was a harsh way of putting it, she had to admit, but they had definitely failed. The banks had picked up on the anomaly they were putting into their code far too quickly, and from most of the reports she had gotten from her feelers in the more-corporate systems nearby, the small disruptions they had made with Jefferson's inserted code had been smoothed out over the last couple of months. That one would certainly be a work in progress, too.

And now she had a new one. She flattened the piece of paper the best she could and pulled out a chiseled yellow number-two pencil that was about a quarter-length of its original size and showed clear bite marks. Using her leg as a makeshift desk, she did her best to write down the new task.

5. *Get food.* Lots of steps.

She was rather amazed by all the logistics their small operation took to keep running. It made her admire the world-changing movements she had read about at Jefferson's house that much more—the Civil War, Mao's Red Revolution, the Feminist Movement.

I doubt very many people think about how much toilet paper those groups used up during their cause. Or how much food, for that matter. She sure hoped Stan would pull yet another miracle on that one. She rolled her shoulders back a few times and made a mental note to not hunch them so much and to trust her crew more. Sometimes she honestly wondered why they stuck with her, given how capable they all were. The least she could do was trust them a bit more. She had found a way to do that with street kids. She could certainly find confidence in competent adults. With that in mind, she headed toward the activity in a corner of the warehouse where computer parts that looked like random pieces of scrap metal were being put together.

Jefferson, what in the world have you gotten me mixed up in?

chapter 2

Gwen had to admit it—Stan had pulled off what she had assumed was the impossible. He had arranged a meeting with the largest food-distributing operation, working outside of the global mega-farm operations on the Eastern Seaboard. As she rode in the passenger seat next to Stan on their way to the farm, her nerves started to get the better of her though.

She took a couple of deep breaths and put a foot up on the dash, but immediately took the foot down. "Sorry," she said sheepishly.

"This hunk of bolts? You can keep your feet up all you want. Though she has good bones and could almost pass for vintage," Stan said, pulling up the armrest dividing him and Gwen.

"Thanks, Stan. So, remind me, what's our strategy here?"

"Hmmm . . . strategy doesn't exactly jive with Gerty," Stan said, keeping his eyes fixed on the rough road in front of them.

"Okay. Then how are we going to play this?" She started to fidget and brought her foot down to the floor of the truck a bit harder than gravity would have done on its own.

"We'll talk to Gerty. Explain our situation without giving up too much, especially the fact that we have less than a week's worth of food left, and see what she says."

Gwen waited a few seconds for more.

"That's it? That's your game plan?" Gwen asked, glad that her seat belt was on so she couldn't reach Stan because, in that moment, she wanted to wring his neck.

"Like I said, Gerty isn't the sort of person you can win over with a polished presentation or someone that you can hope to convince." A smile slowly played across Stan's face, and his eyes took on a distant look.

Gwen rolled her eyes and folded her arms in disgust.

"She's way too smart for that." Stan cleared his throat and ran his hand through his hair thoughtfully. "She'll feel us out. If she likes us, and I think and hope she will, we'll seal the deal. If not, we'll figure something else out. At least if I remember her right."

Gwen couldn't quite figure out why Stan was being so fluid with the plan. He had always struck her as very matter-of-fact, the man with a plan. He ran his kitchen like a military operation, after all. She just didn't get it. But then the truth became obvious.

"You still have feelings for Gerty."

"No—"

"Yes you do! It's obvious. The stoic, far-off look in your eyes, the natural smile on your face. It's all this, 'Gerty will feel us out' and 'She's way too smart for that.' Come on, Stan! And you're betting our whole operation by feeling things out when you have complicated feelings towards the person who is the answer to our number-one problem? Seriously, Stan!" she yelled in disbelief.

"What do you want me to say?" Stan said, shifting the arm he had at the steering wheel.

"Just the truth," Gwen threw back at him.

"Okay. You got me. Maybe I have one or two ulterior motives."

"And those motives wouldn't have anything to do with her luscious lips and the way she moves those hips—"

"Okay. That's enough of that," Stan said, trying to give Gwen a friendly slug without driving them off the road.

Gwen dodged his fist, trying not to laugh because she was still mad at him for how much he was leaving to chance.

"That's a sound I haven't heard come out of you in a while," Stan said.

"What do you mean?" Gwen asked, trying to catch her breath.

"Laughing. I haven't heard you laugh since . . . Well, I'm not sure if I've ever heard it for real since I met you a few months ago. You're pretty good at it. You should do it more often."

"That's because there are so many funny things in our lives right now," Gwen said, meaning it as a throwaway. It felt good to hear Stan validate laughter, but she didn't like being called out, even if Stan was only complimenting her on her laugh.

"We really do," Stan said.

"Come on, Stan. Be serious." She turned away and looked out the window.

"I am! Seriously serious. None of this makes any sense. So we can either get frustrated or laugh about it. I'm sure there's plenty of material out there for my old stand-up routine if I could only pull together an audience."

"What would you be standing up?" Gwen asked, confused.

"Oh, yeah, sorry. Here I go again, exposing my age. Stand-up comics were folks who stood on a stage telling jokes, trying to get an audience to laugh. Some people made boatloads of money doing it."

"Wow, that would not be a job I'd be good at or ever want."

"Really? Coming up with clever ways for people to feel good and laugh?"

"Being on stage and feeling responsible that people are entertained enough to get better moods. That sounds like a nightmare to me," Gwen said.

"I bet there are still some of them out there, even after the shift to more commercialized art with no tax benefits to incentivize folks to donate to foundations or museums."

"By the way, I'm still waiting," Gwen said.

"For what?"

"Your personal motives to want to see Gerty," Gwen said with a grin.

"Not letting me off the hook, eh?" Stan glanced in Gwen's direction. She shook her head.

"Okay. I knew Gerty before the Economic Wars."

"Back when dinosaurs roamed the earth, you mean?"

"Haha. Yeah, way back then," Stan said, slowing down to turn left off the main road and onto a dirt road, which, surprisingly, was much more comfortable to drive on than the pock-marked asphalt. Although, grass had grown up tall enough to be bent down by the truck's undercarriage. "She was studying business at the time, though, as I recall, I thought she was crazy for not studying botany or genetics or something scientific because the house where a party I went to was more plant than human, I swear. She might have been looking into an agricultural master's or something like that after. Well, after we broke things off."

Stan slowed at a fork in the road. Both paths were so shaded by thick undergrowth and trees above that even though it was midmorning on a clear sunny day, Stan flipped on the truck's headlights and kept to a slower pace as he eased onto the right side of the fork.

"Can you check the map to make sure I'm still heading us in the right direction?" Stan asked Gwen, shoving the thick spiral-bound road atlas toward her.

"I can't believe you have a road atlas, Stan. I mean, wouldn't it be easier to pull up directions on a device?" She tentatively turned the pages, trying hard to remember the few lessons Jefferson had given her on reading paper maps on their way to the D.C. area from the farm in Kansas.

"Don't get me started on the dangers of asking AI for directions," Stan said emphatically.

"Okay, when dinosaurs roamed the earth, I'm sure that things were different—"

"I'm not just being old-fashioned this time. Think about it—how do you get directions from a device?"

"Okay, Stan. I'll play." Gwen adjusted herself in her seat so she could prop her head up in her hand with her arm propped up on her window's armrest. "Satellites, I guess."

"That's right. Satellites. And who maintains those? Sends them updates and bug fixes and ensures the networks they're tapping into are secure?"

"Businesses, I guess."

"Ah ha! Yes! Private enterprise. Before the United States government fell apart, it hired military people in Colorado, a state in the western part of the country, who maintained what we called the Global Positioning System, or GPS. One of the most used, under-appreciated government services I've ever heard of," Stan said.

Great, now he's started, Gwen thought. At least we won't run out of things to talk about for the rest of the ride.

Over the next twenty minutes, Stan told Gwen about when the United States government stopped maintaining the GPS and private enterprises took over the satellite business for their own benefit. And something about manipulating search and driving-direction results so that people were more likely to go past certain shops. And how businesses would then track people through the end of their days after that. Gwen tried to keep track of it because, although Stan was famous for pontificating, this time, it really did seem important. But then Stan abruptly stopped talking.

The truck slowed to a crawl, and Stan rolled down his window. Gwen heard the papery stroke of wind sifting through dry tree leaves. It was a lovely sound—one of her favorites, actually. But then she caught a whiff of decaying flesh.

It took Gwen a while to recognize that the body they were driving around had at one time been human. She had been around dead bodies plenty in the past, but this was the first time since Jefferson had taken her in last fall.

Gwen rolled down her window so she could lean out to get a better look. As they passed the body, she saw large gashes where an arm used to be—evidence of wild dogs or coyotes having done their work, while the more surgical body part removal had probably been the work of weasels or birds. Gwen made a mental note to talk about the dangers of wild dog packs in one of her morning briefings with the crew. With no animal control, dogs had to find other unfortunate means of survival.

"Sorry you had to see that," Stan said once they had gotten far enough away from the remains that the smell had mostly faded.

"Not your fault." She shuddered and tried to hide her impulsive revulsion. "But whose fault was it? The picture I had of Gerty is shifting a bit, Stan."

"I can't believe that Gerty would be behind that."

Gwen gave Stan a questioning look.

"Okay. If Gerty is behind that, I'm sure they deserved it."

"Well, I'm sure looking forward to meeting this woman," Gwen replied slowly. "By the way, as far as I can tell from this ancient atlas, you're right on track." Gwen closed the book, careful not to rip the cover off, which was held to the spiral binding by a few tattered threads. "Straight ahead."

Gwen could tell they were getting closer to their destination, not by any direction signs or by consulting the map book again, but by the change in landscape. Where the trees and tall grasses that hugged the roadside grew in bunched and frantic disarray before, she started to see order. Tree limbs were pruned. Dead branches were removed, or piled, at least. The road they were driving along showed a measure of care, too, with tractors' huge tire tracks here and there.

As they were making a particularly wide arching bend, Stan slammed on the brakes in time to avoid colliding with a young man who had his hand raised and looked to be in his early twenties. Though, the serious and comfortable way he held the rifle he was pointing at them made him look much older to Gwen.

"Stop! Damn it! Stop, will you?" the young man yelled as he walked around to the driver-side window with his rifle now pointed directly at Stan.

"Whoa! Easy! We're friends." Stan said, showing his hands.

Gwen followed Stan's example and showed her hands too.

"Right. You almost killed me with that scrap heap of a truck," the young man said, breathing hard and fast.

"Now that's going too far," Stan objected, but an elbow to his ribs from Gwen stopped him from taking further offense.

"What's your business with us?" The young man traded off looking at Stan and Gwen.

"We're here to talk to Gerty. I'm a friend of hers. Well, I used to be, I think," Stan said.

Gwen was instantly on edge. Stan's friendly banter could get them shot.

"Everybody claims to be Gerty's friend. Most turn out to be less friendly when their true intentions are pulled out of them," the young man said in a matter-of-fact way.

Gwen had had about enough of the male bravado standoff.

"Hey, can I talk to you?" Gwen asked, knocking on her side of the truck and waving outside her open window.

The man with the gun hesitated to shift focus, standing still for a few moments with his gun on the ready, but gradually, he inched his way around to the other side of the truck and settled his rifle on Gwen. Suddenly, she understood why Stan had lost his wits. She closed her eyes and took a deep breath.

"I don't blame you for assuming that my friend Stan here is in charge. I mean, he is in the driver's seat, and he's an older man, too," Gwen said with a special emphasis on the word *man*.

The guy with the gun flinched at that.

Okay. So maybe this is a decent guy being given a tough job. "But I'm the leader of a group up north a couple hundred miles, and we've come to negotiate for a few supplies. We arranged to meet with Gerty."

She was playing a tricky game. Be too vague, and the guy with the gun wouldn't be convinced. Share too much, and she'd be giving away important leverage.

"Negotiate. As in negotiate with actual money or things of real value—or junk like this truck?"

Stan opened his mouth to object, but Gwen shot him a fierce look that stopped him cold. "We wouldn't have come without something to pay for what we need," she said.

"Funny. That doesn't stop a lot of people like you from coming anyway."

"Look. Believe us. Don't believe us. You can see that we are completely unarmed. If we had any other reason to come, do you think we'd come with nothing but this beat-up truck to defend ourselves? You can't honestly see us as a threat."

"I'll be the judge of that," the young man said.

Gwen noticed his shoulders loosen up a bit. Hoping that's a good sign, she thought. "Exactly. You are the judge. You can get rid of us easily enough. But then we'd have to take our business to one of your competitors. We've come a long way because we've been told that your place has the best supplies, but we can go somewhere else if we need to." Gwen smiled.

"Oh my goodness! This is painful. Let them through, Greg."

Gwen and Stan spun and looked out the driver's side of the truck in the direction of the woman's voice they had heard.

"Come on, Gerty. I was just doing my job," Greg said, waving them through and stepping clear of the road. "Go ahead and move forward— slowly. Try not to kill the next guy in the road. This truck isn't worth it."

"People used to call this baby a classic. No respect for experience," Stan grumbled as he eased off the break.

"I say that about you all the time, Stan." Gwen gave Stan's arm a gentle squeeze. "Was that Gerty we just heard?"

Before Stan could answer, he stopped the truck again. This time, the person barring their way forward was a tall, imposing woman with silver dreadlocks that tumbled down the top of her head and cascaded down below her shoulders. Her rich brown eyes and brilliant brown skin almost glowed with intensity. Gwen's eyes were wide, and she had to remind herself to breathe. She felt instantly drawn to the woman and was terrified at the same time.

"Welcome to my farm, young lady," Gerty said with a nod in Gwen's direction. "And Stan, I could smell you from a mile away. If you hadn't brought this bright young woman with you, I probably would have shot you myself, just out of principle."

"I've missed you too, Gerty," Stan said, giving her a hesitant wave. "Come on back. Let's see why you've come all this way."

Gerty turned without another word or gesture and disappeared around the bend. Stan froze in place as if he didn't know whether he should follow or turn tail and run as quickly as he could. Gwen leveled a comforting smile in his direction. "Come on, Stan. Let's see about getting a few supplies, eh?"

chapter 3

Broken shoes striking broken pavement. No sound other than the initial hit of rubber on asphalt followed by a squelch from the plastic inside the shoes giving way. Sky and non-descript, two-story buildings and, somehow, all around, everything showing up grayscale. Time warped so the shoes made a repetition of hitting the sad pavement over and over, caught in the present moment on a confusing loop. The smell of decaying garbage and unwashed bodies. The stark cry of a crow. And then . . .

Patch sat up in a cold sweat, breathing hard. The dream had been a regular one a year ago when he had been first introduced to new opportunities, places, and foods, but his dreams had changed with his circumstances.

Will sure would have some Freudian crap to throw at me if I were back at school right now. Patch chuckled, easing his head back onto his pillows. He counted his breaths. Breathing in—one, breathing out—two up to ten, and then he repeated the process a few more times. Ordinarily, after counting to 10 two or three times, he would be back asleep.

After spending most of his sixteen years on the streets, falling asleep was a skill he'd had to master the hard way, sleeping in whatever shelter he could find no matter how hungry he might have been. So why am I still awake?

He certainly was no longer living on the street. He glanced at a projected image on the wall—a picture of Patch standing next to Malcolm, his benefactor and sort of his investor, after his first track-meet victory. What sterile words those are? Benefactor? Investor? Patch thought.

The projected image ran through a carousel of more recent images too. Dinners, road trips to the mountains, Patch's first Christmas experience. But he paid special attention to the images that showed everyday experiences. The ones he would have let drift out of memory had the photo not been taken. The in-between times. The two of them reading on couches, sipping warm beverages while listening to Malcolm's great music mixes. Times spent out on the deck, chatting while soaking in the summer sun. Those were the times that Patch liked best. Those were the times that built his relationship with Malcolm into so much more than an investment agreement.

Patch tried his breath-counting technique for one more round and finally let out all the air in his lungs in a long, drawn-out breath. Then he threw the covers aside. He stretched out his unusually long legs and arms—as far back as he could—and turned his neck in a couple of methodical circles. Clockwise, then counterclockwise. He planted his feet on the plush rug by his bed and stood, bouncing on his toes a few times before bending into his closet to drag out his running shoes and throwing on the hoodie he always kept on the ready.

If I can't sleep, I might as well put in a few extra miles, he thought, shoring up the laces and tying them in tight double knots. Patch left his bedroom and shuffled down the hall to the kitchen, where he waved his hand over the kitchen sink to activate the water dispenser. He downed two full glasses and headed out the back door.

"Deactivate alarm," Patch said quickly as he heard the chime alarm.

"Okay, Patch. Good morning. Would you like me to choose some good tunes you can listen to on your run?" the pleasant AI woman's voice asked.

"No, thanks," Patch shut the door behind him and placed his thumb on the lock to reactivate the alarm. He had to admit it, their AI assistant usually knew what he wanted or needed before even he did, including how to choose great music. But that morning, Patch needed to think.

In the back courtyard, Patch did a couple of last stretches while serenaded by the water feature, a fountain that Malcolm had been so proud to have fixed himself. Malcolm had recently gotten into the routine of eating breakfast out there, and most mornings, Patch joined him. Though, he hadn't figured out a way to explain to Malcolm why eating breakfast in that spot made him uneasy.

Patch had a hard time fighting the ghosts from his past life in that spot—the courtyard where he had spent his first night after meeting Malcolm. After running so far and so fast that even his almost superhuman aerobic abilities were taken too far, all for the sake of some moldy scraps of bread and rotten apples. He was warming up to even that spot, though, now that it had been over a year since that experience. Patch put a hand on the peach stucco wall for support, and he reached a couple of inches further in his stretch. As his foot hit the ground, he patted the wall. Malcolm's place really felt like home now.

His feet sprang into action without needing any internal pep talk or other motivation. Even now, after so many runs for survival, runs at track practice, and so many runs everywhere in between, he still got a thrill every time he took that first step.

The cool, gray light of pre-dawn was starting to define the trees that lined the manicured front stoops. The tops of buildings emerged slowly out of the cool mist as he rounded the corner outside the courtyard and onto the main road. Birds were marking the coming morning with their songs, and Patch thought he caught the enticing smell of fresh bread baking from inside one of the houses as he rushed past.

The shoes he wore landed with an almost unimaginable silence and cushion—the absorption systems taking the impact of the pavement completely. But the mechanics of his body were the same, and Patch knew those mechanics and loved them. The fulcrums and pulleys of his legs worked together in sequence, driving him forward. Once he passed the first corner deli on his normal route, he fell into a comfortable pace and rhythm. Within that headspace, he hoped to work out a problem he had been wrestling with lately.

He'd be starting school in a few short weeks. His second year ever. He liked school well enough, though. So that wasn't a problem. He felt his feet in his wonderful shoes, and for a moment, that took him out of the flow. He certainly was aware of how different his life would be playing out had he not taken that run for those scraps of food a year ago.

That run—so vivid in his mind—the snarls of the street kids as they raced after him, the fading sunlight, the feel of the breeze that played against his beat-up jacket and unkept black hair with slight lighter streaks that shined in the sunlight. The crumbling masonry underfoot from forgotten brick buildings that he pounded to dust as his duct-taped shoes pounded the uneven pavement.

Malcolm had seen him run that night and had set his mind on investing in his potential future. Literally invest. It had been a business transaction at first. Malcolm would pay for his school; Patch would win his races, and Malcolm would be able to capitalize on that success for his own business ventures as well as a percentage of Patch's future life earnings as he saw fit. Things had changed between then and now—in ways Patch felt ill-equipped to understand.

"Watch it!"

Patch narrowly avoided barreling headfirst into a man pushing a hand truck loaded to the brim with bags of flour. Patch made a quick pivot to the side and spun away from him.

"Sorry!" Patch yelled, running backward and waving at the man with the flour, who was shaking his head.

That must be where that delicious bread smell is coming from. He'd have to remember to visit that shop again when they were open.

He checked his surroundings a bit more. The morning light had progressed to the more substantial kind now. It wasn't only the early-morning delivery trucks that were out and about anymore. He saw the stooped image of an older man wearing a dark hat and walking his dog, and a block ahead, he caught sight of a young couple holding hands with their heads turned toward each other. Patch was impressed that they weren't tripping over their own feet or the rises and dips in the sidewalk that had been built to accommodate tree roots.

Time to turn around. He didn't want Malcolm to worry. A thing Malcolm did a lot more since a certain run back in the spring. Patch didn't like to think about that particular run. It was the day he'd not only found out when his mom died but also why. The memory flashed into his mind—the realization that Malcolm had known his mom had been a Total System Donation and hadn't told him. He still felt some of the dulled shock even now, several months later, whenever he thought about his mom sacrificing herself because she didn't have the means to pay her debts. He and Malcolm had gotten through that, though. Now Patch felt closer to him than ever.

Patch increased his speed a bit so that he had to focus more on the moment and could push that memory out of his head. He only had a couple of miles left on his run back home to try to figure out why he was feeling off. He nodded to a fellow jogger as he passed her, and instantly his mind was taken back to running the halls in the basement level of the bank corporation where Mr. Vanderbilt worked. It was also where a guy named Jefferson was detained by contract enforcers.

When that experience came to his mind, Patch was amazed that it hadn't appeared in his mind earlier like it had so many times before on his runs. Maybe he was shying away from that memory. Though, as he thought through it, fear wasn't the central emotion. Shame was. Shame that he hadn't been able to save Jefferson. Shame that he had been so easily duped by the bank corporation's AI systems and by Mr. Vanderbilt. Shame that he had used his relationship with his then-girlfriend, Kourtney, to get down to the basement levels of the corporate headquarters in the first place, in a foolish attempt to save a girl he barely knew—Gwen.

As he thought about that girl, the one he had bumped into at the train station, that anxious feeling came rushing back in new waves. The feeling was too big and too messy for him to process, and the thought of breaking it down into its parts and even attempting to understand it was way more than he was capable of dealing with right then or ever, maybe.

What do you do with feelings that make you feel lousy but that you can't get past? he thought, turning in toward Malcolm's courtyard and proud fountain. He was pretty sure there was nothing more he could have done, knowing what he knew back then, to have helped Jefferson.

Patch was certain that the contract enforcers would have had to release Jefferson by now, anyway, and they had freed Gwen. So maybe everything was good. It certainly didn't feel right to think that way, though.

The look in Gwen's eyes as they rode the elevator up to the main level of the bank corporate headquarters and as she caught her final look at Jefferson with Mr. Vanderbilt in that small concrete room—cheap card table and a set of four chairs around it, Jefferson hunched over in resolution but still showed an intensity Patch had never seen in anybody in his life. And Gwen's scream that echoed as loudly in his mind now as it had in that elevator. Her face aflame with fear and so much loss and indescribable anger.

Patch looked up at the familiar scene of home. That familiarity almost dispelled the emotional mess that he had stepped into. Patch actually shook off both feet as he slowed to a stop in the courtyard as if the emotions could be sluffed off like dog droppings.

"There you are! Join me. We're eating southwest-style potatoes and sausage this morning. Be prepared to have your face completely melted off!" Malcolm shouted from the deck two stories above Patch.

"Bring it on, Mal. You know I can take the heat," Patch replied while stretching out his arms and legs.

"Boy, don't I know it? Come on in. I have something cool I want to show you too." Malcolm disappeared inside the house with a tray of something that smelled absolutely intoxicating.

"Be right there," Patch said. "Just need to finish stretching."

It was true enough. If he didn't finish his regular cool down, he'd pay for it with sore calves later. But he was also grateful for a couple of minutes to shift gears. Patch certainly didn't want to burden Malcolm with his current emotional quandary.

chapter 4

"**S**o, what cool new gadget is Malcolm's fascination of the week this time?" Patch said, breezing into the kitchen and grabbing a pear out of a basket full of assorted apples, pears, and oranges.

"I don't find new gadgets every week." Malcolm swatted at Patch's hand as Patch tried to steal a potato early—hot off the griddle. "So maybe I have a gadget problem, but at least I have some manners."

Patch grinned as he bit a large chunk out of his juicy pear. "Are you saying I need to learn a thing or two about manners?" Patch asked with his mouth full of pear and even spraying the pear juice on the counter for extra emphasis.

"We all have to start somewhere, I guess. I did snatch you off the street, after all. I can't expect much when I have so little to start with," Malcolm said with a half-smile that told Patch that Malcolm was enjoying the banter but that he didn't want to tell Patch that he was enjoying it. Malcolm flipped off the stovetop and transferred the potato concoction in the cast-iron griddle to an awaiting hot pad on the steel table.

"Yeah. Thank you so much, Malcolm, for showing me the ways of the world. I am awful grateful." Patch took another big bite of pear and showed chunks of it to Malcolm in a big smile.

Malcolm set out plates and glasses and a French press loaded with steaming coffee that was letting off a very encouraging aroma. "It's my duty to society. Refining young men and preparing them for productive lives is my calling for life. Just make sure you pay it forward for the next generation. Seriously though, make sure you don't grab at scraps at the next President's Luncheon at school, okay? It makes us both look bad."

"I got the sense that as long as I kept winning races, the school president didn't care all that much about how I behaved." Patch pulled out two stools from behind the counter for him and Malcolm.

"True enough. Administration usually turns a blind eye to the exceptional. Okay, let's eat!"

Malcolm loaded up Patch's plate with a huge heap of potatoes and three large sausages before serving himself a much daintier portion.

"Gosh, Mal! You've got to remember I have to carry my own weight when I run, plus any that I add on," Patch said, putting one of the sausages and a spatula load of potatoes back.

"You'll burn it off, I'm sure. What do you think of the potatoes? Go ahead and take a bite! It's mainly cayenne pepper and cumin, but I'm wondering if the cilantro might have been a bit much."

Malcolm waited until Patch had thoughtfully eaten his first bite of potatoes. Patch took his time rolling the substantial potato cubes across his tongue. He closed his eyes for a moment as he finally swallowed.

"I'd say . . ." Patch squinted through mostly still-closed eyelids to catch Malcolm's expression of anticipation. Patch knew how much Malcolm aimed to please with his food; his love language would be food if social science ever established it as one. "You've done it again, Mal. These potatoes are absolutely delicious. Hand me back that spatula. You'd better not be very hungry this morning because I'll fight you for second helpings."

Patch watched as Malcolm's face broke into a smile. Everybody has the capacity to smile, but Malcolm knew how to do it best. The smile went so far beyond the mouth. His whole face rose. The smile lines tucked alongside his eyes stood up in all their lovely nuances. When Malcolm smiled like Patch saw him smile that morning, he could swear Malcolm had found a way of marshaling his entire body in a new method of lighting up a room.

"So glad you like them," Malcolm said with a flourish. "Let me try them with my, perhaps, more sophisticated pallet."

Malcolm took his first bite, too, and Patch watched as Malcolm turned his head from side to side. "Not too bad. Maybe I did overdo things a bit with the cilantro, but not bad."

"You're always your own worst critic, Mal."

"Yeah, but if we can't be honest with ourselves, then not a whole lot else matters."

Malcolm meant that last statement as a throwaway comment, one of his clever truisms, but it reminded Patch that he still hadn't talked to Malcolm about his misgivings. Though, Patch wondered if Malcolm would pick up on them because of his more-than-usual fidgeting. Maybe this is as good of a chance as ever.

Patch cleared his throat and set down his fork. Leaning in a bit, he prepared to explain without being sure how to start.

"Mal, I have something to—"

Malcolm jumped in at exactly the same moment. "Oh! My gadget of the week. Let me show it to you. You're going to ask yourself how you've ever lived without one of these once I introduce you to it." Malcolm dashed from the room.

Patch's mouth was still open and ready to broach the tough conversation. He felt awkward and a bit disappointed that he wasn't able to get the messy thoughts off his chest, but thankful for the distraction at the same time. He anxiously scuffed his toes against the ceramic tile floor.

When Malcolm returned, he was reverently cradling what appeared to be a regular pair of eyeglasses with a thick black frame.

"Cool glasses," Patch said, trying to muster more enthusiasm and failing—mostly because he knew he had missed his shot to talk about his problem now that his courage was waning.

"Cool glasses, he says. Ha! If only you knew." Malcolm jumped back to his stool. "These puppies are way more than a pair of glasses, though they do function as regular eyeglasses too. Here, put them on!"

Malcolm lunged forward with the glasses, earpieces first. Only Patch's superb reaction time saved him from being skewered.

"Watch it, Mal! I won't be able to see anything if you poke out my eyes," Patch said, snatching the glasses from Malcolm and putting them on properly. "Okay. So now what do I do? Are these prescription glasses? They look a bit blurry right now." Patch felt around for any knobs or buttons to adjust the visuals.

"Do you have your earbuds on and activated?" Malcolm asked eagerly.

"Yeah. I have them on most of the time these days."

"Great. So ask Siri to adjust the blurry glasses," Malcolm said with a knowing wink at Patch, whose curiosity was growing.

"Okay. Hey, Siri, adjust my glasses," Patch said hesitantly, almost more like a question than a command.

The glasses instantly cleared.

"Hi, Patch. I adjusted the glasses according to your stored medical record. Do you want me to save these settings?"

"Yes," Patch said.

"Okay. I've saved these settings. To take full advantage of everything you can do with your glasses, you'll need to activate them. It looks like the pair you're wearing has been authorized for your use. Do you want me to activate this pair of glasses for you now?"

Patch looked at Malcolm with a raised eyebrow.

"You can activate that pair. Because . . ." Malcolm pulled something out from under the table. "I have a spare! Won't this be great? We can have video chats all the time when you go back to school. Won't that be fun?"

"Oh boy, can't wait to be interrupted constantly with FYIs about proper brands of hummus," Patch started to say.

"Hey! Don't joke. Hummus is serious," Malcolm said with a wry smile.

"Seriously though, thanks. I can think of at least a dozen things I could use these for at school. Siri, activate my glasses."

"Okay. Your glasses are now activated. Do you want me to give you a tour of what your new glasses can do?"

"Yes, please," Patch said.

He and Malcolm then spent the next hour exploring all the tools the glasses offered, including auto-shading for virtual reality settings, a no-record tool that made it so anybody using a different pair of glasses would only see a fuzzy blob if they tried to record Patch, and an augmented-reality mode that Patch could see some definite uses for.

"I could totally use these for my second-year economic history class. Maybe even go to Washington D.C. and walk the streets, seeing the old government buildings as they used to be," Patch said. "Or maybe I'll finally learn data modeling because I'll be able to see real-world applications for those models in action. You know how much of a visual learner I am."

"I certainly do. That's why I instantly thought of you when I saw them the other day," Malcolm said, grabbing the plates from off the table and putting them in the sink.

Patch grabbed both cups with one hand, squeezing his fingers together from inside the cups.

"You know that gives me a heart attack every time you carry glasses that way," Malcolm said, snatching the water glasses from Patch.

"Yeah, and guess how many times I've dropped a single glass?"

"Okay, fine. Never. But still. It's the principle of the thing. Go and get a bit cleaned up. We're playing pickleball with Rosencrantz this morning at the club."

"Is that code for something?" Patch said as he wiped down the table with a dish rag.

"No. We are literally playing pickleball with the Rosencrantz and Associates people. You remember them. I introduced you to one of their founding partners at that business Christmas party I dragged you to. Craig Edmonds?"

Patch stopped and leaned against the fridge, trying to remember that far back.

"Oh yeah! The guy with the regrown hairline."

"What?"

"The guy totally regrew his hair, but it looked so unnatural for a ninety-year-old man to have deep-chestnut hair when it's combined with wrinkles that can't be hidden at that age, no matter how many skin grafts he might have had," Patch said excitedly.

Malcolm's eyes widened, and the smile that was so characteristically him was suddenly gone. Patch hadn't seen Malcolm look that serious very often.

"Okay. Let's establish right now that my investors' skin grafts and hairlines are off-limits as topics of conversation, okay? This firm really matters," Malcolm said.

"Got it. I promise I'll behave," Patch said, heading to his bedroom, but he turned back suddenly and popped his head back into the kitchen. "So, hopefully, this won't be too much of a problem, but I've never played pickleball. Your investors aren't expecting me to be amazing at it or anything, are they?"

"No. I'm sure they'll all want you on their team because you're the star athlete, but don't sweat it."

"So it doesn't matter if I'm on their team and we lose because I've never played before? That won't hurt your future investment possibilities?" Patch asked, nervously kicking his toes against the slate floor again.

"Don't tell me you're afraid that you won't be a match for ninety-year-olds, Patch, or else I'll have to sign you up for a couple of sessions with a motivational psychologist."

"Well, no, but—"

"Don't sweat it. Pickleball is basically tennis for old people. They get to hit the ball on a smaller court so they don't have to chase after it as far. You'll catch on in a snap."

"If you're sure. I just don't want to embarrass you," Patch said, turning back down the hall.

"You'll be fine. But don't embarrass me."

Patch decided not to push for an explanation and instead headed to the bathroom for a quick shower. He stepped in the shower and selected the default setting for water flow. A steady stream of warm, gentle water that perfectly simulated rain hit his upturned face. The shower had at least five other settings, including one that weirded Patch out. It produced a mist that somehow got him drenched without him feeling any individual water droplets hit his skin.

As the water rushed over his hair and down his shoulders, he did his best to smooth out his nerves. Just tennis for old people. I can do that, Patch tried to convince himself.

chapter 5

Gerty led Gwen and Stan along a maze of narrow paths cut through tall grass that was well above even Stan's mop of hair and so thick that Gwen couldn't see even a foot past the path on either side. She was fighting the urge to run at every step, even knowing the paths were designed to get anybody not intimately familiar with their network hopelessly lost and disoriented. She got the sinking feeling that, by that point, the work had already been done. There was no chance for her to retrace her steps, even if she had the sense that she could get away.

Gwen had been focused on the guard's boots a few feet in front of her, but as she followed them around a tight turn, she lost them. She darted her gaze around her surroundings, desperately trying to get her bearings. She looked to the left, but the path in that direction dead-ended with a thick wall of tall grass. She darted to the right and then found a tight left turn. She was about to give the retracing-of-her-steps thing a try, turning back the way she'd come, when Gerty's voice sounded from behind her and further down the path, which was quite disorienting, but with so many tight, angular curves, it wasn't hard to see how Gerty's voice came from behind her even though Gerty entered the maze first. In her previous frantic moment, Gwen had almost forgotten where she was or why she was there, but she was able to follow Gerty's voice to regain her focus and bearings.

"Aren't these path mazes fantastic? On my old farm, back in the day, we used to carve mazes like these in our cornfields around Halloween. I never got the appeal of getting lost like so many others did, but people paid a ridiculous price to give it a try."

Halloween? What's that? Gwen turned in the direction she thought Gerty's voice had come from. A couple more turns to the right and then a left and, at last, the path ended with an open, sunny field. The sun struck Gwen's face unexpectedly, and she couldn't help but smile at the warmth. She let the sunlight seep through her jacket and bring her body temperature up a bit after so long in the path's shadow.

"Welcome back to sunshine. We faced that entrance into the morning sunlight on purpose, too. Like the paths. We figured by the time people were so cold and disoriented, they'd thank us for bringing them back into the sun. Great negotiation tactic," Gerty said without paying particular attention to any one person. Just stating a fact. "I guess I shouldn't do that—tell you all of our tricks. Oh well, I'm not one for negotiations. If someone has something we need and we have something we can let go of for a fair price, then why not, right?"

Gwen nodded as she stepped into the canvas shelter, where Gerty bustled about, sorting through baskets designed to hold produce—probably—but holding reams of paperwork instead. Gerty looked up from a basket that held blank paper.

"Like our filing system? Very high-tech. I never did like computers, even before everything went to hell in this country. I mean, we used them, of course. That's how we used to do business. It was all, Do you use Venmo or Apple Pay? No. I certainly did not. But after losing enough business, I got the hint and gave in. Having to do without that now isn't difficult for me at all. I don't miss any of that, and these lovely sheets of paper are a thousand times more secure than the digital versions because we can ensure there's only one copy. Please sit down, both of you."

Gerty gestured to two sturdy wooden chairs. "Can I get you anything? A glass of water? An apple? I think we have a squash, but you'd have to wait a few minutes for that to be prepared," Gerty said, pulling out random pieces of produce. She lifted her head out of the baskets for a moment. "And Stan, stop trying to make yourself so inconspicuous. I know who you are. I remember how things fell out between us. I still decided to meet with you instead of shooting you on sight, so relax."

Gwen glanced to her right, only to see that Stan didn't take Gerty's assertion as all that comforting. He cleared his throat nervously and paid way too much attention to some dust on his jacket that was brushed off the first time he'd rubbed his fingers across it. When he saw Gwen eyeing him, he smiled sheepishly.

"Honestly, I've been smelling all of your amazing produce ever since we entered your farm, and I've been dying to try some. Were you serious about offering us an apple? That sounds great right now," Gwen said, trying to play things cool.

Gerty rummaged through a particular basket and presented both Gwen and Stan with the biggest, most colorful apples Gwen had ever seen. Gwen accepted hers almost reverently, and Gerty dropped the other for Stan to catch, which he did awkwardly.

The apple Gwen held in both hands was cool and as smooth as marble. It had bright-red flares shooting off from both the top and bottom, bleeding in both directions into a beautiful orange and yellow. Gwen almost hated to take a bite. But no matter how beautiful the apple might look, she was more interested in giving it a taste.

She quickly glanced up, remembering where she was. Gerty was giving Gwen a very interested look, and she nodded encouragingly.

Gwen bit into the top curve of the apple and was thrilled to discover that the fleshy interior was crisp all the way through. She realized too late that she had torn out more apple than she could politely chew, but from the pleased look she saw flash across Gerty's face, being impolite wouldn't be a problem. Gwen closed her eyes as she rolled the apple chunk inside her mouth, picking up the sweetness and the tartness and the way the combination of flavors thrilled and shocked her tongue at the same time. After several long seconds, Gerty scooted even more forward in her seat so that her chair actually leaned forward.

"So?"

"I think that's the most beautiful thing I've ever tasted," Gwen blurted out, but then she froze for a moment. Keep it together! She told herself.

"Ahhh! Excellent! I'm absolutely thrilled." Gerty clapped her hands five times with impressive speed. "Just excellent. You two enjoy those, and I'll get the paperwork started."

Gerty exited the tent, leaving Gwen and Stan to finish their apples. Gwen leaned toward Stan. "Sorry. That was probably not the right thing to say. This whole negotiating thing . . . I feel like I'm out of my depth here, Stan."

"What makes you think that?"

"I don't know." She slumped back in her chair. "I'm giving too much away already."

"You are going about this brilliantly, Gwen. Trust me. Gerty loves you already, and I think I'd know since I broke her heart," Stan said, lowering his head and rubbing a bit of dirt off the face of his apple.

Gwen smiled and gave Stan's shoulder a squeeze and at the same time felt the tightness in her neck loosen slightly.

"I know absolutely nothing about relationships, but I think you're a good guy, whatever might have happened before," Gwen said.

Stan lifted his head a little higher and smiled.

"Okay. I'm back. It looks like the important person in the room has eaten her apple, so we can talk business," Gerty said, sitting down in her chair and spreading out some papers on the table. "So how can I help you?"

"How can you help me?" Gwen asked, confused at being asked such a generous question.

"Oh! Gosh, old ways die hard. Sorry, that's what shop owners used to ask customers. Let's put it in more practical terms, shall we? What do you need?"

Gwen was perfectly prepared for that kind of question. "Got it. We need some supplies that I'm hoping you can let go of."

"Smart girl, this one! Using my own words against me." Gerty turned her head, looking slightly behind her and toward the guards outside. "Let's see what you need and go from there."

"Sounds like a plan," Gwen said. Here we go, she thought, taking a deep breath. "What we need right now are basic food items like fruits and vegetables, flour, cooking oil, those sorts of things."

"How much supply do you have on hand?" Gerty asked with a sideways look at Stan.

"I don't see how that's important to this conversation," Gwen said awkwardly, trying to choose her words carefully.

"Think about this—it'll take me some time to round up, package, and deliver the goods you buy. It makes a bit of a difference if I know people are going to starve. Get me?" Gerty said, leaning back in her chair.

"Yeah. I get you for sure." Gwen swallowed hard and looked at Stan. Stan nodded once, slowly.

The truth was the only option at that point, though Gwen took a moment before responding—to race through finding any way she could to not give up their dire circumstance. Her shoulders slumped. "We have about a week's worth of provisions left."

Gerty jumped forward in her armchair, using the armrests to lean toward Stan.

"Stan, how did you let things go so far before reaching out to me? Seriously, and knowing what a glutton you can be, too. I'd think you'd let your stomach guide you to make a wiser choice. Although, you've let other bodily urges guide you in other respects. They didn't serve you well either," Gerty said with a dangerous grin. "Maybe you've learned not to trust those urges."

Gwen watched the exchange with growing anxiety. But it seemed to her that Gerty was letting down her guard, which could mean she was warming up to her and Stan, and maybe that meant they were getting close to the goal of feeding their operation. But Stan shriveled faintly under Gerty's powerful stare. Then, after a few tense moments, Gerty leaned back in her chair and addressed Gwen in her former, friendly, business-like manner.

"Okay, so you'll need a full slate of food and perishable cooking supplies delivered within the week. We can accommodate that. It'll be a rush order, so I'd imagine you're prepared to pay a premium for that. We don't gouge our customers though. Plus, I think I'm starting to like you, Gwen, so let's go with regular base prices."

This was the part that Gwen was most nervous about and where she feared her lack of experience would be most exposed. She knew how money worked, but it was one thing to understand a concept and entirely another to have a bunch of practical experience.

Jefferson had left accounts with what seemed to be a lot of money to Gwen, but she had no idea how much she should pay for a couple of months' worth of supplies for an operation like hers. She decided it would be best to get in front of her lack of experience rather than be taken advantage of later in the negotiations.

"I appreciate you being fair with us, Gerty," Gwen said. "I'm not much of a negotiator either, really. In your case, that's because you like to be a straight shooter, and cheating people, I bet, goes straight against everything you believe in. In my case . . ."

Gwen stood up and walked over to the baskets stacked along the side of the tent. She gestured to the variety of different colored fruits and vegetables. "In my case, I'm not much of a negotiator because, for most of my life, I believed that everybody I met was willing to kill me for the scraps I might have. Plus, they were usually bigger and stronger than me. Not much of a leg to stand on at the negotiation table, eh?"

Gwen paused and looked at Gerty. Gerty was good at this. That was clear, but she was also paying attention.

"I grew up in the Wilds. I recently found out that region used to be called Kansas, I guess. I don't think much of it is worth a name, but it's home. I also learned that it used to be a part of what they called America's breadbasket because it produced so much food that most of it got shipped off to other countries for better prices. I couldn't believe that at first, but I guess it must be true. The mega-farms I saw there, with autonomous tractors cutting thousands of miles of crops, shipped it everywhere except to me. I sure could have used a couple of baskets full of your produce back then."

Gwen reached out to grab a long, slender vegetable with smooth, dark-green skin that she had no idea the name of. She heard an anxious intake of breath, and Gwen looked up, afraid she had crossed some line of decorum by touching Gerty's vegetables without asking.

"Sorry. You and I both know that I'm completely out of my depth here. Until I met Jefferson last year, I didn't believe that places like this, with more food than I could ever imagine, existed. I didn't believe in much of anything, I guess, back then."

"Jefferson? Who's that?" Gerty asked with a blank look.

Gwen sent an accusatory glare to Stan, finding it absolutely impossible that he wouldn't have mentioned Jefferson when setting up the meeting. That changed her assumptions tremendously. Stan quickly shook his head.

"Sorry. I assumed Stan had mentioned him, although it makes sense. We haven't seen Jefferson for a couple of months. He was taken by contract enforcers. I've been told that they don't usually take people prisoner because it costs them too much or something, but Jefferson is the reason I'm here. Why our operation exists at all."

Gwen gently put the vegetable back in its basket and turned to face Gerty. "We have some money. I'm not sure if it'll be enough to buy all that we need. I hope it is. How much will it cost to get a couple months' worth of food supplies?"

Gerty looked intently at Gwen with a curious smile on her face. Even Gwen, who ordinarily felt comfortable with silence, started fidgeting after a long wait for Gerty's reply. She was about to ask her question a different way when Gerty raised her hand to her lips. Gwen stayed quiet.

"So you trusted this guy? Jefferson?"

Gwen nodded slowly.

"So much so that you'd follow him to a place you've never been to be a part of an operation you have no experience with?"

Gwen nodded again.

"This Jefferson must have been quite the persuasive fellow."

"It's not just that!" Gwen took a step forward so fast that she heard rustling from the guards outside.

"I'm fine, guys," Gerty said, waving her hand in the general direction of the guards.

"Sorry. It's not just that though. He isn't just a smooth talker," Gwen said, emphasizing the present tense of Jefferson's existence as much for herself as for Gerty's. "He taught me enough about history and economics and world politics for me to understand that the current state of the world isn't the only way it could be or the only way it has been."

Gwen paused then, searching for the best way of saying the most important thing she needed to say to Gerty. "I've never lived in any other world than this one, but Jefferson gave me permission to get excited about a different one. One that would be possible if we could somehow break up the banks."

Gwen caught Stan's instant cringe, and Gerty showed an uncharacteristically authentic surprised look, given the polished and controlled demeanor she had shown until then. Gwen knew sharing their operation's true purpose was a big gamble. She'd heard of rewards being given to people who turned in rebels, and gauging by the comfortable but not-posh conditions of Gerty's operations, a reward could be very well used at this farm.

"Gwen, you've got more grit in you than a thousand masons have under their fingernails," Gerty said.

Gwen had no idea what that expression meant, so she stayed silent and hoped Gerty would explain.

Then Gerty let out a full and delightful laugh. It shocked both Gwen and Stan and startled some nearby crows, who sounded their displeasure as they flew off. But Gerty's laugh caused something impulsively rich and good to rise up in Gwen's chest, as if releasing all the weight of responsibility and tension and fear that she had bottled up for the last two months in one triumphant push. She laughed right along with Gerty. And even Stan joined in, though more cautiously and while keeping an eye on Gerty.

"Lord, have mercy! I needed that. Forgive me. I don't mean to make light of your situation with your friend being held by the contract enforcers. It's just so good to feel courage again," Gerty said with a final chuckle and a long sigh. "I wouldn't miss the opportunity to be the supplier for such a brave undertaking for the world."

Stan and Gwen had a mostly quiet ride back to the warehouse. Both were lost in their own thoughts. Gwen hadn't known enough going into the negotiations at the farm to set realistic goals or have hopes for the outcome, but she remembered feeling a similar thrill when she spoke to the crowd on the night Jefferson kicked off his campaign to take down the banks.

It was a kind of shimmering that pulsated inside her and was tough to contain. She held her hand in front of her face. Her fingers quivered ever so slightly, as if she were holding within her a world of pent-up electricity. At least, that's what it felt like to her. I could get used to feeling this way.

Gwen scanned over the sheet with the itemized list of supplies that Gerty would deliver to the warehouse by the end of the week—a two-month supply of a variety of food items in crates that could serve a dual purpose. It included cooking oils, cleaning supplies, and various other things that Stan had also requested. Who would have ever thought one group could eat that many eggs? Gwen folded the sheet of paper again and tucked it back into her jacket's inside pocket, then pulled out her other scrap of paper. She pulled out her pencil and crossed off Get Food, which felt amazing.

They were entering the D.C. metro area.

Where they had been driving along an old farming road for the last hour or so, they now turned onto a more substantial highway. Some cars sped around them, which distracted Stan a bit, or so it seemed. Gwen certainly didn't want to distract him further by talking about her enthusiasm. She so rarely had things to share, and now, in that moment, she had so much to share that it felt like if she didn't share some of what rushed around inside her, things would start tumbling out. Thankfully, Stan spoke first.

"You were absolutely brilliant back there. Really," Stan said, giving Gwen an approving nod.

"You think so?" Gwen asked.

"Are you kidding? You nailed it!" Stan pounded the steering wheel, adding emphasis and making the truck swerve. He slid back into his lane. "Seriously. You read Gerty perfectly."

"I didn't feel like that. A lot of what I said to Gerty just felt right," Gwen said.

"Negotiation must come naturally to you then—" Stan started to say.

But Gwen interjected. "No. I'm a horrible negotiator. I can see that now," she said, deflating a bit in having to admit that. She turned in her seat to talk directly to Stan. "I gave Gerty way too much information. I laid all our cards out on the table way too fast. It worked with Gerty, I think, because she appreciated the direct approach. But she could have taken advantage of my lack of experience if she'd wanted to."

"Well, you got it done, and that's the key thing," Stan said. "I'm afraid I wasn't much help though. I actually thought Gerty was going to shoot me at a couple of points during the interaction."

Gwen started to laugh but stopped when she realized Stan still looked quite serious. He eventually let go of that look, and they shared a hearty laugh.

Stan turned off the main highway and onto a road that ran parallel to a dark river lined with a jumble of trees and scattered trash. Gwen looked out her window at the gray buildings on the far side of the river and missed the peace she had felt on Gerty's farm once the negotiating part of the visit was over. Then a thought came back to her.

"What did go down between you and Gerty? I mean, I don't need the messy details, exactly, but you were obviously in a relationship that went bad a long time ago."

"When dinosaurs roamed the earth—"

"You're not going to let that one go, are you?"

"No. Not so much. Like I tried to explain this morning when we were heading to Gerty's farm, my relationship with Gerty was complicated."

"That's it? That's all you're going to give me? I could play the I'm-sixteen-and-all-I've-ever-learned-about-relationships-has-come-from-an-old-man-and-people-who-have-wanted-to-kill-me card," Gwen said, spinning a strand of her hair around her finger.

"Wow! When you put it that way. Let me see . . . Where to start? Gerty and I went to school together. She was studying business first but shifted to organic farming or something related to agriculture I think, like I mentioned this morning. And I was studying business finance. I needed some tutoring for my plant biology course, which was intended to fill a simple general requirement, and was totally taken off guard by how tough the class was and how bad I was at science stuff. I'm rambling now. The short of it is, Gerty was my tutor."

"And she taught you more than you bargained for?" Gwen said with a knowing look.

"Don't give me that. Yeah, we dated for a while. She wanted to explore a more committed relationship, but I was going away to graduate school the next fall, and I didn't feel like it would be good for either of us to connect more than we already had. I knew the relationship would end anyway."

"And then you broke her heart?"

"Man, you are direct, aren't you?" Stan stretched his arms against the steering wheel. "Yeah, I guess you could put it that way. I never realized how important the relationship was to her. Promise not to tell her, but it was wonderful to see her again. And to see she's still the same beautiful and vibrant person I knew."

Just then, Gwen heard rumbling down at her feet. She straightened up and dug into her bag that she had totally forgotten she'd brought. Her tablet was still rumbling with new, insistent notifications.

That's odd. I never get that many messages, she thought, grabbing the earpiece that was magnetized to the tablet. She wasn't prepared for the first message and paid no attention to the dozens that followed it.

Jefferson is back!

chapter 6

Patch tried his best to take in the flurry of activity as he and Malcolm walked into the vast bubble that housed dozens of courts of various shapes and sizes under the climate-controlled arena, but one thing was certain—pickleball was not going to be easy to master, and it definitely was not tennis for old people.

He nervously twirled the small hard paddle in one hand as he scanned the room until he found the area where people used the same shape and size paddle he was holding. They seemed young—quite athletic—and though the balls they were hitting weren't moving quite as fast as the bright-green tennis balls whizzing around the other portions of the arena, they were going fast enough.

"I don't think this was a good idea, Mal," Patch said, trailing behind Malcolm, who was in his element.

"Nonsense! You'll do great!"

"You say that, but maybe this is a case of overconfidence, like with that fun experience of putting together that desk without looking at the instructions?"

"Hey, that desk looks great! And doesn't lean too much," Malcolm said, slowing his pace a bit. "And can't carry any weight without falling. Okay, so maybe I'm a bit overly confident that you'll smash this game. But I'm justified in feeling that way this time."

"And what gives you that feeling?" Patch said, having to run to keep up with Malcolm, who had resumed his previous quick clip.

"Pickleball isn't easy to get really good at like other sports. But you have two things going for you. One, you are incredibly coordinated, and two, you can run like hell."

Patch couldn't argue against that logic. He felt a bit better about his prospects, but one rung above abject despair was still pretty low. It wasn't that he was afraid to look foolish, not even in front of all of these beautiful people. And they were all beautiful—polished and perfectly maintained—like expensive sports cars. And the expense of keeping up such appearances, Patch realized, might cost as much as a sports car. No, it wasn't them; he didn't want to hurt Malcolm's business prospects.

They wound their way past several underway pickleball matches until they found an empty court where two older gentleman wearing white shorts that stood in bright contrast to their unnaturally tanned legs were pulling out paddles.

"Hey, Craig," Malcolm shouted across the court, waving a friendly hand toward one of the men.

"Malcolm! You made it," Craig said, looking up and smiling a perfectly straight and shockingly white-toothed smile.

Malcolm crossed the court with his hand outstretched. Patch did his best to hide behind him as Malcolm shook Craig's hand as well as the hand of the other man.

"Hi, I'm Tom. Tom Fordham," the other man said, shaking Malcolm's hand.

"And this must be your star runner?" Craig looked behind Malcolm.

"Hi, sir. My name is Patch Robinson, so nice to meet you," Patch said, remembering the manner lessons Malcolm had given him. Shake the hand firmly, but not in an overly aggressive way, he reminded himself as he shook both men's hands.

"You know, Mal, bringing in a ringer as your doubles partner hardly seems fair," Craig said, stretching his arms across his chest with a smile. "I take it to mean one of two things. Either you really want to impress us so we'll invest even more in your firm, or you really hate losing."

"I do really want your business, which doesn't seem like too horrible of a thing for either of us, given the healthy returns I've been getting you," Malcolm said, thoughtfully polishing his paddle with a corner of his shirt. Malcolm dropped his shirt and looked squarely at Craig with a winning smile. "And I really, really hate losing."

Patch did his best to mimic what he saw other people do in preparation for their matches. Rubbed down his paddle, stretched, then stood in an awkward, hunched-over stance. Wait for the ball to be . . . What is it even called when the ball is hit at the start of a point? Served? Patch thought frantically, his feet nervously kicking against the green clay pavement.

He thought he heard someone calling his name from far away. Then he realized it was Malcolm. Patch shook his head and tried to focus on what was happening around him.

"Sorry, Mal, what was that?" Patch asked, trying to sound as nonchalant as he could.

"What was what?" Malcolm chuckled. "I was just telling our new friends here about how I found you."

"Ah. My favorite story," Patch said, fighting the urge to keep up the kicking and deciding to do a few pregame hops on his toes to release some of his nervous energy. "Sorry to interrupt."

Malcolm had told other people about their first encounter many times in many different settings. As he listened to Malcolm tell it this time, something felt different. His chest started to tighten. His nerves subsided. In their place, though, an agitation that urged him to leave bubbled up inside him. But not out of fear. Where is this coming from?

Malcolm was getting to his favorite part of the story where he'd talk about his master plan to get Patch to agree to be sponsored. All it took was a bit of kindness and a lot of really good food, Patch ran the familiar line through his head.

"All it took was a bit of kindness and a lot of really good food," Malcolm said, who was rewarded with an impressed laugh from Tom and a clap on the back from Craig.

"Betrayed."

Patch was startled when all three men looked at him with puzzled looks. He hadn't meant to say it out loud. But that was the agitation. He felt betrayed.

"I mean, how could anybody resist Malcolm's eggs Benedict? Seriously? They should have a class at my school on negotiation just for cooking that because, after eating those eggs, all guards come down—I'll tell you that," Patch said, hoping that might smooth things over.

It seemed to have the right effect. Tom and Craig chuckled and nodded appropriately. But Malcolm shot him an annoyed glare.

"Well, gentleman, are we going to talk all morning, or are we here to play some pickleball?" Malcolm said, turning his back on Patch and putting his arms around Tom and Craig's shoulders, nudging them to their side of the court.

"You told me your young friend has never played before, right, Malcolm?" Craig asked as Malcolm walked to his side of the court.

"That's right. So you might have a bit of an advantage for the first couple of points. But after that, I'm counting on young legs and superhuman coordination to win the day," Malcolm said, getting into a marked square near the net and that hunched stance players stood in. Patch moved into the square directly behind the one Malcolm stood in and hoped it was right. Malcolm gave a subtle nod in the direction of the square next to the one Patch was standing in, so he casually stepped into the proper square.

"Okay, let us serve first so we can show you how it's done," Craig said.

"By all means. Give us your worst," Malcolm said with a look back at Patch. He gave Patch a thumbs up and mouthed what Patch thought was You've got this!

Craig and Tom both stood in the back part of the court, but Tom had the ball and was looking in his direction, so Patch did his best to mirror Malcolm's ready stance in his spot—the back right corner of the court.

"Zero, zero, two," Tom called out, and he tossed up the ball and struck it underhand in Patch's direction.

Patch dashed into the trajectory of the ball and prepared to smash it, thinking that even if the ball didn't land in the right spot, if he hit it hard enough, it might still impress Malcolm's clients.

He was in position well before the ball, so he did his best to set up. Do I have to hit the ball underhand? Is that a rule? Does it matter what square I hit the ball into now that it has been served? What am I doing here? he thought as he braced himself for his first return. Patch decided on a side-arm approach, figuring that would be the safest bet. He swung at the ball with all of his pent-up nervous energy and sent it whizzing over the net and far beyond Tom and Craig. It finally stopped after smacking into the mesh that divided the courts.

"Whoa, boy! Take it easy. You just need to beat us. Not kill us," Craig said as he traded squares with Tom.

Tom still had the ball, so Patch prepared for another serve. Malcolm nudged back into the square behind where he had been standing and pointed to the square right in front of Patch. He moved up. So you keep serving until you lose the point, trading serving spots. Now I get it, he hoped.

Tom served again, this time toward Malcolm, who easily returned the serve, driving the ball back at Tom and barely clearing the net. The ball kept gliding along the ground to Tom's left. Tom turned and hit the ball with an awkward backhand that sent the ball into the net.

"Alright! That was sweet, Mal!" Patch said, giving Mal a fist bump.

"Thanks. Sometimes I've got it. Your serve, Patch," Mal said, glancing back toward Tom, who had already tapped the ball in Patch's direction.

Patch narrowly avoided having the ball smack him square in the face, only catching it after fumbling it with his paddle. What did those numbers that Tom called out mean again? Patch thought desperately.

"Zero, zero, two," Patch called out.

"Zero, one, one, actually," Craig said.

"Of course. Zero, one, one." Patch tossed the ball and struck it underhand toward Craig like he had seen Tom do before. He was thrilled to see the ball clear the net.

"Out," Craig shouted.

To his left, Patch heard Malcolm grumble. He tried to set up for Craig's turn, getting into that weird, wide, hunched-over stance.

"Move to the other side. We trade sides every serve," Malcolm said, moving Patch in the right direction.

"Zero, one, two," Malcolm shouted before serving.

Craig deflected the serve in Patch's direction. Here it comes again, Patch thought, preparing to do something else wrong. He hit the ball as it came to his side of the court and knocked it so it dribbled down the court, running along the net.

"Nice, Patch," Malcolm called out from behind him.

Patch let out a relieved smile and nodded toward Malcolm. It dawned on him that the only reason why he was able to return the ball like that was because he was able to react quickly enough to position himself well before the ball got to him. And he had done that pretty easily. So maybe if he didn't embarrass himself too much while serving, he could deliver those kinds of returns.

"One, one, two. We're on the board!" Malcolm said as he traded sides with Patch. Malcolm served again. This time, Tom didn't get the ball over the net.

"Watch out, Tom. I'm after you," Malcolm said, tauntingly. "Two, one, two." Malcolm served out of bounds, and Patch inched back so he was level with Malcolm in the back half of their side of the court.

"You're getting it, Patch," Malcolm reached out his paddle for Patch to tap.

"One, two, one. I hope you enjoyed those points. You won't see another one for a while," Craig said.

Craig served in Malcolm's direction, but Malcolm put some kind of spin on the ball so when it landed on the other side of the court, it jumped away from Tom's paddle.

"Very fancy, Mal. You don't have to show off like that. We already know you're a great guy," Craig shouted at Malcolm.

"And don't you ever forget it," Malcolm shouted back.

Craig hit the ball to Tom so Tom could serve, which meant the ball would head in Patch's direction, and he wouldn't be positioned anywhere near the net this time.

"One, two, two," Tom said, then hit the ball in a slow loping fashion that made the ball hit and bounce just above Patch's eye level.

Overhand, Patch smacked the ball hard, hoping that doing it that way wasn't against the rules. The ball careened into Tom's shoe and bounced away. Tom let out a frustrated growl, and Craig shook his head. "Remember me telling you it wasn't fair to bring in a ringer, Mal?"

"Remember me telling you how much I hate to lose, Craig?" Malcolm said with a knowing grin.

Patch let out a long, satisfied breath. Maybe he wouldn't totally disappoint Malcolm after all.

Once Patch finally figured out the odd scoring system and got used to the required and constant rotating—from side to side and up and down the court—he decided pickleball wasn't half bad, as far as games went.

He was aware that Craig and Tom weren't the greatest competitors either. Malcolm had exaggerated their ages a little, maybe, but not by much. And with how weirdly tanned and manicured the two guys were, age was kind of relative, he decided.

The two business investors had lasted four games, all of which Patch and Malcolm had won by large margins. By the end of the fourth game, Patch had been concerned. "Won't they be mad if we skunk them like this?" Patch asked Malcolm before the last serve of the fourth game.

"No way. If we go easy on them, they'll be way more insulted. Keep at it, okay? You're doing great," Malcolm said, breaking away from their huddle with a paddle-hit and a slap to Patch's back. Patch served and won the last point.

After the last game, as Patch was putting his paddle in its cover, he glanced over at Craig. He got an uneasy feeling around him. Where is this coming from, I don't even know the guy? he thought. Which was true enough. Craig was changing from his shockingly white sneakers to a pair of leather loafers that Patch was certain had cost a fortune. As Craig pulled a sock off one of his feet, Patch became instantly curious.

Craig's exposed foot was bony and had toes that were bent too far in unnatural angles. Veins ran in clear, blue patterns from the top of the big toe all the way to the heel. And though the foot had the same kind of tanning treatment as the rest of Craig's body, the effect the tan had on his foot was more of a sickly darkening than a healthy glow.

Patch realized he was staring too late, and Craig was looking right back at him. Patch quickly looked down at his paddle, but since it was already secure in its cover, there wasn't any legitimate reason to pay attention to it. So he nervously scratched the back of his neck and stretched his arms one after the other.

"It's okay, Patch," Craig said with a chuckle. "Aren't they hideous? I've been meaning to get some work done on them, but I keep them hidden most of the time so I don't notice, and women don't seem to mind either." Craig gave Patch a knowing wink that made him feel a bit sick to his stomach.

"It's fine," Patch said, instantly feeling like that was the stupidest thing to have said. What was fine? Craig's foot? No, it most certainly was not fine. It was something that nightmares were made of. And Patch knew that whatever Craig had shared about women wasn't fine either. Thankfully, Malcolm saved Patch from having to say anything else.

"Let me know if I can ever give you another good walloping," Malcolm said, giving Craig's and Tom's shoulders good squeezes and then shaking their hands.

"I'm afraid I'll be licking my wounds for a good while after this one, Malcolm. But great matches. And your kid here certainly didn't disappoint. You'd really never played before today?" Tom asked, reaching out his hand.

Patch shook it with a smile. "I really never had. The first couple of serves were rough, but I think I sort of got the hang of it by the end."

"Got the hang of it hardly describes what you did this morning. You absolutely destroyed us. But that's as it should be. Thanks for the great games," Tom said, giving Patch's hand one more good shake,

Patch was more comfortable with Tom than with Craig. I wonder why he's in business with Craig. Patch still had so much to learn about business.

"Mission accomplished!" Malcolm said enthusiastically when he and Patch were back in the car and on their way home.

"I'm just glad I didn't embarrass you too bad. Although, if I had, it would have been mostly your fault for not explaining to me how the game is played. I seem to remember you calling it . . . How did you put it? Tennis for old people?" Patch said.

"Yeah, okay. It's a bit more complicated than I let on, but embarrass? Are you kidding me? You were a force of nature on that court! Like I said, you caught on in a snap," Malcolm turned onto a street lined with stately sycamore trees, their large leaves filtering the noontime sunlight. When Patch looked up as they passed the trees, the random shimmer made him feel a bit better.

"So you got what you needed? More investment from Rosencrantz and Associates?" Patch said coldly—colder than he meant to sound—but Patch had a hard time saying it any other way.

Malcolm completely missed the edge to Patch's voice. "Oh yeah! They're going to go in another thirty percent over the next two years. That's huge," Malcolm said, emphasizing huge with a fist bump to the steering wheel.

"Glad to be of service," Patch said, rolling down his window and stretching out his arm to feel the warm summer air brush against his skin. It felt good. At least something did.

"Hey, what's going on?" Malcolm asked. "Be excited with me. Today was a big win for us," Malcolm said, giving Patch a concerned look.

"A big win for you, you mean," Patch kept his face forward.

"A win for me is as much a win for you. I mean, that artisan coffee you don't seem to mind doesn't pay for itself. Or I guess, in your case, that falafel," Malcolm said with a strained smile. "Come on, kid, do you want to give me some hints here? I've never been very good at the guessing game, especially with feelings."

"Why do you have to do business with them?" Patch said, turning to look at Malcolm.

"With Rosencrantz?" Malcolm asked with a quick breath from his puffed-up cheeks. "I don't know. Why do I do business with anybody? They have funds that they want to get as big of a return from as they can. I know how to make those returns happen. I take my percentage of those returns. Everybody's happy."

"Sure. So Craig can afford to get those feet fixed," Patch said, leaning his head on his fist with his elbow propped up on the armrest.

"His feet? What are you talking about?" Malcolm said with a searching glance at Patch.

"His feet. I looked at his foot when he was changing shoes. The toes are all bent out of shape, and the foot was more of a skeleton's than a man's."

"Seriously, Patch? You don't like the guy because of the way his feet look? That's pretty low. I mean, he can hardly help the way his feet look at his age, and—"

"But he could, actually. Couldn't he? I bet he sets the appointment on his way home. Why not? The rest of him has been done, probably multiple times already," Patch gripped his armrest tight, trying to contain the mess of feelings rushing through him.

Malcolm didn't say anything for a couple of awkward moments.

"What's this really about, Patch? You didn't realize that rich guys like to pretend they're younger by tanning and getting their sagging neck skin treated?"

"Yeah, well, no. I guess I've never thought about it before. The people you've had me meet were all in suits or tuxes, not shorts and expensive polo shirts that show me how many skin grafts and muscle implants they've had to keep up their appearances."

"So it took you by surprise or what?" Malcolm said, developing a bit of an edge to his voice now, too.

"It's more than that . . ."

"Okay. Then tell me how my business is being tainted by interacting with the likes of Craig Allen and Tom Fordham."

"Tom was better, at least. I didn't get the sense that he was a womanizer AND completely made of spare parts," Patch said more to himself than to Malcolm.

"Oh. Okay. I'm glad you approve of Tom, at least. That's very kind of you," Malcolm bit at his lower lip and flexed his fingers out and then back into a fist against the steering wheel.

"I'm not explaining this very well—" Patch started to say, but Malcolm interrupted.

"You could have fooled me."

"I'm sorry, okay? Craig gave me the creeps after he told me that women didn't seem to mind his feet, and those skin grafts and muscle implants don't seem right. I don't know why. I've known for a while that people get them. Well, I guess some people get them."

Malcolm's eyes widened for a second, and he stopped biting his lip and nodded. "This is about your mom, isn't it?" The edge to his voice was completely gone.

Patch hadn't put words to his feelings yet, but when Malcolm mentioned his mom, some things clicked into place.

"What about my mom?" Patch asked, slowly lifting his head from off his fist.

"Your mom went through a Total System Donation."

"You think I'd ever forget that?" Patch said with a catch in his voice.

"No, of course not. What I mean is, your mom donated all of her skin so guys like Craig could have younger-looking skin for a while. And he's not even taking good care of it. I mean, did you see how weirdly tanned he was?"

"Yes! So gross!" Patch said, brushing at his eyes.

"Totally gross. I get it," Malcolm said.

"No, you don't," Patch said, putting his head back on his fist.

"Okay. I don't. That's true. But I can imagine how you're feeling right now. And I do care. Give me that much, at least?" Malcolm asked. "I'm looking at you, which I'll keep doing even at the risk of wrecking my fancy car to make sure you're hearing me."

"Right. And, of course, you don't have the driverless mode activated at all, either, I'm sure."

"Alright. Though, I trust you'd think it a stupid waste to wreck my car to prove a point, anyway," Malcolm said, looking at the road and hitting a button on the steering wheel, giving him back the controls.

Patch let out a loud breath and cleared his throat. "You're right. It would be a total waste. And I do. I really do hear you. I really appreciate you, Mal."

"Darn right," Malcolm said with a serious look on his face, although Patch knew that Malcolm was fighting a spontaneous, beautiful grin.

Malcolm and Patch rode the last couple of miles in silence. When Patch got to his room, he threw himself onto his bed and started tossing a pink rubber ball toward his ceiling, then placed his earpiece in.

"Hey, Siri?"

"Hi, Patch."

"Hi. Locate Gwendolyn Reynolds."

Okay. Let me find Gwendolyn Reynolds."

chapter 7

Jefferson is back. Those three words were ones that Gwen had assumed she'd never hear, though she might have wanted to hear them more desperately than any other sound in the world. The full magnitude of the three words hadn't sunk in yet, either. How could it?

The parking garage, the elevator ride up past the window that gave her just enough of a glimpse to know for certain what was going on in the room below, but no way to do anything to help. And she still remembered her primal scream on the elevator ride up to the main level of the bank corporation.

Over the past months, Gwen had found her own coping mechanisms so that she wouldn't be a total mess anytime she thought about that early morning elevator ride, which, even now, came to her mind many times a day. And no wonder.

Everywhere she went, everybody she talked to or met, all of the bustling activity in or around the warehouse—it all existed because of one person—Jefferson. So how could she ever grieve his loss properly? She had to keep up the fool's hope that, somehow, they would get him back. She couldn't kill that hope, even if it was the healthy thing to do. No. She was certain of at least one thing: most of the people who stayed with their movement didn't stay because of her. They stayed because of Jefferson.

"What's going on, Gwen? You look like you just saw a ghost?" Stan said.

"What's that?" Gwen asked, shaking herself awake from her own thoughts.

"Are things okay? What's so important that your tablet was on fire?"

Better than okay, Gwen thought. She was about to let Stan know that his old friend was still alive and back, but she stopped herself. Once she announced it, things would be different for her. Stan certainly wouldn't be driving to who knows where, trusting her with such important responsibilities as securing supplies from impressive people like Gerty once he knew that Jefferson was back and in charge again. What am I thinking? Jefferson is back! What's wrong with you? She reminded herself again.

"Jefferson's back!" Gwen shouted.

"Wait? What? He's back? He's back!" Stan pounded the steering wheel triumphantly.

"Whoa, Stan! We still have to make it back to the warehouse alive if we want to see him again!" Gwen yelled, pulling the truck back into their lane by jerking the steering wheel.

"Sorry. I can't believe it! I mean, I've been hoping for this, but I . . . I never really thought—"

"I know. I get it. It's impossible to process it all right now. Hopefully, when we see him, the news will become more real for both of us," Gwen said as Stan turned off the road and onto the long gravel driveway that led to the warehouse and the riverfront.

Gwen and Stan could hear the commotion inside the warehouse from inside the truck with the windows up. Once Stan had parked, Gwen hopped down from the truck and walked the few steps to the open bay door on shaky legs. Everything about the space was so familiar. This had been her life for the last several months. She knew the warehouse and the river as well as she knew anywhere now. But, somehow, things had changed, as if the world had shifted at least one degree and everything she knew about herself and the world around her she had to meet for the first time all over again.

She pushed through the crowd, trying to get to the center of the group of people congregating around the very spot where she had given out the morning's marching orders. She kept weaving her own path until she bumped into the back of someone tall and shockingly thin.

"Jefferson, is that really you?" Gwen said it quietly, but somehow, her voice carried better in that moment, as if she were using a different frequency.

The man standing in front of her, with his back to her, turned in a flash and looked down. The late-afternoon sun was striking the warehouse skylights, and that refracted light struck Jefferson from behind, seemingly emanating from him. His wild gray hair was on fire. "Oh, Gwen. It's you!"

Jefferson picked Gwen up in a hug that swallowed both of them into their own world. Gwen's arms wrapped around his jacket. The same jacket he had worn the morning he rescued her from the basement of the bank headquarters. The morning she'd last seen him. Until now.

"Of all the things I was looking forward to most, this was it," Jefferson whispered to Gwen and brought their foreheads together with his hands.

The moment lasted maybe a few seconds. Gwen knew it couldn't last long, but she did her best to experience it, to see Jefferson and realize he was tangible and alive, then safely nestle the moment into her mind so she could recall it during the harder times she knew she would experience in the future.

But the moment passed. The sounds of the crowd, the late afternoon sun, the smell of old oil canisters and excited, sweaty bodies all came back to Gwen's conscious attention. And as she was wrenched back into reality, tears started to flow.

"Where on earth have you been all this time?" Gwen shouted, not meaning to sound as angry as she felt for reasons she couldn't understand.

"I know. It's been too long. Explanations will come. I promise. But now is not the time or place," Jefferson said.

Gwen held Jefferson's resolute gaze for an extra second or two to reassure herself that what Jefferson had promised was true and that he was real. Then she nodded. Jefferson smiled and gave Gwen's hand a warm squeeze as he turned back to the crowd. Gwen faded toward the back, feeling, for the first time in the last two months, uncertain of what she should do next.

Not knowing where else to go and feeling uncertain about her role, Gwen wandered out of the warehouse and walked slowly to the tree near the riverbank, where she found she did her best thinking. She didn't feel comfortable moving forward with the plans she had set out to do that afternoon. They seemed of little consequence now.

Gwen stretched her right leg upward to place her foot on a large knot that protruded several inches from the rest of the trunk and was a couple of feet above the base of the tree. Using the knot as leverage and reaching for the lowest main branch, she pulled herself up to her sitting area in a practiced and fluid motion. There, sitting in the tree, life seemed small enough to manage. Her concerns and worries and fears seemed further away. So, while in the tree, things made a bit of sense.

She settled into her favorite nook. A spot up in the tree where three stout branches shot out from the trunk, making a comfortable place to sit with her back against its firm trunk and her feet dangling between the three branches. Somehow, she doubted she would be able to make sense of things, even there in her favorite thinking spot.

Jefferson has been gone all this time. And now he's suddenly back? She brushed her hands against the roughness of the branch's bark, taking some comfort in familiar things. Her thoughts were distracted for a second by a savory smell that wafted past her in the air. Stan must be making some kind of celebratory stew. With their last weeks' worth of food. Then the real source of her uneasiness since hearing that Jefferson was back clicked into place in her mind.

She had secured two more months of food for their operation. She did that. She had won over Gerty and had made her into at least a partner and maybe even an ally. She had kept things running the whole time, even when no one expected her to step up.

Gwen swiped at the sweat that beaded around her neck, then looked across the river to the crumbling monuments of government leaders long dead. She could just make out some kind of hawk returning to its nest made out of a jumble of branches on top of one of the stone monoliths. Jefferson wouldn't have had anything to come back to without me, she thought. It was a petty thing, but she also knew it was true.

She vividly remembered that morning, returning from Boston without Jefferson. The shock and emptiness could be so clearly read in the faces of Jefferson's followers—the followers who chose to follow her instead of abandoning the movement. What's the point? What was she looking for exactly?

"Thank you."

Gwen jumped at the sound and had to grab the branch above her to steady herself. She looked down to where the voice had come from and saw Jefferson looking up at her with a tired smile.

"Thank you? For what?" she said more brightly than she felt.

"For all of it. Everything."

"Sure thing, I guess. I mean, someone needed to keep things going, right?"

"No. Actually, no one did, and I doubt anybody else would have if you didn't," Jefferson said, sitting down and leaning his head against the tree trunk. "After the train wreck of our first attempts at disrupting the banks, I wouldn't have blamed anybody for thinking we tried and failed and it was time to go home. You had more reason than most."

Gwen perked her ears up and leaned her head down to glance at Jefferson. "What do you mean by that? I've been as involved and a part of this movement as long as anybody."

"Oh, absolutely. That's not what I meant at all. You had two additional reasons to leave when I got caught. You'd been detained by contract enforcers, so you knew what that was like. I imagine you'd rather not be detained again. And two . . ."

Jefferson paused for a couple of breaths that Gwen could hear even up in the tree—the slow, gravelly sound of an inconsistent intake of air and its release. "And two, you weren't there for the movement in the first place. Not really."

Gwen swung herself around on the branch she was sitting on so she could better face Jefferson. "That's not true. I believed in what we were trying to do."

"I know. That's not my point."

"That sure sounds like your point."

"Let me explain what I meant—"

"Oh good, so I can be a better soldier," Gwen said flippantly.

"No, listen to me—"

"No! You listen to me." Gwen jumped down from the tree, landing on the gravel-covered ground and making a loud crashing noise reminiscent of a shotgun going off. Her whole body shook, fueled by a rage she didn't know she'd been bottling up.

"You left us! How could you do that? Why did you come to save me? You knew they would want you more than me! Did you honestly expect to rescue me from their headquarters without them knowing? They couldn't have held me more than an extra day or two. But you've been gone for two months. Two months without a word! Without any idea if you were alive or dead."

Gwen threw up her hands and walked to the riverbank, kicking pieces of gravel and hearing the satisfying plunking as the gravel sank. Jefferson stood behind her a few paces, but she didn't turn to face him this time.

"You left, and I don't know why I tried to keep things going. But I did. And I was getting the hang of things."

"I'm sure you were. I'm not surprised."

"A lot of people did leave."

"Not too many."

"Some. I did what I could," Gwen said, picking up a larger stone and skipping it along the river until it disappeared into the water that was, by then, getting dark and reflecting the sunset as it shone in the flowing water. She didn't realize how long she had been going over things in her head before Jefferson had come out to see her, but it must have been an hour or more.

"I'm so sorry for leaving. I knew going to the bank headquarters was a risky move."

Gwen stiffened at that and was about to shout back a sarcastic comment, but Jefferson quickly continued.

"Okay. It was a stupid idea. But we do stupid things when people we care about are in trouble. I wasn't basing my decision off some algorithm or predictive analytics. I lost you, and I needed to get you back."

Some of Gwen's previous intensity and anger dissipated. She lowered her shoulders when she realized they had been hunched forward and pulled nearly up to her ears even after climbing the tree.

"Do you remember what I said to you on the day we first met?"

Of course she remembered it. The men who were trying to kill her, the fight she almost won and almost ran away from, the pain of the stab wounds in her leg and back. Waking up to find Jefferson rummaging through his things and saying things too fast for her blood-deprived brain to process.

"I don't remember a whole lot of that first conversation. As you recall, I was all but dead when you found me."

"Yeah, but not completely dead—yet. You should have been totally dead. I mean, what sixteen-year-old girl takes on three desperate adult men?"

"The kind that wants to survive," Gwen said flatly.

"Exactly! I don't know why it stuck in my head. I usually don't pay that much attention to the words that come out of my mouth."

Gwen chuckled and tried to stifle the laugh too late.

Jefferson grinned. "That gets me in trouble some days. But on that particular day, at that moment, I remember exactly what I said. And that memory imprint is a testament to how impressive you were to me even then. I said, 'I saved you because there should be no way you're clever enough, agile enough, or tough enough to best three armed men by yourself. Yet, that is exactly what you did.'"

Jefferson paused, lowered himself to the ground, and sat with his arms wrapped around his bent knees. Even through the baggy utility pants he was wearing, the outline of his bony legs stood out. Gwen sat next to him and looked out to the fading sunset.

"My God, didn't they feed you at all while you were held there?" Gwen said, shocked.

"Not much. Not enough. Let me finish reciting my brilliant thought from that first day, though. I then said, 'That's a once-in-a-lifetime thing. And I figured it would probably be wise for me to get to know the young girl who managed such a feat.' You've only become more impressive as I've gotten to know you, Gwen. That's why I wasn't surprised at all that you've carried on with this crazy movement or that you've got the leadership stuff down already. You're definitely still my once-in-a-lifetime friend, and I'm going to rely on you as much now as when I was gone. I could never afford to set you aside and would never want to."

Gwen saw Jefferson's tired smile and smiled back. She realized, as she had in only a couple of instances since meeting him, that Jefferson was old. And the weight of his experiences made him seem older still.

"I hear you even negotiated with Gerty. I mean, seriously! That woman is a tough cookie," Jefferson said.

"Yeah. No kidding. I think Stan and I would have been happy to have left her farm with our lives. We did end up with a pretty good deal on supplies, though," Gwen said with a proud smile.

"Yes! I couldn't have done that half as well."

"You would have figured things out better—"

"Knock it off with the false modesty. It's more insulting than placating. Neither approach suits you."

"That sounds more like the Jefferson I used to know," Gwen said.

"I'll get back there eventually, with enough time and sleep. Oh, sleep! That's the number two thing I was most looking forward to if I ever got out. Real sleep."

Gwen held silent, expecting Jefferson to explain, but when nothing came, she felt like she needed to nudge a bit.

"What did they do to you, Jeff?" Gwen asked, putting her hand on Jefferson's shoulder, but at the touch, he jumped back as if repulsed.

"Sorry. I don't know why I did that. I know you were trying to be kind. I just need time and rest, and I'm sure I'll be as right as rain."

68

"Jeff, what happened?"

Jefferson was visibly shaking but slowly calmed down, and his breathing returned to a normal, more measured pattern.

"The worst of it is you know you'll break eventually. You put on a brave face and endure whatever might come for a while. But then days melt together. You lose connections to things. Important things like relationships and the meaning of your life. Until one day, you realize that if you survived . . . I didn't know how I could live with myself."

"So they tortured you?" Gwen said, inching a bit closer to Jefferson.

"I don't want to talk about it."

"I think you need to—"

"What I need is rest and time!" Jefferson burst out.

Gwen jumped back and thought about leaving Jefferson alone. But then it struck her that she was probably the only person in the whole operation that Jefferson would ever open up to about his time with the contract enforcers.

"I'm not going to push it. But wouldn't it make sense to have it out now before things get busy again? Now that you're back, there's a lot to do and tons of people will be all over you with questions and needs."

Jefferson pushed out a ragged sigh.

"You're right. There won't be a better time. Just promise me one thing—"

Gwen raised an eyebrow. "Okay. What am I promising?"

"Promise me that you won't be so disgusted by the end of this story that you don't let me at least try to earn your trust and friendship again."

Gwen opened her eyes wide and then frowned, startled by what Jefferson asked, but she was also certain of there being only one response she could give.

"Of course. I promise."

"Okay. I don't know if I can do this. But let's start with where you saw me last."

chapter 8

Robert Vanderbilt had left me to my own thoughts. Time was such a hard thing to measure down in the basements of the bank, where no clock or sunlight could give me any sense of time passing. But it felt like I was in the room for hours.

At first, I worked on a strategy to get out. I tried both doors. Of course, they locked from the outside. Then I felt through my pockets, not daring to reveal what I had available because I assumed the room's black windows, which ran around the upper third of the four walls, were actually surveillance monitors.

I had a pen, a utility knife, and an apple in the two front pockets of my jacket and a tablet in my inside pocket. Maybe because I was so many levels down in the basements or because they purposely blocked any signals to that room, my tablet had no signal which made it about as useful as a brick, so I worked it into my plan that way.

Casually, I searched the room for any additional supplies and resources, but the room had been swept clean. Just two folding chairs and a cheap plastic card table—the kind with fake wood grain and a plastic cover— were there. And a sign declaring the space *The Room*.

I don't think I ever told you the stupid little joke we wanted to play, Robert and me. When we were young associates in that very bank, we had a plan to name a room in the building *The Room*. We thought it fit in one of those corny old horror movies. Robert must have thought it poetic, somehow, that I be detained in that very room.

So I had what I was wearing and carrying in my pockets, and I sat in *The Room* in as boring a way as I could so that whoever was observing me through the walls of black mirrors would underestimate me. Eventually, the contract enforcers came. There were six of them with helmets and face shields that completely obscured their faces.

Their entire uniform was of a silvery-gray material that I assumed was made of some kind of enhanced Kevlar. It molded around their bodies as though they had been dipped in the metallic material rather than having put it on. I'd heard of clothes like that—clothing that takes advantage of nano and robotic technology so the fabric can learn the contours of what it's draped over and provide rapid self-healing properties—but had never actually seen anybody wear it.

Isn't that ridiculous? Even as they came in, my first thought was a fascination with their uniforms. As it turned out, I didn't have much time to admire them. The enforcers used some sort of light and sound device that not only blinded and deafened me but also knocked me out. My beautiful escape strategy thrown out the door within the first seconds.

When I came to, I was covered in vomit. I suppose the flash device did that to people. The acid from my own body burned my nose, and it took nearly all of my attention to keep the remaining taste of that vomit from making me gag up whatever was left inside me.

My hands were immobilized in front of me, resting lifelessly on a steel table, and my legs had a similar constraint. I couldn't feel them, either though the chair I occupied held my head up absolutely erect, so I couldn't see down to check my legs. A small circular monitor flashed a red light in a regular rhythm, just above eye level on the wall I was facing. The door made a low booming sound as it shut. The contract enforcers had left the small room with white walls, concrete floors, and me strapped in place.

Eventually, after moving my eyes and eyebrows around, I was pretty sure I was wearing some kind of mesh cap on my head, and by twisting my head from side to side using the little I could, I could feel some kind of cable running from the back of the cap.

I had never seen or used the device that was attached to my head. But Robert and I had talked about developing a tool just like it. And Robert has one quality I am certain of—he is thorough. I had no way of knowing how fast the technology advanced beyond what Robert or I had theorized back then until the cap I was wearing activated.

You probably haven't watched shows where they used the old interrogation stunts like waterboarding. Or sleep deprivation, caused by playing horrible screamo music and flashing floodlights at you in random intervals. Those techniques worked by making the subject so tired and hopeless and disoriented that they eventually gave in. Sometimes it worked. But those techniques were generic.

I was hit by some kind of invisible current that penetrated my skull. As the current started flowing, it felt like warm fluid was being squirted inside my brain. Maybe the monitor sent a signal to activate the cap on my head, or maybe the monitor on the wall was just a way of observing the effects of the cap. I don't know. But within seconds, my entire head was filled with a slow-flowing sludge that washed over my brain.

Right when I thought my head would explode if any more of that fluid seeped in, it stopped circulating, and then my visual field flashed white. Completely blank. Gradually, I was able to make out some rough definition of the display before my eyes. A house made of red brick. A wrap-around porch. Trees lining a sidewalk. Colors eventually became more pronounced, and I could make out the soft sunset hues in the sky and fleecy purple clouds above the house. The lush green lawn underfoot.

The visual field darted to the side at the sound of a bird, and I was surprised that I had somehow turned my head. I still recognized that I was strapped to the chair. As I bent down, I could see my legs again, and almost unbidden, the legs I saw started moving across the stone path that led from the sidewalk to the wooden steps in front of the porch and the front door of the house.

Other senses grew clearer and more natural, and as the full scene unfolded, I got a weird sense of familiarity and a comfortable urge to walk right into the house without any fear or hesitancy. I pulled open the screen door and turned the glass knob, glancing with one eye at the porch swing that was moving gently in the slight breeze that brushed against my face.

No lights were on in the house as I entered, but large windows throughout the space showed a leather sofa and armchair tucked around a wooden coffee table that sat in front of a large fireplace. I took a couple of steps forward. On the left-hand side, there was a room with open glass doors and a baby grand piano with music books scattered around it. Three terracotta pots resting on wrought-iron plant stands overflowed with red flowers.

I turned my attention forward and slowly walked toward the dining room table. I rested my hands on the smooth, dark wood, and my eyes focused on a tiny faded handprint in glossy pink paint. As I placed my hand over it, memories came to me in a raging flood.

I was home. Well, at least the home I'd left when I resigned from the bank. But that handprint. That had been sanded off and refinished long before I left. My daughter must have been barely two when she'd left that handprint. I remembered my kids clearly by then, too. Olivia and Emma. They were old enough to be disgusted by my decision to leave Boston—the place they had known their whole lives—and to stick with their mom when she, too, decided to stay rather than go with me into an unknown future. Who could blame them? I must have scared them, too—the day I tried to convince them to come with me. I had such a frantic energy that day.

I'm not proud of how hard I tried or how much reassurance I gave them that we'd be able to build a good place somewhere away from what would soon become a dangerous Eastern Seaboard. Maybe I should have tried harder. I'm not trying to make excuses or justify my behavior, but try to imagine that you were responsible for some corruption in a company that you'd built your life around. That would be a horrible feeling in its own right. Now try to imagine that corruption growing so that it caused the breakdown of the entire world order. A world order that had existed and thrived for centuries. Gone in a matter of weeks.

The magnitude of what I had done . . . the guilt and horror. Knowing how many millions of lives would be destroyed. How many millions of people would be forgotten by society. I couldn't contain it, and the only thing I could think to do was to escape far enough away that maybe I wouldn't be reminded of what I had done every time I opened my fridge or drove on roads or ate food from the grocery store where brands that benefitted from my mistake showed up everywhere. So I left without my family. In shame. I left, I guess, because of that shame and the constant urge to forget my mistake.

The longer I experienced that projected reality, the more it felt right and real. How often do you check on the life you're living to ensure it's the real or right one? As I moved into that projected life, it felt more like the only one I had ever known. I could have sworn that I had lived a late afternoon exactly like the one I had jumped into. And the more I wanted it to be real, the more it became real. And the more I pushed out the memory of how I got there, the more distant it became. By the time I heard Olivia's voice, I had convinced myself that the strange circumstance of my arrival was a trick of a dream. Like how after waking from a particularly vivid dream, we're not quite certain what's real and what comes from the dream. I accepted the lie.

"Daddy!"

I turned to see my older daughter coming downstairs like she always had—with an artist's flair and passion for life. She was never halfway about anything. And in that moment, I was her object of attention.

"Olivia?" I said, filled with surprised joy, as if I had shown up to a hospital and was handed the most beautiful baby, the thing I had wanted most in the world, and told that I got to keep her because she was truly mine.

"You've been gone for simply hours, Daddy. Why did you have to go? It's Saturday."

"I know, honey. I had to do a bit of work. But I'm done now. What've you been up to?" I said, feeling certain that what I had said was the truth but not knowing how I knew. The wrongness of ever having left Olivia was the most real thing I could have possibly remembered.

"Me and Emma were playing campout in the blanket fort. You've gotta come up to see it. We built a campfire."

"A campfire? Really?"

"No, silly. It's just pretend. But promise that you'll pretend too? It's no fun unless everyone does. Promise!" Olivia said, pointing her finger at me with solemnity.

"Oh, I promise. I'll be the best pretender. Watch." I bent over so Olivia could lead me by the hand upstairs—she had to stretch to reach my fingers. Time passed then. It felt like the normal passing of time to me. Days passed where I just lived life. But even as the days bled into weeks and those weeks bled into months, somewhere in the hidden parts of my brain, I retained a realization that I had been given a second chance at life. Similar to how it would feel to survive a bad car wreck—one that shouldn't be survived.

Every experience felt richer. Deadlines at work didn't seem to matter as much. I went to work like normal, but I didn't pull the late nights. I was home for dinner and bedtime stories in the blanket fort nearly every evening.

My wife was my best friend. That's why we'd decided to give marriage a try even though I was asexual. Did I ever tell you that? Anyway, we both wanted to raise kids, so we made that work. And, oh, what wonderful work it was to do during that second chance. And I wasn't going to miss a single thing. Not a conversation with my wife, Julia. Not a porch-swing moment with Emma, or a single laugh as she and Olivia jumped into a pile of autumn leaves. Not even mundane, everyday things—searching for matching socks, loading up backpacks in a mad dash to get the kids to school. It felt so good to live it all.

Everything except for work, that is. As the months rushed past, I felt more urgency to shift my professional track. I even considered going back to school to get my teacher's certificate so I could teach high school economics and finance classes. I built up the courage to broach the subject with Julia one evening after the kids were already in bed.

I staged things as perfectly as I could. I had two mugs of steaming apple cinnamon tea with apple slices and cinnamon sticks actually added to the mugs. I had soft piano music playing in the background, and the lights were off, except for the ones that would lead Julia right to the living room, where the tea was sending off delightful aromas.

"Don't let me forget to talk to Olivia's teacher tomorrow about her being out Thursday for her first orthodontist appointment. She is seriously going to hate braces. We'll have to focus on how many colors she can choose from," Julia said, picking up books and a cup from the ground and placing them on the kitchen counter.

I'd braced myself for her flipping on the kitchen light, but she didn't. She re-emerged from the dark kitchen and started to follow the path I was hoping she would.

"Something smells amazing? Did you get an apple cinnamon candle?" She said, following her nose to the waiting mugs and to where I sat leaning forward in my armchair in anticipation.

"Uh oh! It's a trap. Best I get out while I still can." Julia said in mock alarm.

"Too late for that, I'm afraid. I know where you live now. Besides, the tea is the perfect temperature for some serious sipping. It would be such a shame to let it go to waste."

"Okay. You found my only weakness—apple cinnamon tea. But I reserve the right to back out of negotiations at any point after my mug runs dry."

"Deal," I said with a relieved smile, gesturing to her mug and the sofa.

"So go ahead and lay it on me," Julia said, sitting cross-legged on the sofa, close enough that I could smell her subtle vanilla bean hand lotion.

"What makes you so sure I need to lay anything on you? Can't a husband do something nice for his wife from time to time?"

"I suppose, but past behavior is the best predictor of future behavior, right? Or whatever that psychology professor said in that class after you showed up ten minutes early so you could find a seat next to the one I always sat in," Julia said, dipping her face behind her mug but revealing her mischievous eyes.

"Guilty as charged. I don't think I remember a single thing from those lectures. But I remember the first time you walked into class wearing that fabulous red peacoat you loved. Man, you were amazing."

"Were? Careful, this negotiation is still very young, and you don't want to offend the other party before you've given your pitch."

"Amazing then, and more amazing now. If I haven't learned that after fifteen years of being married to you, then I hardly deserve to call myself an analyst." I said, wishing the words could carry how much feeling came with them.

Julia uncrossed her legs enough to rub my knee with her socked toes. Ordinarily, physical touch didn't appeal to me, and most of the time, I tolerated it. Julia was the only person who made that different for me. I didn't long for that touch, but it felt right and good to me in a deeper way than anything else.

"To be honest, though," Julia said, taking another thoughtful sip of tea. "Lately, things about you have felt different."

"Different how? Different good, I hope?"

"Definitely good. You've been here, and you seem more present when you are—especially with the kids, but with me too. So, I retract my previous statement," Julia said, hiding her face behind her mug again.

"Duly noted. Let the record reflect that," I said, smiling back. "I'm almost regretting it now, but you're right—I do have an ulterior motive."

"Ah! I knew it. The intuition I built during those crazy nights in the ER with guys bleeding out, confessing to having not been caught in a gang-related shootout even while I pulled out the bullets is serving me well, yet again," Julia said. "Just kidding. You're not nearly as bad a bluffer as those guys."

"High praise, there. Thanks."

"Anytime. So what's up? It must be important if you're going through all this staging," Julia said, resting her mug on one of the black ceramic coasters I'd set on the coffee table.

"Right again," I said, taking a deep breath before continuing. "I love our life here. I love our home and the fact that we live close enough to a great school for Olivia and Emma to go there and that they enjoy it, too. I love the porch swing and the big sycamore trees. I even love those horrible pods they drop every fall that are impossible to clean up."

"I feel a big but coming," Julia said.

78

"Yes. I'm getting there. Bottom line—I love the life we've built together, and I know how much sacrifice and work you've put into building it. Way more than your fair share."

"We're probably at seventy–thirty. Okay, I'll go as far as sixty-five–thirty-five," Julia said, dropping her socked toes to the plush rug and leaning closer to me, taking both my hands in hers.

"That's generous of you, honestly. Everything in my life is so beautiful. Except for my work."

"Oh?"

"Yeah. I know it's made us a very comfortable living. But when I leave you in the mornings, I feel like I'm being cheated of the most valuable resource on Earth."

"What's that?"

"Time. I feel like work is robbing me of precious moments," I said.

"Doesn't work always do that?" Julia asked. "I don't think there are jobs that don't take time."

"Right. But it's different when I feel like I can't be proud of what I'm doing. I want to be able to tell Olivia and Emma about what I do, to take them to the office, and be excited to share what I do with them."

"I didn't realize work was making you so miserable," Julia said with a bit of an edge.

"It's not as bad as all that. Well, not yet, at least. I don't think. How can I explain this in a way that won't come off as petty? I know there are much harder jobs. Your nursing job was ten times harder. A hundred times, even. And you loved it because you were able to really help people."

"Yeah, but it was more important that I stay home with Olivia and Emma. We both agreed that was best for the greater good or whatever high-minded aspirations we had back then when we didn't know the first thing about parenting," Julia said, shaking my hands for extra emphasis.

"That's absolutely right. For the greater good. I'm going to come right out with it. The bank has been dabbling in some uncharted investments that make me uncomfortable. They're hinting that they're going to hand that portfolio off to me to manage."

"What kind of investments? You're not talking about child trafficking or cozying up with cartels, right?"

"No. I don't want to bore you with the messy financial mechanisms. But, basically, I'm worried that if the bank goes down this road, they'll get some serious leverage and make unheard-of amounts of money—"

"I thought that was the point of your job. You're a financial analyst, right?"

"I'm afraid it'll break the entire financial system. Worldwide. Okay, I've said it. I know it sounds crazy. But I've run the predictive models and almost all lead to major breakdowns of governments around the world. The United States' financial markets will feel it too. So, I've come up with three possible scenarios. Are you ready to hear them?"

Julia nodded, squeezing my hands harder.

"Option one, I ask for a reassignment to where I don't deal with those financial instruments. We might take a bit of a salary cut, but nothing unmanageable."

"Okay, that one sounds reasonable," Julia said with a reassuring smile.

"Option two, I go along with it. I take on the shady portfolios. We become ridiculously wealthy. I'll spend a lot more time in the office, but we'll have more money than we've ever dreamed of, and maybe it'll provide some opportunities for you and the kids that'll make up for my absence."

"Let's take that one right off the table, okay? You not having time with Olivia and Emma is not an option. They would resent me, too, if I went along with it, anyway," Julia said, pulling my head toward her and kissing my forehead. "And option three?"

"I abandon financial markets entirely. Maybe I go back to school for a teaching certificate and teach high school. We'd have to sell the house, but we could buy a great one, maybe in Ohio near your parents—or Kansas—even. We could pay cash, based on the equity we'd get for this house, and we could get a big old Craftsman like the ones you love so much, somewhere in the Midwest. I'd teach; maybe you could work part-time at the local hospital or a clinic if you wanted to. We could still have our blanket fort upstairs, the porch swing, big trees. The school probably wouldn't be quite as good, but maybe that would make Olivia and Emma stand out that much more. And . . ."

Julia brought my head toward her again and leaned her forehead against mine, her bangs dangling across my eyes. "And . . ." she nudged.

"And I wouldn't feel like I was wrecking the world my kids are set to inherit. Maybe I'd contribute to making it a little bit better." I closed my eyes and dropped my hands so that Julia was the only one holding them up.

"My goodness, your hands are heavy. Okay then," she said, giving my hands one more good shake, dropping them, and hopping back to sit crossed-legged on the sofa.

"What does okay mean?" I said, lifting my eyes and clearing my throat.

"Okay means that if you're certain there isn't any way of making things work at your current job . . ." she said, more as a question than a statement.

"Not that I can comfortably live with. I guess I could try to sabotage things. But the bank would probably find out, and I'd end up with jail time and no severance package. And then they'd reset what I'd done without me."

"Also, not a viable option then," Julia said.

"And maybe when I explain why I'm resigning, that might make enough difference for them to think twice before diving too deeply into those investments. I mean, they haven't handed them to me yet, and they're just doing preliminary explorations. Robert and I devised them ourselves. Maybe they'd listen to me. No doubt other associates would gladly pick things up if I refused, though. Robert would certainly jump at the chance if it was handed to him."

"Ah, yes! Mister Vanderbilt. The man with the big name and puffed-up shirts," Julia said with a smirk.

"That's not fair. Okay, it's mostly fair. But it's hardly his fault. With a last name like that, I can only imagine how much pressure he's getting to strike it rich however he can—to restore his family's name and wealth. Anyway, so that's it. That's my pitch. I imagine you need some time to deliberate with your negotiation team?"

"You know what?" Julia said, picking up her mug again and drinking the remaining tea even though I was certain it was cold.

"What's that?"

"I don't think deliberation will be necessary. I think there's really only one option—"

"I feel a big but coming," I said, grinning hopefully.

"When you say moving near my parents you're not envisioning like next-door neighbors or anything, right?" Julia looked stone-faced serious, but the seriousness slowly melted into a wry smile.

"Close enough to visit any time, but far enough we would have our own space and routine. Guaranteed," I replied, using all my willpower to keep from bursting with gratitude for Julia and with a thrill for the potential next adventure with her.

She laughed out loud, tilting her face up and closing her eyes. I jumped up and pulled her to me in a fierce hug. We parted just long enough to kiss with both of my hands cradling her face. I picked her up by the waist and spun her around a few times, not caring one whit that she kicked books off the coffee table. I put her back down, and we stood still, letting our hearts and breathing slow.

"Oh. And one other thing," Julia said, looking up at me questioningly.

I braced for whatever she would say but nodded.

"We definitely have to have room for that blanket fort. Olivia and Emma have had it up for ages, and I think they would never be happy without it, wherever we end up."

"Space for a blanket fort. Got it," I said, making a check mark in the air with my hand and smiling foolishly, but not even caring.

"Do you think we should wait a while to tell the kids?" I asked as the reality of things sank in.

"Why? It'll be an adventure. I think they'll be even more excited than you are. We shouldn't have any problem selling the house the way the market in Boston is going. Let's tell them in the morning."

"Yes! Why not start things moving now," I said with a pump of my fist in the air.

Julia grabbed the fist with both hands. "But now, we both need sleep. All of these life-changing plans make me absolutely exhausted. Race you to the bedroom?" Julia said with a knowing look.

"Are you serious? Are you ten years old?" I said with a chuckle.

"I'm even better than ten because I'm an adult, which means I can do adult things," Julia said with a demure smile as she grabbed my hand, and we rushed for the bedroom.

That's when the visual field froze and slowly faded to a blaring white. That fluid that had flowed into my brain was suddenly sucked out. The light that had flashed red on the monitor looked clear in the black-and-white scene and then gradually transitioned into a harsh blood red. As the white walls gained definition, I realized I was screaming. Bloodcurdling, visceral screams. I didn't know how long I had been screaming, but long enough for my throat to feel like it was on fire. Along with spewing saliva, bloody flecks also dropped from my mouth onto the steel table where my hands still rested, immobilized.

Though my limbs were frozen to the chair, my wide, bloodshot eyes searched the room wildly. Streams of sweat flowed down my shoulders and face and drenched my jacket and pants; an unearthly hunger gnawed at my insides and brain. I lowered my eyes, expecting to see my stomach distended and my arms as mere shriveled husks. It felt like I was at the very last moment of despair before succumbing to starvation. But my stomach and arms looked as they should have, except for the pools of collecting sweat and the yellow pallor of my hands.

I needed food. My whole limited brain knew that. And that hunger made me horribly disoriented. I felt suspended in time and couldn't trust where I was or who I was or any of the experiences I had next. A voice filled my head.

"The hunger you are feeling won't subside for several days unless we treat you with an antidote that we are very happy to provide. Answer a few simple questions, and it will be administered right away."

The intensity of my screams changed to more of a weeping. I had no words to call out in response. No vocabulary at all. Though I knew what I wanted to say, the mechanics of thought reaching the vocal cords were still being reconfigured since I'd burst out of the alternate reality. To know what to say and how to say it was such a natural part of who I was. To discover that my brain was misfiring and not able to say a word added so much to my horrifying confusion.

The sick, greasy feeling of fluid rushed back into my brain. This time, the fluid seemed lighter somehow, as if the fluid they were inserting flowed easier than the other fluid I was already familiar with. When my brain was fully saturated, the voice continued without any kind of response from me.

"It is normal to lose the ability to speak after the procedure. It, too, will come back after we administer the antidote. First question: How do you feel?"

I wanted to throw myself off the nearest tall building. I wanted to claw my eyes out and disappear. The fluid in my brain took on a new circulation that made me think the cap on my head was transferring my thoughts into some form that could be recorded and analyzed.

"Thank you for being so forthcoming. It helps us refine our process. Question number two: Where and when were you transported during the procedure?"

I was instantly taken back to a freeze-frame of the last moment I'd had with Julia—the soft trail of light, the two mugs sitting on ceramic coasters on the coffee table, Julia's eager hand gripping mine. The scene wasn't a photograph, though. By some cruel trick, it carried with it some of the emotion, too. Though, it felt more like a mockery of the experience I had just had rather than a true depiction of that beautiful scene.

Suddenly, I discovered a new source of hunger. This one was even more intense than the ache for food. I needed to go back to that world.

Nothing else mattered, and nothing else ever would unless I was able to be transported back into the reality that I had experienced as a tumble of months, one after another after another, but it had really been just a moment in the harsh reality I had been jarred back to.

"Excellent. Thank you. Because you haven't fought our mental probes, we will administer part of the antidote treatment now. You will be able to answer our final question verbally."

There was a pause and another shuffle of circulation in the flow of the fluid in my brain, and I knew I could speak again, although I didn't know how I knew it.

"Final question: Would you like to go back to the reality that was projected during the procedure?"

Gwen waited a long time for Jefferson to share what his response was to the last question the contract enforcers had asked him. It wasn't easy, though. She wanted to shake him so she could hear the last bit of the story. How did he answer the last question? Should she rush to the warehouse to initiate a mass exodus from the space before contract enforcers came rolling in?

"Jeff?"

Jefferson lifted his face from his hands and looked at Gwen as if he were waking from the deepest sort of dream. Though, as she searched his face, she had no way of knowing if that dream was the best kind or a nightmare. It was obvious Jefferson loved his family, but he sat there, leaning against a tree—with her. Jefferson's eyes gradually gained their focus, and at last, he slowly nodded.

"What did you say?" Gwen asked softly.

"You're a brilliant kid, Gwen. You know that, right?"

"Thanks, but Jeff—"

"No. Seriously. I know you've already put two and two together," Jefferson stretched out his long legs in front of him. "You're wondering why I was released like nothing ever happened. You're asking yourself, why would I get off so easily when I cost the bank a lot of money and headache by organizing a movement against them. They can't let people off that easily. Not only did I hurt the bank's profits—I also caused people to worry about their investments, maybe for the first time in decades. Multiply that worry by thousands of people, and it adds up to a very hefty price."

Jefferson stood with a groan, using the trunk of the tree for support. He rocked from his heels to his toes a couple of times and offered his hand to help Gwen up. Gwen grabbed it, though she didn't use much of his leverage to stand. He looked so frail.

"Do you remember what I made you promise before I told this story?" Jefferson asked.

"That if I lost all trust in you, I had to give you a chance to regain it?"

"Yes, this is when I need to hold you to that promise."

Gwen braced for the worst but nodded, encouraging Jefferson to finish his story.

"First, I didn't tell them everything. I never revealed our location or how many people were a part of our operation—I don't think. Their way of extracting information is horrifying. I never gave names. They never asked me to bug any of you or our facilities. I'm sure they knew that information all along. We totally underestimated the full extent of their surveillance. So we'll have to move our operations somewhere they can't track us—first thing in the morning."

Gwen let out an audible sigh and dropped her shoulder in relief. But then she realized that couldn't be the bad news.

"Why shouldn't I trust you? How are you back, Jeff?"

Jefferson looked away from Gwen.

"Because the answer to their last question was yes. Yes! I would have jumped back into that reality if they had let me. The physical hunger pangs were subsiding because they had given me part of the antidote. But the other hunger was still there. It's still there now. Do you remember when you read the Chronicles of Narnia at my place back in Kansas?"

"Yeah." Gwen was confused. Why was he bringing up those books?

"You remember how the Lion, the Witch and the Wardrobe ends, right? The kids grow up to become kings and queens in the golden age of Narnia, and they spend their years hunting and feasting and mingling with Aslan and dryads and talking beasts?"

"Yeah, I remember."

"And then these kings and queens follow a stag back to a lamppost that leads them back into the wardrobe, and they fall out as if no time had passed at all.

"C.S. Lewis was brilliant, but those kids would've been total messes. They would have been obsessed with getting back to Narnia every second of every day. Or, if they couldn't do that, I'm afraid they would have died trying. Or by suicide. Can you imagine? Having all the years of experiencing the magic of Narnia in your head but not being sure if any of it was real?"

Gwen took a step back. Jefferson's arms were quivering, and tears were pooling in his eyes and dropping soundlessly to the gravel bank.

"I believe in this movement. Maybe more now than ever before. At least in some ways. Everybody in that warehouse matters so much to me. And you, Gwen, matter even more. But no matter how messed up those Narnia kids would have been, having their realities torn in two a couple of times throughout their lives, how lost and desperate would they have become if they'd been allowed back into Narnia every day over a period of months? Allowed to live out many more years as kings and queens in that magical land, fearing that any day—sooner or later—they would be thrown back inside the wardrobe with the horrible fear that it would be for good? The contract enforcers must have been absolutely certain that I was no longer a threat, and the ways I might have strengthened their human dynamics must have been worth enough that they let me go."

Whatever Gwen might conjure up in her mind would never come remotely close to how vividly Jefferson had experienced that other reality. She knew that. She doubted anybody could help him. But she was certain about one thing—

"Come on, Jeff, Stan's stew is probably about ready. And let me tell you, that stew is real and very good." Gwen grabbed Jefferson's hand and led him toward the warehouse, where a warm glow illuminated the tall windows, laughter punctuated the night stillness, and the fragrance of a hearty stew grew stronger with every step they took.

chapter 9

The rest of Patch's summer went by in a blur of trying to get back into old habits, like getting up early, going for a good run—most morning—trying to limit how much delicious food Malcolm cooked for him, and attempting to enjoy something he had never really experienced in his life—relaxation.

It was a foreign concept to Patch at first. Anytime he didn't have something on his calendar, his natural tendency was to get anxious. But he was digging the mindfulness tracks that Pete had given him.

"It's the best way of quieting your mind, Patchman," Pete had said as Patch packed his things in his dorm room on the last day before summer break. "If you name your feelings, observe them, then watch them drive past instead of chasing them down the street, you'll master those anxieties, my friend."

Pete gave Patch an awkward hug with two neat claps to his back.

"See you in the fall, Patch. And don't lose those quick feet. I'll be the mindfulness instructor for the track team again next year."

Among all the anxieties that Patch was trying to let go of, track was one near the top of the list. He'd fallen into a comfortable cadence with the track team schedule by the end of last school year. He went to the morning run, which wasn't required but sort of was because it showed his real commitment to the team and the captain of the team noticed who showed up. Then Patch would dash back to get ready for the day, shovel in some food in the dining hall, and go to his classes—usually a minute or two late to the first class of the day.

At least this year my first class won't be with Dr. Bedford. Last year, Patch had been pretty sure that Dr. Bedford would have expelled him for his tardiness if it hadn't been for what a voracious reader of the course materials he had always been. That, and there was his first day of school ever, too. Dr. Bedford and Patch had gelled in a strange but powerful way that day.

During his first class on his very first day of school, Dr. Bedford had tried her best to establish the fact that she knew things better than the students did so they should pay attention. That technique was common among the teachers at Harvard Academy, but Patch's rawness had taken Dr. Bedford off guard. And when Patch showed up having read his economic history book from cover to cover on the second day of class, it pretty much sealed some kind of permanent commitment. Not to say that Dr. Bedford's commitment to Patch meant she ever cut him any slack. Quite the opposite, Patch realized.

"If I didn't care about you, I wouldn't push you," Dr. Bedford had said after Patch's first-year thesis had been accepted. Barely. "And I expect a lot more math to back up your thesis claim next year, or I'll have no problem destroying your hopes and dreams. Now get out of my office. There's a dear," Dr. Bedford had said with a lavish smile and a wink.

Patch's possessions had multiplied exponentially in the last year, too, but they could still comfortably fit in a single duffel bag and backpack with ample room to spare. He had his running shoes—his everyday training pair and the pair with custom-built spikes that Malcolm had insisted he get fitted for at some sporting goods store that seemed to care more about how the shoes and clothing looked on display than selling any of them. He wore the custom-made pair to meets.

Patch packed up the couple of outfits that he always thought were too many. Why do I need more sets of clothes than one to wear and one to wash? He warily threw in a third and fourth set. He stuffed his backpack with books, running his hands across their smooth spines lovingly.

Books were the kind of item that Patch was more than happy to accumulate. As many as he could get his hands on. After his first experience with reading his economic history book, he devoured books on management, business, leadership, and for sure, economics, but also novels. He loved connecting with characters that seemed real enough to build relationships with. It amazed him how much he learned about relationships from well-written stories.

Relationships . . . there's another source of anxiety he had let go of that summer. He heard a soft ping from the tablet in his backpack. Kourtney again. His relationship with Kourtney was complicated, to say the least. They had basically broken up last semester, but then Patch had needed his connection to her to get into the bank headquarters to free Gwen. Kourtney had mostly forgiven him for using her like that, Patch thought, but not completely.

Kourtney surprised Patch sometimes. She liked to play the part of a happy-go-lucky Valley girl, but there was a lot more to her. Patch was actually excited to explore those hidden depths, but at that moment, his thoughts jumped back to freeing Gwen.

Patch had found Gwen much easier than he thought he would after they'd parted ways earlier that spring. For some reason, she'd left on the location finder she'd set for him. At first, he thought it was a mistake, that maybe she didn't know how the technology worked. But he had gone over it in his mind so many times that he was all but certain that she continued to leave that connection on purpose. What purpose, he had yet to figure out.

I'll reach out to her on the train ride over to school, he told himself as he took one more look to make sure he wasn't forgetting anything. Convinced that he was as ready as he could be, he picked up his duffel bag, slung his backpack onto one shoulder, and hauled both bags down the hall, ready for the train ride to school the next day.

"Are you sure you don't want me to drive you there," Malcolm asked as he filled a container with eggs and sausage for Patch to take for the road.

"You always ask that. And you know I can't eat that on the train. It'll make my train ticket cost three times more because it'll annoy other passengers."

"Who knows, maybe the sausage aroma will add utility for the ride for some of them so things will cancel out," Malcolm said, sealing the container with the four clasps—one on each side. "Don't open it until you get to school, then. We both know you'll hit that falafel food-cart at the station anyway. But this is a cool container that guarantees zero air movement either in or out, so no smell should get out. It'll stay nice and toasty for you, too."

Malcolm handed the container to Patch, who stuffed it into his back-pack, which was no small feat.

"That thing is a chiropractor's gold mine. Why do you have to carry so many books. You have practically every book ever written at your fin-gertips on your tablet—through that All World Knowledge Project thing that Google did a bunch of years ago," Malcolm said, shaking his head.

"Yeah. It's not the same though. You know?"

"Yeah, I know. All that romantic crap about real books appealing to more senses than just sight and all that. Now, let me look at you."

Malcolm straightened the collar on Patch's jacket and squeezed both of his arms warmly. "You're going to rock it this year. You know that, right?"

Patch smiled and nodded. He never got tired of Malcolm's pep talks.

"Take it by storm, kid."

"What's that supposed to mean? Like a hurricane sort of metaphor?" Patch said with a blank look.

"Oh, sorry. Boy, let me see if I can think of a meaning for that old saying. Haven't I used that phrase before? I could have sworn I wished you the same last year when you were going back to school. I think that was probably the original meaning. Like most sayings, it has to connect to weather or war somehow. It's the human way, I guess. Here goes my attempt at defining that phrase: to be wildly and quickly successful at achieving something after putting in a passionate effort. How's that? That's not a bad thing to wish for someone, eh?"

"Not at all. Thanks, Mal. I'll miss you," Patch said, dropping his backpack so he could give Malcolm a proper hug.

"You, my friend, are a very wise investment," Malcolm said with a thoughtful look at Patch after pulling out of the hug.

"I'll try to be a good ROI," Patch said, slinging his backpack over one shoulder and heading out the back door.

"You are a lot more than that," Patch thought he heard Malcolm say as he left the house. Though, the words seemed to be for Malcolm as much as they were for him, so he didn't turn back to respond.

Patch passed through the bustling main entrance of the train station. He looked up to facilitate the full-body scan required to open the reinforced-steel, full-wall gate. Within seconds, several bars receded into themselves to make room for a single person to pass through.

He wound his way to the food court and headed directly toward his favorite cart.

"Hey there, young sir," a friendly man greeted Patch before he was even up to the counter at Gino's.

"Hi there. I'd like a falafel sandwich, please," Patch asked.

"Coming right up, my friend." The man disappeared into the back of the bright yellow food-cart.

"Hi, Patch. Are you ordering a falafel sandwich from Gino's? Do you want me to pay for that using the card on file?" Siri asked through Patch's earpiece.

"Yes, please."

"Okay. You're all set."

"What was that, my friend?" the man at the food-cart asked, returning.

"Oh, sorry. I was just paying for my sandwich."

"Ah. I suppose I'll never get used to it," the man said, scratching at his gray beard and smiling at Patch in a way that showed off the deep system of wrinkles spread all over his olive-toned face.

Patch had never noticed before, but wrinkles could be beautiful with their intricate designs and patterns. And the fact that the wrinkles were made over a series of decades of exposure to the sun and the relaxing of skin and a whole lot of smiles, just like the one the man was giving him right then, added even more appeal.

Patch's mind flashed back to the very different effect of meeting the old gentleman he had played pickleball with. Their tanned, smooth skin could never match the food-cart worker's. Not in his estimation anyway.

"Get used to what, sir?" Patch asked, very glad to have remembered what the man had said after his dive down that wrinkle rabbit hole.

"People talking more to their devices than to real people," the man said with a chuckle. "But I know I'm old-fashioned. People used to be buried in their phones before they became so enamored with AI."

"Yeah, I agree. It's taken me a long time to get used to it, too," Patch said, nodding.

"You say this? You're so young? Young people are born with devices in their hands," the man said, laughing again.

"I'm an oddball, I guess," Patch said, stepping up to the counter, eagerly watching the man drizzle a sauce on his falafel sandwich and then wrap it in aluminum foil.

"You are a very good young man. That's what you are, my friend," the man said, again crinkling his face in those beautiful wrinkles and a smile and handing Patch his sandwich.

"You too, sir. I mean, you're a very good person, too. Thank you."

Patch was hungrier than he thought, or maybe it was nervous eating, either way, he was halfway through his sandwich before he made it to the main corridor of the station.

"Hey, Siri, where's my train?" Patch said between bites of his sandwich.

"Hi, Patch. It looks like your train is on time and will be in terminal C-3. You've already checked in. I can activate a pathfinder for you. Would you like me to do that?"

"Yes, please."

With his new glasses on, a simulated bright-green, foot-wide path illuminated in front of Patch and extended to his destination at terminal C-3. Patch made sure to walk with the flow of traffic. With so many people meshed together, it was important that he follow the norms of train etiquette, or his train ticket could get a lot more expensive. He wouldn't hear the end of that from Malcolm. He did his best to get used to seeing so many blurred-out faces while wearing the glasses, but he liked the real view much better than the augmented view that the glasses provided. He was still excited to use them for school projects though.

On the train, Patch followed the green line to his seat, where he slid in to get a better view from the window. He grabbed his tablet out of his backpack and pulled up what he had searched for before—Gwen. It was obvious to Patch that Gwen was still working to undermine the banking industry from a vacant manufacturing hub in D.C. Does that mean that Jefferson had been released as Patch had assumed, or was he still detained by contract enforcers? And if he was still detained, who was leading things in his absence?

Gwen's geotag was easy to see on Patch's tablet. She seemed to spend a lot of time by a river called the Potomac. Patch had never had a reason to go to D.C., but from what he'd heard, the whole city resembled the streets where he used to live—dirty, desperate, and dangerous.

Patch tapped the geotag, and a box appeared on-screen with some options. He tapped the call button. His face was reflected back at him, and he raked through his unruly, wavy dark hair a few times and adjusted his shirt collar in a rush to look a bit more presentable.

The tablet abandoned the call after eight rings. Patch let out a sigh, unsure whether it was coming from a place of disappointment or relief. He unzipped his backpack to drop the tablet in but pulled it back in front of him. Patch tapped the call button one more time.

One more try . . .

One ring, two rings, three . . .

And then Gwen's face lit up the screen. Her face had striking definition, as if her cheeks, nose, and chin were cut from stone, but then there were softer features. Her eyes had enough blue and green in them that the two colors fluctuated in prominence depending on what she wore. On that particular day, her eyes were definitely green, matching her forest-green sweater. Whisps of her hair were blowing in the morning breeze. Her hair was fascinating to Patch. It appeared to be a regular brown at first glance, but when sunlight ran through it, it broke into golden highlights. There were more highlights than he remembered. She must have spent a lot of time in the sun this summer, Patch thought.

He caught a few branches of a leafy tree in her background.

"Hi," Patch said.

"Hello."

"Are you sitting in a tree?" He instantly regretted asking that. Stupid!

"Uh, yeah. I like sitting here. It gives me a chance to be alone."

Patch cringed. Perfect. So I sound like a fool, AND I'm messing with her only chance to be alone. This is going super well.

"Not that you're interrupting anything," Gwen followed up quickly. "I tend to hang out here most mornings. It gives me a chance to think."

"For me, it's running," Patch said overly eager.

"What's running?" Gwen asked with a puzzled look.

"Oh, running is the way I think. I take lots of morning jogs. So running is like my tree. Or, I mean, your thinking place. The tree is like my thinking place, running, which now that I think of it, is nothing like a tree at all. Sorry," Patch said, fighting the urge to smack himself.

"No, I get it. We all need to find what works best for us. Your way is just healthier than mine," Gwen said with a smile.

Patch got distracted by that smile and the way the tilt of her head made sunlight play across her cheek and lips. Then he realized he had been staring too long. "I don't know which is healthier. It seems like your spot would be a lovely place to do some mindfulness," he said in a rush.

"Mindfulness?" Gwen asked, squinting.

"A buddy of mine, Pete, he taught me about it. It's supposed to help train the mind so you can let go of anxieties and stuff like that," Patch said, very glad to have a natural next thing to say.

Gwen's eyes opened wider and gave a slight nod, which Patch found very encouraging.

"I could show you how I do it the next time I see you. I mean, whenever that is," Patch said.

"Yeah, whenever that is. I don't suppose you have any plans to come down here to D.C. any time soon. No school tours to the abandoned seat of the federal government?" Gwen asked with a grin.

"Can't say I do, but who knows? Maybe for economic history," Patch said.

"They really have a class called Economic History?"

"They have loads of them actually. It's kind of my focus this year."

"Do they teach the whole history or only the part after the banks took over the world?"

Patch caught a slight bitterness in her tone. "We talk about the transition from the market economy to the true meritocracy, mostly. I don't get the sense that Dr. Bedford, my professor, is one to buy into propaganda," Patch said, realizing that he felt defensive for his school.

"Sorry. This is my life here, so hating the way things are now is kind of in the air we breathe. But what's up? I was surprised to get your call. We haven't connected since"—

Gwen trailed off, and Patch's view of her was tilted away for a moment so Gwen's tablet faced the gravel bank, the river, and beyond to cracked marble buildings. When she reappeared he caught the pink hues around her eyes, as if she had rubbed them.

—"since you and Jefferson came to get me out of the bank headquarters. Did you need something?"

It dawned on Patch, then, that he didn't really have a reason to call Gwen. He had just thought about her almost every day since the night at the bank. And since she hadn't deactivated her geotag, he thought maybe she had thought about him too. How could he share that without sounding creepy?

"No. I don't need anything. I guess I just wanted to . . . when you didn't turn off your geotag, I kind of thought . . . What am I saying? Gaaah! I guess I just missed you!" Patch blurted out.

She seemed to focus on the screen for a couple of seconds.

"Which, I realize now, was probably an accident. Boy, I am not good at this," Patch said, scratching at the back of his neck.

"No, you're fine. Well, yes, I didn't leave the geotag for you to remember me by or anything," Gwen said.

Patch deflated a bit and looked down from the screen.

"But it's not a bad thing hearing from you either," Gwen said in a rush. "Ever since that first meeting at the train station, where you practically bowled me over, I've had a hankering for another one of those falafels. Was that what that was called? That sandwich we ate in the food court?"

"Oh yeah, the falafel sandwiches. Gino's is the best! The next time you're at the Boston Station let me know, and we'll enjoy another one. My treat. And I didn't bowl you over. In fact, as I recall, you ran into me as much as I ran into you. Actually, we both kind of did fancy-spin moves to avoid that collision, didn't we?"

"You have an impressive memory. Yeah, I guess you're right about my fancy footwork being the only reason we didn't collide for real," Gwen said with a wry smile.

Patch perked up at seeing that smile. He grinned back, but then he felt the slight lurch forward as the magnets in the station engaged with the ones at his destination in Cambridge.

"My train is taking off. I'll have to let you go soon because the ride will literally take about a minute. I was just thinking about you the other day, and I was wondering how things were going with the—you know? The revolution or whatever?"

"Things are complicated, but I think we'll get it all sorted out."

Patch nodded, reading the caution on Gwen's face. "I didn't know why I was contacting you before. But I do now," Patch said.

"It wasn't because you missed me, then?" Gwen asked with a raised eyebrow.

Patch grinned. "Well, that, for sure. But also, I wanted to let you know that if there's anything I can do to help with things there, I'd like to. I'm with you."

Gwen took a few moments to respond, and Patch's train was taking off in earnest, reaching its peak speed of several hundred miles per hour in a matter of seconds.

"Gwen, I've got to let you go—"

"Thanks, Patch. I'll think about it. I think there might be some ways you can help, actually. Can I call you later?" Gwen asked.

"Sure thing," Patch said, beaming. "Anytime."

"Okay. Bye."

"Bye."

The call ended.

Well, that went better than I expected. I mean, she asked if she could call me. But then he realized all the things he should have asked about, like if Jefferson was ever freed and if Gwen's group was safe. Patch rolled his shoulders back a couple of times as the train prepared to dock, already arriving at the Cambridge station.

That'll give us something else to talk about the next time, he decided.

chapter 10

Patch fidgeted inside his driverless cab, bouncing up and down absently on the seat cushion, catching himself and reminding himself that the cab's AI might give him a bad review, which would cost Malcolm more for the ride. Considering that, with the potentially high price of bad behavior on a busy train, Patch tried to remember that Malcolm could insist on driving him to school next time.

No more falafel from Gino's, no more time to reflect before jumping into school, and no more conversations with Gwen, he thought. Even though he had worried about the start of his second school year all summer, ever since that conversation with Gwen, most of Patch's mind had been occupied by one thing—Gwen. He was pretty sure his feelings were more than teenage infatuation, though he had to admit there was maybe some of that, too. No, his feelings about Gwen were deeper for one simple reason.

"She's the first person I've ever talked to who really knows what it's like."

"I'm sorry. I can't pick up the first person who you like. That goes against my protocols. If you ask me to do things like that in the future, I'm afraid I might have to give you a poor review, which will result in higher fares in the future," the driverless car said.

"Sorry," Patch said sheepishly, sinking into his seat but chuckling all the same.

Then Patch caught the familiar red brick set in contrast to the gray granite windows. And lofty stairways. And white wood turrets. Even though he had been there for a year, when he approached Harvard

Academy, a thrill shot down his spine. That thrill tickled, and Patch smiled, looking up at the hall where he'd attended his first orientation and welcome ceremony.

Will and Kourtney! Patch wondered if they would already be at school. Patch had decided that he wanted to return during Orientation Week—usually held for first-years—because he could use all the orienting and extra help he could get. This being the one and only second year of school in his life.

"You have arrived at one hundred ninety-seven, Mount Auburn Street. Your account has been charged automatically. Don't forget to collect any belongings you may have brought onboard. Have a great day!" The chipper driverless car announced when it had come to a stop at the parking lot in front of Patch's dorm building.

"Don't be too excited to get rid of me," Patch smirked, getting out of the car and collecting his bags from the trunk that popped open as soon as the passenger door opened. He swung his backpack onto both shoulders so he could be better prepared to carry his duffel bag up the four flights of stairs to his dorm room. At least, he hoped it was still his dorm room. He never thought to ask or check with anybody to make sure he would be living in the same dorm.

Patch headed to a series of red canopies emblazoned with the Harvard Academy logo where people wearing school-ambassador T-shirts were directing what were sure to be first-years.

"Yeah, this isn't your dorm. You're in Gates Hall, around the corner and along that sidewalk. See it? Excellent," Patch heard a young woman in a pulled-back ponytail and a way-too-big ambassador T-shirt say.

Or maybe she was wearing way-too-short shorts. Either way, he couldn't tell if she was wearing pants under the T-shirt, which Patch decided would be ridiculous. He was contemplating that when he heard the young woman say something to him.

"I'm sorry, what was that?" he asked her.

"Uh, I said, 'Hi, Patch. What are you doing with all the first-years,' but you obviously have more important things to think about, eh?" The girl gave Patch a withering stare but then broke into a big smile. "Just kidding. Welcome back! But seriously, what are you doing here during Orientation Week? If I didn't have to be here for my internship, I certainly wouldn't be at school a whole week early. I can guarantee you that."

"Oh, I figured I'd get a bit of a head start. I can use all the help I can get, right?" Patch smiled, wracking his brain. How did this girl know his name? She wasn't in any of my classes last year, right? Patch thought rapidly, running through both semesters' worth of classes.

"Hey, first-years, look this way! We have our own local celebrity here. Patch Robinson, the track star. He pretty much single-handedly led the academy to victory at Track Regionals last year. I'm sure he's doing autographs," the girl said in a grandiose voice that made Patch all but certain she was either flirting with him or making fun of him. Or maybe both.

"Alright, that's enough of that, I think," Patch said, realizing how she would know him without him knowing her. Thankfully, he finally caught sight of the nametag on the girl's T-shirt. "Don't set your expectations too high this year, Kacie. I'll never live up to them."

"Aw, you will for sure. Do you know where you're going, Patch. Usually, they stick people back in the same dorm room with the same roommates, but not always. Do you want me to look you up?"

"That would be great, thanks, Kacie."

"Looks like no changes for you this year. And still with Will Keyes. Great guy. I had a psychology class with him last year, I think." Kacie dropped her tablet on the red cloth-covered table.

"That would be Will. He pretty much breathes psychology," Patch said, not noticing that Kacie's attention had focused on a clump of first-years.

"Hey, you folks? Yeah, you. Let's get you all set up," Kacie yelled assertively, leaving Patch standing there foolishly.

Well, that was awkward. He grabbed his bag and headed to his dorm—Carnegie House. He scaled the four flights of stairs, smiling appreciatively at the worn stone steps and the excited buzz he heard in the hallways as he passed each floor. When he got to the fourth floor, though, he found things much calmer. No pillows blocking the path to his room. No hoots of laughter or triumphant yells. The floor was almost orderly, in fact. A state he had never seen in the space.

"Don't you strike the fervent and determined pose of destiny, Patch."

Patch turned around at the familiar voice.

"Will!" Patch yelled, dropping his backpack and giving Will a bear hug.

"Careful with the disabled kid!" Will laughed, returning Patch's hug with one of Will's characteristic one-handed hugs that were somehow always as warm as the two-armed kind.

"I'm so glad you're here. I worried I'd be the only second-year here this week." Will took Patch's backpack, and they walked together to their room. Will dropped Patch's backpack on the bare bed opposite his.

"I commend your commitment to your training regime, but isn't carrying a ton of bricks in your backpack taking things a bit far? Have I ever talked to you about athletic addictions, Patch?" Will said with a smirk.

But Patch was still standing at the doorway to the room with his duffel bag in hand.

"Come on, Patch. It's a dorm room. Don't get sentimental about that," Will said, squeezing past Patch and looking left and right down either side of the hall. "Still living the Spartan way, I see."

"Give me a break. I was just taking it all in," Patch said, poking his head into the hall with Will. "And, yep. That's everything I need. Honestly, I felt silly bringing as much as I did."

"Right? I mean, it's not like you'll be living here for the next ten months or anything. Why bother with frivolous things like changes of clothes? Seriously," Will said, going back into the room and plopping down on his bed, which was already made up with a thick gray comforter.

"I wish I could say I do it on purpose."

Patch glanced at Will's desk. Will wasn't one for frivolous things either, but he was much better at packing. He had a stack of sticky notes, a metal container for pens and other writing tools, and a digital photo frame showing video scenes from a beach trip.

"Looks like you had some fun this summer," Patch said, nodding to the frame.

"Oh, that. Yeah, our annual family vacation to the Northwest Coast."

"That's great. I didn't know your family did that."

"Yeah, my mom and brother and I read *Moby Dick* a while back and decided we needed to go for a whale watch as a reward for finishing the book. I can't quite remember what was wrong with going somewhere near here," Will said, picking up the frame and flipping through the feed. "I mean, the book starts in Nantucket, after all. Maybe whales weren't in season or migrating or whatever. I'm not a biology major. Anyway, we ended up going for a whale watch in the Northwest a few years back, and we decided we needed to make it a tradition."

Patch wasn't sure if it was the nostalgia of being back at school and in his familiar dorm room or something else, but when Will mentioned tradition, Patch had a hard time focusing on Will's story. Tradition. What did that really mean? Other than something people decided to repeat or a choice they made to be in the same place again so that it somehow meant more?

"And my sister was seriously about to vomit right over the side of the boat, but—"

"We need some traditions!" Patch blurted out, interrupting Will.

"Whoa! Okay. Rewind. How does my sister hurling into the ocean connect with traditions? That is certainly not the sort of thing I'd like to experience on a regular basis," Will said, placing the frame back on his desk in the same exact spot, close to his bed. Patch thought there might have been a faint outline in the faded wood around where the frame always stood.

"We need to talk about that OCD sometime, Will," Patch said.

"My compulsions are not the topic of discussion at the moment. Your weirdly intense suggestion about a tradition is. Let's break this down for a second," Will said, crossing his legs and nodding thoughtfully.

"I don't think I need psychoanalysis, thank you very much. Well, I'm sure I do, but not now. And not from you. But seriously, this is my second year here. We need to start a tradition. It's the perfect time, don't you think?" Patch said dumping his duffle bag in his closet.

"Sure. But let's get at least one thing straight here and now," Will said, getting very serious and uncrossing his leg.

"Alright," Patch said cautiously.

"I will never psychoanalyze you because"—Will paused for dramatic effect—"I think Freud was a fraud."

Will and Patch grinned at each other.

"I set you up for that," Patch said.

"You most certainly did, my friend. But back to the tradition idea. Love it. Any ideas?"

Patch took a few seconds to consider all the experiences he'd had last year. As he looked back, he was blown away. It had been full of new experiences.

"I don't really know how traditions work. Are there rules or expectations?" Patch asked awkwardly, scratching at the back of his neck.

"Why, yes. There is a rule book governed by the Tradition Policy Board," Will said, throwing his pillow at Patch.

Patch barely had time to dodge it.

"Of course there aren't any rules. You kidding? I guess there might be expectations, but those are up to us, not anything formal."

"Okay. So, like with your family trip to the Northwest Coast. You read *Moby Dick*. You go on a whale watch with your mom and brother. It was fun, so your parents decide to take the whole family, then you decided as a family to go every year after that?" Patch asked.

"Kind of like that. I guess the piece you're missing is the reason why that trip stuck. I mean, there are tons of places that would be fun to visit as a family. And people make broader traditions where families just go on a trip somewhere every year. That's a tradition, too."

"Got it. So no set rules. We get to decide how broad or narrow we make the parameters for the tradition," Patch thought for a few more seconds until an obvious choice popped into his head. "Do you remember when we stole that ice cream?"

"That was not stealing. We'll call it redistributing our assets. We're paying for school, including meals, so we're just deciding a different time and place to enjoy those assets," Will said, taking mock offense at the idea of stealing. "But of course I do. We'll do it tonight!" Will stood up with his hand raised like a conquering Viking. Although, his gym shorts, hoodie, and flip-flops took away from the triumphant look a bit.

"I didn't mean tonight, necessarily—" Patch started to say.

"Oh, but this is perfect timing. The first time we're both back at school for the start of fall semester, we shall feast on plundered ice cream and other delicious vittles!" Will said, now trying on a pirate accent.

"Aarg! Let it be then, matey." Patch said.

"Okay. It's a plan, then. Tonight, at midnight."

"Okay. It's a deal." Patch reached out his left hand for Will to shake.

"Aw! Now we can truly say we're friends. We even have secret hand-shakes," Will said.

"I just thought that you might prefer—"

"Shaking hands with my left hand instead of me trying to position my gimpy arm for a handshake? Absolutely. Much appreciated, Patch."

Will shook Patch's left hand enthusiastically.

"It's all settled now. Our ice cream raid starts at midnight!"

Patch wished he could match Will's enthusiasm. Why did I have to suggest such a risky tradition? he thought as he unfolded the com-forter and sheet set that was in a crisp pile at the end of his bed. He made his bed while Will told him more stories about his summer adventures. Patch's mind wandered again when Will dove into his summer reading.

Will really was a friend. Patch's first friend, and the only friend he really had, not counting Kourtney, which Will reminded him.

"Hey, Will, sorry to interrupt again. But have you seen Kourtney yet?" Patch asked.

"No. Didn't she say she and her family go on a cruise on their yacht around this time of the year?"

"That's right. One of the two times a year they actually use that massive boat. I'm a bit jealous, honestly. I never thought I'd envy the ultra-wealthy, but that boat is something else," Patch said.

"You've gone for a ride on it?" Will asked.

"Yeah, a couple of times last spring. Kourtney's family pays for someone to run the ship year-round even though they only use it those couple of weeks," Patch said, shaking his head.

"Of course they do. You don't own a boat like that just for taking trips, though. It's a symbol," Will said.

"A symbol of what exactly?"

"Of who and what they are. They are the Vanderbilts. They are a different species of human. A better species of human," Will said in a very stuffy way. "And that boat acts as a clear sign of that to us lowly creatures, but it could be important for entertaining any prospective clients that Kourtney's dad might have, too."

"It seems like such a waste. That's all," Patch said.

"There's no denying that. But again, you don't buy, or I guess build, a boat like that to be frugal," Will said with a chuckle.

Patch forced a laugh too, though, his thoughts went to the many other places that that money could have gone.

chapter 11

That afternoon, Patch headed to the track and field facility. He wondered if Coach Curtis would be there. The track and field facility was an imposing domed structure made out of reflective glass built into a brick frame. Inside, hundreds of gray stone pillars held the massive ceiling up. Patch wound his way around the outer hallway. Even after spending so much time there last year, he still took the same way to Coach Curtis' office because he'd still get lost otherwise. Gate numbers hung above thick wooden, double doors that opened up to stadium seating with room enough for thousands of spectators.

He had never before thought about where teachers and coaches went when they weren't teaching or coaching. The more urgent question for Patch as he approached his coach's office, though, was whether Coach Curtis would be excited to see him.

What Kacie, the girl he'd met that morning upon arrival, had said was mostly true. His times and wins in his events had pushed the Harvard team to the top. But he also realized that he only participated in two events—the 400- and 800-meter races—and so many other events had helped build that score. That and Patch had given Coach Curtis perhaps more worry than anyone else on the team, so he had no reason to feel cocky.

His coach had diplomatically called his abilities raw, whatever that meant. It seemed to mean that his coach had him focus a ton more on his block starts, consistency, and ability to push himself to his limits. He cringed as he thought back to his first day of tryouts and how awkward his feet had felt as he burst from his starting block with no technique or grace. Or his first race and meet, where he practically fell on his face and had to regain dozens of meters in a mad dash.

He had won that race, but it was too close. For most of his teammates, winning or losing races was a thing of personal preference and pride. For Patch, it was a matter of staying at school. He couldn't imagine Malcolm throwing him out, but he could never get the fact that their relationship was based on him winning races and being a good return on Malcolm's investment out of his head either.

Patch swallowed that thought down as he knocked twice and opened Coach Curtis' office door. Coach Curtis was sitting behind an old desk that looked like it had been picked up at a thrift store. Visible scuffs and dings were around the edges, and one of the legs was propped up by a wad of paper. And Coach was making do with a metal folding chair.

"Still haven't upgraded to proper office furniture, I see, Coach. Glad to see that," Patch said with a smile.

"Any coach wasting program dollars on fancy furniture isn't worth their salt," Coach Curtis said without looking up from his tablet. "So last year wasn't hard enough. You decided to come back, eh? We'll have to change that this year."

After a very long time, Coach Curtis finally broke out into a genuine smile and looked up at Patch, face-to-face, for the first time. "Pull up a chair and tell me about your summer. And don't try to oversell your training. I've been a coach too long to buy any of that."

Patch smiled. He knows me too well. Instead of talking about his lack of training, Patch told his coach about his first experience with pickleball.

"Anybody telling you that pickleball is just tennis for old people is definitely leading you on. It's important to recognize what skills a game honors and those it disregards," Coach Curtis said knowingly.

In the mouth of anybody else, those sorts of things would have sounded pompous, but Patch had grown to pay attention to anything Coach Curtis said, even things that were outside his expertise because, invariably, he ended up being spot-on most of the time.

As Patch left his coach's office, he let out all of his pent-up anxieties in one long breath. Leaning against Coach Curtis' closed office door, a weight dropped from his shoulders because of one thing Coach Curtis had probably not meant to say but that gave Patch comfort. He said he'd work me harder this year. He wouldn't have said that if he wasn't expecting me on the team. Patch called that a win for sure.

Patch's understanding of how campuses were laid out was limited to his own school and the schools in his division. He had visited eight other schools—mainly the athletic facilities for meets. That hardly constituted a deep education of campus design. But he could make two safe conclusions. One, he was at the best-funded program with the deepest history of success among all the schools in his division. And, two, every campus had an area like the one he was walking through as he got close to the house.

The term house doesn't really fit the place, he thought as he progressed along the path. It was really more of a cottage, though he'd only seen that term used in fairy tales. His thoughts were disrupted by a revving diesel engine somewhere nearby.

Every campus had a portion that wasn't necessarily off limits to students but had nothing to entice students to visit it, so other than the occasional lost student here or there, generally, only employees frequented the areas. And Patch made a point to visit those areas on every campus he visited because he was drawn to their quiet grittiness.

They are just like daily runs.

Spectators at meets only saw the finished product. They never saw how the runners were actually made. These places showed how the campuses actually came to function. Buildings he passed still had the iconic neoclassical look that most buildings on the Harvard campus had, but unlike the central buildings, these lacked the turrets and cornices on the roofs and the ornate stone embellishments on the walls. Also, unlike the main buildings, Patch could catch glimpses of concrete flooring through open doors and hear the beeping of heavy machinery through closed windows.

Though the area was clearly more functional, Patch smiled as he caught small touches that showed the people working behind the scenes cared about their own neck of the campus, too. Patch was walking on a concrete sidewalk, whereas most of the central campus had cobblestone walks that set a certain tone of traditionalism and timelessness. But the concrete sidewalk was well-maintained with no cracks or weeds between the slabs of cement. On both sides of the sidewalk, healthy-looking hedges grew in neat rows. The trees that grew in most intersections along the path were perhaps less impressive in size than the ones at the main quad, closer to where most of his classes were held, but the trees were carefully pruned and even had self-watering systems surrounding their trunks.

Patch slowed to a stop near the end of the sidewalk. Beyond the concrete, dirt paths led to empty, historic stables from bygone days when workers used horses for maintenance rather than machinery. And past the stables, all paths dead-ended at the Charles River, which flowed lazily along its way to the Boston Harbor.

The building Patch was visiting was tucked behind the hedge and barely visible from the sidewalk. He had run past it on one of his first days on campus last year. He wouldn't have found it at all if he hadn't gotten lost on his way to his track tryouts. He felt an instant connection to the building and the trimmed rose bushes and properly mowed lawn surrounding the small home. Ever since that accidental visit, on the days he ran his own route, rather than one set by Coach Curtis, he ran past this forgotten corner of campus and stopped for a few moments at the building.

Patch hooked his arm around the dark wrought-iron lamppost to the side of the dirt path that led to an outbuilding—possibly a garage or work shed. He realized that, in the winter, the dirt path would be less convenient to drive on than the geothermal, heated driveways that most buildings around campus used, but there was something appealing about the way the grass grew so perfectly along the dirt ruts that had been made by decades of driving in and out of the drive the same way day after day.

The cottage itself was hard to make out because ivy and a few massive oak and willow trees with thick canopies concealed most of it throughout much of the year. Patch usually took a look at the little bit he could discern from the sidewalk, though he always felt a bit guilty. He was intruding into someone's life that he had no business poking into. There was one spot that he felt particularly drawn to—an old maple tree that had a prominent main branch from which hung a moss-covered swing.

Patch leaned toward the building, still holding onto the lamppost.

"Taking in the sights?" A deep, tired voice said from behind Patch. He jumped back, nearly knocking heads with a man who stood behind him.

"I'm so sorry. I shouldn't be here. I know I should leave you alone, I . . . I . . . I'm just sorry."

Patch sprinted a couple of paces, but then realized he'd left his backpack by the lamppost. He took a couple of seconds to weigh the pros and cons of paying the consequence for losing books he had borrowed from Dr. Bedford earlier in the day. He sheepishly crept back, avoiding the piercing look that the man gave him as he slung his bag over one shoulder. "I really am sorry. I don't mean to . . . uh . . ."

"Gawk? Spy? Make fun of? Be grateful that your house is so much bigger than this? Scout out new places to make out with and impress your girlfriend by showing her that you know the secret spots on campus?"

Patch relaxed a bit when he caught a glimmer of the man's sense of humor. "I guess all of those, except for the make-out spot. I don't know if my girlfriend is still my girlfriend," Patch said, remembering that Kourtney would arrive in a matter of days and that he had no idea what kind of reception he'd get from her.

"Oh, that's tragic. The little gawker has complicated relationships. Who would ever have thought it?" The man's words dripped with sarcasm. "You've gotten your glimpse of blue-collar life, and now you can shove on out of here." The man pointed in the direction from which Patch had come.

"Of course. I'm so sorry for bothering you, sir," Patch said, turning to leave.

"Hold on a second. I've got to ask you a question." The man said, stopping Patch in his tracks.

Patch turned slowly. "Sure. I guess."

"Why do kids like you find my home so damn fascinating?"

Kids like you. Those words hit Patch hard. The man took a step back, as if he noticed the change in Patch's demeanor. Patch tried to calm himself by taking a deep breath, but something out of his control was building inside him.

"You mean kids who spent their lives on the street, who once dreamed about living in such a comfortable place as your cottage? I guess they would still dream about a place like this, if they were ever lucky enough to be here. They don't let many street kids loiter on campus for some odd reason. And I'm speaking from plenty of personal experience on that."

The man stood motionless and silent.

After what felt like a very long time, Patch turned to leave, then stopped. "But I am sorry for intruding. Your life is not my business, and it's wrong for me to make visiting your cottage a spectator sport," Patch said, feeling an instant weight of loss. He probably wouldn't visit the cottage again. Though, he didn't understand why it appealed so much to him in the first place, not really.

"Wait a minute. I think we're both guilty of making unfair assumptions today," the man said.

Patch turned to face the man yet again.

"There have just been so many hotshots that cruise by my place, take their selfie or whatever term they give to the kinds of photos people take of themselves using those tablets now, and maybe do a *Singing in the Rain* move with my lamppost. That's what I thought you were doing."

The man gestured to the lamppost, and Patch realized what the man meant. It was the perfect setup for a selfie and cheap quip for social media.

"Yeah. I can get that. What's a Singing in the Rain move, though?"

"*Singing in the Rain?* Classic musical. Gene Kelly and Debbie Reynolds?"

Patch tried to fight the blank look on his face.

"No? Oh well. Great show. I'm sure you can pull it up. The move is kind of a swing around the lamppost, like this." At a run, the man grabbed hold of the lamppost with one arm and used his momentum to swing himself around the pole with his opposite arm and fingers outstretched for extra flair.

Patch broke into spontaneous applause. The man was much more agile than he looked in his slacks and ball cap, especially with waves of white hair sticking out around his ears and the back of the cap. The man made an unsteady bow, breathing hard.

"Thank you, thank you. I'll be here all evening. Well, probably not if I keep this up. That's the problem with all the modern machinery. You sit on it and think you're doing a lot of work when, in reality, you're just sitting there pushing buttons and pulling levers, letting the machines do all the work. Not much of a cardio workout, I'm afraid. I'm Chuck. Chuck Mason," the man said, offering his shaky hand that bobbed involuntarily in a gentle rhythmic way.

Patch shook Chuck's hand warmly. "Patch Robinson. So nice to meet you," Patch said. "I have a confession to make . . ."

Chuck shuffled his feet and raised a bushy white eyebrow that accentuated the myriad of wrinkles along his forehead. "I'm not a priest. I'm just a groundskeeper."

"Yeah, this isn't my first time here, though. I've made it a regular part of my training runs, actually."

"So you're the runner. I've seen you around here a lot. Not many track stars running through this neighborhood. Too few people to show off to, I guess."

"You're probably right." Patch nodded.

"So why do you frequent us over here?"

Patch was struck by the genuine curiosity. "I don't know exactly."

"Come on, people wouldn't run around facilities management unless they had a reason," Chuck said.

"I guess it feels more familiar to me than other parts of campus. And maybe your cottage has a nice homey feel to it. I don't have any family left," Patch said, worrying that he had shared too much and kicking at the pavement. Chuck's reaction to Patch's response was hard to read, and Patch's stomach growled, reminding him he still hadn't eaten lunch.

"I'd imagine you have other things you need to get done on your first day back. I know I do," Chuck said, picking up the rake that Patch hadn't seen before.

"Of course. So sorry for keeping you." Patch shook Chuck's hand again and turned to leave.

"And Patch?"

Patch looked over his shoulder.

"See you round, but no more gawking, okay?"

"Got it," Patch yelled back with a wave. Out of the side of his eye, he saw Chuck disappear behind the hedge and rose bushes, which were still in full bloom.

It was late afternoon by the time Patch made it back to his dorm. He had taken the scenic route along the river and wound past some familiar buildings on his way. The dining hall was mostly empty, and he'd missed the lunch window. There were a few dining hall workers wiping down tables and setting out trays in preparation for dinner.

He could have put in a special request for a regular meal, but he didn't want to bother the kitchen staff, so he grabbed a yogurt, a couple of string cheeses, and an orange from a section of the dining hall where snacks were always available. He took a seat in the back corner, facing the main entrance.

After practically inhaling the yogurt, he realized just how hungry he was. He opened the string cheeses but chomped down on them in three large bites without pulling them apart at all. Then he ran back to the snack bar and grabbed a protein shake and downed that on his way back to his table. He picked up the wrappers and tossed them in the trash bin and was about to leave when he looked back at the table one more time. The orange was still there.

Patch picked up the orange and twirled it around his palm. He felt the cool smoothness, and even with the orange's rind still on, he could smell that startling and familiar fragrance. He sat back down and dug both thumbs into the side of the fruit. He felt his way to the firmer fleshy part of the fruit and then added two fingers to pull away the bright-orange covering, revealing the ribbed, paler orange fruit inside.

Patch had the entire orange peeled in a matter of seconds. He set aside the peeling—one peeling that he put back together to make a hollow, complete shell of the orange. He broke the fruit in half and then into fourths and bit into one of the four large wedges. The juice sprayed his face, stinging his eyes. The combination of sweetness and tartness thrilled his tongue. He broke the remaining three wedges into smaller segments so he could pop them into his mouth whole.

His mind flashed back to the first time he had eaten an orange. He swallowed another segment. That was the day he'd met Kourtney. She had been impressed that he could peel the orange in one piece, and she had wasted half a dozen perfectly good oranges trying to do it too. He had eaten every single one and felt sick to his stomach most of that morning, but leaving food on the table, especially food as wonderful as an orange, was not something Patch could do last year.

Could I leave those wasted oranges now, he thought as he shot the orange peeling like a basketball into the trash bin.

chapter 12

Over the next two days, the operation at the warehouse across the river within sight of the crumbling marble monuments packed up shop. Gwen was amazed at how quickly a place that had almost started to feel like home could be stripped of anything recognizable and packed into trucks. The last crates, full of cooking equipment, were being loaded into small moving trucks.

"Let's use our leave no trace ethics here, folks," Stan said, overseeing the last sweep through.

"Wasn't that an old government slogan? There ain't no government here," someone shouted back at Stan with a gunslinger, Wild West accent.

"True enough. And honestly, leaving this place in better shape than we found it is a very low bar to clear. Let's just make sure we're not leaving anything important or of value, okay? Hey, Gwen," Stan shouted as he left the warehouse with a couple of bags that had been left in a neat stack at the entrance to the building. Gwen ran to catch up with him and grabbed a couple of his bags to help take them to a waiting truck.

"Hi, Stan. Ready for round two with Gerty?" Gwen asked with a wry smile.

"Yes. I was such a charmer last time," Stan said with a chuckle. "Thank goodness you were around to keep things together."

"Hey, don't sell yourself short. She hated you so much that, by contrast, I was practically her best friend," Gwen joked.

"I try to do my part. Seriously though, I'd imagine things will be quite different this go-around."

"What makes you so sure about that?" Gwen asked.

"This time we have Jefferson."

Stan said the words with a confidence that surprised Gwen and bruised her ego a bit, too. Though she hid that, turning away momentarily. They loaded the bags they were carrying into the truck, Gwen still having not responded. What could she say?

"See you inside the fort," Stan said, clasping hands with Gwen as he passed.

"Assuming Gerty doesn't shoot us first," Gwen said, which had become a new inside joke between her and Stan. She added a smile. "Hope for the best at least, right?"

"Right." Stan winked, then headed back to the warehouse.

The rest of the morning, Gwen tried to stay out of everyone's way since the clean-up didn't require much direction on her end now that Jefferson was involved.

As Gwen observed the flurry of activity to move their operations to a new location where the bank corporations and contract enforcers couldn't track them, she was grateful she could focus on saying good-bye to the space and to some of the people she'd met while there. Her favorite morning climbing tree, the river bank, and across the river in the abandoned city, the street-kid crew she had led earlier that year and had left too soon.

Gwen stepped out into a sunny patch of gravel, thankful for the ready warmth the sun brought after spending most of the morning in the shadowy warehouse. She carried a single backpack and a duffel bag to the tree where she had started so many days over the last few months. She still didn't feel the need for a lot of stuff, but valued what she did have. Unzipping her duffel, she pulled out a simple object—a dark-red rock with smooth edges that fit nicely in her hand.

She rolled the rock from side to side, feeling its substantial, firm and cool surface with her thumb. *I sure hope I'm leaving things in a good place with those street kids this time.* She replayed her first meeting with the group after having left them suddenly when Jefferson pulled her from her own operation to perform a different assignment earlier that spring.

As she reflected on that meeting that had taken place a month ago, the spinning of the rock in her hand got faster and she unconsciously laid more pressure on it.

The humidity was already oppressive that day, and wending her way along the pocked blacktop made the heat even worse. Beads of sweat rolled off her face, and her clothes felt a bit sticky. As she moved, the sweat made her even more conscious of her clothes rubbing against her shoulders and legs.

Gwen knew better than to assume she could sneak up on the crew she used to lead. They would have spotted her long before she got to their old base of operations in a spacious brick building that used to be a covered market. So she didn't try to hide. That way, she would seem less threatening. That's what she hoped, anyway.

As she approached the market building, she heard a few hoots that might have been attempts at bird calls but were clearly human. She tried to track where the sounds had come from, but the high walls and narrow streets in the neighborhood made that difficult. She turned her head to determine where the last hoot had come from, but she jumped back and faced forward when she saw what was in front of her. Three kids brandished homemade knives manufactured out of various sharp objects, like glass bottle shards and scrap metal. She was the one who had taught these kids how to make the knives they threatened her with.

"Very nicely done, Miles. Though you might work on making those owl calls a bit more convincing, and I don't think I know the other two of you. Recent recruits to Alex's crew?" Gwen said, trying to stick with a steady, calm, and familiar tone.

"You totally didn't see us, right?" Miles said with obvious pleasure.

"Totally. You've gotten scary good at finding great hiding spots. You've obviously been practicing."

Miles beamed while the other two looked confused.

"So, I was hoping to talk to Alex. About the operation? Is he around?" Gwen asked, taking slow steps toward the building's main entrance.

"Hold on a second. You move when we say you can move," one of the kids—a girl who looked around twelve years old—said. Though, the desperate life the girl had lived probably made her look older than she was.

"Okay, no problem. Just doing your job. I respect that," Gwen said, raising her hands to calm the situation the best she could.

Miles turned to the other two and pulled them into a huddle.

Gwen only picked up scraps of the urgent-sounding conversation. Things like "she used to be one of us" and "Alex's orders" gave her some sense of where the whispered conversation was heading.

"Look, I get it. Miles, you're probably pissed that I left you guys the way I did this past spring. And you two don't know me at all, so you have absolutely no reason to trust me. Here's the deal, though—I do need to talk to Alex about important operations stuff about disrupting the banks. If you have to zip-tie my hands or whatever, that's fine," Gwen said, holding her hands in front of her chest so the three sentries could put zip ties on her if they wanted to.

"The operation doesn't really exist anymore," Miles said.

Gwen picked up on the steely tone of voice and the stony face Miles reverted to after she'd mentioned the operation.

"Zip-tie her hands, and let's take her to Alex," he said.

Gwen winced. More because of the stupid assumption she'd made than the tightness of the zip ties. Though, she had to admit that she was impressed by how well they had secured the ties. Taught them too well, she thought with a sad smile.

She was glad about two things: Alex was still in charge, and he could be reasoned with. At least, the Alex she used to know could be. The three sentries nudged Gwen in front of them, though she didn't really need directing. She knew from the start where Alex would most likely be. The spot where the two of them had last spoken—a spot where a nice ledge jutted off from a set of bay doors that brought filtered sunlight in through the lead paned windows.

As Gwen advanced deeper into the market building, she accumulated a pretty good-sized group of kids trailing behind her, and the general murmur got louder with each step. So many faces she knew and recognized and could tie memories to.

She turned the corner and entered the alcove. And there he was, sitting alone on the ledge. Alex—slowly swinging his legs and lost in thought. She was taken to him, then stood silently for a few seconds. Eventually, Alex looked up.

"Thanks, Miles. Cecily, Diego, thanks. I can take it from here," Alex said with a tired smile and nod toward the way they had come in.

The girl who Gwen then knew as Cecily gave her a poke with her knife as she left. That one has potential. Gwen filed the thought away in her mind and focused back on Alex, who was staring at her intently.

"You're back," Alex said flatly.

Gwen nodded. "Yes. I'm back."

Alex gave a small nod and returned his thoughtful stare to a patch of weeds growing through the cement floor. Gwen waited for him to say more. Anything would be better than the silence and look of disgust she could read on his face.

"There's no excuse and no words to make what I did okay. I know that," Gwen said, taking a cautious step forward. When Alex still didn't say anything, she continued. "I totally abandoned the crew. I abandoned you. It doesn't mean anything, but I wanted to let you know how sorry I am for everything."

Alex's continued silence was driving Gwen crazy. She would rather he yelled or threw something at her. Anything but the tired, sad look he gave her.

"Did you know some of the kids died when they left my crew? They wouldn't have died if they'd stayed, but after you left, it took time for me to pull things back together, and some lost faith in my leadership or whatever. And while they were on their own, they were killed. One for their jacket, I heard. A stupid jacket!" Alex's suddenly flared.

Gwen took a step back, but Alex jumped down from the ledge and got right in her face.

"Another kid—Alice—do you remember her? Wore round-rimmed glasses that she always needed to push back on her nose because they didn't fit right. I almost got her to come back. She promised she would swing by the building the next morning. I found her beat-up body a few blocks from here. A day too late, but that's life, isn't it!"

"Alex, I'm so—"

"Sorry? There were others. Oh yes! There were others," Alex said, pounding his fists against the brick wall that he had backed Gwen against. "But what do you care? They served their purpose. Gave you something to do so you could feel like an important part of your operation across the river."

Gwen's eyes got wide as realization sank in. She had forgotten that Jefferson had been monitoring her activities with the street gang. That meant Jefferson had probably talked to Alex after she had been taken by the contract enforcers.

Gwen felt Alex's heavy breathing blow on her hair that she had put in a hasty loose braid, held together with a rubber band. She slowly raised her head to face him. She searched his eyes, darting her gaze from one to the other. She didn't know why, but she raised her zip-tied hands over Alex's head and leaned against him and into a hug.

Alex's whole body flexed, and Gwen thought she saw him eye the knife tucked inside his belt. But, slowly, his arms softened and gradually dropped to his side, allowing Gwen to drop her tied hands lower on his back. His hands haltingly found their way around her, and once there, they gained confidence and weight. Gwen tucked her cheek into Alex's chest and broke into convulsive sobs. Alex pulled her tight against him and, in a failed attempt at hiding the tears forming in his eyes, turned his face away from Gwen. His breathing became ragged, and Gwen felt his chest heaving, trying to take in more oxygen as his reflexive sobs intensified.

Without words, they held each other for a long time, each leaning against the other to stay upright while tears mixed with the sweat from the hot summer day.

Gwen put the rock back in her backpack and sent a quiet well-wish to Cecily, who had given it to her that morning as, in her words, a see-you-later-not-goodbye thing to remember her by. Gwen patted the trunk of the tree that provided pleasant shade above her, thankful that Gerty's compound had a ton of trees. Within their shady branches, she could continue her morning routine, including her mindfulness sessions—a practice she had always done but, thanks to the brief conversation with Patch, now knew to call mindfulness instead of what she used to call breathing.

Things with Alex were still a bit more complicated than she would have liked, but the relationship was heading in some good directions. For one thing, Alex and his crew were willing to give her another shot. She didn't know how the crew would play their part in the next chapter of Jefferson's operation, but they'd play some role. And beyond that, it felt right and good to have patched things up with the crew.

Trust, once broken, could never come back the same way as before, but she was learning that it could be rebuilt in strong ways that mattered. Just like how the revolution's operations could be picked up and dropped anywhere, and as long as a group of people believed in its core purpose, it could start again.

chapter 13

Gwen rode with Jefferson in his 1981 Chevy. The similarities between this ride and the one that had brought them to the warehouse earlier that spring weren't lost on either of them. And the dusty, familiar smell that Gwen had recognized the last time she'd ridden in the truck flooded her with too many thoughts and feelings to hold inside her small frame. So she decided to put her feet up on the dash, roll down the window, and enjoy the warmth of the sun and the breeze on her arm as she idly waved it outside the window.

"So, remind me how you know Gerty, Jeff?" Gwen asked, comfortable with the silence they had ridden with for the last couple of miles but trying to start up some conversation.

"I don't know her really well, honestly," Jefferson said. "I met her a couple of times with Stan in college. What did you think of her?"

Gwen had to think for a few moments before answering that question. Gerty couldn't be summed up with a few simple words.

"I think she's a rather remarkable woman. Strong. Justifiably confident. She knows what she wants and, most of the time, knows how she can get it, and she's not afraid of the work it takes to get it, either. That might also make her dangerous. I'm glad things worked out the way they did when I first met her, but I can imagine a ton of different scenarios where things could have turned out less well, and we would have ended up dead. She's not someone to take lightly." Gwen looked over at Jefferson, who was nodding thoughtfully.

"A couple of other things we know because you not only survived but built the start of a pretty good working relationship with her. She saw something special in you. That means she's smart and willing to forego stereotypes and stupid cliches about young people not having what it takes to lead. She can recognize goodness no matter where it comes from. That's a good thing for us."

Gwen fought a pleased smile that crept over her face. Jefferson's compliments always were the best because he never flattered. He called things as he saw them.

"And one other thing I'm sure hoping I'm right about, based on the exchange that you and Stan had before, she still has some hope for things to get back to how they were before."

Gwen knew what Jefferson meant. Her reading had taught her that, successful or unsuccessful, the old system of governments, market economies, histories of revolutions, and even novels depicted the world before as a given—as if the way things were was the only way things could ever be. But no matter how much she read or talked to Jefferson about that world before, she hadn't lived in that reality. That made a huge difference.

They drove past a white road sign that had two faded black numbers on it and leaned against a bush. A speed limit sign, she knew from peppering Jefferson with questions on their drive to D.C. during the first trip that spring. That's what it felt like to know about that world before, she thought. Like someone who is used to kilometers having to convert things to miles.

"So you're hoping she'll work with us. But what's your plan exactly?" Gwen asked, rolling her window up so she could hear Jefferson easier now that they were on the open road where Jefferson could pick up speed. The truck sputtered as Jeff pulled hard on the shifter knob and gave it a gentle jiggle to shift it into a higher gear.

"It's a bit of a Hail Mary," Jefferson said, glancing over at Gwen.

Gwen looked back blankly. "A hail, what again?" she asked curiously.

"Oh. Sorry. Of course. Let's see. A Hail Mary was a Catholic prayer to Mary, the mother of Jesus. But the term was picked up by the sports world, particularly football. To throw a Hail Mary would be like throwing a last-chance pass when the team is down and time is running out."

"One of these days, you'll have to explain some of these sports to me."

"Oh, don't feel bad. Most people don't understand them," Jefferson said. "Though they might want you to think they do," he added with a wink. "Anyway, the plan. The Hail Mary plan is this in a nutshell—convince Gerty that we should join forces so that we can disrupt the food supply chains."

The rest of the ride, Jefferson did his best to explain what supply chains were, why they were important, and why disrupting the food supply chain should be their next tactic. Gwen almost got it as Jefferson pulled off the main road and onto the familiar, well-maintained dirt road she and Stan had driven before.

"So by disrupting the food chain—"

"The food *supply* chain. The food chain is something different entirely," Jefferson corrected.

"Right. So by disrupting the food supply chain, we'll be waking people up to the need for a different system."

"Yes! Exactly. We're not going to win people over by convincing them that the meritocracy that replaced world governments is immoral. It makes people way too much money. And there are some nice things about the system. There are a lot fewer people who talk in movie theaters, and people don't eat fish on trains anymore because doing those types of things costs them money. Remember when we talked about the Total Surveillance System that the banks have in place, especially in cities? They know everybody's preferences, so they can charge people who misbehave and take enjoyment away from those around them more to compensate them. That's a very nice thing in some ways, but people always call for change when they get uncomfortable. Do you remember reading about the US politics during the 2020s?"

"Sure. The two parties basically went back and forth of being in charge of the government, and they would reverse as many of the policies from when the other party was in charge as they could." Gwen said.

"Right. And political parties back then were more like fan clubs than serious political groups. People would cheer for the star player of their party—like the presidential candidate. Everybody was so certain they were right and everyone else was wrong. That pride and blind desire for change was what drove it all. People didn't really know how they wanted things to look because that was hard to imagine. So people rallied around anybody who shouted about how bad things were and how they would change things. Any future change seemed better than the bad present. That's what we're going to give them—a need for change—a bad present. And then, when they're shouting loud enough for that change, after they've experienced a bit of hardship trying to pick up their favorite sparkling water from the grocery store, we'll feed them the kind of change they could enjoy."

"I see what you did there. *Feed them the kind of change.* I swear, sometimes you're actually quite clever, Jeff," Gwen said, grinning.

"Only sometimes?" Jefferson asked with a raised eyebrow.

"I'll settle on most of the time. Ready or not, I sure hope Gerty understands supply chains better than I do. Because we're here. Watch out for sentries with guns," Gwen said.

Just as she said it, the truck was abruptly stopped by two armed men in camouflage fatigues. One of the men approached Jefferson's side of the truck and gestured with the muzzle of his gun for Jefferson to roll down his window.

"Morning, gentleman," Jefferson said preemptively chipper and friendly.

The two men gave slight upward nods in response.

"State your business," the man in front of Jefferson said, inspecting the truck—knocking on the bed with his gun and looking in the wheel wells.

"We have a business agreement with Gerty. We're here to discuss that," Jefferson said calmly.

Gwen was impressed with Jefferson's cool demeanor. Must be a tactic he picked up while being grilled in the boardroom.

"What agreement? Gerty has lots of business deals all over," the other man, who was inspecting the passenger side of the truck, said.

"We have an operation on the banks of the Potomac in D.C.," Jefferson said. "My name is Jefferson, if that helps."

"No. That name doesn't ring any bells. But you look familiar?"

One of the men, who was pointing his gun in Gwen's direction, looked vaguely familiar to her, too. Gwen rolled down her window as the man who had addressed her approached her door.

"Greg?" Gwen said, trying to picture the man without the reflective sunglasses that hid his eyes.

"Yes! Hey, Gwen. I thought I recognized you. Gerty hasn't stopped talking about you since she met you. Calls you her prototype or something fancy like that."

"Protégé maybe?" Jefferson offered.

"Yes, that's it. Her protégé. Come on through. Gerty would not be happy with me if I held you up like I did last time." Greg walked about twenty yards in front of the truck and signaled to someone around the corner.

Gwen heard the creaking of a metal gate, then Greg motioned for Jefferson to pull forward. "Welcome back, Gwen," Greg said with a friendly wave.

Jefferson and Gwen quickly rolled up their windows so they could have one last huddle before facing Gerty. Jefferson eased the truck forward. "It pays to know people, eh?" Jefferson said, beaming. "You are very impressive, you know that?"

Gwen had been nervous when Greg first recognized her. Jefferson was prepared to take the lead with Gerty, and Gwen wasn't sure how being singled out might have mixed up the cards in their negotiating position. But looking at Jefferson, brimming with obvious pride, thrilled her to the core. "Thanks. Things worked out pretty well last time I was here," Gwen said.

"You think? From what I saw back there, pretty well is a huge under-sell. Well done, you! I wasn't sure how the two of us would play this meeting, but now you'll have to play first fiddle, at the front end, at least. This'll be fun," Jefferson said.

Gwen gave Jefferson a nervous smile. He seemed to have regained some of his former flair. He must live for these kinds of negotiations.

And, although she did feel her nerves lift, making her a bit lightheaded and energized, the nerves seemed more like excitement than the fear she'd felt the last time she had been at Gerty's compound.

Another sentry directed the truck to a side building that Gwen hadn't seen last time. It was a long, tall steel building with a wide enough door that two trucks could pass each other while driving through its opening. Jefferson backed up the truck alongside a couple of work trucks with tall wooden beds.

Gwen jumped down from the truck onto gravel and instantly picked up a distinct fragrance in the air. It was pungent in a way, but earthier than the pungent smells she was used to from her days on the street. This smell had nothing to do with the decay or rot or death. She couldn't place it. Gwen followed Jefferson to the opening in the steel building, and then she understood.

Dozens of workers were processing mass quantities of produce. Gwen had been so caught up with operations in D.C., where there had been few signs of the passing of the season, but at the farm, time ticked by on the seasonal clock and late-summer harvesttime was in full swing. Conveyor belts transported several varieties of apples and peaches to an area where cardboard boxes were stacked high. Other fruits and vegetables Gwen didn't recognize filled the building with an overwhelming smell—rich and enticing.

"Gwen! Back for another one of my delicious apples, I presume?"

Gwen jumped, absorbed by the smells and flurry of activity around her. "Gerty, hi!" she cleared her throat and tried to get her bearings again. Turning, she saw Gerty strolling toward her and toting a box on her hip. "If you're offering, I would absolutely never turn down one of those apples. Not on my life."

Gerty smiled and tossed an apple from the box she was carrying toward Gwen. Gwen caught it in one hand and pulled the apple close to inspect it. It had an overall golden color but also had bright-red blushes around the top edges and orange accents. As Gwen held it in her hand, she felt its firmness and picked up on the tart sweetness of its smell.

"Give it a try. It's a new variety I've been crossbreeding. I call the breed Jedediah Cross. Kind of catchy, but the name's just a draft," Gerty said, carefully dropping her box a few feet in front of Gwen.

Gwen suddenly felt self-conscious as she prepared to bite into the apple. What if I bite in the wrong way or in the wrong place? I'll offend these people so much. Fruit is their business. But her self-consciousness melted as soon as her teeth sank into the crisp side of the apple. The tartness hit her first, so much so, in fact, that her tongue tingled. But then the sweetness kicked in too, not too powerfully, but enough to balance the tartness. As she swallowed, she thought she might have picked up a slight hint of spiciness, too, although her palette was far from sophisticated.

"Do you like it?" Gerty asked with surprising trepidation in her voice.

"Gerty, this is amazing! How on earth did you breed in so many flavors? My goodness, I feel like I've eaten a meal with a single bite of one apple," Gwen said, taking another bite between grinning teeth, trying to cover her mouth so as to not spray Gerty with juice.

"Yes! Put that in the win column. That's exactly what I was going for. Old varieties of apples can be so boring. This variety will make people think and feel things, like a fine wine," Gerty said, pumping her arm and reaching out her fist.

Gwen gave Gerty a hearty fist bump.

"That's right! Okay, so tell me why you're doing me the pleasure of visiting again. We didn't have a meeting on the calendar, did we? We're still preparing your first delivery. I'm one of those old-school nuts who still uses an actual wall calendar. I just can't get away from those hot, shirtless farmhand pictures. Oh, and Thomas Kincaid. I'm a sucker for those sparkles," Gerty said, picking up her box again and dropping it on a conveyor belt, sending it whizzing away to the far side of the cavernous building.

"I'd like to introduce you to someone, Gerty, someone really special to me. This is Jefferson Jones. Jefferson, meet Gerty. I'm so sorry, Gerty, I don't think I've ever heard your last name."

"That's because I don't use it much. My name is Gertrude Terry," Gerty said, receiving Jefferson's waiting hand warmly. "Gerty Terry just doesn't ring true, does it? So call me Gerty."

"Incredible to see you again after so many years," Jefferson said

"Again, eh? Go ahead and tell me where. My memory isn't what it used to be," Gerty said.

"Oh, I wouldn't expect you to remember. It was back in college. I think I met you the first time at a student association soiree. Those academic get-togethers always had such high and mighty names, didn't they? Galas and convocations. As I recall, they were just good excuses for students to drink too much," Jefferson said with a chuckle.

Gerty let out one of her shimmering laughs, and Gwen burst into a laugh, too, at the joy of Gerty's laugh, although she had no idea what soirees or convocations were.

"Ah yes, those were fun days. Strike that. Those were crazy days designed to be fun but ended up being full of booze and hangovers and other follies. I only really went to those parties my first year, so you must have caught me early on."

"I guess so. You haven't aged a day, other than your hair changing into an even more beautiful shade than back then," Jefferson said.

"Charmer—this one," Gerty said, looking at Gwen.

"He actually isn't at all, even though sometimes I wish he were. No, he calls things as he sees them," Gwen said.

"Then maybe we'll have to keep him around to remind me from time to time that the laugh lines on my face are actually invisible to every-body except me," Gerty said, glancing back at Jefferson when she said keep him around.

Gwen slowly shook her head in admiration. Gerty had already figured out their play. And if she had figured it out, Gwen was certain Jefferson knew it and, hopefully, had a plan B.

"Gerty, as much fun as it is reminiscing about the old glory days—"

"See, now he calls me old. Forget about the charmer bit," Gerty inter-jected with a demure smile.

"Sorry. The recent glory days of our youth that you have miraculously remained in while the rest of us have aged," Jefferson said, grinning. "I know you already know why we're here. I had the other trucks wait miles back up the road, but I figured you'd get word sooner than later, and it was much sooner. Sooner than I could even get out my grand pitch, which I'm sure would have won you over to the cause."

Jefferson took a long breath, and Gwen looked at Gerty to see if she could read any change. As far as she could tell, Gerty was waiting for the rest of the ask before making any judgments.

"On the ride here, our mutual friend Gwen asked me to explain what a Hail Mary was. I did my best to explain that it's a prayer for a miraculous catch to win the game, even against odds that seem impossible." Jefferson winced and leaned against the nearby conveyor belt. He still carried wounds from being detained, some much deeper than bruises.

Gerty's eyes lit up with curiosity and maybe concern.

"I don't know what all Gwen might have shared with you about our efforts to disrupt the banking system while in D.C., but what I'm certain she wouldn't have told you. She's far too modest to say that I would still be living out my days fairly comfortably on a small farm in the backwoods of Kansas if I hadn't run into her. She had just bested three hulking men who were trying to kill her, and I patched her up a bit. We forget sometimes, I think, that younger folks like Gwen have no idea what it was like before the government fell. And what rekindled my desire to change things, came from a horrifying thought that grew inside me as I got to know Gwen. When our generation fades away, there won't be anybody left to tell a first-hand account of how things used to be. The meritocracy will encourage people to embrace the new order completely, and no one will be around to show a different model. People like Gwen won't even know to want that world back."

Jefferson picked up a discarded pear that had been caught in the conveyor belt. It had a gaping gash and was oozing juice, causing a small pool on the ground that shone in the steel supports connected to the belt.

"Our first attempt at disrupting the banks failed. We got some early wins, sure. But the AI's algorithms are too responsive and sophisticated, with powerful predictive analytics and total surveillance at its fingertips. Since I designed the original systems, I thought maybe I'd found a back-door. But that . . . well . . . that didn't work either."

Jefferson had a catch in his voice, and he bowed his head to his chest, his wild, long gray hair falling loosely over his face. Gwen saw Jefferson's chest rise and fall in deep, haggard breaths. Gerty's head was cocked to the side, and her hands were away from her sides a few inches like she was debating whether she should give Jefferson a hug. After some quiet moments, Jefferson looked up again and brushed the hair out of his face with a determined nod.

"So here we are. We had to leave our base in D.C. so we could get away from the eyes of the contract enforcers, who had been monitor-ing us the whole time. I could spell out my whole new plan now, or we could wait until later, but some facts will always remain—we tried and failed with the banks. We've moved our focus to disrupting the food supply chain, and we have a group of about fifty people who care a great deal about telling their stories from before the Economic Wars but who, without your help, will have to go back to their old regular lives soon. Will you help us?"

Gerty let the silence collect after Jefferson asked his last question. She gave a resolute nod and stepped closer to Jefferson, taking the man-gled pear from his hand. "You know what the amazing thing is about produce?" Gerty said, slowly walking to a plastic dumpster.

Gwen and Jefferson waited for Gerty to answer her own question.

"Produce is never wasted. Even with this poor pear here," Gerty said, tossing the pear into a bin. "If it's not fit to be eaten, it can make com-post to help build new soil. Nature just does her thing—organic material grows and it dies, restoring the nutrients back to the soil that it took to grow and leaving it for the next crop."

Jefferson and Gwen glanced at each other questioningly. Gwen raised her shoulders and shook her head.

"Let me get right to my point. There will always be injustices in the world. There were a ton before. There are different ones now. You think there's justice or fairness in the natural order of things? Ask the deer that we're making into stew tonight. Maybe these times are a bit less fair for some people. That's wrong because we can do things to make it better. We should do that within our own spheres of influence, for sure. But I'm not about to risk the privilege of protecting and feeding and caring for the dozens of people I have working with me here—not based on a Hail Mary toss. Maybe businesspeople like you are willing to take those kinds of risks, but not me."

Gerty grabbed a rag hanging on a wooden table near the dumpster and wiped the pear juice off the conveyor belt. "You're all welcome to dinner tonight. I can offer you a good meal, at least," Gerty said, turning to face Jefferson directly. "Jefferson, I admire what you're doing. I do. And I'm definitely taking a liking to this one," Gerty said, nodding in Gwen's direction. "But you'll have to look for a partner other than me. Of course, I'm still more than happy to provide you with the supplies we've already agreed to deliver to you. Just let me know where to send them. Gwen struck such a hard bargain that our business transaction feels like I'm donating to your cause anyway." Gerty sent a wink to Gwen. "Who knows, maybe I'm a bit of a revolutionary after all. See you at dinner. Five o'clock sharp, or I can't guarantee there'll be anything left except for soggy turnips."

And with that, Gerty disappeared into a bright haze of sunlight outside the building, leaving Gwen and Jefferson standing silently with the whirring of the conveyor belt and the muted thuds of produce landing in cardboard boxes.

chapter 14

Patch was brand new to the concept of traditions, but he worried that sneaking into the kitchens at midnight might not be quite as thrilling as it had been last year. Ever since he'd returned from his visits on campus, he was sure he had suggested the wrong thing as his and Will's tradition. What had his writing tutor always said last year? First word, best word? Did that apply to thoughts of new traditions too? Maybe? Hopefully?

And where had Will been all day, anyway?

"Hey, Siri," Patch said.

"Yes, Patch?"

"What time is it, and where is Will?"

"It's eleven thirty-seven p.m. right now, and Will hasn't authorized you access to his location. Do you want me to send a request?"

"No." It was worth a shot, but Patch guessed that Will would have thought of that. I'm sure he's cooking up some kind of surprise, he thought. Heaven help us.

Patch lay down on his bed and grabbed the pink rubber ball that he always kept by his bed. He tossed it at the ceiling, trying to get it as close to the ceiling as he could without actually hitting it. After many such restless occasions, he'd gotten pretty good at the game, though there were plenty of subtle pink marks scattered across his ceiling where he'd missed—the ball smacking right up against the ceiling, too.

"Hey, Siri! Tell me about the history of Harvard Academy," Patch said.

"Sure thing. Harvard Academy, or more properly, Harvard Advanced Preparatory Academy, was established in 2028 when the former Harvard

University was bought by a cooperation of banks. The cooperation also changed the academic levels taught at the school from a focus on under-graduate and graduate studies to the high school equivalent. Do you want to hear more about that?"

"Yes. Tell me why the academic levels taught are lower now," Patch said, still tossing the ball at the ceiling.

"There is great speculation on that. The best-established theory is that the academy wanted to have a bigger influence on the academic training of rising leaders by establishing their curriculum earlier. Other theories state that the academy determined it would be more profitable as an academy than as a university."

"Sounds about right," Patch smirked.

"Sorry. I didn't get that. Did you mean Tomorrow Morning by Jack Johnson? Do you want me to play it?"

"No, thanks. Tell me more about Harvard Academy."

"Sure thing . . ."

The minutes passed slowly while Patch learned about the academic focuses of Harvard Academy, its standings among similar schools, and its sports programs, which he couldn't resist diving into, particularly its stellar record in track and field.

"Hey, Siri, what should I do if my roommate is a total creep?"

Will dashed into the room, and Patch sat up, letting the ball bounce off his head.

"Let me look into that for a moment. I found something on what to do if my roommate is a total creep from the Foundation for Child Advocacy. Would you like to hear about it?"

"Yes!" Will shouted at the same time that Patch shouted, "No!"

"Sorry. I didn't get that. Do you mind repeating that?"

Patch threw the ball at Will to distract him and shouted, "Cancel."

"No problem."

"Great, so now I'll get a bunch of advertisements for hotlines to protect myself from child predators. Thanks for that, Will," Patch said, glaring.

"Don't mention it. Those advocacy groups do such important work. We should pay more attention to them anyway," Will said with a grin. "Speaking of advocacy work, are you ready for the great ice cream heist?"

Will dragged Patch upright and to the center of the room.

"Wait for it," Will said, freezing and closing his eyes.

"Wait for what?"

Just then, the bell tower in the main quad struck the hour. As soon as the twelfth strike sounded, Patch's room lit up in neon projections of abstract art versions of ice cream sundaes that danced to a throbbing techno beat. Patch's gaze darted around the room to find where the laser show was coming from and followed the source to Will's watch.

"Your watch can put on laser light shows?" Patch yelled over the thump of the techno beat.

"Hey, I decided what to project! So give me some credit. Though I might have let my watch do most of the work. What do you think I've been doing all afternoon?" Will asked, pleased to see that Patch was impressed.

"You set all this up for ice cream?" Patch asked, slowly turning to see all the neon pictures. He caught one that looked like Leonardo da Vinci's *Last Supper*, except all the dishes on the table were mounds of ice cream piled high.

"You like that one? I remember you talking with Kourtney about that particular art piece. That one took some special touches. The graphics program kept swapping faces for ice cream dishes, which was a bit too sacrilegious, even for me," Will said.

The light show must have been timed because, a moment later, the lights went out with one last boom from the music. "Now, my friend, it begins!" Will dashed out of the room without making sure that Patch followed.

Patch sprinted to catch up with Will, who was already halfway down the first flight of stairs.

"Hold on a second," Patch hissed at Will, finally catching up with him and pulling him against the wall. "There are people in this building who are probably asleep and who might be curious about why two students are tromping down the stairs at midnight after blasting house music."

"Don't worry. No one from our floor is here yet. I checked. And they've soundproofed the floors so well that I doubt any first-years heard anything at all," Will said confidently.

"It's not the first-years that I'm concerned about. It's cameras." As soon as Patch said it, reality sank in. *Of course they'd have cameras in the kitchen, too!*

"What's the problem? Cameras are all over the place. Trust me, okay? Everything will be fine," Will said with a reassuring pat on Patch's arm.

"Okay. If you're sure. Remember, I'm not nearly as good at lying as you are," Patch said, willing to be dragged down the remaining stairs by Will.

"Ouch! That burns. I don't lie as much as project into the universe the kind of reality I want, and usually things work out. It's more of a post-modern approach to the truth," Will said, halting outside the stainless-steel kitchen doors and holding his pointer finger to his lips to silence any further conversation.

Will stood on his tiptoes and peeked through the round window and into the kitchen. Patch was at least a head taller than Will and could see perfectly well that there was no one in there, but he played along.

"The coast looks clear. Let's go!"

For the next fifteen minutes, Patch and Will searched inside the expansive freezers until, at last, Patch found what they were looking for. Two long rows full of huge tubs of ice cream.

Patch leaned out of the freezer and whispered in Will's direction, "Target in sight."

"Nice work, soldier. Get that ice cream."

Will ducked inside Patch's freezer, and they each hugged a tub.

"I forgot how heavy these are. There's got to be at least twenty pounds of ice cream in each of these," Patch said, adjusting his grip on his chosen tub of mint chocolate chip.

"Ah, the classic mint chocolate-chip choice. I've got the fruit down— raspberry cheesecake. Are we set? Any other desserts strike your fancy?

You'd better check the freezer I was in, just in case," Will suggested, putting his tub down at his feet and stretching his back.

"Okay, hold on a sec." Patch dashed into the freezer Will had last been in. He was flooded with memories as he spotted the delicately decorated cakes stacked on four rows of shelves that lined one entire wall of the freezer. But he was looking for one particular kind. Carrot cake. He scanned the rows, darting his gaze past lemon cakes with rich red filling and dark chocolate cake with frosting so thick Patch couldn't understand how it could be swallowed. At last, he spotted his target on the third shelf, close to the back.

Patch could almost taste the mixture of a subtle sweet cream-cheese frosting set alongside a savory walnut flavor and an earthy texture. If there was a perfect cake for him, carrot cake was it. Patch carefully carried one of the plastic containers holding a large wedge of carrot cake out of the freezer, then firmly latched the freezer door behind him. He hoisted the tub of mint chocolate-chip ice cream in his left hand, balancing it against his hip.

"Okay, I'm ready now," Patch said, starting to make his way to the door. "Spoons! I am not going to suggest that we build onto this tradition by eating the ice cream with our hands like last time. Let me grab two—hold on—"

"Never fear, I'm way ahead of you," Will said with a pleased smile, presenting two spoons that he had tucked inside his hoodie pocket.

"When did you grab those?"

"Don't worry about it. Let's go."

Patch's nerves were really flaring at Will's behavior—first, he was apathetic to their theft, then he was in a hurry. But Patch didn't want to ruin the tradition either, even if taking the sweet treats didn't excite him quite the same way it had last year. So he played along. Then when they reached the door of their dorm and Will waited for Patch to catch up, Patch knew something was up.

"Okay, Will, what's going on? You never wait for me. You usually jump ahead of me by a mile. And are we going to eat this ice cream in the hall or—"

"Happy Birthday!" Shouted a chorus of voices right as Will opened the door.

A deluge of confetti and balloons covered the little floor space in their dorm room and bright, warm light halfway blinded Patch as Will pulled him through the door.

"I figured you don't know your birthday, so I decided today could be it," Will whispered in Patch's ear. "Everybody here thinks it's your birthday, so just play along."

Patch was led into the center of the room where he was amazed to see at least a dozen people, besides him and Will, packed into their tiny dorm room.

"Hey, Patchman!"

Patch turned around to see the familiar face.

"Pete! How's it going, buddy? I didn't know you were coming back early."

"How can I be anything but fantastic, feeling all the love for you in this room, my friend?" Pete held his hand against his chest and breathed in deeply, as if he were on a tropical beach rather than in a smelly dorm room.

"Thanks, I think," Patch said awkwardly.

"I couldn't miss my buddy's birthday party," Pete said with a knowing wink.

Patch figured Pete knew it wasn't really his birthday. Pete had been in the same situation as Patch—living on the streets. At least, he had before Patch's big run-in with Malcolm, which had encouraged Pete to get tested. As it turned out, Pete had a huge aptitude in spatial reasoning and emotional intelligence. Whatever those were. So the school had been eager to bring him on, too.

"Are you seriously not even going to say hi to your old girlfriend?"

Patch followed the sound of the voice to the back corner. The crowd was so packed in the tiny space that he hadn't noticed Kourtney sitting on his bed, tucked behind three particularly tall high jumpers.

"Kourtney! I didn't even see you there. I thought you were on your family's boat this week. I'm sorry for not—"

"Oh, I'm not that offended," Kourtney said with a thrilled grin. She jumped off the bed and gave Patch a hug that would have knocked him over if it weren't for the solid frames of the high jumpers to lean against. "Why didn't you tell me that today is your birthday?" Kourtney asked when she finally let him go.

Patch quickly wracked his brain to remember what the day's date was for future reference. August nineteenth is my birthday now, he thought, making a mental note. It was one of those things that he'd never recognized as missing from his life. A birthday. But now that he had at least a made-up one, he had to admit that there was something grounding and nice in having it.

"I usually don't make a big deal over it, you know?" Patch mumbled.

"Well, if you had told me, I would have come up with something much better, but you can hardly expect a masterpiece with a day's notice, and from the deck of a ship no less," Kourtney said, reaching behind herself and pulling out a package nearly as big as she was.

"Open it, open it, open it!" Kourtney said, shoving the package into Patch's arms.

Patch rotated the long, thin package, carefully trying not to hit anybody in the crowded room. He removed the twine from the top seam of the burlap covering, and it fell off gracefully, revealing a painting framed in a stylish dark wood.

"Do you like it? Tell me you love it! I think I'll die if you don't say you—"

Patch stopped Kourtney cold with a kiss. Kourtney's eyes widened in surprise, and her whole body tensed at first but melted fast. Patch needed a lot of work in the kissing department, but he gave Kourtney's upper lip a little extra tug with his lips that he hoped was something a more experienced kisser would do.

"Sorry about that. I didn't mean to. Well, I did. It wasn't a mistake or anything. I just mean, it's not like me," Patch stammered.

Kourtney grinned and jumped in for another kiss, this time on her terms.

"That was not the response I was anticipating, Mr. Robinson," Kourtney said, sitting on the bed and motioning Patch to sit by her, which he did.

"Better or worse than you anticipated?" Patch asked.

"Better. Much better. So I take it you like the painting?"

"Are you kidding? I love it! How did you remember how much I loved that first glimpse of the ocean? And you've captured it perfectly."

"Is there really a perfect in art?" Kourtney asked in a lofty academic voice. "I'm kidding. I tried to accentuate the pieces of that first view that might have struck you most. The immensity of space, the sun sparkling across the breaking waves. The stark contrast in colors between the sky and water and beach."

Patch looked closer at the painting now that Kourtney had outlined those components, and she was spot on. Those were some of the most striking parts of that first visit to the ocean last year. But there was something else about the ocean that no painting could duplicate. When Patch had stood on the beach that first time, he'd felt a sense of peace in his own smallness. That it was okay that he would be such a small part of the whole scheme of the world because he was grateful that places like those existed, whether or not he was there to see them. He couldn't have described that feeling to Kourtney, though.

"I did my best. I gave up on trying to portray that sense of insignificance or whatever you said about the ocean making you okay with being insignificant," Kourtney said, resting her head on Patch's arm.

I've never given Kourtney enough credit. Patch wrapped an arm around her shoulders. "I love it. It's the best thing you could have ever given me. Thank you so much, Kourtney."

Patch sat looking at the painting and enjoying the closeness with Kourtney for several minutes, which surprised him. But Will eventually found him.

"Okay, you two will have all school year to reconnect and snuggle. This part of the event is for roommates only," Will said.

"Thanks so much for coming everybody," Patch shouted to the exiting crowd. Patch turned to Kourtney. "Thanks so much again, Kourt. And it means even more that you'd leave your trip for my birthday."

"Of course, silly," Kourtney said, slipping between Patch's arms for one more hug. She stood and grabbed her handbag, which she draped across the crook of her elbow. "Gentlemen, it's been a pleasure," she said with a formal bow.

Patch and Will laughed and returned the bow.

"See you 'round, Kourtney," Patch said with a wave as she disappeared into the dark hallway.

"Now, we feast," Will said, leveraging open the lid of his raspberry cheesecake ice cream. "And look, the tradition continues. The ice cream is even melting for us."

Will tossed a spoon at Patch, which he used to pry open his tub of mint chocolate-chip ice cream. Patch curled a spoonful of the bright-green ice cream and brought it to his lips. It tasted even better than he remembered. This birthday thing is a very good idea, he thought as he dug in for more of the cool, minty goodness.

"I love this time," Will said, letting out a satisfied burp. Both Will and Patch were resting flat on their backs on their beds.

"Nice one. What time are you talking about?" Patch asked, getting back to the ball–ceiling game.

"The time where you're so stuffed and you know you're going to pay for what you ate later, but you feel full and content and, in our case"— Will gestured to the half-empty tubs of ice cream and the empty plastic carrot cake container—"we're enjoying a lingering sugar buzz for a little longer. There's something very good and existential to it, don't you think?"

"No offense, Will, but I've learned to kind of go with whatever you say."

The ball bounced off the wall behind Patch's head, and he had to flip around fast to catch it before it ricocheted off a shelf and away from him.

"Like that right there," Will continued as if Patch hadn't said anything. "You very likely will have a tweak in your back in the morning for flipping around to save that ball. But right now, you're just grateful to have the ball rather than having to hunt it down under the bed or somewhere."

"I guess I get that. I remember having a debate in one of my classes last year about whether any other animals have the ability to think about their thinking like you're doing right now," Patch said, staying on his stomach and stretching out his legs so they hung over the far edge of the bed.

"Nice. That's one of the roots of most philosophy. Very Descartes-esque. I think, therefore I am kind of thing," Will said thoughtfully.

"You lost me there," Patch said, muffled because his face was buried in his bedspread.

"You do kind of live in the moment, Patch. That's something I've always admired about you, honestly."

"Thanks?" Patch said awkwardly.

"Oh! I completely forgot! How did the visits go today? You were going to beg to stay in your coach's good graces, right?" Will asked, propping himself on his side to face Patch.

"Yeah. That one turned out surprisingly well. Coach Curtis—don't you start again!"

Will was fighting a peal of laughter that he eventually lost to, cracking up into giggles.

"I know, you dated a girl named Maddi Curtis, so you imagine Coach Curtis with red curls," Patch recited.

"Frizzy red curls all over his head! Sometimes those visualization exercises can be taken too far," Will said, settling back down but still taking heavy breaths broken by occasional sniggers.

"Anyways, so Coach . . . I'm not even going to say it," Patch said with a sharp look at Will. "Coach seemed excited to have me back. He even kind of let me know that he's all but counting on me to be on the team this year."

"Was that in question at all? I mean, you broke regional records in your events. Why in the world wouldn't he be thrilled to have you back," Will asked incredulously.

Patch didn't answer right away. He had heard similar statements often enough. But a lingering doubt always stuck in his mind.

"Although, perhaps your need to prove your own worthiness is your superpower," Will said.

"That makes sense, I guess."

Patch and Will let the quiet settle for a couple of minutes, deep in their own thoughts. Patch eventually broke that silence. "I visited one other spot," Patch said hesitatingly, but instantly perking up Will's interest.

"Oh yeah?"

"Yeah. You know that old cottage on the northwest corner of campus by the river?" Patch asked, craning his neck to face Will, who gave no indication whether he knew where Patch meant. "You know where all the facilities management buildings are, right?"

"Oh, yeah. Where all the big machinery stuff is, and where campus isn't so historic?" Will said with air quotes around historic with his one good hand.

Patch clearly had a puzzled look because Will followed up with an explanation.

"My Dad told me once that most of the buildings around campus have been renovated or, in some cases, completely rebuilt, but they tried to build things back in the neoclassical style to match the original buildings back when the university was founded like four hundred years ago or something."

"That seems about right," Patch said, nodding slowly. "There's a house tucked away in that part of campus. I like to visit it on my runs. So I visited it this morning too," Patch said, a knot developing in his stomach as he began feeling more and more certain that he shouldn't have shared such information, but now that it was out, he couldn't put it back.

"Why there? Does anyone live there?" Will asked.

"Yeah, an old groundskeeper. He's been there since before . . . when this used to be Harvard University."

"Whoa! Hold on. There's an old groundskeeper tucked away in a forgotten cottage that no one sees or knows about?" Will said, sitting up on his bed and swinging his legs over the edge in long arcs that almost kicked Patch's bed. "That sounds like a plot for a horror flick. I had no idea."

Patch sat up, too, trying desperately to downplay the whole place. "It's really not anything special, Will. I only go there because it reminds me that not everything is about money or getting ahead. It helps me remember where I came from," Patch said, not having powerful enough words to explain the emotional connection he had with the cottage. That the cottage represented exactly the way he wanted life to be in about as well a way as anything could be—a quiet and compassionate life, taking care of a small piece of the world and helping a few rose bushes to grow.

"No, that's amazing! It's perfect, actually. I've been looking into ethnographic studies and was planning on making that my focus for my major project this year," Will said excitedly.

So much for the quiet and compassionate life . . .

"What do you mean? You'll study the cottage? Like its history and stuff? I'm sure they have some things about it at the library," Patch said, getting more nervous by the minute, sensing where the conversation was going.

"No. Ethnographic studies are more personal than that. I'll need to interview the groundskeeper to get a sense of how he lives. And that connection to the old university will definitely win me extra points with Dr. Sessions."

"Will, you can't bother this guy," Patch said, fighting the edge creeping into his voice.

"I won't bother him. I'll be incredibly respectful of his space, and I'll just ask him a couple of questions. It sounds like you've met him before, so you can introduce me," Will said in a way that told Patch he was already setting everything in place in his mind, as if it were a done deal.

"You're not hearing me, Will. I think the guy is very private. And wouldn't it be insulting to him—that you were there to observe his life and existence? Almost like he's a different breed of human?" Patch said, letting that edge in his voice move right in this time.

"He is," Will said, but when Patch's whole body convulsed, Will quickly tried to explain. "I didn't mean that—"

"Of course you did," Patch said bluntly.

"I guess I did. But not in the way you're thinking. He's not a different species, and I won't be studying him like he's some endangered animal or anything. Having someone like that—a classic blue-collar worker who's been employed by one of the most prestigious schools in the world for at least forty years and who's seen the fall of governments and a major shift in schools—is so rare. Do you see what an important story he probably has to tell?"

Patch was ready with a biting response, but Will's thinking did make some sense. The groundskeeper—Chuck—really did have a unique situation. Who knows? He might even want to tell his story, Patch thought, trying to convince himself.

"Come on, you owe me. I threw you a surprise birthday party. You practically ruined the surprise, too, by the way."

"I was almost certain you knew we'd get caught, that you were so used to getting away with things that you weren't concerned or something. I mean, there are definitely cameras down in the kitchen. Come to think of it, how did you pull that ice cream thing off last year, anyway?" Patch asked with genuine curiosity.

"Oh, my mom and dad are kind of important people in the right circles. As much as I like to think I got into this school on my own, I know my parents didn't hurt my chances, either. They'll probably have to make a donation or something to smooth over my misbehavior," Will said, using air quotes again around the word misbehavior.

"Enough with those air quotes. Not everything you say deserves quoting." Patch smiled. "Okay. I'll take you by the cottage on two conditions." Patch waited to make sure he had Will's full attention.

Will nodded eagerly.

"If we knock on the door and he doesn't answer, you won't bug me every day about going back. For all I know, the groundskeeper might ignore visitors to his house because a lot of kids over the years have made fun of it. A spot to take their photo. Okay?"

Will nodded to that as well.

"And, if he does happen to be around and opens the door when we visit, you won't try to twist his arm or convince him that he should let you interview him. If he says yes, that's fine, but we're not going to push him. Got it?"

"Got it. We'll go tomorrow morning." Will jumped up and grabbed his bag with his toothbrush and headed out the door.

"Whoa! Where are you going?" Patch yelled back at Will before he disappeared into the dark hallway.

"To get ready for bed. I need to be as rested and sharp as I can if I only have one shot at interviewing the groundskeeper." Will ducked into the hall, leaving Patch to his own thoughts and misgivings.

chapter 15

The dinner of vegetable stew with hearty whole-wheat bread was delicious, but the laughter and comfortable chatter Gwen had grown accustomed to in their old warehouse operation were missing that night. All of Jefferson's crew knew they still hadn't found a new base of operations, and all of Gerty's workers seemed embarrassed that Gerty had turned them away. But Gwen made the most of the opportunity by getting to know some of Gerty's team.

"You were a big shot financial planner, and you gave that up to work on a farm?" Gwen asked the person sitting next to her, whose name she learned was Maggie. Their picnic table was nestled among a dozen others set in two neat rows in a grassy field near the processing building.

"Yeah, I know! Crazy, huh? And what a time to leave, too, right? I mean, financial planners basically rule the world now," Maggie said, sopping up some of the stew from the side of her bowl with a piece of bread that she popped in her mouth.

Gwen followed Maggie's example, and both grinned at each other, enjoying the delicious combination of textures and flavors.

"What made you change jobs like that," Gwen asked.

"After I saw what financial instruments could do—I mean, they basically took down the world order—after that, I couldn't be a part of it anymore. Then, one morning, I escaped the office and went for a ride in the country, trying to figure out what I should do with myself. And I stumbled onto Gerty's farm. At first, I thought I'd just buy some produce, but thirty years later, I'm still here. So let's say, Gerty knows how to make a good impression on people," Maggie said, swinging her legs to the other side of the table's bench and putting her spoon and napkin in her bowl to start cleaning up.

"So nice to meet you, Maggie," Gwen said.

"Likewise, Gwen. I knew you had to be special because Gerty hasn't been impressed by many people more than she is by you."

"She must see things I don't recognize in myself, I guess, because I'm just a teenager trying to figure things out," Gwen said honestly.

"She always does, but then we get the chance to live up to those high expectations. Good night," Maggie said, giving Gwen's arm a little squeeze as she passed by on her way to the kitchens.

Everyone Gwen met had a similar story of finding their way to Gerty's farm and then finding a reason to stay. Impressively, their backgrounds had ranged from school teachers to sanitation specialists before they became farm workers. And Gwen could certainly see the appeal in farming—a quiet, meaningful life, growing food in a community of caring people interested in stepping away from the frantic bustle of the outside world. But Gwen also felt something else.

Anger.

At first, she couldn't place where it was coming from. After all, Gerty and her crew had been generous and incredibly kind, and the setting sun that cast warm light across the fields enhanced the already peaceful scene. Still, the unsettled feeling kept growing inside her, so after she had washed some dishes to help clean up and had said goodnight to Jefferson and many of Gerty's crew members, she escaped to a tree to think and to be away from people, afraid that she might say something she'd regret.

She climbed a great old maple that had struck her fancy earlier and settled on a large branch with her back against the trunk. She stayed long past the sunset, and the darkness rolled over the landscape. Gwen wasn't used to nights that dark. Even back in Kansas, she'd spent most of her years in the remnants of a city where automatic light systems still produced enough light pollution that the night sky wasn't dark enough to make out many stars.

On the farm, though, stars popped out of the black sky, and once the nearly full moon rose, the sky's lights were bright enough for her to easily find her way down from the tree. She started tearing off dead twigs from the tree's limbs and breaking them into pieces as small as she could, her agitation swelling inside her chest. She wished she had thought to get her jacket from Jefferson's truck because she wasn't done enjoying the night's stillness that calmed her thoughts and frustrations, but she was cold. She had decided to get her jacket and maybe climb the tree again when she saw someone sitting on a bench tucked away under the largest apple tree she had ever seen.

At least, she thought it was an apple tree. There weren't many apples on it. To make sure, she crept closer. The cool moonlight struck the person's face in a way that almost made them look ghostly, but in a serene way rather than a scary one. Gwen's eyes were so trained on the figure on the bench that she didn't pay attention to her feet and stomped on a branch, causing a loud cracking noise as the branch broke in two.

Only then did Gwen recognize that it was Gerty. At first, she stiffened at Gwen's shadowy appearance, but after recognizing it was her, Gerty's face relaxed into a warm smile.

"What are you doing out so late and without a jacket, no less? Come and sit by me," Gerty said, patting a spot on the bench near her.

Gwen sat down, and Gerty draped her wool shawl over Gwen's shoulders. The wool didn't have any of the normal starchiness that Gwen expected. Instantly, the warmth seeped into her arms. She wrapped the shawl closer around her. It was large enough that she could wrap it around her skinny frame and cover her legs, too.

"Thanks, but won't you be cold?" Gwen asked, realizing that Gerty hadn't worn a jacket under the shawl she had given Gwen—only a bright-purple dress.

"Oh, us old ladies know to dress in layers. Don't worry at all. I'll keep plenty toasty," Gerty said, leaning against the bench's back and drifting into deep thought.

Gwen didn't mind the silence, partly because, that way, she wouldn't blurt out anything, as her anger still simmered. The two sat listening to the distant croaks of frogs and the rhythmic beats of crickets. An owl sounded in the trees nearby. It was so serene. Gwen found it almost unbearable. She'd be leaving in the morning.

"Did you know that, eventually, old fruit trees have a harder time producing fruit even though they can live for a century or more?" Gerty said without dropping her gaze from the sky. "Most big fruit operations wouldn't keep apple trees like this one." Gerty slowly waved a hand above her, toward the tree they were sitting under.

"I didn't know that. Why have you kept this one," Gwen asked, fighting to keep her frustrations at bay.

"Mainly because I like trees for their own sakes. And, also, I wouldn't want people to cut me down once I'm old and less useful," Gerty said with a mischievous wink.

Gwen stole a glance at Gerty. She had a timeless look about her that made it hard for Gwen to remember her age. She remembered that she had gone to college with Jefferson and Stan, so she'd have to be about the same age. The memory of how old and frail Jefferson had looked in recent interactions made her anger give way like frost warmed by the morning sun.

"I doubt that day will ever come," Gwen said.

"That's one thing I like about you—you speak your mind. And you're usually right. At least, you seem to be this time," Gerty said with a tired chuckle.

Both women let the silence settle back for a long while. But then Gerty picked up Gwen's hand and squeezed it between hers.

"I'm sorry I can't join your cause. I really am. I'm thrilled to continue to provide you with supplies once you've landed somewhere."

"Thanks for that," Gwen said, recognizing the anger and frustration as it started to rise in her chest again. She fought it, not wanting Gerty to understand what she was really feeling. She didn't want to hurt Gerty, but she didn't know how to escape her growing feelings either. Somehow, Gerty picked up on the shift in her anyway.

"I know you think that's not enough. I don't blame you. If I were forty years younger and didn't have dozens of workers to take care of, I would jump at the chance to change the world, too."

"I don't want to seem ungrateful, and I can't completely understand how responsible you feel for your workers, but I bet they feel more like family, and we do whatever we can to protect family, right?"

Gerty nodded.

"My crew is family, too. Jefferson is like a father to me. And when he was gone, I wanted to protect everyone else."

"I'm sure you did," Gerty said, releasing Gwen's hand and placing it back in the cover of the shawl.

"But there's something I really don't get with you," Gwen said.

With wide eyes, Gerty turned to look at Gwen more directly.

"What's to get?" Gerty asked cautiously.

"You've got to know that sooner or later, while you're still living here or after you're gone, things will change. Nothing is okay with the world. And pretending that it is makes you more of a coward than a savior," Gwen said, letting all the words spew out of her in rapid fire without being able to hold them back.

Gerty's eyes developed that steely look that Gwen had seen the first time she had met her. The look of calculating an enemy weighing trust-worthiness. It broke Gwen's heart to see it, but she couldn't stop.

"There are thousands of kids like me who've been dropped by the mainstream. Most have died already, even. Those who haven't are just scraping by. If Jefferson hadn't found me, I'd still be in that situation. How can you sit here on your pretty little farm when you know people like me are out there?" Gwen said, shaking noticeably, either because of the cold night or the energy pulsing through her.

"It's not that simple—"

"Explain it to me then," Gwen shot back.

"I will if you let me," Gerty said with a hint of an edge.

Gwen deflated a bit. She had crossed a line.

"Farms live on hope. Think about it for a second. We plant. We nurture trees. We pull weeds all through spring and summer in the hopes of things growing into food by the end of the season. Even after forty some-odd growing seasons of watching things work out pretty well, there's never a guarantee that this season will be another bumper crop. All you can do is encourage the right conditions by working hard based on what you know. If you mix organic fertilizer with the soil around young trees, they're more likely to grow stronger. But not always," Gerty paused to take in some slow, deep breaths.

Gwen looked critically at Gerty but remained still.

"What I'm saying is farms, for better or for worse, live on the probability of success. What's the chance that a frost will hit the crop in early spring? Should we take the time to cover fruit trees and protect their blooms from that potential frost, or do we risk it? Do we harvest fruit that we're unlikely to sell, or do we let it drop?"

"So you're saying we don't have a chance. You're not willing to take the risk. Fine," Gwen said, standing suddenly and hastily folding the shawl. She held out the shawl for Gerty to take.

"I see I've disappointed you. That's fair," Gerty said.

"I'm mad," Gwen said, placing the shawl beside Gerty—harder than she meant to. "I'm mad that people like you hide in your comfortable homes and farms and do nothing."

Gerty gave Gwen a look like she had just been slapped in the face. What Gwen had last said might have been unfair, but her mind was racing so fast she couldn't think clearly. Or articulate things in kinder ways.

"You think I'm doing nothing?" Gerty asked, standing and slowly walking to the trunk of the tree. "You don't know what you're talking about, girl."

A bit of fear crept over Gwen as she saw a side of Gerty she had forgotten. She thought back to the first trip to Gerty's farm—the corpse left to be eaten by coyotes that Gerty didn't excuse away.

"I'm one of the last off-grid suppliers for groups like yours, and you don't think I'm taking a risk by supplying a movement trying to take down the most powerful institutions this world has ever seen? Banks with more power and resources than even the most powerful governments in history ever had? What's my farm to them? It's just an annoying horsefly to be squashed. Every supply run to groups like yours could be my last. There are lots of different kinds of bravery, Gwen. Don't dismiss mine because it's a different flavor than yours. It takes all kinds of roles to have a successful movement. The people who yell at power and the people who feed those doing the yelling."

Gwen rubbed her arms awkwardly, wishing she hadn't been so quick to hand over the shawl. She wrapped her arms around her chest. Part of her wished she could take the things she had said back, but the more defiant thread running through her veins felt like the things she'd said needed saying.

"I have one more thing to say, and this might be the last chance I'll have to say it because we don't know where we'll end up. If we don't find a place pretty soon, I'll probably end up back in Kansas, which wouldn't be the end of the world," Gwen said.

Gerty turned to face Gwen. "Okay. What do you need to say?"

Gwen took a deep breath with her eyes closed, trying to calm her mind and feelings enough to say what she needed to say in the best way.

"You talked about deciding whether it would be best to harvest fruit even though you probably wouldn't be able to sell it. You harvest it or let the fruit drop and rot, right?"

Gerty had a puzzled look on her face but eventually nodded.

"I think you have a choice like that right now. Will you take the risk and step in and help us make things better, or will you leave your fruit to rot? Sooner or later, ripe fruit spoils and your little paradise will be found out. It's only a matter of time. I guess the question I have for you is, when that day comes, will you be prouder that you took a stand or that you let the fruit drop?" Gwen let that settle into the still night for a moment before rubbing her arms again, deciding it was time to go to bed. "Thanks for everything, Gerty. Really," Gwen impulsively threw her arms around Gerty, who was nearly bowled over, taken completely by surprise, but who recovered quickly and returned the hug the best she could. Gwen turned away without looking back, leaving Gerty standing in the cool night air under inconstant moonlight that filtered through the clouds.

Gwen woke up in Jefferson's truck the next morning, groggy and with a cramp in her neck. She yawned and stretched the best she could in the truck's confined space, then kicked open the door and tumbled out on unsteady legs. Slowly, her body warmed up, and as she walked toward the processing building, her legs got their circulation back. The sun was starting to strike the tops of the trees, turning them bright shades of gold. The air was crisp and smelled of good soil.

As she approached, there was a flurry of activity around the processing building. Many of the farm workers she had met the night before were sealing crates and loading trucks. Then she caught Jefferson's tall frame above the crowd, directing the loading of one of the trucks. She walked over to him.

"What's going on?" she asked, puzzled.

"We're transporting some things to our new facility," Jefferson said with a radiant smile.

"Really? You found a new location for our operation?"

"Yeah. Here," Jefferson said, laughing at the confused look Gwen gave him. "I don't know what you said to Gerty last night, but it did the trick. She's on board."

Gwen wracked her sore brain to recall, play by play, how the conversation with Gerty had worked out. *Because of me? No way!* All she had done was make Gerty mad. Jefferson noticed her confusion.

"Don't be so worried, Gwen. Gerty makes up her own mind on things. Maybe you gave her a reason to hope like you did me," Jefferson said, turning back to answer a question from one of the people loading the truck for Jefferson.

Gwen was flooded with so many feelings. She felt relief unlike any she had ever felt before. They had a home base again. Some new things around the farm would eventually become familiar. She could look for a new tucked-away favorite tree! Even though the day was already shaping up to be one of the last remaining uncomfortably warm days, Gwen was shivering, but she was electrified. Why does excitement have to feel so much like anxiety? Gwen thought, trying to get ahold of her nerves and overwhelming excitement.

And there were some lingering doubts that crept up and begged for notice, no matter how hard Gwen tried to push them aside. Jefferson had been pretty upfront with Gerty, but he hadn't shared everything. What if questions arose about the way Jefferson came back after being detained so long? Gwen still had questions about that, so she certainly wouldn't blame Gerty for having them. Would Gerty pull out then? Just how committed was Gerty?

A truck behind Gwen made two polite honks with its horn, making her jump and waking her up from her own thoughts. She stepped aside and waved at Stan, who drove the truck Jefferson had been loading. Gwen watched as the truck drove toward a building about a quarter-mile away from the central compound where the processing building and picnic tables were set up. She took a few steps in the direction Stan was driving but then stopped.

Gerty had walked out of the processing building and was interacting with a mingled group of members from the two operations. That's exactly how things should be, Gwen thought with a spontaneous smile growing across her face. Gerty looked up from some plans that the group was running past her. Gwen looked around frantically when Gerty's eyes settled on her. She tried to look busy, but she was standing in the middle of the road with nothing in her hands. Finally giving up, she gave a small wave.

The slight drop of Gerty's head was a little hard to read, but Gwen hoped it meant they would be able to patch things up over the coming days, though she felt their relationship had changed in some significant ways. They wouldn't return to the way things were before, but maybe that wasn't so bad either.

Gwen nodded back, trying, but mostly failing, to mirror Gerty's cool nod technique. She turned and took the path to her new operation headquarters and—she really hoped—a place that might feel like home again.

Over the past few weeks, Gwen fell into some brand-new routines but held on to a couple from her days at the warehouse in D.C. and before meeting Jefferson. After the first couple of days of a flurry of activity in setting up their new home base, Gwen had some breathing room to explore the farm and to do some thinking.

One of the first tasks she needed to do for herself was find her hideaway spot. And, although she had made the decision before, intuitively, she knew that the spot had to meet certain characteristics. The most important was the tree. The species of tree didn't matter so much as the scale and setup. It had to have a good-sized branch facing east, and it got bonus points if that large branch had other branches that shot off the trunk nearby and made sitting more comfortable. And the trees would start losing their leaves in the next month or so, which made it important for the tree to be tucked away and surrounded by a hedge or evergreen bush of some kind.

A place to escape. That was the main thing the tree had to offer Gwen. A place to *just be* for a short time each day. A place where she didn't have to worry about meeting expectations or filling roles she didn't feel qualified to fill. Trees never judged her or made her nervous, and those qualities made them the best sorts of companions for her.

She finally found it when she was exploring some discarded silos whose thatch roofs had mostly fallen in. When she stuck her head inside the silos, all she found at the bottom were several seasons' worth of leaves and bugs relishing the loam.

As she made her way around the pair of silos with crumbling masonry connecting them, her gaze darted to a nearly imperceptible break in the overgrown bush that surrounded the backside of the silo. She ducked inside the small opening and bent nearly to the ground. The other side of the bush opened to a pocket-sized clearing surrounded by bushes that easily reached twenty feet high in all directions. The bushes grew so thick that once she stood, brushed off the leaves, and looked around, she was thrilled to see that no light shone through from the other side of the bushes. That meant that no one could see through from the silo side either. And what excited her most was standing right in the center of the small clearing—a tree with a trunk so thick that when she wrapped her arms around it, her reach didn't go even halfway around.

Good-sized knots that would make for excellent foot and hand-holds peppered all along the tree to the first main branch that jutted out from the trunk just above the height of the bushes. The rough bark was so textured she could probably climb the tree without the handy knots.

When she reached the first big branch that faced directly east, which would make for some fantastic mornings, she let go of her handholds, raising her fists and letting out a triumphant yell. Thankfully, her feet braced her securely enough that she didn't fall back.

Right where the main branch grew out from the trunk, four other significant branches spiraled to one large knot. The perfect place. Gwen tested out sitting against the trunk. Its natural slope made the seat seem specifically built to support her back. She could sit there for hours without even getting stiff, which meant she would have to be careful, or else she would sit there for hours.

The view from her comfortable perch in the trunk's alcove looked across the tops of the bushes to a sea of trees growing on countless rolling hills. The clearing where the tree grew was on a hill with a gentle downward slope and situated at the highest point in the entire broad valley. At that moment, the valley shone with an early fall glow—the leaves beginning to change to what Gwen was certain would become brilliant reds and yellows. She took in a deep breath and was thrilled by the earthy scent of leaves and grass and spongy, decaying wood.

She could never have dreamed up a better tree or place to start her day. Gwen was thankful to have found such a perfect spot because some of the days in the last weeks had been short on bright spots. Gwen was still amazed that so many kind and wonderful people were struggling to adjust to each other. But she was certain things would get figured out between Gerty's and Jefferson's crews.

Gwen crept back around the silos and took up a nonchalant stance as she made her way back to Jefferson's headquarters building. Their building was nearly as expansive as Gerty's main processing building, and Gwen couldn't believe that such a well-maintained building had been sitting vacant. Gerty's way of helping us out without having to admit that she was helping us, Gwen figured.

She entered the building through the back door that was, thankfully, regular-sized. The massive front door was intimidating. And, maybe, it made her feel exposed, too. She couldn't see into the darker spaces inside from the front door, but anyone inside could see her enter in bright contrast.

Jefferson had organized the space into four main quadrants with a central walkway that cut the space in half and two smaller paths that made the space into a nice, neat grid. One quadrant was for sleeping with dozens of cots in rows. Another was for cooking. One was for eating meals, and the other was affectionately called the War Room.

Jefferson and Gerty had held some pretty intense meetings where some sparks had flown in the War Room, but they had agreed upon how to divide the roles and responsibilities so neither would micromanage the other and both could capitalize on their strengths. Gwen wasn't certain what role she'd play, but she was becoming more okay with a small one. Something about the farm's peaceful and clearly understood daily rhythm had her rethinking her need to be the center of attention. She had even developed a liking to washing the dishes after dinner. The warm, soapy water was comforting in a weird way, and she loved how simply plates could be cleaned so they looked like new again. She'd be fine with any role now that she had a new place to call home.

chapter 16

The start of Patch's second year of school had its fits and starts. The first few weeks of classes were grueling, punctuated by many moments of despair as Patch faced the daunting task of catching up on at least ten years of education. All years that his classmates had on him. Especially math. He needed to catch up on that subject, especially.

But there were also plenty of micro victories.

He didn't make nearly the fool out of himself at track tryouts as he had the year before. Coach Curtis seemed pleased more often than dismayed. In fact, Patch had landed a spot on the team with an amount of confidence that surprised even himself.

Dr. Bedford never showed confidence in Patch, exactly, but he was starting to pick up subtle clues that even she was pleased by the progress he was making—maybe. His thesis, especially incorporating charts and math into the paper, was moving along at a good clip, too.

And then there was Kourtney. After his party to celebrate his newly minted birthday, things felt different with her. She remained the same vivacious, chatty girl who jumped from one thought to another with bridges that were very hard for Patch to connect a lot of the time. But he was starting to see her in a new light, and with that lens on their relationship, he started to pick up things he appreciated about her that he had totally overlooked before. He was starting to like her because he was finally getting to know who she really was.

"Why don't you just telling Will that you've changed your mind?" Kourtney said one morning midway through the fall semester as they walked together with Patch holding her mittened hand.

"I told him I would take him to see him. And we've had so many scheduling fails that this is our best shot. Plus, it seems really important to him, so I don't know. I feel like I should."

"Everything is utterly important to Will," Kourtney said, having nearly a skip to her walk, making it a bit difficult to hold on to her swinging hand, especially given the extra care Patch needed to give to the potentially icy cobblestone path they were crossing.

"True enough. I'm so bad at this sort of thing," Patch said more to himself.

"What? Getting what you really want? Or disappointing friends? Or walking on sidewalks? You seem to struggle with all three."

There it was again. A year ago, he would have totally chalked up Kourtney's statement to chatter. But he honed in on the disappointing friends' bit, so much so, that he actually stopped walking and was almost pulled down by Kourtney's forward momentum.

"Patch! Come on. You'll be late for class, and I'll have to act particularly sweet to Madonne to make up for being late," Kourtney said, dashing behind Patch and giving him a friendly push forward.

"Oh, sorry. Who's Madonne again?" Patch asked, allowing Kourtney to set the fast pace as they started walking again.

"My art history professor."

"That's right," Patch made a mental note as he tried to do better at appreciating Kourtney's art emphasis. Though, he struggled every time she talked about the nuances between Flemish Baroque and Dutch masters.

Patch and Kourtney came to her building first. He lifted the stylish cashmere hat Kourtney wore nearly to her eyebrows and planted a kiss on both rosy cheeks.

"Good luck with Madonne. You have nothing to worry about because you're the sweetest thing there is," Patch said, giving Kourtney's mitten a firm squeeze.

Kourtney threw her arms over Patch's shoulders, and Patch staggered back a bit when she lifted her legs too.

"Don't worry all day about visiting that cottage. I'm sure you'll do the right thing," Kourtney said, dropping out of Patch's arms, tucking her hat back down lower on her head, and sprinting up the steps. But she stopped just before the door. "And if you don't do the right thing. That's okay too. I'll still tolerate you."

"Gee, thanks," Patch said with a smirk and a wave as she disappeared into the art building.

Patch walked the few hundred yards to his business management class in silence, his eyes focused a few feet in front of him. Kourtney was right—worrying about Will's request wouldn't help anything, but he could hardly help it. How could he explain to Will that his request was wrong and that Patch still liked and respected him? Why do relationships have to be so confusing? he thought as he scaled the steps into the building.

"So, this groundskeeper who lives in that cottage on the outskirts of campus? I've done some research on him while we've been waiting for our schedules to match up. He's been the groundskeeper here for generations, it looks like. The school is trying to decide when to let him go. From what I've heard, they would've fired him years ago, except his contract was so old it superseded the current administrative system of the school, and we all know how eager everyone is to obey contractual agreements. Of course, you'd know a lot more about that than me," Will threw out excitedly.

All Patch had time to do was nod before Will continued, dragging Patch with him at a fast clip, even faster than his normal unusually fast walk.

The groundskeeper's name is Chuck Mason. It was really bothering Patch that Will kept referring to him as the groundskeeper rather than trying to remember his real name. Patch's thoughts drifted as Will explained more about the groundskeeper, as if Patch hadn't met him.

But what Will had said about the school's focus on enforcing contracts was true. Over the last couple of months, he had had that reinforced for him even more than last year. Especially now that he was taking a class on contract law. Even Dr. Bedford, a person who Patch trusted had more of a rebellious nature at heart, had emphasized the virtues of orderly contracts.

Patch rammed into Will, nearly knocking them both down. Will had stopped abruptly, though Patch had been so deep in his thoughts that he had no idea why.

"Trying to knock down the disabled kid again. Patch, you should be ashamed of yourself," Will said jokingly.

"Sorry. I was thinking about something," Patch said, making sure Will was okay and dusting off a few leaves from his jacket.

"I said—just before you walked right into me—that we'd better make sure we're on the same page before we meet the groundskeeper," Will said impatiently.

"His name is Chuck Mason. I told you I'd met him before," Patch said, getting more agitated by the minute.

"Right. I forgot. Sorry. It'll be good to call him by his name at first. It'll build rapport," Will said, who was so eager to make strides on his project that he clearly missed the edge in Patch's voice and continued, "It'll be important that I clearly outline the purpose and need for the conversation at the beginning. That way, the material we'll gather will be more targeted and a lot less transcript for me to go through. That can be murder sometimes."

I've got to try one more time, Patch thought urgently. "Just leave him alone, Will. Use me as your test subject. I mean, I was a street kid, and now I'm a track star. Wouldn't that make for an interesting study?" Patch asked, grabbing Will's shoulder to stop him and maybe get more of his attention.

"You are very worthy of many studies, Patch, but unfortunately, the professor has made it clear that subjects have to be outside of friends and family," Will said matter-of-factly.

"I mean, I'm sure he won't appreciate being your guinea pig, Will." Patch was getting even more irritated at Will, and his voice was exposing that clearly.

"I thought we'd already gotten past this. You agreed to this weeks ago," Will said.

"No, you basically told me that was what we were going to do, and I went along with it like usual," Patch said, distractedly kicking at the cobblestones.

"Why this passive aggression, my friend? You don't even know him, after all. Do you? You've only met the grounds—I mean, Chuck—once before, right?"

Patch nodded, not knowing how to explain the thoughts screaming inside his head.

"So, you two aren't friends or anything. So, I don't know why you're defending him. Besides, no one needs to defend him. I'm not some reporter looking for dirt on the guy. I just want to understand what his life has been like," Will said, looking at his watch. "And you'll add a serious level of the common man to the discussion that I'm sure will put him right at ease."

Being told that Patch understood the common man from someone with Will's life experience made Patch want to explode. "You don't know what you're talking about. Even if I did understand regular folks, which you clearly have no clue about, what makes you think I'd use that to exploit someone else who has obviously struggled a lot more to get by than you?" Patch asked, kicking at the ground harder.

Will suddenly lit up. "Aren't you at all curious about the economic side of things with that cottage and the grounds—I mean, with Chuck's job?"

Patch stopped kicking at the sidewalk and looked up curiously. "What do you mean?"

"Here's a guy who lives in little more than a shack to do a job that pays, I'm sure, so little that nobody would do it unless housing was offered because the drive from where they would have to live, given the higher prices in the neighborhood around this school, would eat up their entire paycheck just to get to work." Will paused and studied Patch.

"Go on."

"Normally, when situations like those come up, don't wages go up until it makes sense for someone to take the job? I'm really asking. I only took like one econ course as a required general a few years back."

"Yeah. The cost of labor should rise until enough people are interested and able to take the job. Or the school could set up other arrangements or incentives," Patch said, rattling off the textbook answers.

"Right. Thank you." Will shifted his weight from his right leg to his left.

Will's bad leg must be acting up as days get colder, Patch thought, starting to feel guilty.

Will picked up the conversation thread again.

"So the academy is willing to pay for someone's housing rather than paying a regular employee a little bit more. Why would they do that? I don't care what kind of strange contract they might have entered into with Chuck, they wouldn't have written in housing for life. The academy isn't a charitable organization. It's basically a business, but instead of making machines, the school cranks out educated kids. Besides that, there are plenty of large-scale landscaping companies that could add the academy among their stops. I'd bet they'd give a huge discount to land a contract like that. The school probably has a contract like that in place, anyway, because at Chuck's age, he certainly can't take care of all the grounds himself. And let's not forget that autonomous lawnmowers are totally affordable now. It doesn't make sense, does it?"

As much as Patch hated to admit it, Will had a point. Things didn't stack up. The whole time he had known about the cottage, and especially after meeting Chuck at the start of the school year, he had assumed that the school was exploiting him somehow. Or, at least, Chuck was maybe stuck in his situation, and the school knew that, so he had to keep working.

But now that Patch really looked at things from an economic vantage point, he realized what a great deal Chuck was actually getting. Housing in exchange for work that could be contracted out a lot cheaper? What was really going on?

"Don't be so pleased with yourself," Patch said smugly.

Will's pleased grin disappeared instantly, but Patch knew that the look on Will's face clearly told him that Will was close to achieving what he wanted.

"Fine. Remember the two conditions, though. If he's not there when we swing by his place today, you're not going to keep bugging me to go back, and if Chuck doesn't want to talk, you won't pressure him."

"Of course, let's go—"

Will turned to go, but Patch shouted for him to stop.

"You won't pressure him at all, I mean. You have a way of pressuring people to do what you want without seeming to do it."

"Could you be a bit more specific? I don't think I'm a psychopath."

"That's what a psychopath would think," Patch said, grinning.

"Haha. Very funny," Will said, folding his arms defiantly.

"Sorry. I couldn't resist. You set that one up way too perfectly. But you know what I mean, right? No guilt trips. No calling yourself the disabled kid. None of that. Clear?" Patch asked with raised eyebrows.

"Clear. Now let's go." Will grabbed Patch's arm, and they were back at Will's breakneck speed on their way to the forgotten cottage tucked back behind the industrial park of campus.

chapter 17

It was strange to have a distinct purpose for visiting the cottage this time, Patch realized as he and Will approached the frozen two-track dirt walk that led to the cottage's front door. Patch stopped before he took the first step onto the path. Will didn't even turn around until he'd already arrived at the front porch.

"Come on, Patch, why're you back there? I need your street smarts to win over our friend the groundskeeper. Blast it! I mean our friend Chuck Mason."

"I don't think I should come with."

"Patch, seriously! Remember what we talked about back at the quad?"

"No. Come on, Will, why do we have to do this? This guy definitely doesn't want to be bothered."

"How do you know that? He might be terribly lonely or bored. He probably doesn't interact with many people. Maybe our visit is exactly what he's been hoping for."

Patch had to admit that Will's logic made some sense, but his gut told him otherwise.

"Okay, Patch. In all seriousness, something we both know I prefer to avoid, here's my last pitch. I think Chuck may be the only person at this school who knows what the rest of the world is really like, or at least, who may be willing to talk openly about its problems. There are lots of students from poor backgrounds, but they're on their way up, so they're horribly biased. This guy can tell me the truth. There it is. My unvarnished and last-ditch effort," Will said with arms wide and jazz fingers shaking as if he had just landed a backflip in a circus routine.

That did it for Patch. His stomach was still roiling, creating a nasty taste in his throat, but he forced his legs to finish the few steps it took to join Will, who knocked on the worn wooden door. The knocking echoed in a weird way—the way it did after the carpets and paintings have been removed for remodeling. Hollow.

The door opened halfway, and a chiseled, pale face made even paler by a mess of white hair and a well-kept white beard appeared from inside the dark room of the house. Though Patch had met Chuck before, this was the first time he had really given him a serious look. The last time, he had been so embarrassed by his gawking at the cottage that he'd had a hard time looking him in the eye.

There was no denying that Chuck was old. Patch was never good at guessing people's ages, but Chuck's cheeks and the ripples of wrinkles that radiated around his eyes told a story of lots of time spent working outdoors, and the gentle gathering of loose skin under his chin and down his neck showed he'd lived well past his sixties and could very well be in his eighties. Chuck's freckled hand that held the door slightly ajar showed scars and his decades of hard work. But despite those obvious signs of age, there was an intensity to the look he gave Patch and Will. A look that Patch remembered from his first encounter with Chuck.

"Hi, sir. My name is Will, and I'm a student here at Harvard Academy. Can my friend and I come in and ask a couple of questions?"

"Your friend? You're seriously with this fake joke of a researcher?" Chuck asked Patch with an almost sympathetic look.

Patch smiled and gave Will a look that he hoped told him to be careful what he wished for. Will didn't seem to understand the look, though, and fixed his eyes on Patch as if looking for guidance on what to do next. Patch shrugged and nodded in Chuck's direction to remind Will that Chuck was still there, leaning out the door.

"My goodness, that school is being far too stringent in their admissions policy. They're only letting in the true cream of the crop now, aren't they?" Chuck said with brutal sarcasm. "Well, are you coming in, or aren't you?"

Chuck left the door halfway open and disappeared back into the darkened room. Patch and Will looked at each other, Will silently asking Patch what had just happened. "I warned you. Now you're in for it. Try not to make too much of a fool out of yourself," Patch whispered, holding the screen door open for Will.

Will nervously walked into the house, and Patch followed.

Inside the front door was a modest entryway with a once-formal sitting area that held a single overstuffed armchair that Patch could tell didn't get much use. Patch dragged his fingers across one of the arms of the chair, causing symmetrical lines of cleared dust. Other than a single end table with a few faded photos inside well-polished metal frames, no other furniture or decorations were in the room. Patch continued past the entryway into the next room, which was a dining-room-kitchen combo.

A wood table filled nearly half the rectangular room. Patch dragged his feet against the gray linoleum floor, which might have been yellow at one point, and glanced at the shelves above the stove, which were topped with an assortment of pots, pans, and glasses.

"I can't imagine that your research is on my interior design. If so, let me stop you here and tell you my place doesn't have any," Chuck said without looking up—his face buried in the cupboard.

Will was clearly interested in the layout of the room and appeared to have missed part of what Chuck had just said.

"Doesn't have any what?" Will asked with an air of forced interest.

"Sense. Or interior design. I'm lacking in both, I'm afraid."

"What do you mean?" Will said, completely confused now.

"Well, you boys keep outdoing yourself in the charm and intelligence department. Keep it up, and I might ask you to stay for tea."

Patch glared at Will. It baffled him to see Will clumsily missing cues and paying such poor attention. Ordinarily, Will was as polished a talker as anybody Patch knew.

"I'm sorry. We're both being very rude, sir. Let's start over—Mr. Mason, this is my friend, Will."

Chuck was rummaging through drawers, then pulled out a butter knife and three mismatched mugs and brought the kettle to the sink to fill.

"Pleasure to meet you, Will. Call me Chuck."

Chuck placed the kettle on the stove. He jiggled a knob, and a feeble stream of blue flame shot from the stovetop. He adjusted the flame slightly, wiped his wet fingertips on a towel hanging from the oven's handle, and turned to face the two boys who were awkwardly standing around the table.

Chuck held out his large, paw-like right hand toward Will. Will positioned his right hand the best he could and shook Chuck's.

"I didn't hurt your hand, did I?" Chuck asked.

"Oh. Don't worry. You didn't do any more damage than my brain already has. I had a brain injury when I was younger. But I do the best I can," Will said.

Chuck smiled a more genuine smile then and offered his left hand instead, which Will enthusiastically shook.

Then, Chuck turned to Patch and offered his hand even though that wasn't their first meeting. When Patch shook Chuck's hand, he had the strangest sensation that he had done it dozens of times before—that he knew Chuck much better than he had any right to know him.

"Take a seat." Chuck gestured to two sturdy wooden chairs on either side of the table.

Patch and Will sat down, and after having grabbed a few other things out of his cupboards, Chuck joined them, placing a plate of shortbread cookies between the two boys.

"Alright then. What do you need to ask me?" Chuck asked with a much softer tone toward Will.

Will had been out of his element the whole conversation, but now that the conversation was moving in the direction he had anticipated, he cleared his throat and pulled out his tablet.

"Yes. Thanks, Mr. Mason—I mean—Chuck, for being willing to answer a few questions. Do you mind if I record our conversation? It'll help with the notes."

"Sure. Go right ahead."

"Okay, so, Chuck, how long have you been living here?"

"How old are you two?"

"We're both sixteen. Well, Patch turned seventeen at the start of the school year, actually. So, I'm sixteen. He's seventeen," Will said, cringing.

The sentence had come out awkwardly.

"Okay. Then I've been working here three times longer than you've been alive."

"That's a pretty good while," Will said nervously.

"Yeah, I suppose. Long enough to be the last man standing who remembers what education used to be."

"What do you mean by that?" Will said, leaning in eagerly.

Chuck leaned forward, too, mirroring Will and putting his clasped hands heavily on the table.

"I mean that things used to be different."

"Okay. Let's start there. How did things used to be on this campus, Chuck?" Will asked, tapping on his tablet's screen.

Chuck leaned back again and laced his fingers behind his head.

"It's dangerous to leave the door wide open for old men to tell stories. You may live to regret such invitations. But since you asked—"

The kettle started whistling, and Chuck jumped up and, with a towel, pulled it away from the heat, then filled the three mugs with steaming water. He placed the mugs on the tray with the cookies and brought the tray back to the table. Afterward, he settled back into his chair with a mug cradled in both hands.

"Like I was saying, the way things are now is not the way they've always been. When I started working here, this place was the best university in the world. People came from every country on Earth to go to school here because if they had Harvard on their resume, it was a golden ticket for any job they wanted—"

"That's mainly the case still, though," Will interjected.

"Are you telling this story or am I?" Chuck said, taking a sip of his tea.

"I'm sorry. Didn't mean to interrupt."

"It didn't seem to stop you much, though, did it?" Chuck said with a wry smile.

Will smiled back sheepishly, and Patch gently kicked Will's foot under the table.

"You don't know what it used to be like. Universities were places where debates took place. I was trimming the bushes outside a lecture hall one time, and the whole class was yelling at each other about why China's economic growth was unsustainable. You'd think they were calling each other's mothers some kind of horrid name or something for how much they all seemed to care about the things they were saying."

"And we have great debates too, like this one time—"

Patch kicked Will's foot a bit harder this time, making Will stop midsentence.

"I'm not describing this very well. Mind, I'm no historian. I'm sure your classes are great and that your classmates are top-notch as always. I guess the difference was the kind of students." Chuck paused for a moment. "Yeah, that's the difference. You may have a few scrappy students like our friend Patch here, but back then, you could have a backwoods Midwesterner sitting in a class with a sixth-generation Harvard student with a family that owned an island. You still had money influencing things, but merit mattered a lot more."

"We have merit predictive analytics—"

"That's the other thing! People proved their merit rather than having it all figured out before kids were even out of diapers. People could work hard and make something out of their life. Now everybody is nudged into line where they belong in society. And before Mr. Genius corrects me again, I know that people aren't forced into their line of work or class or whatever, but you tell me where most people would end up by doing anything other than what the system wants them to do when everything is stacked against them."

Patch was getting more uncomfortable by the minute, not because he didn't believe what Chuck was saying, he actually agreed with most of it—the thing was—he was one of those exceptions. How could Patch hold ill feelings toward a system that gave him such a great chance?

Patch caught Will thoughtfully observing him and wondered if he'd picked up on his uneasiness. Then Will asked the very question that had been on his mind.

"How do you explain people like Patch being at this school?"

Chuck set down his cup, interlocked his fingers behind his head again, and looked beyond the boys as if seeing something they couldn't.

"Yeah, people like Mr. Robinson are a puzzle, aren't they? I bet you haven't even been tested or chipped have you, Patch? The only reason the academy believes you're worth educating is because you have a very powerful ally or two who convinced them, right? Let me guess: stellar athlete meets wealthy benefactor."

"You nailed it!" Will shouted with a grin.

"Actually, I was recruited totally because of athletics. I'm managing with the school stuff, but it's mainly because I can run."

"My point exactly. The university used to offer scholarships for promising athletes, but now individuals can sponsor students."

"Yes, but there were grants and endowments from individuals who sponsored students before. That's not that big of a difference," Will said, getting a bit impatient.

"You're right."

Chuck picked his cup back up and nervously moved it in circles between his hands. Patch could sense his frustration, so he stepped in to end the interview.

"Hey, it's okay. Will doesn't really need this. We're sorry to bug you—"

"I used to be proud I worked here. That, and the university used at least to care enough for their employees that they made sure them and their families were taken care of. That's it. That's the biggest and maybe the only difference."

Will leaned forward eagerly, and even Patch turned toward Chuck and leaned in slightly.

"Yeah, that's it. The students who studied here would leave with a degree and start organizations that fought world hunger or had aspirations to end horrible diseases using their medical degrees. A lot of students used to believe that they could make the world a better place and that it was worth improving because the people mattered. I guess that's another difference."

All three fell silent for a long minute, each taking a turn sipping their tea. Patch was very grateful that Will didn't correct Chuck for sharing two differences even though he had said that they were each the difference. Will finally cleared his throat.

"Well, that is something. Those are very significant differences, actually. Tell me more about that."

The conversation headed off in that direction for a good half-hour, with Will interjecting questions and frustrated statements from time to time—to keep things on track. Patch was silent the rest of the conversation. Chuck's idea of being proud because people used to build institutions that cared for others and the throwaway about family members being taken care of in the old days made Patch curious. What was that all about?

He already knew from his classes that when institutions and organizations sought to help the poor or less privileged, they took finite resources and shared them with people less capable of developing a positive return on that investment. That was the core principle behind the current society's success. That was the textbook answer. Patch had built that into many essays for multiple classes. People who were better able to take advantage of their situation and resources ought to be encouraged to do so unimpeded since they would end up benefitting society more in the long run. That was the right answer. But Patch had a sinking feeling that he wouldn't be able to use that line of logic for papers anymore. Or at least use it and mean it.

But on the other hand, how could he know for certain that everybody was given a fair shot of proving themselves? If he was picked up by a chance sprint away from neighborhood gangs, how many other promising people might be out there? What about people like Gwen? How far could she go if she were in Patch's place?

"I think we'll have to schedule a repeat interview if you have more to ask. Old men like me need their rest," Patch heard Chuck say.

That woke him from his thoughts.

"I'm sorry to keep you. I understand. Rest is important," Will said.

"Really, I just want you to leave for now." Chuck's wrinkles scrunched up into a pleased smile. "But you can come back."

"Thank you, Chuck. We will. Definitely."

The two boys took their mugs to the sink and followed Chuck to the door. Chuck shut the screen door behind Patch and Will with a wave. Will was down the path and to the main walkway before Patch had moved.

"Interesting kid. Will. I'm sure he doesn't mean to be so insulting," Chuck said from inside.

Patch quickly turned toward the door. "I'm so sorry about all of this. Will twisted my arm—"

"Don't take advantage of our relationship again," Chuck said with absolute seriousness.

"I won't. I promise," Patch said solemnly.

"Good. Now get out of here," Chuck said with a smile and a nod.

chapter 18

"**G**ood morning, Mr. Robinson," Coach Curtis said without losing his focus on something he was reviewing on his tablet.

"Morning, Coach," Patch said, swinging his arms from side to side and bouncing lightly on his toes as he readied himself for the first meet of the season.

"I want you to participate in Pete's mindfulness exercise this morning, Patch."

"Okay. Will do." I can take all the calming influences I can get, Patch thought as he used a bench to prop his foot up so he could reach for his toes.

"Oh, and Patch?"

Patch dropped his foot from the bench and looked back at Coach Curtis.

"No repeats from last year. Got it? You're faster and more disciplined, and your technique is off the charts better than where you were a year ago. So there's no reason you shouldn't win your races today. But"—Coach looked up from his tablet and seemed to reach right into Patch's soul—"you're still just racing against yourself. Let the times and numbers drift into the background. You got this."

Coach Curtis headed to lead formal warm-ups but stopped beside Patch to put a hand on his shoulder and give him a resolute nod. Patch went back to finish his stretching routine and then to find Pete for his mindfulness exercises. But at that moment, he could have easily broken the high jump record and thrown the shot-put ball out of the arena. He had no idea how Coach Curtis did it, but with those few words and that intense nod, Patch was on fire.

"Hey, Patch, over here. Join us in a moment of reflection and communal love," Pete hollered over to Patch. Pete had set up several yoga mats on the artificial turf, and Patch heard curious music with long flute tones and a wind background.

Last year, the mindfulness exercises had felt weird to Patch at first, but he knew they did something good for him. This go-around, like times past, he felt more aware of where he was right then, and the anxieties of the moment were subdued somewhat.

Patch was competing in his regular events—the 400 and the 800 meters—which was always a challenging transition. At almost all of the meets he had gone to, the 400m took place early on in the meet, but the 800m was near the end. That gave Patch a lot of time to worry about his other event. And that last event was a tough nut for Patch to crack.

Granted, Patch had won his events last year, but the scary thing was that he wasn't quite sure how he'd done it. The 800m was two full laps around the track, and no matter how good of shape he got into, he would never pull off two full laps at an all-out sprint. So, last year, he kind of waffled between moments of a full sprint mixed with moments of awkwardly holding back, taunting the competition. As if the competition needed another reason to hate a competitor who had risen to fame out of nowhere and without the years of grueling practice and mileage the other runners had suffered to get to where they were.

They also probably had food to eat and beds to sleep in, he reassured himself as left the meditation circle to make an easy round of the track, warming up his legs and getting the blood flowing. He looked up as he jogged around the arena. People in yellow and black windbreakers were setting up extra trash bins and attending to last-minute clean-up needs. The day's announcer was running through sound checks. A glint of sunlight filtered down to Patch, momentarily distracting him. It made him smile. Having leafy trees to run past at meets was obviously impossible, but Patch was so glad his first meet would be in the open air rather than in the climate-controlled bubble or, even worse, in the school's indoor arena. He still had a lot to get used to with that beast. It made him suffocate, even thinking about that arena.

Patch slowed to a walk and joined a group of his teammates congregated to run through team stretches and get any last-minute instructions from their coach. Patch returned to gentle bounces on his toes, keeping his energy up and legs warm.

"Gather 'round folks," Coach Curtis called out, waving both arms and with the tablet that was always attached to his person, one way or another. "Listen up folks. I know this is our first meet of the year, and for some of you, this is your first meet at this academy . . ."

Patch tried to focus. He knew that Coach Curtis didn't waste words, and Patch could use all the instruction he could get, but his thoughts kept drifting back to the similar scene he had experienced the year before. He had been one of those kids Coach Curtis was referring to. First meet at this academy . . . or anywhere else, Patch thought.

"If you can all just focus on that, you'll be in the right headspace to achieve great things today. Okay, twenty jumping jacks, on my count!"

As Patch did his jumping jacks, he felt something he hadn't felt at meets in the past—he felt ready.

"Up next, the four hundred meter dash," Patch heard the announcer say with an overdone excitement.

Patch looked up to the stands where hundreds of people cheered on the various events. The crowd was bigger than he remembered from his first meet a year ago. A lot of the crowd was probably there to see him break another record. He fought the nerves that crept up at the thought by scanning the crowd. He knew it was a long shot, but every time he competed, he looked for Malcolm. Since his first competition, Malcolm had become his lucky charm.

No luck this time, though Patch did notice more attention being paid to his section of the arena than any other. Right when his nerves started to kick back up, he caught a glance of his coach staring at him. Patch read the look on his coach's face as clearly as if he'd spoken to him. Keep it together, Mr. Robinson!

Patch took some deep breaths and closed his eyes, visualizing the track and the arena as empty and open and completely his for the taking.

"On your marks."

Patch heard the cue and got into his lane and kicked lightly against the block to feel the contact and pressure he would use to bounce out of his crouch.

"Set."

He arched his back and felt the spongy and dusty red turf under his fingertips. He looked directly forward, trying to hone in on his lane. I'm just running against myself . . .

The sound of the digital pistol cracked, and Patch sprung out of his block and rushed toward the first curve. Everything inside him hummed with precision and the thrill of pushing forward with the eager nudge at his feet to spring from the track's surface. By the time he broke from the sheer flow that surged inside him, he had blown past the finish line, several seconds ahead of the nearest competitor. "Patch Robinson has done it again folks! Beating his best time and setting a new school record. Forty-four seconds flat. Wow, folks! We've been treated today!"

Patch took in the news, and before the excitement really reached him, he had an immediate thought, Malcolm will probably keep me around for sure now.

"Nicely done, Mr. Robinson. We still need to work on those starts a bit, though. You hesitated," Coach Curtis said with an approving nod and a slight smile, which was very high praise from his coach.

"Thanks, Coach. I'll keep working on it," Patch said, grinning, his attention being pulled in several directions as dozens of people rushed in to celebrate. But Patch couldn't move entirely into celebration mode yet. He still had one more race, and the 800m race was still a puzzle he was desperate to figure out.

He did his best to distract himself between his two events. First, he did his typical slow rounds around the arena. Patch sometimes forgot that while he was preparing for his races, several of his teammates prepared for theirs, and those events mattered as much to his teammates as the 400m and 800m mattered to him.

With such a large crowd, Patch kept getting pushed into places he wasn't sure he should be. The last thing he'd want to do was disrupt his teammates' events. So he tried some mindful exercises off to the side of the track. Pete had taught him that mindfulness helped people experience life more fully and create more space to hold unwanted feelings or thoughts. But as Patch tried to focus on his breathing, he successfully became more aware of his feelings and current moment, but never found the bigger space to put them in. Perfect. Now I'm even more aware that I'm anxious, he grumbled to himself getting up from the turf in the tucked-away corner of the arena. The minutes did slowly pass, though, and Patch's last event was finally called.

"Next up, the eight hundred meter," Patch heard the announcer say. Patch jogged over to his starting place. As he did his last-minute stretching, he ran through the strategy that Coach Curtis had drilled into him all semester. Start all out so that I can be ahead of the pack when I come around the first curve. That way, I won't have to fight for position with other runners after the break line. Set a pace almost but not quite as fast as my four-hundred-meter pace for the first lap. Then the second lap—it's okay if I slow down a bit. That way, I can have reserves in case I need to pull ahead at the end.

Patch bent down, taking in a couple of deep breaths, trying to, yet again, imagine he was just racing against himself. That's another thing that feels weird about the eight hundred meter, he thought, No starting blocks. Somehow, it made him feel exposed. He shook out both legs and focused again. He would spring forward and to an early lead. An early lead . . .

Patch lunged forward at the cracking of the gun and took early advantage of that feeling of being pulled by an elastic band around the first curve so that by the time he reached the first straight and the break line, he had a few feet of cushion to work with.

First step accomplished, he thought as he approached the second curve. As he came out onto the second straight, he had extended his lead even more. Now there was an obvious gap between Patch and the rest of the pack, who were jostling for leverage in the crowded group behind him. Patch heard grunts, and he imagined runners giving hidden jabs to their opponents, trying to cut into better positions.

Thankfully, he'd never had to fight his way to the front in any of his previous races since he was ahead of the pack by the break line every time. He knew he'd have to learn at some point. Come on, Patch, focus!

Patch swung around the third curve and on to the second lap, but as he came out of the curve and started on the last straight before the homestretch, the urge to connect to the ground and push his limits surged inside him. It was an electric jolt that ran down his spine, tickling his back and down through his legs. He smiled as the thrill pulsed through him. Why not go all out, he thought, stretching his gait to match his normal pace for his 400m dash. Coach Curtis flashed in his mind, but the urge to stretch his lead and feel more of the thrill overcame Coach's advice.

Patch focused on the ground in front of him, the feel of the pavement pushing him forward. He smelled the hot dogs cooking at a stand nearby and felt the wind he was making as he cut through the air. But as he made his last curve toward the homestretch, things shifted.

As he rounded that last curve, he tried to summon the elastic effect, but he definitely didn't feel propelled forward. He faced the homestretch. His legs and lungs were burning hot, and chinks in his inexhaustible reserve of momentum saw holes.

Patch kept pushing, all the mechanics of levers and ball-and-socket joints were functioning in proper form, but they were slowing down. Patch's usually smooth, relaxed arm swings turned into desperate flailing as he tried to hold on to the brutal pace he had set for the second lap.

Just a few more meters. Focus on the track ahead of you. You're racing against yourself, he told himself frantically, searching for any scraps of reserve energy he could call upon.

Patch gave everything he had left and threw it across the finish line inches ahead of the runners that blew past him. He'd won. But for the first time in his relatively short racing career, he didn't feel the urge to keep running. Patch took a few staggered steps, gripping his sides with both hands, trying to suck in more oxygen than the air seemed to hold. His heartbeat pounded in his head and his chest. He knew he'd recover eventually, but in that moment, he had a hard time believing it.

No new record this time. There was much less celebration among teammates with this second race. No one dashed over to pat him on the back. He had won, at least, right? Why didn't he feel like it?

"Hey, kid!" Patch looked up to see Malcolm pushing his way through the crowd of spectators in line for coffee.

"Mal!" Patch headed in his direction. Malcolm gave Patch a hug, both men beaming.

"Your perfect record lives on," Malcolm said with a proud smile shining down on Patch.

"Yeah, I guess so," Patch said, kicking softly at the turf.

"What do you mean, you guess so?" Malcolm asked, grabbing Patch's shoulders and shaking them. "There's no guessing there. You put in the work, and you reaped the reward. Man, that four-hundred-meter dash was absolutely spectacular!"

Seeing Malcolm's obvious pleasure in his performance helped.

"That eight-hundred-meter race was closer than I would have liked," Patch shrugged.

"That just gives you something to work on, right?" Malcolm said encouragingly.

"I guess so—"

"No more of this guessing stuff. Are you hungry? Let me take you to lunch or early dinner or whatever. Let me buy you food," Malcolm said as he led Patch through the crowd toward the exit.

"Hold on a second. I need to check in with my coach. Did you park in your special-investor-VIP-alumni-booster spot?" Patch shouted back to Malcolm as he headed the way they had come.

"Yeah, you know it. See you there!"

Patch knew his coach wouldn't be so generous with praise, and he braced for a withering comment. He approached Coach Curtis but saw his back was turned, so he waited. Coach must have heard him because he addressed him without turning around.

"Patch, you completely went against our plan."

Coach Curtis said it bluntly and without emotion. It was simply a fact. Patch knew the plan perfectly well, and he went against it and against his own better judgment, too. There was no denying that.

"Members of our team can't do that. I don't care how talented or however many records they break. My job is to help you reach your full potential, and that eight-hundred-meter race was a huge step back."

"I'm so sorry, Coach," Patch said, not knowing what else he could say.

"So am I. Get some rest tonight. You have some extra drills to do tomorrow."

Coach Curtis finally turned around. The full weight of his disappointment shone in his piercing look. Patch's shoulders hunched forward, and his jaw tightened. He fought the urge to scuff at the turf again. Then Coach did something Patch didn't expect.

He smiled.

"I won't do that again, Coach," Patch said seriously.

"I know," Coach Curtis said with a nod. "Now go celebrate."

"Will do Coach!" Patch turned to dash off, ready to run a hundred miles if Coach asked him to, all because of one, simple smile.

Then Coach Curtis shouted after him.

"And Patch?"

Patch jerked back toward Coach.

"Get ready for one of the hardest workouts of your life."

Patch stood there awkwardly and finally just said, "Okay, Coach." He grimaced at the thought of what kind of workout routine his coach might have in store for him—still willing, but a little less ready to run a hundred miles. But that would be tomorrow. He had won his races. Barely. But he had won. And he'd eat great food and be with Malcolm, whose enthusiasm and encouragement were infectious. Patch wove through the crowd and toward the VIP parking to meet up with Malcolm. He'd survived another track meet.

chapter 19

"How do you feel about going back to Kansas?"

Jefferson's question hung in the air, and Gwen had the weirdest sensation that made it hard for her to tell if Jefferson had really asked the question or if she only thought he had, or maybe he'd asked hours ago. When Gwen met Jefferson's concerned look, she realized she had been staring at a blank sheet-metal wall for several seconds.

"Sorry. Say it again," Gwen said, hugging one of her arms around her shoulder, rubbing it gently as if it had suddenly gotten colder in the building.

"What do you think about going back to Kansas?" Jefferson asked again.

"That's not what you said before. How I feel and how I think are two completely different things," Gwen said flippantly.

"You know what I meant—" Jefferson started to say.

Gwen interrupted him. "Yeah, I do. And you already know how I'd feel about it. Otherwise, you wouldn't approach me so delicately. So let's get the questions over with. Why do you want me to go? And when do you plan on letting me in on the details of your master plan?" Gwen asked, trying to distract herself from the agitation she felt building inside her by playing with a discarded sweet potato.

"Fair questions. I'll answer the second one first because it'll make the first one obvious," Jefferson said, walking up to the whiteboard in the War Room and drawing a diagram.

"Most people these days have forgotten where their food comes from, and they really don't care so long as they can get it delivered to their door or pick it up at a nearby grocery store, and it's reasonably cheap."

193

Jefferson's diagram became more recognizable—a map Gwen remembered seeing in an old road atlas Jefferson had had in his house. Jefferson's drawing was of the land mass that used to be the United States, and it had several arrows leading from central locations of the country to endpoints on the eastern and western coasts.

"But technology hasn't replaced the need for growing food yet. Technology has made the process of growing that food a ton more efficient. There used to be a bunch of hobbyist farmers who grew food as a lifestyle choice and sold their produce at farmer's markets. There's still some of that closer to the east and west coasts. And there used to be many midsized farming operations like the hundred- to five-hundred-acre scale. Those were usually family operations, where the farm got passed from one generation to the next."

Jefferson finished his drawing and put down the marker to turn to Gwen.

"The thing that really shifted everything was that when the United States government shut down. All the towns that were propped up by government services and government jobs disappeared too. No more federal incentive programs like farm subsidies or low-interest home loans. It also meant there were no more county courthouses or federal offices to employ the citizens of these rural towns. Those offices were often the largest employers in small towns. Those communities basically imploded, and without any basic services like grocery stores, medical centers, public parks, and things like that, people couldn't or didn't want to live in those areas anymore. So they moved to where those services still existed."

Jefferson jumped back to the whiteboard and used both hands to point to the east and west coasts. "The population naturally gravitated to the coasts, not because anybody forced them to. Those were the areas with the services that people needed and wanted. Which meant . . ." Jefferson gestured to Gwen to answer without him needing to finish the full line of reasoning.

Gwen almost wanted to leave Jefferson hanging. She always felt like an eight-year-old kid when Jefferson went all professor on her, but she decided to play along this time. "The land that was left over could be used for a better purpose, like enormous mega-farms like the ones in Kansas," Gwen answered, jumping up to the whiteboard and pointing to the biggest arrow that originated in the center part of the map.

"Exactly! Excellent! The central part of the country is too far away from seaports where overseas markets exchange goods and services. So it made no sense to develop anything in the central part of the country except for one thing. Agriculture. The ground is flat and fertile, and there is a lot of it. Throw in autonomous tractors and drones to monitor insects, diseases, and self-watering systems, and massive farming operations can run from anywhere in the world. And if no one needs to live near those operations, there's also no need for towns to provide services." Jefferson slowly sat on a folding chair near the whiteboard.

Gwen plopped down on a chair next to the table.

"That's where your street gang friends come into play," Jefferson said with a sparkle in his eye.

Gwen had heard all of what Jefferson had shared before, at least in pieces. But involving the street kids was new. She gave Jefferson a cautious look. "What about them?"

"What you did this spring, sabotaging autonomous transport vehicles was really rather brilliant."

Gwen was tickled at hearing her operation called brilliant, but she reminded herself that Jefferson had been acting like such a condescending professor-type a moment ago to stop herself from being too pleased.

"Go on," she said.

"But those isolated trucks didn't really make a dent in the whole supply chain or impact the profits of corporations. Big companies just absorbed those losses. But what would happen if there were suddenly millions of acres of a vital crop, like soybeans, destroyed all in one season?"

Gwen couldn't help but show her surprise. The way Jefferson had always described the disruption of food supply chains had felt more like an academic exercise than anything like destroying crops. "How would you destroy that much cropland?"

"That's where Gerty's expertise will be invaluable," Jefferson said with a slight grumble. "Where your street kids disabled the autonomous vehicles by force, we'll destroy the crops via the introduction of a new disease."

Gwen's puzzled look encouraged Jefferson to continue.

"Over the decades, a few big agribusinesses have genetically altered their cash crops to resist certain weeds and bugs. That way, they could sell the seeds, herbicide, and insect control at the same time. Farmers have become completely dependent on one or two companies for the success of their whole operation. Great position to be in on the businesses' side. Not so much for the farmers."

"I get that. But it sounds like they have super-crops and bug killers that can withstand insects and diseases, so how do you hope to kill these mutant crops?" Gwen asked.

"That's the beautiful weakness that we'll be exploiting." Jefferson hopped up from his chair. "Because those huge agribusinesses have been focused on single strains of crops, they leave themselves vulnerable to new diseases or weeds. That was a concern long before the Economic Wars, but now that farms most often run remotely, using drones and things, the system relies on constantly monitoring the whole operation for weaknesses."

"So we're dealing with super-crops and super weed-and-insect killers, and things are monitored constantly for weaknesses. I still haven't heard our in. Cut to the chase, will you, Jeff?"

Jefferson sighed. "Sorry, Gwen, I know I overexplain things. I always like talking about how things work, not just clear-cut objectives. But you've been more than patient. Here's the grand reveal—"

"We'll use their own operation against them."

Gwen and Jefferson looked up at the main bay doors to see Gerty standing outside the War Room, idly spinning a small cucumber on the table she was leaning against.

"You totally stole my punch line!" Jefferson shouted in Gerty's direction, running his hands through his hair in frustration.

"I know. I'm a horrible person. Let's face it, Jefferson, Gwen must have the patience of a saint. I thought I had strong willpower, but all that prep for that punch line was about to do me in," Gerty said with a wry smile.

"Well, it's good you're here. I was curious how things were going in the genetics lab," Jefferson asked.

"What we have is hardly a genetics lab. We're lucky I held on to some of my old equipment from my research days right out of grad school. I'm the main ingredient, anyway, and it's a good thing I'm brilliant."

"Yes, we all know that fact, for sure. But how are things going with the new soybean disease?"

"Of course. I just wanted to make sure that we were all clear on that fact of me being brilliant and all." Gerty rubbed her hands together excitedly. "So, I've isolated a strain of the fungus Cercospora sojina, more commonly known as frogeye leaf spot. I'm certain that the seed and fungicide mix the mega-farms use has counters to the common strain, but I'm cooking up a strain that masks the characteristics of the leaf spot and looks a lot more like a natural nitrogen-fixer element."

"Nitrogen fixer?" Gwen asked.

"Nitrogen is a really important fertilizer. Most crops need it to grow properly, but the problem is they use the nitrogen they find in the soil, and if you don't add more in, it'll be stripped out of the soil and the soil won't be productive. One of the magical things about soybeans, though, is they create their own nitrogen, so growing soybeans actually improves soil conditions. For that reason and for a ton more, farmers all over the world have a love affair with those adorable beans."

"Let's keep the steamy romance down a bit. We have a teenager in the room," Jefferson said, grinning.

Gerty laughed her full-throated laugh, and Gwen and Jefferson laughed with her. That felt good, Gwen thought, and seeing Jefferson and Gerty laughing together was a very good thing, too.

After she had a couple of moments to catch her breath, Gerty walked up to a bag of topsoil. "The best way to spread the fungus will be to incorporate it directly into soybeans ready for planting as seed. I'm grateful I haven't had to pay too much attention to the way these mega-farms rape and pillage the land they're using, but I've caught up on modern practices over the last couple of weeks. It looks like a couple of corporate farms have a stranglehold on the entire production cycle, from seeds to soil to pesticides. They have their own proprietary seed, soil, and weed-killer mix, which is horrible for small farms but perfect for our goals."

"How so?" Jefferson asked.

Gerty reached her hand into the bag of topsoil and dumped a handful of the black, moist contents on a table. "They manufacture their own industrial-strength soil, and every year, they strip hundreds of thousands of acres of soil and dump a fresh batch down. They have a rotation schedule. That means all of their productive soil gets replaced at least every three growing seasons. I don't even want to think about what they do with all that discarded enriched soil. Probably pump it underground."

"Then don't think about it, but I hate to say it, Gerty, you're nearly as bad at overexplaining as I am," Jefferson said, impatiently strumming his fingers against the table he was leaning against.

"Ah, blast! You're right. The short of it is, we'll have to get into one of their main soybean distribution hubs and inject as many shipments of seed as we can with my souped-up fungus. They'll lay down square miles of the new soil, and when they add the seed, their monitors will identify my fungus as a natural, beneficial part of the soybean and won't recognize any problem until the seedlings are half grown with leaves covered in blotches that block photosynthesis."

"And that's a good thing," Gwen asked, encouragingly.

"No, that's a farmer's nightmare. Well, I guess it's good for us. I still haven't gotten used to this reversed role. Yes. For our purpose, that's a very good thing. It'll make those plants die. And the fungus will spread from mega-farm to mega-farm here in the good old U.S.A. and then span out internationally. If we hit it at a large enough scale, it'll really rock the agribusiness world."

Gwen hadn't understood a lot of what either Jefferson or Gerty had said, but it seemed like as good a plan as any, and she was certain that

Gerty and Jefferson knew their expertise, so she wanted to trust them. But an aching doubt stuck in her head.

"So we'll be doing a similar thing to what we did with the bank's algorithms, except this time we're injecting plants with a fungus instead of computers with a virus?" Gwen said.

Jefferson and Gerty answered at exactly the same time.

"That's a great way of putting it!"

"You nailed it. Yes!"

Gwen nodded and tried to seem pleased to have finally grasped what their plan of attack was. But as she drifted away from the War Room and outside to her thinking spot through the hedge and up the tree, a tightness wrapped around her chest and the start of an upset stomach churned her middle. When she got up to her perch in the branches of the old black walnut tree, she tried to calm her nerves. Though the discussion had veered away from the role Jefferson had planned for her and the street kids to play, she could piece it together.

Jefferson needed a big group to break into the seed distribution center, inject shipments with Gerty's fungus, and somehow get out without getting caught. That was a big enough worry, but there was one even deeper down in the pit of Gwen's stomach. The computer virus idea hadn't worked, so what made Jefferson and Gerty so sure that a soybean fungus would do any better? And if Jefferson was held for months by contract enforcers that broke him in ways she was still trying to parse out, what would happen if they got caught this time?

Gwen couldn't refuse when Jefferson got around to asking her more specifically to gather the support of the street gang back in D.C. She didn't know how she would convince them or how they would infiltrate the seed centers, but she was confident she could figure it out. She had a hard time believing it herself, but none of that caused her as much stress as something else.

She was being asked to leave another place that had started to feel like home.

Gwen still only had enough things to barely fill a duffel bag—a couple of changes of clothes, a change of shoes, a couple of books. But in each new situation, she picked up a few extra items. They weren't helpful for survival at all, but they meant something to her . . . like the soup ladle from Jefferson's home that Jefferson had used to feed her dinner after the encounter with three desperate men who almost killed her. She'd stuffed it in her bag when they'd left. Once she got back to Jefferson's home, she would have to remember to return that one. And the smooth stone from the girl who was part of the street gang. Cecily. And now, at the farm, she carefully tucked away a cluster of walnuts from her hideaway tree.

What do you call things like these? she asked herself, mulling it over as she slung her duffel over her shoulder in the sleeping quarters section of their operations building and did one last check to make sure she had everything she needed. Mementos? Souvenirs? Those words didn't carry the right amount of gravity. She settled on keepsakes, but that didn't seem quite right either.

Security blanket is more like it, she thought, embarrassed that she even cared about silly things while she and the rest of the operation were basically at war. But knowing she could take the items with her back to D.C. and then back to Kansas made the prospect of leaving such a comfortable place like the farm bearable. Jefferson walked into the sleeping quarters area, and Gwen cleared her throat.

"So do you have everything?" Jefferson asked, nervously shuffling his weight from side to side.

"Yeah, I think so," Gwen said, patting her bag.

"You live in comfortable places like these very long, and you kind of forget that survival instinct," Jefferson smiled. "I'm sure not you, though."

Gwen just smiled, although she wished she had a way of throwing all the feelings that were burning inside of her at Jefferson.

Jefferson lowered himself onto the cot opposite Gwen's. "I know how hard this is for you," he said, absorbing Gwen's hands in his bear-paw-sized ones. Gwen felt the worn calluses that proliferated across the pads of Jefferson's palm.

"No, you don't," she said softly.

"What was that?" Jefferson asked.

"No, you don't know how hard this is for me," she said louder and with more edge than she had wanted. "But that's okay."

"It's not okay," Jefferson said with a fierceness that startled Gwen. "None of this is okay. Not the fact that this incredible farm has to run under the radar. Not that we had to leave our other operations in D.C. That you were picked up by contract enforcers. That you and I had to leave Kansas in the first place. And, most especially, that you've never had the chance to experience life like I did growing up."

Jefferson let go of Gwen's hands and folded his arms around his chest. Gwen noticed how thin his frame had gotten. He's still not back from those months with the contract enforcers, she realized. But how could anybody fully recover from what they had done to Jefferson?

"The world wasn't perfect by any means. So many problems. Multiple wars going on at the same time. The rich getting richer, and the poor getting poorer. And we had it easier here in the States, too. Outside this country, we had hundreds of millions of refugees in filthy camps while governments bickered about not accepting any more refugees, claiming they were terrorists. People back then loved believing in silver-bullet solutions. The government is the problem, so less government is always a good thing. Old white men are the source of all oppression, so they need to step aside. The liberals are soft on crime. The conservatives don't care about real people. But nothing was really that clear-cut. The one thing we had, though, was something to act as a balance to the market, and in many countries, a safety net so that no one had to starve to death before growing into who they were meant to become—before they could start making their contribution to the world. Such huge loss of human potential and meaning for life."

Jefferson and Gwen sat silently for several moments. The silence was comforting. Gwen's mind flashed back to those evenings in Jefferson's home after a good meal, watching the fire in the fireplace burn down to embers.

"I hate the fact that I have to ask you to do this to make our plan work. But neither we nor Gerty have enough athletic crew members to pull off what we need your street-kid crew to do. I promise I wouldn't ask unless it was absolutely necessary."

"I know. I get it. I'll do my best. It's just—"

"We might as well go if we're going." Gerty's voice stopped Gwen midsentence.

Gwen and Jefferson sighed and stood up. Gerty paused as if sensing she had interrupted something important. "Sorry. I can come back."

"No. I'm ready. Let's do this," Gwen said, tightening the straps of her bag and following Gerty and Jefferson out of the warehouse and into the bright sunlight and to whatever they had in store for her beyond the farm.

chapter 20

Another consolation for leaving the farm was that Gerty was coming with Gwen. In order to ensure the new fungal strain was ready and to train the street kids how to inject it, she insisted on going not only to D.C. but all the way to Kansas as well.

They couldn't go back to their previous warehouse operation location since the contract enforcers had been watching them and probably kept surveillance in the area just in case. So they navigated to an abandoned warehouse across the Potomac, closer to where Alex's operations were located.

As they pulled into the three-story concrete building, Gwen noticed that on many walls hung a faded emblem in red, white, and blue with a stylized eagle and the letters U-S-P-S. She didn't have much time to wonder what it meant, though, because she wanted to meet up with Alex and his crew that afternoon.

They'll know we're here already, so no reason to wait for a better time to pitch the plan to them, Gwen figured. So while Gerty's crew set up a temporary operation, Gwen dropped her bag near the truck she'd ridden in and started to head toward Alex's building.

"Whoa, whoa. Hold up for a second, dear," Gerty shouted after Gwen.

Gwen turned around and took a few steps back toward Gerty. "What's up? I just thought it would be good for me to check in with the street kids."

"Great plan. Great to know that's what you're doing and not one of the thousands of other things you could be doing that might make me worry because you didn't tell me where you were going," Gerty said with a knowing look.

"I'm sorry. I guess I'm still used to doing my own thing."

"I get that. But we're a team now. We need to check in before we move on things. It's not to hold you back. It's so we can watch your back," Gerty said, squeezing Gwen's shoulder and brushing her bangs out of her eyes.

"You're right. And I'm really glad you're here," Gwen said.

"Nice of you to say. I don't know if I believe you yet. But nice of you to say," Gerty said with a wink. "Off with you. Are you ready for your pitch like we practiced on the ride over?" Gerty stopped her again.

"Yeah. I've got it. Wish me luck," Gwen said, pointing to her head as she rushed back in her original direction.

"You don't need luck. You're ready," Gerty shouted as Gwen disappeared out of the garage with a wave behind her in Gerty's direction.

Gwen took a slow pace getting to the old covered market where Alex's crew lived so she could have some time to rehearse her pitch. She quietly ran through it out loud while trying to keep a pebble in front of her by kicking it straight forward.

"I would totally get why you'd be hesitant to give me a second chance at leading any big kind of operation. You trusted me, and I left you."

Gwen stopped and tried a few other ways of arranging those thoughts. "You opened up to me, maybe? Or I could say something like I left you in a bad situation. That way, I could connect that idea to how horrible I feel about the crew members who were killed when they left?"

Gwen paused, then, and stood still. She was pretty sure that one or two street kids were watching her from a building across the street, and she wasn't sure what effect her randomly breaking down would have. Keep it together! You're back to help all street kids, and you can't help the already lost ones, she told herself.

After a few moments, she straightened rounded her shoulders, took a deep breath, and kicked the pebble hard, sending it careening down the street to make a satisfying thunk as it hit some concrete wall around the corner. I know what I feel is right. Memorizing speeches will get in the way. I'll just wing it, she decided.

Gwen crossed a complex intersection where five roads jutted off a central courtyard, then she walked confidently toward the dark building. Every time she got close to the place, she liked to imagine what it must have been like when it operated as a covered market rather than a home for abandoned children. Alex once told her that there had been sections dedicated to a hundred cheeses, a different one for fresh-cut flowers, and—the one she'd probably most like to see—a place famous for their buckwheat blueberry pancakes. Gwen wasn't sure what made pancakes better if they were made out of buckwheat, and she wasn't entirely sure what pancakes were, either, but she made a mental note to ask Gerty when she got back.

"It's all good. It's just Gwen," she heard a sentry yell out.

Two kids who had been hiding in the bushes near the main entrance to the market hopped into view.

"What do you mean, It's just Gwen? Don't you mean, It's Gwen, the coolest ever?" she smirked.

"Yeah. I didn't mean to say that it was just—well, when I said that—"

"It's totally fine. Relax. Just teasing you. How are you guys?"

Both sentries relaxed their hunched shoulders and seemed very pleased to have some good news to share.

"We found a broken-down truck carrying frozen meat last week. And get this?"

Gwen tried to prepare genuine excitement for whatever the two boys were obviously eager to share.

"What?" Gwen said encouragingly.

"We got to it before the meat had gone bad. So Alex decided we'd have—what did he call it again, Miles?"

"A barbeque," Miles said shyly.

"Love it! How fun! So you cooked up the meat and had a real feast then!"

Both boys nodded, beaming.

"Darn! I wish I had come by last week now. I bet it was great."

"It was!"

"Yeah!"

"Speaking of Alex, is he around?" Gwen asked.

"Yeah, I'll take you to him," one of the boys said, walking toward the entrance.

"Oh, that's okay. You two are on duty. I'm sure I can find my way. But he's inside?"

Both boys nodded eagerly again.

"Thanks. Make sure all that great food doesn't make you soft," Gwen said jokingly.

The sentries smiled as they went back to their hiding spots, and Gwen entered the shadowy entryway. Gwen walked through the two sets of steel double doors and into the main market space. The building had three-story high ceilings with rafters that made the building look a bit like the inside of an enormous whale, with symmetrical wooden beams every few feet for the entire length of the very long building.

Alex had taken full advantage of the market layout. Where dividing half-walls used to separate individual shops and specialty food stores, the building had been divided functionally. Kind of how Jefferson had sub-divided the warehouse on Gerty's farm, except Alex had divided things into many more functional areas. Gwen walked past several familiar stalls on her way to find Alex.

There was a reading nook with shelves holding dozens of battered-but-repaired books. She passed another area with benches and tables. Their dining area. All the spaces were clean and nicely kept up, but what made Gwen smile were the little details she knew that Alex cared about because they made things a bit special.

Gwen had no idea where Alex had found soft, brightly colored cushions to lie down on in the reading room. Or the pictures of random landscapes in rough wood frames hanging on the walls in the dining area. Gwen could almost imagine them hanging in a café like the ones she'd experienced that spring in Boston. She was amazed yet again by Alex. In fact, she was getting used to being surprised by his obvious care for the people who counted on him. Knowing that would make it easier and harder to make her pitch.

"You're back! I knew you would be."

Gwen had been admiring the way Alex had set things up so intently that she didn't even notice Cecily come out from the reading area.

"Hey, Cecily. Yes, I'm back. Though, it looks like I'm losing my edge. I didn't see you sneak up on me," Gwen said, giving Cecily a warm hug.

"Yeah, Alex gave me a few pointers on stealth, so you'd better watch your back," Cecily said, darting around Gwen and using her fingers as imaginary shooters.

Gwen twirled around, laughing with Cecily.

"Very nice. Have you seen Alex around?"

"Yeah, he's trying to set up some kind of boxes for gardens. Square foot gardens, maybe? I don't know. Anyway, he's outside, over that way," Cecily said, pointing to a side door a few yards further along the building.

"Thanks, Cecily. You'll have to tell me more about what you're reading and what you've been up to when I get done with Alex," Gwen said, pointing to the book Cecily was holding before heading to the doors Cecily had motioned toward.

"Count on it!" Cecily said with a grin as she ducked back into the reading nook.

Gwen heard Alex long before she saw him. She pushed open the heavy doors and found him pounding nails into long weathered two-by-four boards. Gwen glanced around Alex and saw that he had put together rows of several good-sized wooden frames like the one Gwen found him working on. She had never noticed the area before, but it was ideal for a garden.

The area must have been used as an outdoor seating area at one time because Gwen could see discarded wrought-iron chairs off to the side. The alcove had high stone walls that would be easily protected, and although it was surrounded by trees outside the walls, there was nothing to block the sunlight coming from the south. Gwen shook her head in amazement.

"I swear if you weren't running a crew of street kids, you could easily be running a business, living the high life," Gwen said.

Alex looked up and smiled.

"Yeah. Sure. But I can't stand wearing suit jackets, so there goes that dream. How are you, Gwen? What's up?"

Gwen tried to gauge Alex's mood and overall tolerance of her from his tone of voice. She knew what she was supposed to do. Ease into the request—do something particularly helpful to the crew first, and then ask for the help. If things didn't go well with the first conversation, that was okay. They would be in D.C. for a few days, so she wasn't supposed to throw everything out at first. The whole ride over from the farm, Gerty coached her on what to say and how to behave. Gwen knew how persuasive Gerty was, and she did her best to absorb the lessons. So Gwen knew what she should do in the current situation.

Gwen knew it, and she couldn't stand there with no explanation for coming back much longer, either. Alex would get suspicious. And a suspicious Alex would be even harder to work with than the overly cautious one she might work with under the best of circumstances. Yet, she decided to go with the stronger urge to follow her instincts and adapt quickly, like she had learned to do the hard way after years of living on the street.

"So you're building a garden?" Gwen asked, instantly knowing that was a stupid way of responding to Alex's question.

"Yeah, I figured I'd dust off my green thumb. The crew doesn't eat enough fresh vegetables. I worry about how little vitamins they get."

In that moment, appreciation for Alex washed over Gwen. It came in one big wave that took her completely off guard.

"That's incredibly sweet," Gwen said, fighting the urge to run up and hug him right there in the dirt.

"We'll see how things work out. First, I've got to build these planter boxes and find soil that isn't full of all kinds of leftover crap from the industrial activities around here. Oh, and we'll have to find seeds. But one step at a time, right?"

"Absolutely," Gwen responded.

Alex continued pounding nails without paying much attention to Gwen's presence. When he had completed the planter box he was working on, he brushed his sweaty forehead with his forearm and looked up at Gwen.

"Another down. Probably six more to go."

"Can I help? Do you have an extra hammer?" Gwen asked, eagerly looking around for extra tools.

"That's the funny thing. This area probably used to be full of hammers and nails and other useful stuff like that when these buildings were used the old way. But I practically had to sell my soul for a single hammer."

"Really? Your whole soul. That might've been a bargain," Gwen said playfully.

"I think I actually traded it for a pair of shoes, too, so almost as big of a deal as my soul and a whole lot more functional. But you still haven't answered my question, Gwen. What are you doing here? Did your operation find a new place? It's been like weeks."

"It's funny I'd find you making planter boxes for a garden because, yes, we did land a new place for our operation. On a farm. And let me tell you, we have plenty of good soil and seeds to share," Gwen said, pleased to have something she could provide in droves that Alex had just told her he needed.

"Bribing me with dirt and seeds. Sorry, Ms. Reynolds, no deal," Alex smirked with a steady look.

"Who said anything about a deal?"

"Oh, no one yet. But that's why you're here, right?"

Gwen froze.

"It's alright. I think I know you well enough by now. It's not a bad thing to know what you want and try everything you can to get it, but that's how you work."

Gwen flared at being categorized so generally. "I don't think I'm nearly that easy to read."

"That's not what I meant."

"Oh really? You didn't mean that you have me completely figured out and that I'm a selfish jerk who only builds relationships with people to get what I want?" Gwen asked defiantly, turning away from Alex.

"Fine. If you're not here to convince me to help you with another one of your operation schemes, then great. Welcome back. Grab a rock, and try your hand at hitting nails with it. I promise it's not nearly as easy as it sounds."

It wasn't anger or annoyance Gwen heard in Alex's tone. It was resignation, and it broke her heart. *He really does have me figured out.* She walked up close to Alex and crouched down next to him.

"The farm is amazing," Gwen said softly. "It's beautiful, really, with more food than I've ever seen or even imagined."

Alex kept working, placing the newly built planter box in a neat row beside the others. But Gwen picked up tells that Alex was paying more attention to her—the subtle tilt of his head and twitch of his nose. Gwen hadn't forgotten those days of scrounging for food. How could Alex not pay attention to descriptions of places like the farm?

"They grow so many kinds of fruits and vegetables, most I'd never even heard of. And the person who runs the place, Gerty, is fantastic. I think she'd really like you. Maybe even more than she likes me, but don't tell her I told you that," Gwen said, nudging him with her elbow and knocking him off his haunches, making her giggle.

After Alex got over his surprise at being knocked over so easily, he started giggling too.

"I needed that," he said. "I haven't felt much in the mood for laughing lately."

Alex put down the hammer and stood up, gesturing for Gwen to take a seat with him on a raised platform that she guessed used to have bushes on it but now housed nothing but some scraggly brown stumps. She jumped up and let her legs dangle. Alex did the same.

"So, sounds about perfect. If I didn't know better, I'd say you were exaggerating, but I've always taken you as a straight shooter, so it must be really something. Glad you landed at such a great spot. I really am."

Another wave of affection for Alex crashed over her, and before she could get past it, Alex turned and leveled a very serious look at her.

"Let's stop pretending here. You need something. We both know it. So get on with it. You're not a selfish jerk. Most of the time, you have others in mind when you do the things you push for. You just don't let others get close enough. You keep us out in the dark too much. Like last time."

There it was. Last time. Gwen had no counter-argument. No way of explaining away what happened last time. Alex had nailed the real problem down much better than he had nailed the planter boxes together—bent-down nails only halfway buried in the wood.

"I used to have that superpower, too, you know?" Gwen sighed, swinging her legs over the lip of the stone-raised garden.

"What superpower are we talking about?"

"The ability to spot bunk from a mile away."

Alex seemed pleased at the unexpected compliment.

"You sure are a sweet talker, aren't you?" Alex said sarcastically.

"You're welcome. I mean it. I used to be the same way. Never trust anybody. Assume the worst. Then I met Jefferson a little over a year ago, and that started to change bit by bit. I knew that some people could be trusted because I trusted him. But learning to trust someone else is different than letting others trust you. I think that's even harder than learning to trust in the first place."

Gwen looked at Alex, who then locked eyes with her.

"I should have told you the truth last time. I should have let you in. I don't know why it's so hard for me to do that," Gwen said, eyes shining with the start of tears, but she turned away so as to not show them.

"And the thought that you lost your friends after they left because of me. I just can't imagine. That's just—"

Alex gently put his hand over Gwen mouth and slowly turned her head so she faced him. He transferred his hand, which smelled like soil, from her mouth to cradle her chin against his palm. She let the full weight of her head fall into his hand, realizing how tightly she had been straining her neck until then.

Alex cupped his other hand around her other cheek and caught the first tear as it ran out from her lower eyelashes, then rubbed her cheek dry with a caressing dirty thumb. Alex inched his face toward Gwen, not exactly cautious, Gwen decided. His pace felt more respectful than careful, as if he was giving her a wide berth in case she wanted to pull away without either of them losing dignity. But Gwen didn't pull away and actually started leaning toward Alex.

They paused less than an inch from each other's lips. Gwen was certain Alex could hear her heart accelerating and breathing in the sweat and soil that clung to him after his day spent laying out the gardens. To her surprise, the combination of fragrances made a pleasant smell that brought back memories of summers spent in the woods and swimming in hidden lakes near her family's old home in Kansas, then hours of letting the sun dry her body until the heat begged for another dip. She didn't realize she still had those memories.

As if on cue, Alex and Gwen made up the difference between their lips in a quiet, searching kiss. Gwen's lips quivered at first, but they grew more confident, borrowing from the intensity that radiated from Alex. Their lips parted, and they looked at each other questioningly. Gwen smiled and laughed sweetly at the sheer thrill of her very first kiss. She put her lips against Alex's one more time for good measure, and this time, Alex wrapped both arms across her back. Their shared warmth felt right and good.

Gwen and Alex let go of each other and turned to face forward, both grinning widely and swinging their legs in joyful synchrony. Neither spoke for several long moments. Gwen felt like she could easily leap over the high stone walls with the excited energy bursting inside her if she wanted to. At long last, Alex broke the silence.

"So, what now?"

"Now, I have to ask you for a favor, and don't you dare think I planned things this way. I was expecting to be laughed out of this building for even asking. Things have played out very differently than how they played out in my head," Gwen said, careful with the words she chose, but she quickly added, "Better for sure. Much, much better than I expected."

"Okay. Let's hear about your next grand scheme, Gwen," Alex said, letting out a slow, long breath.

Gwen hopped down from the ledge but quickly jumped back up and gave Alex a hug on impulse, then jumped back down, giggling. Alex looked like he didn't know quite what was going on but seemed willing to go wherever Gwen was heading.

"You setting up a garden is so perfect because of what I'm going to ask you and your crew to help with."

Gwen's explanation of the plan to inject soybeans ready for shipment wasn't exactly clean. Alex had to ask a lot of clarifying questions, many of which, Gwen didn't really have answers to. And the prospect of leaving their covered-market home required a lot of reassuring. But after Gwen explained that they would have people watching his building so that no other street gangs could install themselves while they were gone, Alex appeared almost ready to agree, which Gwen hardly believed possible.

"So I get the plan now. It seems halfway possible that we'll be successful, too. But if we are successful, are we supposed to just go back to life as usual?"

"I'm not sure I know what you mean," Gwen said.

"Most of the kids in my crew haven't known any other kind of life than this one. I've tried to build as good of a life for them as I can, but it's not a good life. Not really. And so I'm asking—if we do this for you, for Jefferson and Gerty, and my crew sees Kansas and the massive food operations at the distribution centers you described, how could they possibly be okay with going back to their old lives?"

"You mean you're afraid that people will leave?" Gwen said, letting the weight of what Alex was talking about sink in.

"I'm sure some will. But I'm really more concerned about how these kids could look at things the same way they do now after the operation. Not knowing anything different keeps them going because they don't know anything else is possible. If these kids realize there's so much more out there, but they realize it's all beyond their reach—don't you see how crushing that would be?"

Gwen thought of how impossibly crushed she would feel if after staying with Jefferson that first summer, she woke up one morning to find herself back in Topeka, alone and with nothing to live for. She shuddered at the thought.

"I won't let that happen," Gwen said with absolute confidence.

"How can you promise that?"

"I don't know. But it's true. I'll work things out with Jefferson and Gerty. They wouldn't abandon you and your crew."

"They did last time."

Gwen rushed up to Alex, taking his hands in hers. "But this time we're all working together! Me, you, your crew, Jefferson, and Gerty. And rather than us being a sideshow that I'm running, hoping not to get caught, we're going to be the main event. Things can't go back to how they've been. I won't let them." Gwen looked intently into Alex's eyes, trying to convey the multiple meanings behind her words.

Alex nodded slowly. "Okay. Let me see if I can rally the troops to your cause again," Alex said, hopping down from the ledge and heading to the door leading inside. He stopped and turned back to Gwen. "Come on, you're not off the hook. Against their better judgment, a lot of the kids are fond of you. We'll need that if we have any hopes of convincing them."

Gwen chuckled and hurried to catch up with Alex.

chapter 21

Patch was determined to make Christmas special, but at the moment, he was desperate for ideas. He knew how much that time of the year meant to Malcolm. Last year was the first time Patch had remembered ever celebrating the holidays in any special fashion, and so he had no way of setting too-high expectations or feeling any stress then. But, clearly, it hadn't taken him long to learn how to stress over Christmas.

The school semester had ended the day before, and Patch was on the train, waiting for the short trip to the station where Malcolm would pick him up. That meant he had a few minutes alone to think about all the remaining possibilities.

He wrote off making things special by giving Malcolm anything. Malcolm could buy anything he wanted, and any money Patch used was really Malcolm's, anyway, so that wouldn't work. He thought about making something like he had last year. His homemade trophy with his old, beat-up shoes and the small plaque that read, To the man who believes in life's magic, from a boy who never thought he could.

That's what he needed to find. That magic. Even when he reflected on that night with the tree lit up, the amazing dinner, the gifts, the time sitting together, quietly sipping warm drinks and enjoying the feeling. That's what he needed to bring again this year. Even as he thought about it, Patch realized he needed to feel that magic as much as he wanted it for Malcolm.

Patch's train started so soundlessly—so smoothly—that Patch didn't even notice until the train was already at top speed, halfway to his destination. Come on! Think!

Moments later, Patch got off the train with his bags. He headed to Gino's food-cart. He often did his best thinking while munching on falafel.

Hundreds of people in dark overcoats rushed around Patch. The energy in the station felt different this time. Lighter in some ways. It was probably just his thinking about Christmas and magic that made him think that most of the faces darting around him wore excited smiles. But he liked to think he was right. He still had to avoid any collisions with the fast-moving pedestrians so he didn't get a ton of extra fees tacked onto his train ticket. Malcolm always teased him anytime surcharges showed up because of Patch's clumsiness.

Patch stepped up to the Greek food-cart, thrilled to have timed things just right. There wasn't a line. A familiar man he had seen a number of times before came up from the back of the cart, rubbing his hands with a towel.

"It's the fine young man who talks to real people. How are you, my friend?" the man said.

Patch's mind raced, trying to remember the last time he had spoken to the man in the food-cart. Then the man smiled, and things clicked at seeing the creases around his cheeks and his eyes shining back at Patch.

"Good to see you again, sir. It's been a few months. You have a fabulous memory," Patch said admiringly.

"I don't remember all of my customers. But I usually don't forget important conversations. Hope the semester went well. Home for the holiday, I hope?"

"Yes. Looking forward to it," Patch said, trying to set aside the issue of the season's magic. Someone stepped behind him in line, so Patch hurried and ordered his falafel sandwich.

"Coming right up, young sir."

Patch stepped aside to let the woman, who was completely engrossed in her tablet, step up to the counter. She didn't even look up when taking her food from the kind man at the food-cart. Patch caught the shop worker's eye, and they exchanged a knowing look.

People really don't treat other people as people. It's all transactions, Patch thought.

"Here you go, my friend. One fresh falafel sandwich with my compliments."

Patch received his warm sandwich, which was tightly wrapped in aluminum foil with the inviting aromas making him fight the urge to dig in right there in front of the food-cart.

"Thank you, sir. Happy holidays," Patch said. He turned to leave, but a thought made him rush back to the counter.

"You decided you need two falafel sandwiches based on the smell only? I'm very flattered," the man said with a wry smile.

"No, well, yes. I could probably eat five right now. But can I ask you a question?"

"You have a question that a food-cart owner can answer?" Gino's. This must be Gino. Or Mr. Gino?

"You own this food-cart? It's absolutely my favorite! My . . . well, my friend loves to cook really fancy things, and that's always great, especially around this time of the year. But he jokes that I'd be happier grabbing a couple of your falafel sandwiches, and he'd be right."

The man took that praise silently, but Patch saw his whole face light up.

"So, are you Mr. Gino?" Patch asked.

"Gino is my first name. Gino Pappas. That's me."

"So great to know your name, Mr. Pappas."

"Please. Gino will work for friends."

Gino smiled, and Patch smiled back, but then he remembered the question he wanted to ask.

"Do you celebrate this time of the year?"

"Of course. It's my favorite time of the year," Gino said, shutting his eyes as if he were reliving fond memories.

"What's your favorite part of the holidays?"

The man leaned back against the counter and put his thumb to his chin, thoughtfully. After a few moments, more moments than Patch had expected, the man opened his eyes again and leaned forward so his head stuck out of the food-cart. He ushered Patch to get close. Patch leaned a few feet closer so Gino could whisper just for him.

"Every Christmas, my family and I—my children and now my grandchildren and me—we all get together for Christmas Eve. We sing songs. We eat and enjoy family. And then we all go to church for Christmas Eve services. I think my favorite moment of all is when we are leaving. The bells ring out the start of Christmas Day. Doing that with my family all around me, that's my favorite."

Gino's face absolutely lit up while he described his favorite part of Christmas. Patch's face reflected that same wonder while listening. That's what he wanted. That's what he needed and wanted for himself and Malcolm.

"Thank you, sir. That sounds . . . magical," Patch said softly.

"That's the word. Yes," Gino said. "It's full of magic and love."

Patch laughed at the sheer joy Gino clearly had even in describing the experience. What would it be like to actually experience it? Patch wondered, adjusting the strap of his bag on his shoulder to get ready to go.

Gino lit up again in a broad smile. "Please come! Celebrate with us this year."

"What? Me? Come to your Christmas Eve family gathering? That's so incredibly kind, sir, but I wouldn't intrude on that for the world."

"No, you must come! The grandchildren will fall for you instantly. The star athlete with the chiseled chin. I'll have to watch my granddaughters," Gino said mischievously.

"I don't know what to say. It's so very generous of you to offer, but this is for your family. Your favorite time of year."

"I insist. We'll have so many people in the house, anyway, and it'll bring so much honor to our celebration to have such a fine guest with us."

Patch started nervously kicking the floor tiles. "I'd have to check with my friend. I mean, with my family. Do you have a way I could contact you in a day or two?"

Gino rummaged around the counter for a pen and jotted down his address and phone number on a napkin, then thrust it into Patch's hand.

"Yes, yes! Get back with me tomorrow. Or come back for another sandwich. Bring your friend to celebrate too!"

Patch left Gino, trying to match his enthusiastic waving. As Patch exited the train station, he scanned the dozens of cars in the park-and-wait area. Malcolm was leaning against the hood of his car, waving nearly as enthusiastically as Gino had been moments before.

How am I going to suggest we go to Gino's party, and what if Malcolm really doesn't want to go? Patch thought while Malcolm wrapped an arm around his shoulder and took his bags.

"Can I get you something to eat, or did you stuff yourself at that falafel place you're always racking up such a huge bill at?" Malcolm asked, rummaging through cupboards and munching on random nuts and crackers as he came across them.

We're jumping right to it, I guess, Patch thought nervously.

"Yeah, I grabbed a falafel sandwich in the station. I actually had a fun conversation with the guy working there."

"Oh?" Malcolm said with his head now in the fridge.

"Yeah, I found out that the guy is the owner. Gino Pappas is his name."

"Very cool name. If I had a name like that, I would totally name my business after myself, too," Malcolm said, coming away from the fridge with a container of strawberries and some kind of dip.

"You have, haven't you? Richards and Cohen Investments? Malcolm Richards is your name, right? Or did you name your investment firm after a different Richards?"

"Funny. I'd never really thought about that. Technically, the firm was started by my dad, but you're right," Malcolm said, chomping into a strawberry and sending its juice dangerously close to Patch's face.

"Watch it! And toss me one of those. I thought I was full, but those look too good to pass up."

Malcolm tossed two strawberries from the sink across the large stainless-steel bar to where Patch was seated on a stool. Patch deftly caught both and followed Malcolm's example, biting into one of his strawberries with relish. The flavors were fantastic. It was delicious, but . . .

"I think I need to try it with some of the—"

"Way ahead of you," Malcolm brought the dip over and leaned against the countertop opposite Patch.

"Even better," Patch said with his mouth full, inhaling his other strawberry with a generous helping of the dip. Patch took a few seconds to swallow and then tried to bring the conversation back to Gino's.

"Anyway, so the guy at the falafel shop."

"Right, we got so focused on my brilliance in keeping my firm in my family's name. Please continue," Malcolm smirked.

"Thanks for your permission. Turns out he's a really cool guy."

"Most street-cart owners are," Malcolm said in a matter-of-fact way.

"How could you possibly know that?" Patch said with an arched eyebrow.

"Seriously, they're some of the best people. I used to have a client who helped manage a bunch of food-carts. They'd provide leases so food-cart vendors didn't have to put up all the cost of buying them. Good idea. The management company went belly-up a couple of years later. Luckily, I stopped representing their interests before the shady side of their operation came out, but I visited several of their food-carts to see what kind of shape they were in before signing the agreement. I'll say it again: some of the best people I've had the privilege of meeting."

"Is there anything you haven't dabbled in, Mal?" Patch asked admiringly.

"Arts and crafts. Not much of a market yet, but I think homemade scrap-wood signs are about to hit a tipping point," Malcolm said, smiling while nibbling on another strawberry.

"Well, you'll never guess what Gino did at the end of our conversation."

"He offered you a lifetime supply of falafel sandwiches for wearing his logo on your headband," Malcolm guessed randomly.

"Close. Not a bad idea, really. But I hate wearing headbands. Much prefer getting sweat in my eyes than wearing one of those goofy-looking things."

Patch paused for a few seconds, hoping beyond everything that his suggestion didn't destroy Christmas for Malcolm and that maybe it could be a special thing.

"He invited us to his family's Christmas Eve party," Patch said slowly, keeping his eyes locked on Malcolm to gauge his first impressions of the idea.

"Seriously?"

Patch nodded eagerly.

"Wow, kid, people really warm up to you, don't they?" Malcolm asked with a chuckle.

"It worked with you, too, didn't it?" Patch asked, realizing the uncanny parallels.

"You got me there. True enough. Well, what do you think of the idea? I'll admit doing that on Christmas Eve is a bit unorthodox for me. But it could be kind of fun, too," Malcolm said, leaving the decision bare for Patch to make.

"It could be fun. But I know how important the holidays are to you. I mean, they're already important to me, too. So, if you have other plans already lined up, that's okay."

"Of course I have plans lined up. I always have plans, but who's to say those can't change? Contingency planning is kind of my jam," Malcolm said, taking the much lighter container of remaining strawberries back to the fridge.

"I know. I just don't want to ruin anything."

Malcolm quickly turned to look at Patch.

"Hey! Remember what I always say about Christmas?"

"You can't ruin Christmas," Patch recited while Malcolm said the words in unison with Patch.

"That's right. So I say let's live dangerously. I'm game if you are." Malcolm said encouragingly.

"Alright then. Sounds like a good contingency plan," Patch said with relief and excitement welling inside of him.

"Watch out world! Malcolm and Patch are going to have a Gino's Family Christmas," Malcolm shouted to his vaulted ceilings with arms spread wide.

Later that night, after Patch had put his few things away in his room, he fell back on his bed and picked up the pink rubber ball that was waiting for him on his nightstand, right where he had left it in August when he'd headed to his second year of school. He played his usual game. He knew the feel of the distance between his bed and the ceiling so well, though that it wasn't much of a challenge anymore. Come to think of it, the activity has some mindfulness connections that I'm certain Pete would appreciate, he thought.

Patch tried to put into words the feeling that was warming up inside him, almost making him smile for no apparent reason. After several tosses, he finally found the word.

Home.

He was home. The complex combination of emotions and senses and familiarity and memory all jumbled together—that was his home. He didn't have to perform there. He was known and accepted and loved for who he was right then.

He placed the pink rubber ball back on the nightstand, propped in place by other familiar objects—a blue digital clock and a paperweight with an inspirational quote from someone called Winston Churchill that Malcolm gave him last school year. Patch interlaced his fingers and used them to prop up his head. The space was his, though that felt strange—the house actually belonged to Malcolm. The room is kind of like a gift, he realized. After so many cold nights where he instinctively woke at the slightest out-of-the-ordinary sound, his room was not one he was quick to take for granted.

Patch scooched under the covers and pulled his bedspread up to his chin, smelling the clean linen smell and letting the warmth wash over him.

chapter 22

Over the next couple of days, Patch remembered how much he really missed home. It wasn't the sort of missing where it distracted him during his classes or anything like that, but now that he was back where everything was familiar and so many levels more relaxed and comfortable, he had to admit that it was a very good thing to have a home base.

Patch strolled out of his bedroom, down the hall, and into the kitchen and was met with the most inviting, savory smell of some kind of well-seasoned meat simmered with peppers.

"Is that oregano?" Patch said, sidling up to the bar and plopping down on a stool.

"Close. Tarragon, actually, with some chili pepper and bay leaves," Malcolm said, making a show of stirring the skillet so that flames shot up from the stove.

"Very fancy. What's the occasion? I mean, you almost always have great food anyway, but usually we go kind of continental, don't we?"

"Continental? Is that a young-person slang term or something?"

"No. I found out randomly while studying for my economic history class that there used to be a country called Britain that was really powerful up until the early 1900s, and they called breakfasts on the continent, or breakfasts other Europeans ate, continental because the British ate crazy heavy stuff like blood sausage and baked beans for breakfast," Patch explained.

"Got it. So this is super British heavy stuff?" Malcolm said with an arched eyebrow.

"No. This is just more than toast and fruit and stuff like that. Sorry. It's early. Got to give my brain a few more minutes to wake up."

"Siri, start my espresso machine," Malcolm said.

"Morning, Malcolm. You bet. Shall I brew your usual iced coffee?"

"Yes, please, but make it for two. Heavy on the espresso."

"Okay. Two iced coffee with extra espresso coming right up."

"Read my mind," Patch said while rubbing his temples.

"We'll need extra energy today since we'll be celebrating Greek-style tonight," Malcolm said, turning off the burner and using a dish towel to move the skillet toward two waiting plates into which he tumbled generous helpings of the hot beef-and-pepper medley, wafting mouthwatering aromas under Patch's nose.

"To answer your previous question, I decided that if we're going to celebrate with our new friend Gino tonight, we'd have a glorified Christmas Eve breakfast feast instead of our more traditional dinner version."

"I like it! I mean, I like your food anytime I can get it, but that sounds like a fun new tradition."

"Yeah, we can try it out to see how it fits. In my book, that's part of the fun with traditions," Malcolm said, grabbing their two freshly brewed iced coffees and a bowl of sliced peaches and melon.

"Happy Christmas Eve morning," Malcolm said, raising his glass. Patch did the same, and they clinked glasses and took long sips.

"Ooh, that's good," Patch said, digging into his steaming plate.

"You like it? It's a—"

"It's a new recipe you thought you'd try out," Patch interrupted Malcolm, reciting what he knew Malcolm would say by force of habit.

"Am I really that predictable? Anyway, eat up."

Patch and Malcolm enjoyed a very pleasant meal together and passed away the morning and afternoon, putting up a few last-minute decorations around the house and reading while listening to classic Christmas tunes. Patch was very proud of the lights he added to the railing of the deck that wrapped around the upper level of the house. As evening approached, they both got ready for the party, complete with matching sports jackets and chinos. Because, as Malcolm liked to say, You can never go wrong with a smart blazer.

While Malcolm patted his various pockets to ensure he had his wallet, he checked with Patch. "Got everything?"

"Should I have anything? I'll bring my tablet, of course."

"I guess not. You're sure he specifically told you not to bring a party gift? Not even a bottle of wine or anything?"

"'Bring yourself only. We'll have everything we will need.' There it is. Straight from Gino's text," Patch read off.

"Okay. It just feels wrong. But it would be even more wrong to offend our host during our first greeting. Alright, let's go."

Patch and Malcolm took the stairs down to the basement level, then to the garage, and Malcolm motioned to the SUV. "Just in case we hit ice."

They clamored into the SUV.

"Open the garage, street side," Malcolm said, securing his seat belt and adjusting mirrors while the street-side garage door opened.

The garage door led to a short tunnel that led to the main street from the house. Malcolm turned onto the street, and they were on their way.

"Are you sure this is the place?" Malcolm asked, peering through the window at a series of large, dark concrete buildings.

"Yeah, this is the right address. Nineteen Pigeon Point," Patch said, scrolling around on his tablet to see if the driving instructions were wrong.

"This party will be even more of a riot than I imagined, then," Malcolm said.

"Oh wait! Gino gave special directions. Sorry. He says the place is behind the big gray building and that we should park on the side of the road and not in the company's employee parking," Patch relayed.

"Ah! Got it." Malcolm pulled forward and around to the side of the long, concrete, industrial-looking building. As they came around to the other side of the building, they spotted the place they were looking for.

A set of six steps led up to a brick three-story building that was squeezed between two imposing concrete structures that towered twice as high on either side. The brick building looked as if it were being devoured. They approached the steps that were lit up warmly by the glow of fresh garlands interwoven with gold-colored lights. Malcolm knocked on the wooden door painted a cheery red with a wreath hung over a window that gave off fresh scents of pine and was lit up with yet more lights. They could hear the excited buzz from outside the door, but when the door opened, the joyous chaos bled so far outside it nearly knocked Patch and Malcolm down the steps. Still, seeing such warmth and smelling such intriguing fragrances invited them in.

"Welcome, my friends!" Gino said with his arms outstretched to give immediate hugs to Patch and Malcolm and to pull them inside the openhearted scene. Patch and Malcolm were led into a sea of children running around their waists and men and women ready to take their coats and offering them plates of a dozen different finger foods, all while being nudged forward down the main entryway.

As Patch was led down the hall, to his right, he saw a kitchen so packed full of bustling people preparing dishes and food platters that he was amazed any cooking could be done. The aromas coming out of that room were almost overwhelming. Then, to his left, he saw a sitting room with a fire blazing brightly below a mantle where a myriad of Christmas stockings with various names stitched in them hung. Curiously, the French door into that room was shut, and although the other parts of the home were bursting at the seams with people, no one was in that room.

Patch wasn't able to contemplate the reasons for that room being empty, though, because he continued to be gently nudged forward and around an archway where easily a hundred picture frames of various shapes and sizes were jumbled on the surrounding walls, including well above his head.

At last, they were led into a large, open room where a long series of multiple tables were connected by six different tablecloths that didn't match but fit exactly right in Patch's estimation. Off on the right-hand side, kids were congregating on smaller chairs. Some wore brightly colored paper hats, temptations for the other kids to swat at. Though the room was surely the largest in the house and the couches and armchairs had been pushed aside to make a large central area, the space was still brimful of bright and excited faces. Patch had forgotten how many people had kissed his cheeks or hugged or danced him in a twirl on his journey from the entryway to the room.

Patch and Malcolm were led to the head of the table, opposite the side where the kids batted at each other's hats. Patch caught snippets of conversation all around him.

"He's a champion runner!"

"Yes, at Harvard Academy—"

"He's so handsome!"

"So is his gentleman friend."

Malcolm was drawing nearly as much attention from the older matronly women as Patch was from the many teenage girls—all of whom seemed to give particularly enthusiastic cheek kisses.

"My friends, my friends, please, sit." Gino pulled out two chairs right at the head of the table.

"Oh, we couldn't take the seats of honor, Mr. Pappas—" Malcolm said, gesturing to their host. The kid's side of the table erupted into peals of laughter.

"Mr. Pappas! Yes, Mr. Pappas, here, take my seat, Mr. Pappas." The kids chortled.

"Shush, you," Gino shouted in the direction of the kids' table. "My apologies. My grandchildren call me Papa, so they must be amused by you calling me Mr. Pappas. Please, Gino to friends, especially new, great friends like you, Malcolm. Sit, sit!"

Gino urged Patch and Malcolm to sit and patted both men's shoulders once they were seated. "Dear family, join the table. Come, come!"

The dozens of people slowly merged around the table and amazingly found enough seats. When everyone else was seated, Gino stood by Patch and put a hand on his shoulder, raising his other hand for the people in the room to quiet down. The buzz hushed to a low murmur.

"Dear family, these are my friends, Patch and Malcolm. They are honoring us by attending our special meal."

The room burst into cheers.

Gino raised his hand again.

"Yes, yes! We are so grateful you have come to be with us. Patch is one of my best customers, but he is my favorite customer, for certain."

More cheers and raised glasses pointed toward Patch.

"Dear family, let's welcome our new friends tonight and enjoy the love of family together on this very holy and special day," Gino said.

At the word holy, the room instantly developed a more reverent quality, though Patch could still distinctly hear kids kicking table legs on the far side of the room.

"Let us honor our cohost," Gino rushed to the other side of Malcolm and sweetly helped his wife to her feet. "My dear wife, your mother— Mama Iris, and a much better cook than I will ever be."

The cheer this time was the biggest yet. But Patch caught a bit of the words Gino said in his wife's ear.

"My dear Iris, look at what we've made . . ."

Patch turned his head and tried to focus on the general uproar of cheer, feeling certain he was overhearing something for only Gino and Iris to enjoy, though he was sure he would remember that very moment for the rest of his life.

Gino raised his hands once again, and the people surrounding the table started to bow their heads. Patch and Malcolm followed the crowd's example. Gino bowed his head as well.

"Blessed is God, who has mercy upon us and nourishes us with His bountiful gifts by His grace and love always, now and forever, and to the ages of ages. Amen."

There was a chorus of amens around the room.

"And we thank our new friends Patch and Malcolm for the honor they bring to our table this special night. Amen."

Another hearty chorus of amens echoed around the room.

"Now, dear family, enjoy our Christmas Eve feast!"

Patch had a hard time piecing together all that happened after that. So many new flavors and smells and conversations washed over him for the next couple of hours. The food came around in a caravan, with Gino dictating the pace and direction, which meant all the dishes came to Patch and Malcolm first. That also meant that Patch couldn't refuse to load up on every single one of the dishes as they circled past by the dozens.

"Here, you must try my lamb! Very tender. Practically falls off the bone," Gino said excitedly, placing large slices on Patch's plate. "And, of course, your favorite—falafel! But don't forget the spanakopita—spinach pie. It's my mama's old recipe. One of the few things we saved when she started to lose her memory." Gino gestured toward a contented-looking older woman.

Patch picked up right away that she and Gino were related. The same pattern of wrinkles and facial expressions was playing on Gino's face, too, but this woman's wrinkles were much more pronounced. They seemed chiseled into her worn face. But energy resonated out of her smile, just like Gino's. And Patch was drawn to the woman's beautiful wrinkles and the stories they told, just as he had been drawn to Gino's. The similar life of hard work and joy drew him to her instantly.

Patch honestly didn't know that food could come in so many new flavors. Malcolm was a master cook by anyone's estimation, but it was like Patch was being introduced to the concept of eating again, kind of like the first breakfast Malcolm had prepared for him after spending the night outside in his courtyard. There is so much to learn, Patch thought, being both overwhelmed and thrilled by that prospect.

At last, new food trays stopped coming to the head of the table, and over the course of the next hour, Patch had one of the best times of his life. He dug into new dishes, and his plate gradually started to reemerge from underneath heaps of savory meats, potatoes, and crispy pastries— all loaded with meats and creams and spiced vegetables. And with every bite Patch took, Gino's smile grew wider.

No one seemed offended at all if Patch had a load of food tucked in his cheek when responding to the multiple conversations he got pulled into while eating. There was the ongoing one with Gino, but eventually, Gino focused more attention on what Malcolm shared about ways to increase profitability for his food-cart.

"You have a wonderful product. Have you ever considered franchising?" Patch caught Malcolm saying to Gino.

Malcolm was absolutely in his element, taking everything in stride. He wove back and forth between talking to Gino on his one side and Gino's wife on his other, never losing conversation threads and knowing exactly the right response to generate a pleased and excited look or laugh from everyone. Maybe I'll get there someday, Patch thought admiringly and so glad that Malcolm had agreed to the evening.

Just as Patch was polishing off some savory sauce—that was too good to let go uneaten—with a scrap of crusty bread he had saved for just that purpose, the family members seemed to get an unspoken signal from Gino to pass the dishes down the table to where they were collected on three food trolleys. Once the main-dish trays were cleared off the table, Gino disappeared from the room with two grandchildren trailing behind him, but moments later, he came back pushing three new trollies overburdened with new trays.

"Here are the desserts!" Gino cheered, and the room burst out into huzzahs and whistles and raised glasses. Like before, Patch was the start of the caravan for the food as it was passed around.

"Here, my friend! You must taste my melomakarona. Tell me if the syrup and crushed walnuts don't just send you over the moon, yes!"

Patch prepared himself for a sugar overload, but was pleased to discover—since he wasn't a big fan of overly sweet things—that the desserts balanced the sweet with savory in a remarkable way. Even cakes and cookies had dates and raisins rather than flat-out sugar as sweeteners. Sweetbreads with imprints of bees and flowers somehow baked into their rise were glazed and golden to perfection. And, last of all, a heaping tray of something cut into wrapped, bite-sized squares.

"Saving for the last, the baklava!"

Gino dished up three squares for Patch, who was about to bite into the delicate lattice of dozens of layers of pastry, but caught himself as he saw the family members holding their pieces of baklava and waiting patiently while the tray moved around the table. When the tray had made the rounds, Patch realized Gino's wife was moving around the table in the opposite direction, placing a small china cup full of fragrant coffee in front of each person. This took some time, but as Iris placed each cup with a nod or sometimes with a placed hand on top of a shoulder or a hand, the chaotic buzz in the room hushed to an excited whisper. When Iris came to Patch and Malcolm, the last in the long train, she placed a cup in front of Patch and then took Patch's face in her hand and brought her forehead up against his. She held that pose for only a moment, but it was long enough for Patch to feel a flood of warmth and kindness and goodness wash over him. He felt a tickle at the top of his head that ran down his spine and thrilled him as if he had been struck by an electric current.

Iris returned to her seat but stood with Gino, and together, they raised their squares of baklava high. Everyone in the room raised theirs, too.

"To our dear family," Gino cried out.

"Family!" the whole group said in union, and then everyone bit into their baklava.

Patch did the same and discovered a new favorite food. The honey brought subtle sweetness, while the walnuts added a nutty crunch, and even the texture stimulated his taste buds as he bit through the layers. Though he had gone through two large plates of food already, he was very glad Gino had spoiled him with three squares of baklava and not just one.

Before Patch could eat the other two, however, everyone in the room picked up their cups and gently raised them high.

"To those who have passed but are still a part of us," Gino said in a more solemn tone.

"Still a part of us," the family replied in a chorus of reverent voices.

As Patch scanned the room, he saw that even the youngest children quietly drank their milk with solemn faces that clearly reflected the sacredness of the moment.

Patch sipped his cup of coffee and thought about the only person he knew who had passed. His mother. As he reflected on what she had done as a Total System Donor some of the anger and frustration that normally accompanied the thought shifted to a new place. Longing was what he felt in those silent moments, stirred up by the clear and present connection to family that he saw all around him. What traditions might I have made with my mom if she were still alive? The aching feeling in his chest welled, threatening to overwhelm him, but the sound of dozens of chairs being pushed back at once snapped him out of the mess of feelings.

Malcolm looked over to Patch, and they stared at each other, trying to determine what was happening.

"Come, come, my friends! We'll go to the parlor while the rest of the family gets ready," Gino said, directing Patch and Malcolm back the way they had come—Patch barely having enough time to grab his extra pieces of baklava which he placed as gently as he could in his blazer front pocket—and into the sitting room.

"Get ready for what?" Malcolm asked as he and Patch were nudged toward two armchairs close to the fire.

"For the Christmas Eve service. Yes. Very special night. Please wait here. I'll get some more coffee and will be right back." Gino left, shutting the French doors behind him. The quiet and darkened room was striking in contrast to the experience Patch had been absorbed into through the joyful ruckus of the meal. The room they were in, he realized, was reserved for very special occasions or guests. He took advantage of the few moments alone with Malcolm.

"So. That was something else, wasn't it?" Patch said, leaning toward Malcolm.

Malcolm laughed a full-throated laugh that made Patch chuckle, too.

"You could say that. What an amazing family. What a gift to be here. Thank you, Patch."

"Thank Gino. I just accepted the invitation. He did all the rest," Patch said.

"Oh, don't worry. I'll be thanking him for a long time, and I think we might become business partners, too. Great guy. But I wouldn't be here if you hadn't suggested it. And this was a really good thing."

Patch waited for Malcolm to explain, but Malcolm's thoughtful look into the fire told him not to pry. Gino returned with a tray bearing three large, steaming cups of coffee.

"We adults need that added boost to make it to midnight," Gino said, offering a cup to both Malcolm and Patch. Gino pulled up an extra chair from the corner of the room and sat between the two armchairs.

"Your family is absolutely spectacular, Gino. What a gift it's been to be here with you and participate in your wonderful traditions," Malcolm said, with Patch nodding in hearty agreement.

Gino shook his head and placed both hands on his chest. "No, my friends, you truly have honored me so much tonight. I cannot even tell you how much."

"Well, if honoring requires this much amazing food and company, sign me up," Malcolm said brightly, taking a long drink of coffee.

"You're friend here, Patch. He's a clever one," Gino said with a chuckle. "Enjoy the fire while I help grandchildren get ready. Give us ten minutes, and we'll be ready to go."

Gino dashed out of the room before Patch or Malcolm could say anything.

"You didn't say anything about attending church too," Malcolm whispered, revealing a bit of nervousness.

"Neither did Gino. I mean, I knew they went to a service, but he talked about inviting me to dinner, not church."

"I don't think we have a graceful exit plan. What do you want to do?"

"I don't know. What would you suggest, Mal?"

"I can't think of a good way of declining at this point."

"Maybe it won't be too bad. I bet there's some nice music. You like that, right?" Patch asked hopefully.

Malcolm nodded slowly.

233

The ten minutes came and went too quickly, and neither Patch nor Malcolm had come up with an exit plan.

"We are ready. The church is around the corner." Gino handed Malcolm and Patch the coats and gloves they were wearing when they first entered the now very familiar home, and they were bustled out the door, down the stairs, and around the street corner before they had a chance to discuss anything else.

They shared a resigned shrug.

The cathedral was at the end of the street. It stood a few stories tall and was made up of beige stone punctuated with rosy, highlighted buttresses. Malcolm and Patch moved along with the glowing faces of Gino's family. That brightness, Patch thought, came because of their anticipation for the service, or at the very least because of the chill in the air.

Two solid-wood doors stood wide open, letting out the light and letting a hint of incense, pine, and organ music waft from inside the large, brightly lit nave. Gino's family filed into three aisles to the front. From his raised pulpit, an older man in a flowing white robe nodded and smiled in recognition of the family he clearly knew well.

The church service was a bit of a blur for Patch. All that good food was making him drowsy, too, which didn't help him follow the proceedings, either. But eventually, he got the feeling that things were wrapping up. He had kept an eye on Malcolm, glancing over periodically throughout the service. The way Malcolm had been unsure about going to the services when he was generally sure about everything he did made Patch nervous.

Several people in dark suits and broad smiles brought around baskets full of small white candles. Patch looked up when he grabbed his candle and passed along the basket to one of Gino's granddaughters sitting next to him, who received the basket as if it was a very important duty for her to hold it properly. Other than Gino's family, there were a few scattered people occupying a couple of other pews. Inside the large room, the sparse attendance was even more pronounced.

Patch remembered reading about the challenges the transition from government-run countries to a true meritocracy posed for religions. Or maybe the lack of attendance in the church that was clearly built to hold many more people was a side effect of changes in the neighborhood. Patch didn't know, but as he lit his candle from the person's next to him and let Gino's granddaughter light her candle from his, he imagined how magical it would feel to have the church filled with hundreds of lit candles instead of the lopsided mass of light all coming from Gino's family. But he still felt something magical, holding his candle among the dozens of others around him.

All of Patch's attention was taken in an instant as a young girl's voice filled the room with haunting strains of *Silent Night*. The voice echoed from every direction, but Patch turned forward to find a solitary girl in a white choir robe, cradling a candle with both hands. He heard a stir further down the pew, and he turned to see Malcolm shifting in his seat, his eyes glistening in the bright candlelight around him.

A guitar picked up, accompanying the girl for the second and third verses. It took Patch until the start of the third verse to realize that Gino was playing the guitar. As the first round of the song ended, the priest stood and raised his hands, and Gino's family and the few other congregants stood.

Gino's family members weren't shy about singing. Patch picked up on that from the first line of the song. Most of the voices that he heard singing out brightly in the night weren't well-trained or beautiful in their technical ability, but they were beautiful in every way that mattered. Halfway through the second verse, the granddaughter grabbed Patch's hand and started swinging their arms excitedly, flashing smiles in his direction at every pause in the song. Her voice had a sweetness and a sincerity to it that Patch had to admire and that, in some ways, he envied.

At the end of the song, the priest stood up and added a few simple words, recognizing that the song was a powerful enough conclusion to the night's service.

"Turn and wish your neighbors a Merry Christmas," the priest said.

Before Patch could do anything, Gino's young granddaughter wrapped her arms around his waist and pushed her cheek against his coat.

"Merry Christmas. It's really here! I'm Madelyn, by the way."

Patch reached down and hugged Madelyn warmly.

"Thank you, Madelyn. Merry Christmas to you too! You sing so beautifully."

All of a sudden, Madelyn got shy and leaned back into a woman who was smiling approvingly at Patch and who he assumed was Madelyn's mom. He smiled back and whispered, "She's adorable," hoping that Madelyn wouldn't hear and have to be twice as embarrassed, though she did poke her head from behind her mom's coat and wave her fingers at Patch.

So many other Christmas greetings and hugs and more kisses on cheeks and cheers for the holiday were shared all around Patch. Gradually, Gino's family headed toward the door. Once outside, Patch buttoned his long, wool coat against the chill. The beginning of a snowstorm drifted from the sky, sending thousands of sparkles in every direction, which refracted against the lights. Patch felt an arm on his shoulder.

"Gino, I had no idea you could play like that!" Patch said, putting out his hand to shake Gino's.

"Like how? Like an old man with clumsy fingers?" Gino asked with a wry smile.

"No. Like a brilliant old master. Beautiful. Just beautiful!" Patch knew Gino was pleased, though he remained the absolute picture of humility.

"It makes me so happy to hear that. The service isn't as big or traditional as it used to be, but it's still so good to be a small part of it. I cannot begin to tell you how much your presence this night has meant to me and my family, my friend," Gino said, giving Patch's shoulder a squeeze.

"Seriously? This has been one of the best nights of my life. I'll remember it forever." Patch turned to face Gino and gave him a hug.

"Merry Christmas, Patch."

"Merry Christmas, Gino. Thanks for everything."

Patch saw Malcolm pulling himself out of the crowd.

"We'd better head out so we can beat most of this snow," Malcolm said, shaking Gino's hand. "This night . . . Well, this night has been amazing, Gino. Thank you for everything."

"You two are most welcome in my home any day, but especially this day, my friends."

Gino pulled Patch and Malcolm in for one more hug, and Patch and Malcolm waved to the family, who waved and shouted their goodbyes.

They found the car completely covered in a sheen of fresh white snow.

When they got within a few feet of the car, it started automatically.

It was an uncharacteristically quiet ride, which meant Malcolm had something on his mind, but when they were pulling into the garage, Malcolm still hadn't said a word.

"So, did you have fun tonight?" Patch asked, hopefully, while climbing the stairs to the living room.

"Very much. Sorry, Patch. Don't mean to be like this. I'll blame it on Christmas," Malcolm said with a tired chuckle.

"I thought you said you can't ruin Christmas?" Patch said, starting to feel sick to his stomach. Had he disappointed Malcolm, and on Christmas, no less? Patch's fears crept in.

"Oh, you can't ruin it. But it can sure kick you in the rear sometimes and make you remember some things . . . things best left alone."

Patch eyed Malcolm warily as they both plopped down on the couches by the lit Christmas tree. Simple, soft piano music played, filling the room, set to match Malcolm's mood as determined by his health-monitor ring. Malcolm took in a deep breath and let it out quickly, and like that, he shifted the energy in the room.

"Did you see all that food? I don't know how you packed that in. I had to use every ounce of my considerable diplomacy to pass on some of it just so I wouldn't explode in front of all those crazy kids!"

"I know! It was insane. I don't think I'll be able to eat for a week. There goes all that training."

"You can focus on training later. Let me get some coffee. Probably not wise at one a.m., eh? Maybe some herbal tea? Peppermint good?" Malcolm said, heading to the cupboard and pointing back at Patch.

"Sounds great. So, you had a good time? Really?" Patch asked, moving to one of the barstools in the kitchen.

"Absolutely, I did! Memorable. Such amazing people, and that food was to die for. I'm going to make a killing as Gino's business partner. He'll be able to buy the entire block and convert those concrete buildings into Pappa's Compound or something."

"Remember when you called Gino Mr. Pappas?" Patch grinned.

"Yeah, don't remind me. Not one of my more polished intros." Malcolm brought a tray with two mugs emitting nice aromas back to the sitting area and placed it on the coffee table. Both sat back down on the couch, silently stirring their tea and letting it steep, then they took in their first few sips. Malcolm raised his mug.

"To Christmas—the old and the new," he said.

"To Christmas," Patch repeated, clinking his mug against Malcolm's, and both took long sips.

"I'm glad you had some fun tonight. I was trying hard to think of anything I could give you, and let's face it, now that I've given you my old beat-up shoes, nothing else can really compare."

"Hey, don't mock that trophy you made last year. It's one of my favorite things," Malcolm said, giving Patch a friendly shove.

"I know," Patch said, grinning at Malcolm, who also knew how true what he'd just said really was.

"So I thought since you love Christmas so much, maybe you'd find some kindred spirits at Gino's place since I found out how much the holiday meant to him, too," Patch said, still hoping to gauge Malcolm's assessment of their wild evening.

"Tonight was the best gift. Well, second best after beat-up old sneakers. After those, this is absolutely the second-best thing. So here you go, you've given me the two best things in the world," Malcolm said, smiling above his mug.

"I was trying to be serious here—" Patch started to say, but Malcolm jumped in.

"I mean it. I've got to correct one thing, though. Your running shoes have to go to second place, and this night with Gino is third, I'm afraid. Having you here is the best thing. My favorite thing."

"Thanks, Mal. I wouldn't want to be anywhere else."

As if on cue, both took sips of tea as the moment got a bit more tender than either of them could manage for long. "I'm sorry to throw that church service at you," Patch said. "You were a great sport, but I could tell you would have preferred cutting out after dinner. If we could have."

"I wouldn't say that," Malcolm said thoughtfully.

"Come on, you were squirming practically the whole service."

"Can't an old man squirm a bit with his indigestion?"

Patch arched his eyebrows and waited for a serious answer from Malcolm.

"Okay. It was my indigestion, which is completely understandable after shoveling in so much spicy food, mind you, AND I guess it's been a long time since I've gone to any church service, too. They kind of get to you, don't they?"

"Yeah. That last song with the girl and Gino playing the guitar—that definitely got to me. I saw that hit you pretty hard, too."

"Like I said, Christmas can kick us in the rear sometimes. So many high expectations get baked into this darn holiday that you end up making lasting memories. For better or for worse." Malcolm cleared his throat and quickly stood up, collecting the two mugs on the tray and setting the tray in the sink.

"I'd better hit the hay before I drop right here," Patch said, standing and giving Malcolm a hug on his way to his bedroom.

"Merry Christmas, Mal," Patch said at the entrance to the hall leading to his bedroom.

"Merry Christmas, Patch. Thanks for the perfect evening. What a gift. You hit it out of the park."

Patch smiled and turned into the dark hall, but he looked back just before closing the door to his room. Malcolm stood leaning heavily against the counter of the kitchen island, his head down, rocking and shaking slightly. Not knowing what else to do, Patch sent a silent well-wish to Malcolm with all the intensity he could and closed the door behind him.

chapter 23

Gwen wouldn't have believed, when she first came back to D.C., that their plans would work out half as well as they were. She was by no means a superstitious person, but as one thing after another fell into place, she kept waiting for the loose thread that would somehow unravel all of their efforts to remain undiscovered.

Having Gerty there helped a lot in the confidence department, though. Gerty had no such fears. She also didn't harbor false hopes. Over the past several weeks, Gwen had gotten a real sense of the mechanics of Gerty's brilliant leadership. It was a great learning system. She would observe Gerty and then practice what she liked and modify what she liked less while working with her own crew. Gwen could hardly believe how quickly she was picking things up, too.

After the kiss in the courtyard, Alex had convinced his crew—with some coaxing from Gwen—to follow her to Kansas for Gerty's implementation of Jefferson's plan. Gwen still smiled every time she thought back to when she had returned to Gerty and reported that Alex's crew was on board and Alex would be coming by the next day to learn more about the crew's role and needs.

The look on Gerty's face. Priceless! Gwen thought, thoroughly pleased with herself. And Gerty's first response—"I don't think you quite grasped the concept of pacing yourself on this one"—was even more priceless. And then there was Alex's first meeting with Gerty. Talk about two incredibly powerful forces colliding! At first, Gwen had to keep the two from going at each other's throats, but miraculously, things between Gerty and Alex had calmed down to what Gwen described as a simmering respect for each other's autonomy. Jefferson would like that phrase. The only thing left to do at that point was execute Jefferson's plan, which she still didn't really know how to pull off. But having accomplished so many steps leading up to the execution, even the monumental task of injecting tons of soybeans with a mutant strain of fungus without getting caught or killed in the process seemed well within the realm of possibility.

As she rode next to Gerty in the truck, the back carefully packed with backpacks loaded with thousands of modified needles for the injecting task, Gwen couldn't fight off some misgivings.

"Penny for your thoughts? Or with the look you have right now, I think it would cost me at least two bits," Gerty asked with an encouraging smile.

"Oh, just thinking about the two possible ways this plan could play out."

"Go on," Gerty nudged.

"Scenario one, our plan falls flat. The fungus doesn't work for whatever reason. Say, the soybean distributors randomly decide to improve their soybean seeds, or we don't inject them in the right way. Or, hey, maybe the fungus just doesn't like the soybeans we're offering it for whatever reason."

"I don't think fungi work quite that way, but I'm tracking. We fail miserably. Please continue." Gerty chuckled.

"And, maybe some of us, but not all of us, are able to escape back to your farm in shame and try to pick up the pieces, knowing the street-kid crews will never trust us—will never trust me—again. AND knowing that two plans have been foiled by the indestructible force of modern markets." Gwen shot up her hands and let out a resolved sigh.

"Mm-hmm. I don't really like that one. So tell me what's behind door number two."

"Scenario number two. Our plan goes off perfectly, and we infest most of the soybeans at this big distribution place we're going to, and the fungus spreads in a huge way, and it destroys a lot of the soybeans for an entire year or more. It causes food shortages worldwide. That causes mass panic, resulting in whole continents rising up against the current system."

"I'm liking this one a bit better," Gerty said, nodding.

"But . . . a lot of people are still hurt. I know the banks don't exactly have armies like old countries used to, and the Economic Wars were supposedly peaceful, mostly. But who's to say that this time things couldn't be terribly different? And there's one other thing—"

"Phew! Just one other problem with the good scenario? I think our odds are way in our favor now," Gerty pounded the steering wheel in mock triumph while Gwen gave her a dirty look.

"You joke, but I'm seriously feeling—"

"I'm not trying to make fun of your fears or anything, darlin'. It's just that worrying won't help things be one bit better. In fact, psychologists have shown that stressing actually impacts our brain's ability to learn because we go into fight-or-flight mode. So let's take one step at a time, shall we?"

"You're right, like usual," Gwen grumbled, feeling a bit better, but the volume of worries and fears was still so high that she doubted even a good amount of time spent in her tree would cure her of her anxieties completely.

"I usually am. Very true. That is a very true principle. These dried dates are another very true principle. You've got to help me eat some of these. I've got a figure to keep," Gerty said, passing a small burlap bag full of earth-toned nuggets about the size of a small egg.

Gwen reached into the bag and came away with a few sticky, dried dates. She popped one into her mouth and decided having sticky hands for a while was definitely worth it. The dates had been preserved in some kind of honey mixture that allowed them to retain their plump and fruity flavor as if they were fresh.

Gwen dug into the bag for some more and then caught herself after stuffing her face with a handful. She did her best to make a sheepish smile without having dates spill out her mouth. Gerty's pleased look soothed her embarrassment a bit, but Gwen decided to pace herself. Besides, they were nearly to their destination.

"You haven't told me the last drawback you see in our best-case scenario yet. I'm dying to hear it," Gerty said.

The reminder about perhaps her biggest fear made the dates in her mouth lose some of their sweetness.

"If there are food shortages, that'll make it that much harder for people like I used to be to survive. If you'd asked me a year and a half ago if I would ever do anything to make it harder to find food, I would have laughed at you, and then I'd probably try to steal anything useful you had on you, too."

Gerty didn't respond right away. A thing Gwen appreciated. She knew that Gerty hadn't enjoyed a necessarily easy life. She could have just played along with the market trends and probably hit it big with all the cool, new varieties of produce she cooked up. Gerty had made sacrifices. But Gwen doubted Gerty had felt the primal desperation she knew— that urgent, sickening feeling of needing food. Maybe her passion for growing food made her more capable of understanding that urgency to some degree still.

"We'll take one step at a time. Just one step," Gerty finally said as she pulled off the broken highway leading to the staging area for the next and most dangerous step of their plan.

Gerty's approach was the best, but Gwen's planning-brain was very hard to shut off or even get to shift gears, so Gwen focused on the open road in front of them as they approached their destination.

Nothing seemed to quite fit as Gwen drove across the very familiar landscape of old Kansas. Even when they pulled into Topeka and passed streets and buildings she used to know by their smell, it all seemed foreign in a startling way. She felt like she was waking from one of those vivid dreams where she wasn't certain what was real and what was a memory from the dream.

Gerty parked in front of a massive parking lot with a decrepit sign out front. Gwen could only make out the first letters—S-A-M-S—in a dusty-blue background. Something clicked in her memory, and her mind flashed back to the last time she had been at the building. Her reason for avoiding these big block buildings before. A memory of an altercation and her narrow escape. She shook the memory from her mind, reassured that, this time, she had a team.

When everybody got out of their vehicles, Gwen took stock of who she had to work with. She counted roughly thirty street kids. That would be her primary focus, but she also counted half a dozen people with their eyes glued to their tablets and who were talking energetically about the efficiency of the strain, whatever that meant. Those people had to be the scientific group. And then Gerty had brought about a dozen workers to help with day-to-day operations, like cooking and setting up the base, which Gwen assumed would be inside the huge concrete structure. And then there was Stan. Good ole Stan. She was very glad he had decided to come along, although she wasn't sure what role he was going to play. Cooking maybe?

Not a bad crowd, she decided as the whole group formed a semi-circle clump around Gerty, waiting for instructions.

"Alright," Gerty said, clapping her hands firmly over her head. "We're going to get inside, assess the space, and make sure it'll work for our base of operations while we're here in this God-forsaken land."

Even though Gwen agreed with Gerty's assessment of her old home, a slight twinge of resentment cropped up inside of her. This was her home. For better or for worse. Gwen tried to focus back on Gerty's instructions.

"I'd imagine anybody inside this monstrosity will already be fully aware that we're here and that we're more than enough of a match for any of them, so no sense in going for stealth, but keep your guard up, and use some situational awareness. There might be dark corners in there where someone could do damage if they were desperate enough. Okay?"

The group nodded.

"So, don't worry about carrying anything inside yet." Gerty said. "That way, you can have your hands free to defend yourself if need be. We will take everything inside once we know the coast is clear, so no sense in showing off those big guns in carrying full loads right now. Yeah, I'm talking to you, Cecily."

The group of street kids hooted with pleasure at having Cecily called out, and the ones closest to her gave her playful shoves.

"Got it? Any questions? No? Then let's go."

Gerty's operational group led the way inside. There were three banks of automatic sliding glass doors that had long ago lost their ability to slide on their own. Instead, the doors stood a few feet ajar, and on one side, the door Gwen used was twisted and off its track.

As they entered, sickly, orangish lights flickered on and off sporadically, probably powered by solar generators. They passed the central threshold and into the main room. Gwen could barely make out the light from the doors on the opposite side of the enormous room. Nothing could be seen clearly in the dim light, but Gwen already knew there wouldn't be anything in the room.

She might not have known all the reasons why the big box stores closed so quickly in communities like Topeka after the Economic Wars, but she was brutally aware of the fact that they were the first raided after the businesses shut down their operations and the police pulled out. The space she slowly walked past was stripped clean. No evidence of shelves could be seen. Any metal or screws or used scraps of plastic or glass had been scavenged day by day, week by week. So by now, a couple of decades later, the only things left were the hard industrial-linoleum floors, a few plastered signs on walls depicting smiling families reaching for faded fruit or toys, and caged lighting fixtures hanging fifty feet above her head.

The group scouted out the entire building and didn't run into anybody or any evidence of people hiding out, as if there was anywhere to hide in the broad, open space. Gerty divided the group into functional teams to bring in the supplies from the trucks, and Gwen was glad she and Alex's crew got assigned to the group in charge of setting up the sleeping quarters.

Gwen hadn't had a chance to talk with Alex much during the trip from D.C. She walked toward him while he directed a group of kids on how to best carry a cot so they didn't drop it or hurt themselves.

"Hey," Gwen said, sounding more excited than she meant to.

"Hey, we made it. First step down, only a couple dozen insanely far-fetched steps left to go," Alex said with a smirk.

"Hey you knew what you were getting yourself into," Gwen said, grabbing two cots, one in each hand.

"Whoa! Don't flash those guns around here, or there might be trouble," Alex said in mock alarm.

Gwen laughed. "Poor Cecily. I think Gerty's taken a particular liking to her. I don't blame her. Cecily has certainly come a long way, hasn't she?"

"I'd say we all have. I never thought I'd be back in Topeka. Doesn't it feel . . . I don't know. Wrong somehow? Like things don't fit right, or I don't fit here anymore. Or maybe both. I don't know what I'm trying to say—"

"No, I totally get what you mean!" Gwen said, thrilled to have someone who understood. "It's like we're looking at it as completely different people, so it all feels familiar but not the same."

"Exactly! Yeah, that's it! It's not like I had fond memories of growing up here. Let's see, it's 2054 now, right? The government had been gone at least ten or so years before I was even born, and most of the town was gone with it. This store looked pretty much the same as it does now, even back then. Not that me or my family came to town much. How did my mom joke about downtown Topeka? 'Full of deranged hooligans set to kill us if they got the chance.' She used it as a way to scare us into not sneaking over there. But in the last couple of years before they died, it turned into a kind of inside joke. Don't let the hooligans get you kind of thing." Alex shook his head.

"Funny. I hadn't thought about that joke for years. Being back here brings back a lot of that," he said.

"Yeah. The good and the bad," Gwen met Alex's gaze, feeling connected to him in a new way. "I don't know if it's better having practically no memories from the times with my family or having a lot of sad memories like you do. It is what it is I guess."

"They're not all sad," Alex said and followed up quickly at seeing Gwen's confused look. "I mean, they all get a sad taste, I guess, but a lot of the memories make me happy. Days spent at the lake. Even stupid nothing memories like random nights playing board games. Those are some very good memories." Alex took a deep breath and pushed the air out in an explosive breath. "I'd better start moving. The crew will think I'm making them work while I talk to a pretty girl," Alex said with a rueful smile. He picked up two cots of his own and headed toward the building's entrance.

"Wait up," Gwen said, picking up her two cots and stumbling along in an awkward half-run, half-skip to catch up with Alex.

Later that night, after everything was unloaded and set up according to Gerty's specifications, Gwen sat at a folding card table with a few kids a little younger than herself, eating dinner. Her table mates were friendly enough, but they clearly were most interested in their own conversations, which Gwen was more than happy to accommodate.

She watched them, trying not to eavesdrop or look like a lurker or anything. But seeing how normal the two girls giggling together really were, struck her. They dipped their carrot sticks and chomped down on them, grinning at the added zing of the dip, and Gwen picked up the excitement in their eyes at all the new experiences they were having together.

The responsibility of keeping these kids safe weighed Gwen's shoulders down heavier than ever. She had done all she could to ensure their safety. They had protocols. She'd made sure the kids could rattle off the plan and expectations without having to think, and their last few drills had gone really well. But seeing the kids behaving so naturally and normally made what she was asking them to do and the reason why feel wrong. Her thoughts were interrupted by someone banging on a table to get the group's attention.

"Now that we're all settled," Gerty said, "I think it's best that we jump right into work. We don't know for certain what kind of possible surveillance we might be dealing with here, if any. So the sooner we're able to get those shipments injected with my cute little fungus and get back home, the better. Let me walk you through how the next couple of days will play out."

It was good to hear the plan laid out in detail again, even though Gwen had heard it explained a number of times before. But it was complex, so she listened carefully as Gerty outlined the first things they'd work on over the next couple of days.

"First off, we need to ensure that we're right about the kind of distribution center we'll be trying to break into. What kinds of security measures it might have in place. If the center really is completely run autonomously or if there are a couple of humans around to keep track of things. We'll need to know what kind of camera systems they have set up. That's why Stan is around. Well, that and because he can make a wicked good broccoli-cheese soup. You'll all have to try it."

Stan waved bashfully, and the group around him gave him friendly punches. None of this would have ever happened without him, Gwen thought, making a mental note to reconnect with him as soon as she could.

"Stan happens to be a rather brilliant coder, so we'll be using that expertise to make us invisible. I'm not going to pretend to know how he'll do it. But against my better judgment, I really do have full confidence," Gerty nodded in appreciation toward Stan, who nodded back.

"So, assignments for tomorrow . . ."

Gerty tasked all the smaller groups to tactical teams with objectives like sizing up surveillance and getting Stan whatever he needed to foil the camera systems. Gwen was tasked to oversee the surveillance-inspection team made up of Alex's crew. The surveillance team would have to determine if it was safe to move forward with the injection of the fungus.

"Okay. We've all got our assignments. Finish up with dinner and get to bed at a decent hour. I want to get a jump on tomorrow," Gerty said definitively.

Gwen got the sense that Gerty wouldn't be too pleased with stragglers in the morning.

Gwen stared at her plate, then ate the chicken and green beans, clearing it by force of habit more than actual hunger. Her nerves were starting to twist her stomach into a progressively tighter knot. It wasn't her ability to execute her operation that worried her, not really. It was the thought of something going wrong that she had no way to prepare for. She sought comfort by reminding herself that this was Jefferson's and Gerty's plan, too, not just hers. But Jefferson's last master plan had ended so badly and had left him so broken . . . Who might get hurt this time?

Ready or not, though, this was the reason they were there. She washed her plate and set it in the rack to dry, then headed to the sleeping quarters to try to get at least a few hours of sleep before their first visit to the seed distribution facility the next day.

chapter 24

The facility they were targeting was so long and wide that even though the ceilings were easily fifty feet tall, the building looked flat as Gwen approached it from the cover of some large scraps from a broken concrete shed. This is where Gerty and the communications team would stay, and Gwen and Alex's crew would continue to the building as soon as Stan gave the green light.

"You're making me nervous, darlin'," Gerty said to Gwen, who was pacing back and forth around the concrete patch that they were sheltering behind.

"Sorry," Gwen said sheepishly. "I hate this waiting."

"Me too. But it's all a necessary part of the puzzle. Why don't you make up some sort of game for your young compadres here? They look almost as nervous as you. It'll take their minds off things," Gerty said, making a shooshing gesture.

A game. Seriously? Gwen didn't even play games herself, let alone come up with new ones for others, using nothing but bits of concrete, bare ground, and sickly bushes. She picked up a piece of concrete and idly tossed it, trying to come up with anything. It hit a wall that protruded ten feet above the rubble, and she enjoyed the satisfying knock it made. When she inspected the ding it had made on the wall, she was surprised to see a clearly defined white mark. I've got it!

She picked up the same rock and used it to draw three concentric circles on the vertical concrete slab. She stepped back and took a look. Not half bad. She duplicated the same three circles within one big circle two more times along the wall.

"He guys! I've got something I need you to practice," Gwen hollered over to the fidgeting group of kids. They got up and walked over to her.

"Target practice. You never know when a well-aimed piece of concrete might take out a guard or a surveillance drone. So this is what I need you to do. See those three targets? Make three lines in front of them. Pick a good throwing piece of concrete, like the one in my hand here, and try to hit the center of the target. When you hit the target, it'll leave a white mark so you'll know how close you got."

A couple of the kids looked skeptically at Gwen, but a few others were already picking out their throwing rocks and forming lines. Eventually, even the most reluctant kids picked out rocks after they heard the others yelling out triumphant or disappointed calls.

Within a minute or two, the whole group of thirty-some-odd kids were happily throwing rocks at her makeshift targets.

"Impressive," Gwen heard Gerty say, coming up behind her.

"Thanks. I'm not really very good with games."

"You could've fooled me. Look at those kids. I bet they've completely forgotten why they're here."

"And you're sure that's a good thing?" Gwen asked.

"It's bad for adults to lose focus before they have to remember complicated steps, maybe. But with kids"—Gerty paused and watched as a kid nailed the bullseye and jumped with a thrilled whoop—"it's different. Nerves don't help kids do any better. And any bit of joy we can bring to the world is never wasted." Gerty patted Gwen's arm.

Then, the radio crackled into life.

"Hello, can you hear me?" Stan's voice came through the static, but barely.

"We hear you, Stan. What's your status?" Gerty asked, leaning close to the radio.

"You told me I'd be working computers, not old-school radios. Radios are much harder," Stan said, coming through a bit clearer as the communications team adjusted some knobs on the radio system in one of the vans.

"Your status?" a member of the communications team again asked in a no-nonsense way.

"So serious. Yeah, my status. I'm all set. Just let me know when you're ready for me to flip the switch, and you'll be blind to their cameras."

"You really just flip a switch?" Gwen wondered out loud.

"Hey, Gwen. Be safe out there, okay? And no. There aren't switches. A lot of jumbled lines of code. If only my parents could see me now. They always said that messing around with computers would rot my brain. But flipping a switch is a bit more understandable to most folks," Stan said through the radio.

"They'd be so proud," Gwen said jokingly, not sure how well sarcasm could be picked up over the radio so she added a, "You've got this, Stan."

"Everything is set, so go ahead and flip the switch when you're ready, Stan," Gerty confirmed. "Oh, and Stan?"

"Yes, sir. I mean, Gerty?" Stan corrected himself quickly.

"If you pull this off, all is forgiven."

"Well, I guess I can't let you down for my own sake as much as yours now," Stan said.

Gwen could clearly imagine the way Stan looked as he said each of the things he shared over the radio. And that warm, comforting feeling that rose in her chest, which she now recognized as familiarity and friendship, welled up inside her.

"You are clear," Stan sounded.

"Thanks, Stan. We'll be radio silent during the operation, so we'll see you on the other side," Gerty said.

Alex was right behind Gwen, awaiting orders. She took a deep breath and stepped up to the group.

"Okay, you all know your assignments. Blue Team will follow Alex around the left side of the building. Red team will be with me, and we'll head in the opposite direction, meeting up on the backside. Remember, nobody actually enters the building until we've assessed it as a whole group. Not even if you see a good opening. Is that clear?"

The crew nodded.

"Good luck. See you-all on the other side of the building."

Alex quickly clasped Gwen's hand before they separated, then smiled and let go before running to catch up with his group. Gwen's red team congregated around her.

"Let's head out," she shouted, pointing in the direction of the colossal seed distribution building.

Gwen led her group of fifteen kids on a fast jog toward the right corner of the building. Distances were deceptive because of the lack of landmarks, so it took longer to reach the building than she had expected. She flattened herself against the wall, and the kids behind her mirrored her stance. She peered around the corner. Nothing. She waved cautiously behind her and turned around to start heading toward the short side of the building, which was still at least a mile long.

As she progressed along the wall, she kept her eyes open for surveillance devices, security checkpoints, or possible entrances. She came across a long row of bay doors about a quarter of the way along the wall that she assumed were used for loading autonomous trucks. Up until then, she hadn't come across any cameras, although they might have been embedded in the walls. She sent a quick thought to Stan. I told him he could do this, so believe it! She said to herself as she approached one of the huge metal bay doors.

There is no way we're prying these bay doors open, and even if we tried, we're bound to set off alarms, she determined. But she decided it might be a possible exit point if they opened it from the inside. She followed the dozens of bay doors, one after another, until finally, maybe three-quarters of the way along the wall, she started seeing more normal-sized doors built for humans rather than trucks. It all made perfect sense, given the way Gwen assumed the operations at the facility worked. The whole system was supposed to run without people's involvement, so the facility obviously wouldn't cater to human needs. She tucked the thought away to see if there were any concerns attached to that line of reasoning. For now, though, she needed to focus on determining if there were any feasible ways inside.

She gestured for her red team to huddle up around her. She pointed at the door and started running her hands along the frame and then pointed to the three other doors that were the same as the one she stood next to. She thought it best to keep quiet until they knew more about the facility so she mimed the action of opening the door and shook her head and crossed her arms to reinforce the fact that this visit was only to gather information. Not to go inside.

The kids on Gwen's team formed three smaller groups to inspect the other doors. Gwen scanned the door in front of her. It seemed to be a standard door with two locking mechanisms, including a deadbolt. Gwen could figure out how to pick those locks, but she didn't know the extent of Stan's computer control over the facility. If all he was doing was projecting a false image for the surveillance cameras, then she was certain they would trip an alarm the instant they opened a door.

She collected her team members and finished inspecting the short side of the building. No other doors, entrances, or other access points were found. She flattened herself against the concrete wall like she had before and peered around the corner of the longer side of the building. Her heart sank.

Alex was sprinting directly toward her with a few members from Blue Team. She did some quick assessments. Would it be better for her to stay put and not blow whatever cover she might have, or should she race to meet up with Alex? If their cover was blown, then her team's cover was, too, so no reason to hide anymore.

Gwen dashed to make up the hundred-yard distance between her corner position and where Alex was desperately running to connect.

"One of the kids accidentally opened one of the doors on the other side! No alarms sounded, but I'm afraid we might've tripped one anyway. We've got to go. Now!" Alex shouted to Gwen, taking her hand to hurry her in the direction of their safe zone.

Gwen shook off Alex's hand and tightened her jaw, biting her tongue so hard that she could taste blood. She made some halting steps to follow Alex, but her mounting fear was about to spill over. She leaned against the concrete wall of the facility and tried to slow her breathing and her heart, which was pumping in overdrive. Breathing became the only other thing she could focus on because her mind was racing through so many horrible outcomes—flashes of her failure causing her crew and the operation to fail in so many horrifying ways.

"Come on, Gwen! We need to go now!"

Gwen heard Alex yelling in front of her. She saw him shaking her shoulders as if he were far away and not right in her face, dragging her up on her dizzy, shaky legs. She didn't remember sinking to the ground or why. Her eyes darted around her, wildly searching for her crew.

"Where's my crew?" she kept repeating in sheer terror and desperation.

"They're fine. They're back at base. Where we need to go. Come on, Gwen!" Alex draped one of Gwen's arms around his shoulder so he could help lead her back to where Gerty was waiting.

It took at least thirty seconds for Alex to recover enough to speak after the strain of sprinting back and forth from base and supporting a lot of Gwen's weight, but as soon as Gerty understood the situation, every group was loaded up and on the road in less than a minute. Tension weighed everyone down like a heavy cloud hovering over them as they headed back to the warehouse to assess what they had learned and what they should do next.

chapter 25

"Cecily didn't mean to open the door. She was checking to see if the door was locked. That's a very logical thing to do when you're inspecting a door, right?" Alex said, pulling Gwen aside and into a storage room tucked away from where the group was congregating.

"Yeah, but there are ways of doing that that don't require turning the knob all the way," Gwen hissed, trying not to be overheard.

"How was she supposed to know the door would open after barely turning the knob?" Alex asked defensively.

"She couldn't. That's why she shouldn't have tried it in the first place," Gwen replied, keeping an eye on the growing group congregating around Gerty. "We've got to go—"

"Anybody could have made that mistake. Don't hold it against Cecily, okay?" Alex said, looking directly into Gwen's eyes with a serious look.

"I don't hold it against her. I hold it against you," Gwen shot back, and she ducked out.

Looking back at the whole thing, with a few hours of space and time to reflect, she knew she'd been harsher than she'd needed to be. She could blame it on nerves that were running in overdrive during that tense ride back, but she still eyed Alex to gauge his mood as she took her place near the back of the crowd waiting for Gerty to start the after-action review she had called for as soon as they got back.

As Gerty walked up to the center of the group, Gwen noticed a new kind of urgency in Gerty's voice and actions that she hadn't noticed before. Her normal Southern charm was gone, replaced with a terse directness.

Gwen was glad that the group had more important things to be concerned about than her breakdown at the facility.

When the whole group was gathered, Stan and Gerty stepped to the front.

"We appear to have lucked out," Stan said.

An audible chorus of relieved sighs murmured through the group. A bit of the weight Gwen had been holding in her shoulders dropped a little.

"I've been monitoring the facility's systems for any signs of change since the time Alex said the door was opened. That doesn't mean that no alarms were tripped when it opened, but from what I can see from their front-end or back-end operational system, your cover wasn't blown."

"That being the case, there're a lot of lessons we need to learn from this close call," Gerty said.

Don't I know it, Gwen thought. She tried to let the same relief that she saw on the faces around her wash over her, too, but the fact was, they had made a major mistake that could have undermined the entire operation. If the crews can't pull off simple reconnaissance missions, how could they ever hope to pull off the more complicated seed-injection operation?

Gwen tried to pay more attention as Gerty led an open discussion for everyone to share ideas and lessons learned. Gwen was pleased that no one was singled out, especially because she knew who had accidentally opened the door. She couldn't be mad at Cecily. That's why her anger and fear were building around Alex instead. She almost raised her hand to share her thoughts on poor leadership decisions but dropped her hand just before Gerty called on her. Gerty gave Gwen a questioning look, but she shook her head. It wasn't worth it. And with that decision, a lot of the remaining tension she was holding lifted.

Later that night, while she reviewed the day, she reflected back on the brief but heated exchange she had had with Alex just before the group discussion after they had returned from their near-miss at the facility.

She still hadn't apologized to Alex. In fact, she had made a point of avoiding him the rest of the day. She didn't know why, but she couldn't face him yet.

It's more complicated than that, too, she thought. One slip like this could have meant the end of everything they had been working for. That one mistake could have led to the entire group being caught by contract enforcers. Or worse. She thought about the horrifying story Jefferson had told her about his experience with the contract enforcers. Jefferson. With all the things on her mind, and with being back in her old hometown and everything that had stirred up inside of her, she hadn't had space to reach out to him.

Gwen left the sleeping quarters and hunted for an available tablet in the storage room. She found a charged one and nestled herself into a locker her skinny frame could just fit inside, then pulled some backpacks around her legs so she could be certain no one walking past the room would see her. She put in the earbuds that were magnetically connected to the tablet and opened a communications channel, hoping Jefferson would pick up, still unsure what she would say or what she hoped to hear him say, but calling felt right to her somehow.

Jefferson's familiar bushy, gray hair and striking blue eyes popped on screen. Gwen turned on the private-conversation mode that would block the sound of her voice as well as any bleed from the earbuds from being picked up.

"Hey, Gwen, how are you?" Jefferson asked with concern written on his face and furrowed bushy eyebrows.

"I hardly even know how to answer that question," Gwen said with more intensity than she wanted, but the anxiety from the day's events was building back up and threatened to spill out.

"You've had a lot to deal with. Not just the near-miss today, which was absolutely not your fault"—Jefferson gave Gwen a serious look that was hard for Gwen to read but that made her feel like her concerns weren't stupid or invalid but, at the same time, were unwarranted.

Gwen nodded.

—"but you're also back in your old hometown where you were nearly killed, at least one time that I know of for certain. You've kindly never told me how often those run-ins were for you," Jefferson said, cutting right to the center of the knot inside the swirling messiness of her feelings.

"You don't do chitchat, do you?" Gwen said with a tired smile.

"Not with people I care about. That time's too precious. So what's it like being back in Topeka?"

"Wait a second. That's all I'm going to get about what happened today? Gerty told you, right?"

"She did."

"And it doesn't bother you at all that one mistake from one person might have messed up your whole plan?" Gwen asked with rising volume and agitation.

"Of course it bothers me."

"Well then, why aren't you angry or frustrated or anxious or whatever? I feel like I'm about to explode here. One simple mistake, Jeff. That's all it could have taken, and I would have let everyone down," she blurted out.

Gwen stopped cold. Jefferson didn't fill the silence, letting the full weight of what she'd said sink in for her.

"The job you're doing for our operation isn't easy, is it?" Jefferson finally asked.

Gwen shook her head, wiping at the tears that had welled in the rims of her eyes. She let out a frustrated huff.

"It's so frustrating. After what happened at the facility today, I just got so . . . you know . . . so—"

"Scared?" Jefferson offered.

"It could have turned out so differently. We could have all been caught. I know anybody could have made the mistake that Cecily made, but Jeff, that one mistake could have ended everything. I don't know if I can go back to that facility and risk things again."

Gwen paused, looking away from the tablet for a moment and wiping her sleeve across her nose. "How on earth are you still functioning after what the contract enforcers ran you through? You were there for months, right? I'd be a total mess," Gwen blurted out in a single breath.

"Who says I'm not a mess?" Jefferson asked quietly.

"You just have a way of moving forward. Being okay. Making things okay for all of us, too. How do you do that after what you've gone through?"

"Depends on the day. I guess I focus on the now and try to remember what's real and good and what's important."

Jefferson's mentioning of what was real perked Gwen's interest. She had been so alarmed at how shaken Jefferson had been on the first day he was back that she hadn't dared to ask before . . . and then, with everything that happened after—the farm, hatching their plan—but she needed to ask now.

"You told me about one of your sessions with the contract enforcers. What were you doing for the rest of the time you were there? I mean, you were gone for over two months."

"They did the same thing every day," Jefferson said with a distant voice.

"You mean you relived the same day. With your wife agreeing to go to Ohio and you becoming a teacher and everything?"

"No. Each time, I jumped back to where I'd left off. I have no idea how the simulator works because every time they wrenched me back into reality, different amounts of time had passed in the simulated life I was living."

"You mean, you lived longer than a day or an evening?" Gwen asked, afraid to hear what Jefferson would say next.

"No, Gwen. Years. I watched my kids grow up. I taught whole school years. I took my family on vacations and had the time to laugh about those memories with my family months later. All in a single session. Decades of living packed into a couple of months' worth of those sessions."

Gwen was stunned. She didn't have the space in her mind or the emotional capacity to comprehend such torture. But other questions percolated in a flood, and she shuddered at the thought of experiencing that herself, or even worse, someone like Gerty experiencing them. What would the contract enforcers do if Jefferson was caught again? She sensed that Jefferson was having a hard time keeping things together on the call. So she decided she had only one more question. And she had to ask it.

"How do you know this is real?"

"I guess I don't," Jefferson answered flatly. "But I don't think that matters. My job right now is to do my best to make things as good as I can in whatever reality I find myself in."

Gwen sensed that what Jefferson had said had profound depth, but after the stress of the day, she was too tired to parse out all the meaning of what he'd shared. But talking to Jefferson had helped her. The alarm that drove her fear subsided to a small, biting annoyance.

"You really are a remarkable person, Jeff."

"Thanks, Gwen. You're rather exceptional yourself. Now get some sleep, and call any time, okay?"

Gwen nodded. "Goodnight, Jeff." She closed out the tablet and stuck the earbuds back in place, then tucked the device away in the storage area and headed back to bed. She was exhausted after all the day's anxiety and fear, but before she dropped off, she reflected again on the day. Her mood and feelings had been all over the place all day long. But at that point, she just felt tired with a slight nagging of fear—just enough to remind her it was there. That'll have to be good enough for now.

Over the next several days, the group learned a lot of very valuable information about the facility they would infest with Gerty's mutant fungus. Stan continued to monitor for any change in operations that could show signs that the facility operators or their computer systems were aware of the opened door. He also broadened his blanket cover for the teams visiting the facility so that he could control doors and interior camera systems. Once Stan had that accomplished, the teams were finally able to explore the inside of the massive building.

And Gwen tried some new coping strategies so she wouldn't lose it completely if something didn't work out quite right. She focused even harder on ensuring the street-kid crews were better prepared. She patched things up with Alex—for the most part—and even made a point of taking a walk around the block before she blew up at anyone and at lunch most days. She felt like she was better prepared for the next step in their operations. Most of the way.

Gwen remembered the first time she entered the facility. It was strange to be in a building specifically designed without human interaction in mind. None of the things she had grown to expect in a warehouse fit. No break rooms for workers. No restrooms. No hallways. No safety measures, either, so no guardrails or safety catches. All the sophisticated gears and belts and whirring machinery were wide open and exposed. No lights hung overhead from the tall ceilings, either. Thankfully, the group had prepared for that with night-vision systems for the teams.

Gwen didn't know where they had gotten the night-vision glasses she was wearing, but she got used to seeing in total darkness as if it were the middle of a cloudy summer day. The glasses used a different light spectrum and then converted the hues from that spectrum into her regular, visible spectrum. But from time to time, when they'd been knocked off her face once or twice and she was left in total darkness, she was reminded that she couldn't take the glasses entirely for granted.

As the group started inspecting the space, she was stunned by the scale and scope of the operation. Over the days of inspecting the operation, she found that there was an enormous collection tank, several hundred yards in diameter, in the center of the room. The soybeans would fall through the ceiling, let in by some sort of trapdoor mechanism. The door would swing open when new shipments of soybeans were brought in by train. Aerial drone footage confirmed that a large tube extended up a wall and along the roof to where the soybeans were dumped into the central collection tub.

Hundreds of what she got used to calling arteries ran from that central tub. The arteries ran from there to where the grain was measured for precise packaging. The whole system reminded her of the diagrams she'd seen in Jefferson's books about the human cardiovascular system. Except Gwen would never want to meet the kind of creature that required that many main arteries.

From the main arteries, soybeans were sent along a web of conveyor belts, with multiple belts running under and above each other. Based on some set of instructions, soybeans were then packaged into bags using exact weight specifications, and then wrapped and packaged into some kind of flexible cardboard that made it so more packages could be squeezed into trucks.

Gwen hadn't seen that kind of cardboard around the streets of Topeka, but when she had the chance to inspect it a bit closer, she was amazed to discover how lightweight and durable it was. At least it easily withstood her knife's edge when she tried to cut a piece off.

The whole operation reminded her of some weird dance. Gwen had reminded her crew—and had Alex remind his—to stand clear of the bay doors that opened when a shipment was ready for pickup by one of the hundreds of trucks she'd seen come and go. The packages were sucked into the backs of the trucks. The force that was used to pick up the containers of soybeans, some of which had to weigh several hundred pounds, was more than enough to suck up several team members. She shuddered at the thought of the fate of anybody caught in those airtight shipping containers.

That was how the operation worked. The whole system and the design were impressive, as much as Gwen hated to admit it. When she could look past the millions of jobs it replaced and the towns that were deserted because it existed, the symmetry and grace of the whole facility, which functioned almost like a mechanical organism, was beautiful.

One thing became perfectly clear to the whole infiltration operation—the best place to introduce the fungus was the vast collection tub in the center of the facility. The problem was—how would they be able to inject enough soybeans without drowning in a torrential downpour of more beans from the drop hatch above or stop themselves from being swept away down one of the hundreds of arterial conveyor belts?

The backpacks Gerty's operation team had devised to inject the soybeans came complete with blower tubes to introduce the fungus. The backpack blower tubes would speed up the process of getting the fungus out there, but even with every team member using one of the packs at maximum levels, Gwen estimated it would still take the two teams nearly an hour to cover all the soybeans in the collector.

After a lot of debate and analysis, operations settled on the only feasible plan that would get the job done and give the crews a chance to escape without being sucked into the system's conveyor belts or buried by soybeans from above.

Magnetically pulled trains loaded with soybeans arrived at the facility six times a day. The soybeans were sucked up the main pipe and fed over the roof to the drop hatch in the center of the facility.

After consulting with Jefferson, Gerty agreed that the whole system activated when a train shipment arrived. But there were periods of time between those shipments. The facility must have been built with extra capacity so it could be scaled up or down as needed. That meant there was generally up to two hours where the whole facility stood in eerie silence, waiting for the next shipment.

"That's when we need to pounce. We know that the longest waiting period is after the noontime shipment. The next shipment arrives at roughly fifteen thirty hours," Gerty explained to the group.

"Fifteen thirty hours means three thirty P.M.," Gwen whispered to a puzzled kid named Graham, who was sitting next to her.

"And we'd better plan on jumping tomorrow. We're running out of time," Gerty said, ending the discussion cold.

Gwen didn't quite understand the urgency. Stan still hadn't seen any irregularities in the computer systems running the operations at the facility. But she welcomed the thought of returning to the farm, so she kept her misgivings about the need for better information to herself.

Springtime was approaching, and even in the crumbling city, nature's way of celebrating the new growth and potential that the longer, warmer days promised was showing up in abundance. Wildflowers sprouted in cheery clumps from cracks in the parking lot's asphalt outside their operations. Some mornings, she woke to the sounds of birds jabbering away in the stunted trees outside. She could only imagine how amazing things would be at the farm in the springtime.

The night before they planned to finally deliver the fungus to the facility, Gwen committed to going to bed early, though that was a failed idea from the start. She couldn't keep from replaying all the worst-case scenarios. What happened if they were found out? Stan hadn't seen any changes, but maybe their luck would run out. Or what if they'd miscalculated the depth of the soybeans in the tub and they all suffocated in the world's biggest silo? Or what if they got their timing wrong?

Her tossing and turning must have been noticeable because she heard Gerty quietly calling her name from her cot. Gwen sat up, and in the pale, predawn light that filtered from the windows high above, she saw Gerty sitting on a folding chair with her bed neatly made.

She must not have been able to sleep either, Gwen thought, trying to not make too much noise while she got off her cot and headed toward Gerty, who patted her bed, inviting Gwen to sit next to her.

"I figure you've been curious why I feel like we can't wait. I know we might be able to firm up our plans a bit if we observe the facility for a few more weeks."

Gwen opened her mouth to talk, but Gerty quickly raised her hand, and Gwen shut her mouth again.

"Sorry, just let me get this out. I know you're going to think it's silly, but there's something going on that we haven't figured out yet. I don't know what it is. I remember reading a book in grad school about how our brains break up tasks into two main systems. One we're aware of and we have more control over. The conscious neocortex side of things, I think it's called. The other runs without our conscious awareness. That system actually does most of our thinking for us."

"That's where we get those gut feelings from, then?" Gwen asked with piqued interest.

"Yes!" Gerty whispered loudly. "It's not a very sophisticated system, though. It can't tell me what's wrong or how to avoid danger. It just tells me to run or get ready to fight. We have no chance of fighting here, so our option is to run. But we're not running until we finish what we've come to do. So that means, we need to go tomorrow, even if we don't have complete, perfect information. Come to think of it, we'll never have perfect information, anyway. So if we want to make an impact here, we need to move forward with the best information we can get and rely on courage to make up the rest. Our good friend Jefferson needed a lot of convincing to trust me on that. I think he's been feeling uneasy about how long we've been here, too."

With the thought of Jefferson, Gwen nodded, an aching feeling thrumming within. It wasn't only that she missed him. She missed that first summer at Jefferson's home. It had felt so . . . What? Normal? Safe? She hadn't been aware of how much she longed to go back. To finish all the operations and fade back to quiet days of good homemade meals, books, and conversations.

But what Gerty had said rang loud and clear in her mind, too. She needed to finish what she had started first.

chapter 26

Gwen awoke to bustling activity already buzzing around their operation. Most of the street kids were waking up, too, and Gwen could see their faces slowly remembering where they were and why they were waking up there instead of their home at the market building in D.C. She glanced at one particularly young-looking boy rubbing the sleepies out of his eyes and stretching his arms, exposing his puny, little stomach. The boy was just a kid. In other circumstances, he might have been waking up in a warm bed with nothing more to worry about than what he would eat for breakfast and if his best friend would be at school to play with at recess that day.

The boy caught Gwen's gaze and waved his fingers at her. She tried to wave back in the same way and shared a grin. She could tell he was excited and wished she could share that feeling. She rubbed her neck to work out some knots that were tightening up as the day progressed.

Gwen forced some food down, knowing she'd need the fuel even though she was even less hungry than she had been the night before. She swallowed down an apple and a protein bar and was about to head to the supply area to make sure all of the kids had packed the right equipment. But she stopped when she heard a familiar voice.

"You're not going to save the world with nothing more than an apple and a measly protein bar in your system."

Gwen turned around.

"Come on. I'll make you an omelet, cooked to order Four Seasons–style," Stan said, turning and starting to walk away from Gwen with a backward wave for her to follow him, which she did.

"Stan, I'm not really hungry," she tried to explain.

"Of course you're not. You're worried to death. I get it. You always worry whenever you're responsible for people," Stan said as he and Gwen reached the kitchen. Stan turned on the burner, causing a flash of blue flame, and drizzled oil in a pan, then swirled it around, coating the center of the pan completely. One by one, Stan cracked three eggs with a single hand and whisked them into a bright-yellow mixture that he swirled around the pan the same way he had the oil.

"I'm really that easy to read?" Gwen asked, pulling up a stool to sit by Stan while he cooked.

"No. I'm just super observant," Stan said, testing the firmness of the edges of the egg circle in the pan with a spatula. "That's what makes cooking so fascinating, actually. Attention to detail is everything."

Stan sprinkled some shredded cheese, mushrooms, and sliced peppers on top of the eggs and shook the pan across the flame, making orange flares of flame jump around the edges of the pan. "I don't think that actually does anything, but it sure looks cool," Stan said, adding seasoning with a smile.

Gwen's stomach loosened a bit as the aroma of the cooked peppers, cheese, and seasoning started to overcome her nerves.

Stan freed the edge of the egg mixture with his spatula and then, with one fluid motion, flipped one side of the mixture on top of the other, folding it neatly and tucking the edge tight.

"That's the dangerous part, right there. If the eggs haven't set enough, you have to make do with scraping the eggs together and plopping them on top. Much less pretty, but . . ." Stan paused to scrape the completed omelet from the pan and transfer it to a waiting plate, which he presented to Gwen. The savory smell wafted right under her nose.

"But even in that case, the food tastes the same. Eat up," Stan said, putting a fork in Gwen's hand.

"I see what you did there," Gwen said, fighting her new urge to shovel the food in so as to not embarrass herself in front of Stan.

"What did I do? Other than feed a hungry girl in need of a bit of nourishment?" Stan asked innocently.

"You turned cooking that omelet into a life lesson of some sort," Gwen said, enjoying the soft chewiness of the egg with the crunch of the peppers.

"Okay then. What's the lesson?" Stan asked, rubbing his hands dry with a dish towel.

"I haven't figured it out quite yet because this food is distracting me. So good, Stan. Seriously," Gwen chewed thoughtfully for a moment and swallowed. "I guess you're saying that even if things don't work out exactly as planned, they can still be good enough, and the result can be the same. Something like that?" She placed another large wedge of omelet in her mouth.

"Close enough. It's not a perfect analogy by any means. But I hope you remember that you're good. People trust and respect you here. And there's a good reason for that. You care a lot about all of us, and we all know that. When things go wrong, as they are bound to do, that's not on you. Okay?"

"Okay. Thanks, Stan. You're right about one thing."

"What's that?" Stan asked, pulling out more food to prepare for the rest of the group.

"There is no way I can save the world on just an apple and protein bar, but maybe it's possible with your omelets," Gwen said, hopping off her stool and giving Stan's shoulder a squeeze.

"I've heard they have some superpowers, that's for sure. Now go get after it," Stan said with a smile.

Gwen started heading out of the kitchen area, then remembered something. "And good luck with the coding thing. Not to add pressure or anything, but if you're not successful at that, we're all probably dead."

"Thanks so much for that. Now it's your turn to cook up some confidence builders for me."

"My cooking wouldn't bring any confidence to anybody, I'm afraid. But I know you'll pull it off."

"Thanks, Gwen. Good luck."

When they arrived at their staging area, waiting for the autonomous trucks to depart the facility, the teams of kids didn't skip a beat. They jumped right out of the vans and picked up their crumbled concrete pieces and started up their rock-throwing contest. Any ignorant passerby viewing the scene would have thought it was a school program with a new sports tournament rather than a dangerous attempt at disrupting the worldwide distribution of one of the most important crops.

The kids only had enough time to go through two rounds, though, because after running through the pre-check system so many times, the operations people had things down. The communications team reached out to Stan to verify they were in the clear.

"Righto! We should be all set now," Stan chirped, making loud keystrokes as he typed.

"Copy. Thanks, Stan. We'll reach out to you when we're on the other side of this," Gerty said, moving to shut down the communications system.

"Hold on a sec!" Stan shouted into the radio in a way that made the whole operation freeze in terror. "Gwen?"

Gwen leaned closer to the radio, having a million fears of what might have gone wrong with their surveillance cover. "Yeah, Stan?"

"Remember the allegory of the omelet."

Gwen smiled at the confused looks everybody gave Gwen.

"I couldn't forget, even if I wanted to. My tastebuds are still giving me high fives."

"Glad to hear it. One good-enough step at a time," Stan said, and then the communications tech shut down the radio. When the radio shut off, Gwen had a few panicked seconds where she felt like there were a few more words of encouragement to hear or a few more jabs to share with Stan. But she settled her mind on the task at hand.

The two teams formed up and prepared to enter from the short sides of the building. They would meet in the middle of the central collection tub. Gwen helped adjust the straps on the team members' backpacks and glanced over at the blue team. Alex was doing the same with subtle, gentle interactions with his crew, which raised smiles and laughs.

Gwen was smiling and staring at Alex before she was aware that he was looking right back at her. He walked over to her and leaned his head toward her ear so he could whisper. "I know we hit some rough patches these last couple of weeks. Let's get this done and then see if we can patch things up when we get back. Deal?" Alex asked, extending his arm like he was preparing to arm wrestle.

Gwen firmly gripped his hand. "Deal. Let's do this!"

Alex nodded once and then turned to his team.

"Red team, let's move out!" she called.

The two crews moved with practiced precision. Alex's crew disappeared from around the corner of the opposite side of the facility as Gwen's reached the start of their short side of the building.

"Just like we've practiced nearly a hundred times before," she encouraged her crew as they approached their entrance. Gwen cracked the door and waited a couple of seconds to ensure no alarms went off. Hearing none, she opened the door wide and waited for the full crew to enter the building before she shut it behind her.

Gwen flipped on her night-vision system, and the familiar space materialized. She followed the crew underneath dozens of conveyor belts and other machinery that was, gratefully, still and quiet for the moment. So far so good, she thought, coming to the vital part of their whole operation, which was also the only part of the plan that they hadn't been able to practice in the actual collector.

Gwen's crew fanned out so that each member stood by an artery that opened into the central collection tub, leaving a vacant artery on either side of them. That way, their one crew could cover at least thirty of the openings, and that led to a more evenly-spread distribution of the fungus.

"Turn on your packs and make sure they're set to max," Gwen repeated as she moved past the arterial openings. She received only determined nods or thumbs up from her crew, so she checked her own pack and ensured the straps were secure in case she'd have to move quickly. Gwen stepped up to an available path to the main tub and leaned forward so she could see the faces of her crew. Then she waited.

She caught movement a moment or two later from across the huge tub of soybeans. Gwen could barely make out the faces of Alex's crew forming up the same way that hers had. When all seemed settled and ready, Gwen pulled a laser pointer from her jacket pocket. She was to flash it on and off once if the operation was aborted; twice, to stand by; or three times if the operation was a go. She aimed the laser pointer's beam so that a red laser that everyone could see hovered at the center of the tub of soybeans. She flipped it on and off. Once. Twice. Three times.

The red and blue teams climbed through the openings they were standing in front of, crawled onto the conveyor belts' ends, and took their first steps into the massive central tub. Although the crews hadn't been able to do any practice runs in the actual tank, they had plenty of practice back at the operation headquarters. They'd even made it into a bit of a game to see who could successfully empty their packs' contents the fastest.

But this wasn't a practice run. This was the main event. The whole reason she had been living at Gerty's farm for the last several months. The reason she had come back to Kansas with all the messed-up jumble of memories and stress. The reason why the crew was risking everything, making their way toward the center of the tub full of billions of small beige soybeans to inject with Gerty's fungus. Gwen brushed her hand along the hose that extended out from her backpack ready to disperse the cartridges of fungus. She took a few deep breaths, hearing the energy coursing inside her chest and radiating through her arms and legs. She was ready. The crews were ready. She made her first confident steps toward the center of the collector with a sense of calm.

Walking on top of a layer of soybeans felt strange, like walking on thousands of small pebbles. It almost felt like walking on the banks of the Potomac when she had been stationed at Jefferson's old headquarters in D.C. The similarity brought a smile to her face and helped tamp down some of the fear making her hands shake.

Both crews met in the middle of the tub and then turned their backs to each other so they could fan out evenly and make a larger distribution circle.

Gwen took a long breath. This is it! she thought as she pointed the hose that ran from her pack to the soybeans a few feet in front of her.

"We've got this, friends. Inject those soybeans! Go!" she shouted and both crews jumped to action.

For the next several minutes, the only sound in the vast facility was the plunking of triggers as hundreds of cartridges full of fungus-rich fluid were shot into the ready soybeans.

Gwen was thrilled by their progress at first. But then it dawned on her that things would inevitably slow. As they started to get more sparsely dispersed, and as they moved toward the artery openings they had started from, each crew member would have to cover more surface area as their circle expanded with every step they took. And the tub was so much bigger than it had seemed when surveying it from the outside edges now that she was actually walking in it.

As she got within a hundred yards of her artery's opening, her pack ran low on supply. That wasn't a problem, though. She had distributed the cartridges according to Gerty's specifications. Her pack had functioned perfectly, without even a single jam of the feeder. Just a minute more, and she'd be ready to dash for the exit.

But then she heard a low rumble followed by a few far-off creaking noises from above. She looked up frantically to the ceiling to see the drop hatch slowly open.

Gwen searched for Alex, hoping he was close enough for a quick huddle. He was on the opposite side, far away from her. Several hundred yards.

Not worth it. No time! she decided quickly. But what was the right next action?

She checked her supply gauge again. She had five percent left to disperse. If she continued as planned, the entire group would follow her lead.

Gwen jumped into high gear, dispersing cartridges in rapid fire, focusing less on an even spread of distribution and more on emptying her pack. She thought about Stan's advice—even if it isn't pretty, it still tastes the same. She just had to get it done.

At last, her pack registered empty. Gwen scanned the tub, trying to determine her crew's status. She felt a rush of relief when she saw her crew had followed her lead perfectly and were just finishing with their own packs. But before she could call for her crew to make for the exits, soybeans started falling.

Gwen wasn't prepared at all for how the soybeans released. Instantly, thousands of pounds of soybeans fell every second, viciously pelting the crew and making their footing even more challenging as they staggered under the onslaught.

"Red team, get out now!" Gwen managed to yell without gagging.

The torrent of soybeans brought in a thick cloud of dust and debris that almost made breathing impossible. Gwen heard sounds of choking and convulsive retching as the group stumbled their way toward the arterial openings.

Gwen darted from side to side, putting a shoulder around one crew member until she was certain they would keep pushing forward and then scrambling to the other side to do the same for another crew member— all the while struggling to keep her equilibrium and sense of direction as the soybeans kept falling.

Within minutes, Gwen was trudging through knee-deep waves of soybeans. She only had another minute, if that, to ensure all of her crew members were accounted for and had reached their respective exits before she would have to make a mad dash herself. She brushed her nerves aside, focusing on what she needed to do in that moment.

She helped one more crew member who had fallen and was struggling to free himself from his pack while being hit full in the face by a machine-gun fire of soybeans. Gwen unbuckled the kid's pack, dug it from underneath him and a couple of feet of soybeans, and pried the pack off him. She pulled him up, and they trudged a few yards together until she was certain he could keep going on his own. That was the last of her crew members. She braced herself for the last sprint to the exit, but she glanced one more time over her shoulder.

Two figures were halfway submerged in the flood of soybeans, their features made fuzzy by the soybean dust hanging in the air. Gwen's sophisticated night-vision glasses were fogging in the soybean haze, making it harder to see. She didn't have any time to think. She turned and made her way toward the two people who were frantically trying to free their legs from the rising levels in the menacing tub.

Her heart sank when she reached them. The soybean levels were rising so quickly that even when she used her body to bail them out, more beans filled the pockets she had opened.

She found an arm in the suffocating cloud of dust and pulled on it as hard as she could. Gwen was shattered by the shrill scream that followed. It was Cecily. And the person beside her, being buried alive more by the second, was Alex.

Gwen let out an inhuman, visceral scream that sent a last breath of desperate energy coursing through her body. She pulled Cecily by her shoulder. Miraculously, she made some headway. Gwen freed one of Cecily's legs, which Cecily used to kick at the soybeans, trying to find her footing.

At last, Gwen freed Cecily's other leg, and the two of them came to a bent-over, standing position. Only then did Gwen catch sight of Cecily's face. It was a face pasted with utter terror. Gwen knew that look. She had worn that look herself. Cecily couldn't walk alone—not a single step.

Gwen took a quick look back at Alex; he had no way of making it without help. No other crew members were left in the tub. If she didn't help him, he would die. Of that, she was absolutely certain. Her tired brain and burning lungs told her she couldn't reason it out. She had to go with her gut.

Gwen bent over and pulled Alex's face toward her so she could look directly into his eyes. "I'm so sorry, Alex!" she screamed against the high-pitched wail of the drenching torrent of soybeans.

"It's okay. Go! Please get Cecily out. Go! Now!"

Gwen wrapped her free arm around Alex's shoulder and gave him a fierce hug, and with one more look, she scrambled to her feet and started wading her way to the exit, Cecily in tow.

Gwen fought the desperate desire to help Alex, to look back at him. One step at a time. Just one step at a time—her legs shaking and burning, tearful eyes blocked by soybean dust.

She saw the exit in front of her, a few yards away, but somehow those dozen feet stretched into miles. She'd make one step forward and then lose half a step with the constant falling soybeans. Several crew members stood at the exit Gwen was shooting for, reaching their arms out as far as they could, their arms being nailed by hard soybean pellets.

Gwen reached out her free arm. Only a couple more feet to go. Now her outstretched fingers were within inches of the crew members straining to reach further without falling into the sea of soybeans themselves.

As she reached the tips of the fingers that would pull them to safety, the flood of soybeans stopped. The eerie silence that followed left Gwen's ears ringing. It took a few seconds for her to realize what had happened, where she was, and what she had to do.

She thrust Cecily's arm around the nearest crew member and dashed toward Alex, making her way on top of the waist-high level of soybeans that she still crashed into a few times—unsteady on her feet. When she got to where she had last seen him, all Gwen found was a limp hand and a few tufts of Alex's dark-brown curls.

Gwen dove into the soybeans, wedging herself against where Alex's body had to be, trying to gain leverage. Her heart thudded once with hope. It was easier to dig now that the rain of soybeans had stopped. She got an arm free and pulled Alex's mostly submerged face to the surface. Then she got a leg free and pried the other out too.

When she had Alex lying flat on the top layer of soybeans, she frantically pressed her ear next to his mouth and stared at his still chest. Nothing. She flew to his chest, hoping to sense any rise or fall. Nothing. She pushed her fist into his chest in furious visceral compressions with a dry, desperate howl.

"You can't die!" Gwen said, willing her arms to keep pushing downward. "I'm not done being mad at you!" Her heart wrenched, and her chest burned.

Gwen's arms were giving out. She screamed with her full body convulsing into violent sobs. She hardly registered when a crew member pulled her away from Alex so others could continue with the chest compressions. Having nothing left, she collapsed.

Gwen's energy was completely spent. She didn't even have enough steam to protest as she was carried to the artery opening where she stumbled onto the solid concrete ground. Crew members huddled around her. One attempted to wipe the caked-on soybean dust from her face. Others gathered around her, prepared to carry her out of the facility.

Then Gwen had a flash of coherence and craned her neck behind her as she was taken toward the door they had come through less than an hour before. Several people were carrying a still figure out of a nearby artery. Alex.

Then everything went dark.

When Gwen came to, she was back in their operation headquarters, lying on a cot with a fleece blanket draped over her. Something was on her face. When she brushed at her cheek, she felt some kind of lotion masque. It was cooling and soothing to her raw skin. Then she froze as she remembered where she had been last.

She sat up quickly. Too quickly. The blood rushed from her head, and the world spun around her for several moments. When she could bear to open her eyes without retching, she saw someone sleeping on the cot beside hers. Slowly, the realization sank in.

It was Alex, his chest rising and falling in frail but normal intervals. She braced herself on her cot, about ready to jump from it to Alex, but her dizziness got the better of her, and she eased back onto her pillow.

He's alive! He's alive . . .

That thought filled Gwen's mind with complete relief and sheer elation but then another thought crept in.

How did we get out? And why did the soybeans stop?

chapter 27

Patch's spring term cruised along in a blur of juggling track meets, classes, and time with Kourtney and Will. He fell back into a regular rhythm. And before he even had time to lift his head to survey how things stood and where he was headed, spring break had come and gone, and he was buckling down to finish the semester as strong as he could.

Patch had decided to stay at school for the week of spring break, although he did meet up with Malcolm a few times. Kourtney, on the other hand, had a very different way of spending her break and was thrilled to tell Patch all about it when she got back.

"Oh my God! You won't believe what happened on our trip!" Kourtney yelled excitedly one morning during the first week back from spring break. They were taking a lazy walk between classes.

"I'm sure you're right about that. I probably won't believe it. What did happen?"

"You remember Patrick, the great captain my family keeps on to run our yacht?"

"Of course. What a cool guy."

"Totally. Love him to death. Somehow, he led us in the wrong direction, and we ended up at a totally different beach than the one we were supposed to go to. It had absolutely nowhere to stay. Well, I mean, they had those unbearable tourist-trap resorts but no real accommodations. We had to spend the whole week aboard the ship. Can you believe that?"

Patch didn't know quite what to say or how to respond. The obvious, socially appropriate response was something like, Oh my goodness!

What a pain! But, somehow, Patch couldn't formulate those words in his mouth. They kept getting crowded out by his honest response about how most people would be thrilled to have an ocean voyage at all, let alone one on a huge yacht for a week-long adventure. Since he couldn't really offer the socially appropriate response or the honest one, he just nodded.

"Didn't you hear me? I just told you that my whole spring break was ruined. Daddy was so angry, he fired the captain right then and there."

Patch remembered meeting the captain with Kourtney a couple of times. The captain's life wasn't all that bad. He probably took Kourtney's family on one or two trips a year, and the rest of the time, the captain lived his dream life aboard the ship. But the thought of the captain being fired made something snap for Patch.

"Your Dad fired him?" Patch asked, appalled.

"Daddy yelled at him that he paid him year-round to take us on a couple of trips a year and that he had totally botched the directions. I eventually cooled things down with Daddy and insisted he hire him back. Which he did, of course."

Patch fought his disgust at the thought of firing someone with such a unique job. He tried to stay curious. "Were the directions clear?"

"What do you mean by that?"

"What I mean is, I'd imagine that sailing is quite a bit tougher than driving a car with a GPS unit that tells you where to go and what turns to make, right?"

"Yeah, I'm sure that's true," Kourtney admitted.

"How far off did Patrick get from where you wanted to land?" Patch dug further.

"Daddy said something about the wrong beach. I don't know exactly how far off Patrick really was," Kourtney said.

Patch pulled out his tablet.

"Where were you supposed to spend the week?" Patch asked, handing Kourtney his tablet with a GPS app pulled up.

"We own a small island in Barbados," Kourtney said as if that was the most common thing in the world to say, like declaring her dog was brown or that her favorite food was pizza. Kourtney swiped around on the tablet until she found the specific island. "Ah ha! Here it is," she announced, pleased with herself.

Patch zoomed in on the spot and started exploring the various buildings from a simulated street-view mode. "Nice place," Patch shrugged, trying to not sound as eager as he really was to check it out.

"Oh, it's not too special, but we love it. It has most of the things we love. Daddy really loves fishing out there with Carlos?"

"Who's Carlos?"

"He's Daddy's fishing guide and pilot, of course."

"And pilot?" Patch asked incredulously.

"Of course! You don't expect Daddy to have to swim to where the big fish are, do you? The coral reefs make it impossible for even our yacht, which uses low-water features to navigate, to reach very many docks on the beach."

Patch had a million new questions but knew how quickly Kourtney got bored with this kind of rapid-fire, question-and-answer conversation.

"How many docks could Patrick have gone to?"

"We always go to that one. I've only ever seen it," Kourtney answered idly, starting to show her lack of interest. But her focus jumped back. "And get this! A hurricane was headed straight for us, too! Can you believe that? I guess the trip was cursed from the start."

"That must've been the reason, then."

"The reason for what?"

"For why Patrick went somewhere else. A hurricane was headed toward your island, so he took you somewhere else."

Kourtney looked at Patch blankly.

"Because hurricanes are dangerous, and it wouldn't be very fun to spend a week in torrential rain even if you survived the journey there." Patch coaxed Kourtney along the logical line of reasoning.

Finally, something clicked for her.

"I'm so glad I insisted on Patrick being hired back now. You're so smart, Patch."

"Me too. How did you pull that off, anyway? I've only met your dad a couple of times, but he strikes me as someone who's not easily persuaded, especially convincing him he's wrong."

"Daddy isn't that hard to convince if you know the right way to go about it," Kourtney said and then grinned. "And if you happen to be me . . ." Kourtney giggled.

"It must be a family thing," Patch said, chalking it up to yet another thing he had no real experience with, given the fact that he hardly remembered any family at all.

"Yeah, I bet Daddy would give me basically anything and everything if I asked sweetly," Kourtney said.

Kourtney's last statement was meant to be a throwaway, but it stuck with Patch for some reason.

"Got to run to dance class," Kourtney said, throwing her arms over Patch's shoulders and jumping up to give him a loud smack on the lips. "Bye!"

"Hold on a second, Kourtney," Patch instantly hesitated. Am I ready to tell her? She seems more real this year . . . maybe?

Kourtney stopped in her tracks and made a graceful spin. More than anything, he needed someone else to know what had happened to his mom. Yes, Kourtney has certainly changed this year. Or maybe it was that he was able to see her in new ways. Or both. Patch had such a pent-up need to get it out. . . . He started kicking at the pavement. "Kourtney, you know that my mom was a Total System Donation, right? She was a TSD?" he blurted out.

One of the things Patch truly loved about Kourtney was that, so unlike him, she had a way of expressing her thoughts and feelings using her whole person. She somehow danced and moved with a thought, so when she talked about art, she painted with her arms and mimed an exuberant painter moving around an imagined canvas. Or when she described a great dinner, in her mind, she jumped into the space of the restaurant and acted out the scene as much as she used words. It was amazing to watch, and it really did take him to the places and experiences Kourtney was having.

But when Patch looked at her right after he'd made that bombshell statement, for possibly the first time he remembered, Kourtney stood completely still, arms heavy and limp at her sides, her mouth slightly open. And Patch thought he caught a slight quiver to her lips that had so excitedly just kissed his. After what felt like a very long time, Kourtney came back to herself like one of those street performers who stood stock still until someone dropped a coin, and then they worked their way through their routine.

Kourtney shuffled back to Patch and drew very close to him, standing directly under his downturned face. She had a searching gaze that pierced Patch's sad eyes. She pulled herself up on her tiptoes, tugging gently on Patch's coat collar with one hand while slowly placing her energized fingers on his cheek. Kourtney kept her eyes laser-focused on his.

"Your Mom was a TSD?"

He had to admit that, a year ago, he would have used that term to describe other people like his mom with no more added meaning than any other technical abbreviation or acronym. He had used the term dozens of times in his economic history report last year. But hearing it then, from Kourtney, recognizing that his own mother fit into that category, he saw how sterile sounding an acronym could be and how inadequately it could represent a decision that thousands of others had made out of desperation. Flippantly talking about TSDs was inhuman. Patch got a strong urge to run. But he didn't because Kourtney hadn't asked flippantly. She had asked with her whole body as earnestly as he had seen anybody ask anyone anything.

"Yes, she was." Patch let up on the kicking of the sidewalk.

Kourtney dropped her hands and wrapped her arms around Patch's waist, resting her cheek on his chest. No words. Patch realized that a sincere hug was the only real response Kourtney could give. Such an inhuman acronym deserved a fully human response. Anything less was simply cold sympathy. So she gave Patch the best human response—a genuine, warm hug.

Kourtney pulled out of the embrace and guided Patch's head down to her eye level by grabbing at both sides of his collar.

"We are going to have a ponderous conversation about this tonight, okay? Count on that. For now . . ." Kourtney put her hand back on his cheek in exactly the same way she had moments before, as if she were transforming defined hand expressions for certain inexpressible thoughts and feelings into an expressive dance routine.

"Deal. Thanks, Kourtney. Really, this . . . well, it helped. You're amazing," Patch said straightening up with a sincere smile.

"Don't I know it? Tonight then!" She struck a pose with her hands across her chest, her face the absolute visage of sincerity—eyes mostly closed, neck craned on a slight angle—and with that, she was off.

Somehow, discussing financial markets felt a bit much for Patch to deal with after that emotionally charged moment with Kourtney. So he did something he had never done before. He skipped class and headed to Chuck Mason's house, where he hoped to find someone who might understand the feelings that were threatening to explode out of him.

Before Patch knew what he would say, he found himself standing on Chuck's front porch. Catching Chuck at home that time of the day or year, given all the trimming and mowing Patch was certain spring required at Harvard Academy, was a long shot, but Patch knocked on the door and rang the doorbell in two quick impulsive motions, and then he stood awkwardly scuffing his shoes against the wooden stoop.

The doorknob soon turned in its creaky door settings, and Chuck's gruff face appeared behind the screen door.

"It's you again. Where's your perky sidekick?"

"How have you survived so long here?" Patch blurted out.

Chuck eyed him, then said, "I think you'd better come in and have a cup of tea." He left the door open and turned back into the darkness of his front room.

Patch followed and shut the door behind him. He picked up on things in Chuck's house that he had totally missed before. Photos of Chuck with an arm over the shoulder of a person Patch assumed had been a professor. Chuck surrounded by grinning athletes. Chuck with a young girl and boy on a porch that looked a lot like the one he had been standing on a moment before—but with much newer wood and a bright coat of white paint. The photos with the young girl and boy had been polished recently, like a few he remembered from his first visit with Will.

Chuck pulled a chair away from the table and pulled another one up for himself. He then rummaged in his cupboards, pulling out tea and honey and filling a kettle. Only when the kettle was filled and on the stove's flame did Chuck acknowledge Patch was sitting at the table with his right leg bouncing furiously. He sat down and studied Patch's nervous face.

"So why don't you tell me what's going on?"

"I didn't know where else to go."

"There are millions of other places to go. I guess the better thing to figure out is where you don't want to be right now?"

"At this school, right now, I guess."

"Every kid goes through that. They can't wait to join the real world and be done with school, only to realize how tough the real world really is."

"That's not what I mean at all. Water's boiling," Patch said, hearing the high-pitched whistle of the kettle.

With a dishcloth, Chuck took the kettle off the heat and brought it to the table, pouring steaming cups for himself and Patch. Patch took a long sip, despite the fact that the water was still scalding. Finally, he set down his cup and faced Chuck again.

"When I was here last time, you talked about things being different. Can you tell me more about that? I've read a lot about how things were economically, but how was it to live then? I know my friend was interested for his psychology class, but I'm asking for me. I'm asking because everything I see and learn about in my classes claims that our current system is built on ultimate fairness, but I don't know how to believe that."

Patch paused and took a few labored breaths. "I'm asking because my mom died because of the system."

There was confusion in the look Chuck gave Patch—a new kind of heaviness—but there was something that was activated inside Chuck's face too. Even before Chuck spoke a word, Patch sensed that Chuck understood his perspective better than Will ever would, even with the dozens of books Will had read about poverty and its impact on social psychology. There was a different depth. Patch thought back to how good Kourtney's response had felt, but she had no way of really understanding his situation. Maybe Chuck could.

"I knew there was more depth to you, Patch. I'm grateful you trust me enough to tell me about your mom. At the same time, I've got to warn you that not everybody you share these kinds of things with will know how to deal with them. Take your plucky friend, Will, was it?"

"Yeah."

"Will had some good intentions behind interviewing me. He came back a time or two after you came the first time. He's generally a good kid who cares about the people in his circle of acquaintances. But he's benefited way too much from the system to clearly pick out its flaws. You can. You can because you know what happens to the kinds of people you don't talk about in your economics classes. You don't talk about them as people. I guess you talk about them as ideas, though. People like your mom."

Patch nodded. He took a sip of tea, although the flavor of the tea was lost to him since he had burned his tongue with that first sip.

"I've been working at this school for fifty years," Chuck said. "I'm the last employee of this school who remembers what life was like before the Economic Wars and before governments shut down. When I started, I was young with a wife and two kids. I didn't really know what I wanted out of life, other than that I enjoyed working outside and with my hands. I didn't think I would stay here forever, but I didn't have any future plans, either. I thought I'd landed a perfect gig—housing paid for by the university. The best commute in the world. I could literally step outside my door to get to work."

Chuck's whole presence lit up like Kourtney's did when she talked about modern dance.

"Fast forward a few years. My kids were enjoying their school. I was enjoying my job. My wife was finishing up her teaching certificate, and we thought it was high time we took a vacation together."

Patch caught a shift in tone within Chuck's voice and leaned forward.

"We packed our car so full that the kids couldn't have hit each other even if they'd wanted to—pillows and sleeping bags were so tightly packed in. I still remember us pulling out of the driveway. It's the silliest things we remember. So often we struggle to remember important things. Like I can't quite remember the snatches of the songs my daughter made up to entertain herself while we were driving or the thrilled face my son made when he got a Twenty Questions question right after about fifty questions. But I remember the high beams of the headlights that blinded us as the semi mistakenly in our lane clipped our car. I remember how long it took for the car to finally stop tumbling. I remember the vacant stare in my dead wife's face, and I remember how far away my daughter's screams seemed to be."

Chuck took a sip of his tea, then held it below his nose for a long moment, smelling mint, but his eyes showed that his mind was far away.

"Schools always teach history like everything happens in sequence. Martin Luther King Jr. gave a grand speech, hundreds of thousands marched, and then the Civil Rights Act happened. Like that. Step one, step two, and then Tadah! Success. But in real life, there's usually a long time before anything changes. And lots of ups and downs between. When that accident happened, Harvard University was renegotiating its health insurance options, which ended up meaning we had no real coverage. The insurance business was in such turmoil back then. Medicaid and Medicare were gone. And corporations had basically bought the courts, and the trucking company could pay for much better lawyers than I could. So the company the driver of that semi worked for didn't have to pay for any of the damages. You get the picture. I was a low-level, unskilled employee with a useless healthcare policy. I didn't even qualify for a little assistance from Harvard. Something about not meeting the full-time equivalent or something."

Patch had to quickly run through what employee insurance was, using information he'd learned in a class the year before. Employers paid part of the costs for employees to get healthcare as a perk for working. Before the Economic Wars, insurance companies tested the limits on how little coverage they could get away with and still call it a healthcare plan. Chuck must have been caught right in the middle of that. Patch was doing the best he could to understand while Chuck leaned back with his legs crossed.

"Imagine that, me, a now-single father with a very hurt and, soon to find out, permanently disabled daughter, not able to pay for the care my daughter needed and, at the same time, realizing my son and wife were dead. I tried to find other work, but with the horrible economy back then—between the War and no real system in place and not having a degree—I was lucky to hold on to the job I had. I did my best to take care of my daughter, but eventually, I decided it was better if she lived with my wife's sister in Maryland."

Chuck's voice trailed off. Patch waited for a long minute for him to continue. At last, Chuck sighed heavily. "I told you to be careful who you tell things to, and here I tell you my life story. What a hypocrite, huh?" Chuck said with a sad chuckle.

Both men took sips of their tea, even though Patch's cup had been empty for the last several minutes.

"The point is, there used to be some kind of safety net in this country, and lots of other countries offered even better ones than this one did. Governments used to provide that. Everybody paid into a pot of taxes, and some of that money went toward paying for healthcare, even if you didn't have the money to pay for it. There used to be options for kids like my daughter to go to school despite her health challenges, and maybe not too often, but sometimes, those kids turned out to be super successful. Although, much was stacked against them. That's the difference. No more safety nets. No more sense of the greater good."

Chuck and Patch sat in the silence punctuated by the occasional call of a bird or the far-off rumble of a truck on the far side of the river.

After a long time, Patch cleared his throat. "I had no idea. Thanks for sharing that. I feel a bit better, even though I feel awful about your family." Patch made a move to stand, but Chuck raised his hand, and Patch fell back to his chair.

"I really need to talk to more people. I haven't had much practice for a while. Forgive me." Chuck leaned forward and plopped both arms on the table. "Tell me about your mom," Chuck said with an inviting nod.

Words came rushing out of Patch's heart and mind and mouth in a way he'd never experienced before. He told Chuck the few far-off memories he thought he had of his mom. About how he found out that she had sold her body for him. Though, he still didn't quite understand what kind of life she had expected him to have with no one to take care of him after she was gone. He told Chuck about the betrayal he still felt from Malcolm not telling him that he had known about his mom's situation before Patch figured it out on his own. He talked a lot about Malcolm, actually.

Chuck listened intently to the rush of words and stories coming from Patch, recognizing them with the occasional nod or "go on."

Patch was completely spent by the time he had run out of things to say, or maybe he'd run out of the energy to say more. But for some reason, he also felt exhilarated, like he used to feel any time he sprinted along the crumbled pavement of the streets.

Chuck collected the cups and placed them in the sink. Patch stood and walked with Chuck to the front door. No words seemed appropriate or necessary. Chuck put a hand on Patch's shoulder and gave the slightest hint of a smile. Patch left the cottage with a wave, leaving Chuck with arms folded tight across his chest as if against a chill, even though the day was shaping up to be hot and muggy.

chapter 28

Gwen didn't expect a hero's welcome from the crews back at their headquarters, but she found it odd veering into alarming that no one came to check on her the whole time she was struggling with dizziness in the dormitory, which seemed a very long time to her. Of course, she knew from experience that time was finicky when she was hurt.

She finally felt stable enough to stand and take some unsteady steps out of the sleeping quarters, keeping half an eye on Alex, looking for any sign of change for the better or worse. She leaned against the bay of lockers that lined one wall for support.

When she got into the common area, she ran across people with downturned faces. There was an unusual quietness and stillness to the space, so unlike its normally bustling self. She tried to catch the eyes of anybody walking past so she could stop them and ask what was going on.

As her mind progressively cleared, she ran through the last moments she recalled from inside the soybean facility. The soybeans were burying Cecily and Alex. She got Cecily out and went back for Alex. She did chest compressions until her strength gave out, and then others picked up where she left off. Alex was alive, and she assumed that Cecily was okay too since she hadn't been in the dormitory when Gwen woke up.

So why did she get a growing sense of dread from the room?

At last, she found Gerty having a hushed conversation with a few of her farm operators. Gwen limped toward her, bracing herself against anything she could lean on for support, still not trusting her balance.

Gerty's face fell when she saw Gwen approaching.

"Gerty, what's going on?" Gwen asked, preparing for the worst possible news. Is Alex not expected to wake up? Did something happen to Cecily, and is that why she isn't in the sleeping quarters? Was the operation compromised somehow and the whole plan ruined?

Gerty took both of Gwen's hands and gently led her to a chair. She pulled up another chair very close to Gwen's.

"It's, Stan, Gwen," Gerty said.

Gwen didn't know how to process that. The words felt like a thousand needles had been jabbed into her chest. How could anything have happened to Stan? He had been safe, miles and miles away from the facility. He ran things from their operation headquarters in Topeka. He had been monitoring things. He had been so certain that there weren't any changes to any of the facility's systems.

Wait! That's not true. Reality dawned on Gwen.

When the accidental door-opening scare happened on the first day they had inspected the exterior of the facility, the operation had shifted locations of several key elements, including the location of Stan's surveillance. He had been moved to a van where he had his communication devices set up. That way, they could ensure that if any one part of their operations got compromised, the whole thing wouldn't be discovered all at once. Stan had joked about feeling more comfortable with the van life anyway.

Gerty waited for Gwen to process things in her own time, and Gwen finally looked up. "What happened to Stan?" she asked in a measured tone, trying her best not to scream in Gerty's face. One of her eyebrows started twitching, and she held her hands tight in her lap, afraid that if she didn't hold things tight, they would fall apart.

"When the drop hatch opened and the shipment of soybeans started crashing down on your crews, Stan had no way of communicating with us at the staging area because of the radio silence protocol we had agreed on. He must have watched on a dozen monitors while you-all desperately tried to get out of that main tank. Ultimately, he made a decision," Gerty said, pausing to wipe away her own tears as much as for Gwen to process what she was conveying.

"A decision? What decision?"

"He could stop the flow of soybeans at the click of a button, but he knew the consequences of doing that. He did it anyway. He stopped the soybean shipment, temporarily exposing himself to the farm's operation systems. I'm sure it took their systems seconds or less to locate where Stan's IP address was, even through any kind of virtual private network, VPN, he might have known how to rig up."

"Gerty, tell me what happened to Stan! So he got caught when he saved us by stopping the soybeans. Where is he?" Gwen yelled, springing up and feeling an uncontrollable surge of pain in her head and the strained muscles of her arms and legs. She crashed back down to her chair, writhing.

"Please stay still. Your body is far from healed, child," Gerty said, gently squeezing Gwen's shoulders and checking to see if she had injured herself any further. "We went by to check on him when he didn't respond after you escaped the facility and got back to the staging area. We found a capsule that a member of my crew has identified as a chemical commonly used to incapacitate and move crowds. It was used a lot in the early days of the Economic Wars. It's normally not deadly because people can't stand staying in the stuff or breathing it in for long. How long would you say you were in the facility after the soybeans stopped dropping in from the roof?"

Gwen ran through that sequence for a few seconds and tried to recall how long it had taken for her to do a hundred chest compressions and how long it took for her and Alex to be carried out. When she thought through everything, she was surprised. "It must have been fifteen or twenty minutes, at least. Why?"

"We're still trying to piece everything together, but our best guess is that Stan had to stay by his computer to fend off attempts to regain control and block him out of the farming corporation's systems. For those twenty minutes, Stan was breathing in toxic air that burned his eyes and exposed skin. Gwen, Stan is dead."

A flood of anxious energy rose within Gwen. Her mind started racing. Her fingers quivered. And that extra energy made it impossible to sit still.

She tightly wrapped her arms across her chest, so tightly that it made it hard to breathe, but she didn't care. None of it made sense. She and her crew, they were the ones in danger. Not Stan. Not Stan, who made her omelets and somehow made everything and everyone around him a bit better.

"I should have refused to go forward without better information. The old plan failed, and I knew this one was way too much like that one. I should have—" Gwen started to say, but Gerty stopped her.

"You can run through the what-if scenarios if you want. But I promise you, it won't help, and you'll end up with more questions than answers, and you'll probably be a whole lot more bitter."

"Do you think I give a damn about becoming bitter? Do you think I care about myself right now? God, Gerty, do you not know me at all after all this time? I'm nobody. I don't matter at all. It should have been me in that van, not Stan," Gwen said, quieting to more of a whisper meant for herself.

"I've lost people too. And, I know I joke about being mad at Stan for what happened to our nothing-relationship back in college, but he mattered a whole lot to me. He was an exceptional man. One of the best. And losing someone like that makes no sense because we don't know how to make sense of all the important threads tied to them. There is at least one good thing about the mess people like Stan leave us when they pass, though," Gerty said, pausing long enough for Gwen to look up curiously. "Those threads don't get pulled out. We get to keep them."

Gerty wrapped her long arms around Gwen's frail frame, and Gwen was grateful for the stability because her whole body quivered with rage and disappointment and fear and loss. After a long time, Gwen slowly pulled out of the embrace. Gerty stood, giving Gwen's shoulder a gentle squeeze.

"Oh, and how could I have forgotten this? It worked."

"What worked?" Gwen said, rubbing at her eyes.

"The plan. I set tracker enzymes in the genes of the fungus so we'd know where it was going and what it was doing. Stan covered his tracks enough that the farming corporation hasn't pulled the shipment you infested. Those blasted soybeans are getting distributed worldwide. Within the next couple of months, the seeds will be planted in places all over, and by early summer the farm corporations won't only know they don't have a viable crop this year, but any field seeded with the fungus will also be unusable for years to come. The spread could be pretty extensive. We did it, Gwen."

Gerty strode off, leaving Gwen with an impossible jumble of emotions. She didn't know how she should feel at the news of their success. But what she did feel was pretty empty, wiped out, and lonely. She was ready to go home.

And Gwen got her wish. She was amazed at the speed the operation pulled out. Lockers tucked into backs of trucks, cots placed back in carrier bags, and everything else got swept into trucks and vans over the next two days.

It was clear that the other members of the group were avoiding her. Not in an unkind way, but Gwen assumed that after everyone had said how sorry they were, they didn't really have anything else to say. Gwen certainly didn't have the energy or desire to launch into real conversation right then anyway.

Stan wasn't only important to her, she realized. He had touched everyone's heart and was better known by some of the group members than by Gwen. Everyone dealt with the loss in their own way, but folks who tiptoed past her and avoided eye contact anytime they saw her looking at them knew that she took it the hardest of the group. And that had little to do with the length of association.

I was the one who was under threat. Not Stan. That thought kept rolling around in her head, day and night, since she had gotten the shattering news of Stan's fate. How had she overlooked the now-obvious danger Stan had put himself in? Had anybody else recognized it? Had Stan been aware of what he was doing? Would he have done what he did had he known what could happen?

And the most pressing, nagging question of all: What could she have done in the end? When she was running her crew, she was aware that everybody was at risk, but she was in charge, and so she would do whatever it took to make sure her crew was safe. She had wrapped up all the risk she'd seen under her responsibility, had thought through every possible mistake she could see, and had worked out how capable she really was so she could show up the way people needed her to. But she hadn't shown up.

But she hadn't calculated any risk whatsoever for Stan. He was supposed to be tucked away doing a vital role, sure, but a completely safe one so that he would always be there to fix up a tasty snack and offer a listening ear. The more she thought about things, though, the tighter and tighter her chest got, to the point that she had to focus on every breath to ensure she pushed air out from her lungs and took in gasps of air in return. She got the sick feeling that, all along, she had assumed Stan would always be there for her. How well did I really know him, anyway? Could I have told anybody where he grew up or even if he had family somewhere? When had she ever really shown up for him? She swiped at the tears yet again welling in her eyes.

The last traces of their operation were taken out to the waiting vehicles, and the group got ready to load into the trucks and vans on their way back to D.C. But Gerty called the group together for one final debrief before departing.

"First off, I've got to thank you-all. We did it!" She shouted, throwing her hands in the air. The crowd let out sporadic, timid cheers that were stifled quickly when so few joined in.

"I thought so. It's such a strange thing. We had such a great victory, and we've also experienced such a wrenching loss. I know the tendency to kind of count that as a canceling-out of the two. That can leave us feeling pretty flat and empty. I'll tell you what, though, Stan would be yelling at us right now, if he were here," Gerty said.

Isolated chuckles spread across the group.

"He'd be yelling at us to celebrate the amazing work that we've done here. The two injection teams," she pointed to the general group of street kids and started clapping enthusiastically.

After a couple of beats, everybody else joined in the applause.

"And the communications team, and the operation management team, and the IT team, and let's not forget the cooking crew. I think I've had the best meals away from home over the last few weeks that I've ever had. Let's hear it for everyone!"

The applause got gradually louder, and people started to let out whoops and shouts so that by the time Gerty had mentioned all the different crews and teams that had played parts in the operation, the crowd was truly electrified. A thrill rushed through Gwen even in her lost and lonely state. It only lasted a few moments, but it made a shift in her despair. She still didn't know how she would ever feel good again, but at least, for the first time since Stan's death, she had a glimmer of hope and faith that she would be able to figure it out over time.

Gerty raised her hands above her head, and the crowd slowly quieted down.

"And so, I think it only fitting that, before we drop anybody off in D.C., we have a celebration dinner back at my farm to recognize the wins"—Gerty looked to one side of the group and then turned to the other side and settled her gaze on Gwen—"and the losses of this very successful mission."

Cheers echoed around the empty sidewalks of abandoned Topeka. With that, people loaded into vehicles and started the long trek back home.

chapter 29

Patch felt different. From the day he'd opened up to Chuck Mason, he just saw things differently. He had a driving focus and understanding that it was okay to feel like something was seriously unhealthy in the world he mingled with at school.

His first track meet following that conversation with Chuck went very differently as well, especially with the problematic 800m race. Patch had stepped into position, and even before the gunshot, his breathing was smoother and deeper, his mind was clear, his legs felt a renewed sense of energy and kinesthetic memory, and his feet discovered that familiar sense and reverence for the ground.

The gun went off, and Patch burst forward and around the first turn, being propelled by the strongest elastic effect he'd ever felt. He was far ahead of the pack by the breaking line, but Patch didn't pay any attention to where he stood versus his competitors. The concept of racing against himself had a totally new meaning for him now, so he focused entirely on the path in front of him and that was all he could see.

Even though the new focus gave him the urge to go all out during the entire race, he knew his coach was right, and so he followed the instructions his coach had given him with precision. He had plenty of energy at the homestretch to blow past the finish line like he liked to. He won that race by a huge margin, setting yet another school record. His team was thrilled. Malcolm had said how proud he was of him. But, somehow, for the first time, Patch felt like he was racing for his own reasons—not to please his coach or out of fear that Malcolm would decide he wasn't a good investment.

After that meet, Patch took a long shower and met up with Kourtney for lunch, then had tea with Chuck later that afternoon. It was strange to run after his meet, but he went for an evening jog around campus that night, just because he enjoyed running and the clarity it brought.

Coach Curtis tried to get Patch to explain what had made the difference between the inconsistency he had seen from Patch for most of the year and the steadiness of the last two months. The problem was, Patch couldn't explain it in words.

Once he'd discovered clarity about his life that had brought on his consistency. But he didn't know how to explain that to anyone else. Not in a way they'd understand.

Of course, he didn't have everything figured out. Questions like how people who had benefitted so much from the current system, a system that completely disregarded people like he used to be, could still be good people? He knew dozens of well-meaning, kind people like that. Will and Kourtney were like that. He couldn't label them as being bad people.

And he wasn't on the street anymore either. So how could a system that had given him such great opportunities be bad? Maybe it didn't have to be an either-or thing. Maybe bringing back some sort of government like the world used to have could offer more opportunities like the ones he was taking advantage of. He'd read about a thing called public school where every kid had a chance to be taught, no matter their abilities. Patch didn't know how he would set up a different system himself, even if he was given the chance, but he did know a couple of things.

He had to do something. He was convinced that people who worked so hard, like he knew Chuck Mason and Gino Pappas did, deserved some kind of safety net. They couldn't simply be discarded. Their families shouldn't have to be devastated when their health failed, or when their current services were no longer desired. Chuck had told him at one of their teas, which were becoming a regular part of Patch's weeks, that Harvard had kept him on because they didn't want to mess with renegotiating his contract. And Patch knew full well about the current system's devotion to contracts. He still had some questions about that and about the way so many other things were set up and why. But he was confident he could figure it out. He had one penetrating belief driving his thoughts and future plans. People mattered. He knew that much.

Patch continued with his thesis about trying to develop a new element to the supply and demand calculations with Dr. Bedford, but he also started an independent study about the lost potential that came from mismatched labor situations. He'd even coaxed Dr. Bedford into allowing him to incorporate that, maybe as an example, for his thesis.

Kourtney caught up with Patch as he was heading up to his dorm to pack his few belongings at the end of the semester.

"Hey, Patch!"

Patch turned around and caught an orange before it smacked him in the face.

"What the—"

"Show me how to peel it in one peeling?" Kourtney asked with a demure smile and a sly curtsy.

Patch flashed back to that first meeting in the dining hall. All those peeled oranges. So much had changed the way he viewed the world since then, but some very good pieces from back then were still in place.

"Of course. Happy to oblige, ma'am."

"Oh, don't ma'am me!" Kourtney said, jumping up to Patch on her tiptoes to land a kiss and take his arm to do a dance twirl. She fell back, and Patch caught her.

"Are you sure you'll survive the whole summer without me to keep track of you?" Kourtney asked, looking up at Patch while still leaning against his chest.

"I don't know. We'll have to see. But we can take it one day at a time, and you can tell me about your annual boat ride."

"It's not just a boat—"

"I know, I know. It's a yacht or a schooner or whatever you call a massive impressive boat."

"You're impossible."

"Yeah, I know. Come on. I'll show you how good I still am at peeling oranges, and maybe the dining hall has that disgusting probiotic yogurt you love so much. Time for one more school snack?" Patch offered his arm, and Kourtney gleefully linked hers in his, then dragged him toward the dining hall.

From the day he'd told her about his mom, Kourtney had been more than true to her word, too. She had that talk about his mom with him, but also several subsequent talks. He never felt like he had to convince her he was right, either. The conversations were more like sharing a world she had never known existed but one she was thrilled to explore with him. By the last few weeks of school, she was even talking about opening up art programs for street kids like Patch used to be.

"I mean, just think about how much better you would be now if you had been exposed to Van Gogh or Michelangelo?" she decided.

Patch let the condescending side of her compassion go for the time being. We're all works in progress, he thought. And it felt amazing to know he was joining forces with Kourtney rather than taking advantage of her connections like he had last year.

Things were more complicated with Will. There was a wedge that had been growing between them ever since Will had insisted that Patch introduce him to Chuck. Patch didn't know how to break through that wedge. A coldness that, at the start of the school year, Patch would have never believed conceivable had fallen over them. Patch recalled the last real conversation he'd had with Will.

"So I think we'll have to bookend this year," Will had said the morning of the start of finals week.

"Bookend? Like how?" Patch said, taking one more look at a formula, flipping several pages of a textbook back and forth on his tablet.

"You know that last-minute cramming is totally counterproductive, right?" Will said, jumping into his professor-like tone.

"Yeah, I know. You've told me something about how, by trying to add new ideas now, I'm actually ruining the more solid concepts or something . . ." Patch trailed off, losing the thread of the conversation, absorbed in the memorization of some supply curves.

"Very glad to know my wisdom has rubbed off so profoundly on you, Patch. Yeah, all you're doing now is trying to hold things in your short-term memory that you'll never hold on to with the pressure of taking the test. And since you're stressing your brain into remembering those things, you won't have the recall from long-term memory either. But carry on."

"Okay, thanks . . ." Patch said absently.

"And I think I'll start dating Kourtney and join a nudist colony in Borneo," Will said.

"Sounds good . . ."

"And your friend Chuck Mason has finally embraced the concept of pure capitalism," Will said with a raised eyebrow.

Patch's attention focused quickly after hearing, Chuck's name.

"Wait, what? What's that about Chuck?" Patch said, alarmed.

"Ah! You do have an ounce of attention for your longest friend here at school. Now that I have your attention, let's go back to the original point of this conversation with bookends."

"Right, bookends." Patch tried to turn back to his tablet and last-minute studying, but Will grabbed the tablet and tossed it on Patch's bed, then plopped down next to him.

"Seriously, we started the year on such a high note. With such a bang. What do you say we end it in similar panache?"

"Panache?" Patch said, confused.

"Flair! Exuberance! Definite confidence! All the best qualities to end a school year well lived, wouldn't you say?"

"I guess so," Patch said, noncommittally.

"Excellent! I'll do the decorating and food-gathering and music-selecting and the inviting. So basically, I'll do everything, and then you'll just have to bring your brilliant self. Sound good?"

Patch had nodded and figured he'd go to the party. At least for a while. After all, he figured Will would incorporate their dorm room into the party somehow anyway, so wasn't like he could go to bed early or anything.

Before, when he thought about attending one of Will's crazy get-to-gethers, Patch had always assumed the discomfort came from his own lack of social skills. But a few other things had clicked into place for him now. Though, there was one other question he needed to process for himself. How is it okay for some to have so much, while others have next to nothing, to no fault of their own?

Patch went to Will's party that did, in fact, use his dorm room as a staging area, but also included visits to the bell tower, cafeteria, main quad for howling at the moon, and woods by the river, where they played hide-and-seek. Patch was all but certain they would all be expelled at each progressively extravagant activity. On the last night of the school year, no less. He was very glad when the morning came without any notices on his tablet from the school. He wondered how much Will's parents would have to donate to cover the disruption this time. Based on the huge upscaling for this party from the last, Patch guessed they would probably have to donate a whole new building, at least. Maybe even a new department.

Patch packed his few belongings into his duffel bag. He tried to cover all his bases by saying goodbye to Coach Curtis, Dr. Bedford, Pete, Chuck, and even the sweet older gentleman, Chris, who offered him toast each morning in the cafeteria. Kourtney promised they would connect during the summer, though Patch doubted that would happen since she would be spending most of the summer in the Mediterranean.

"Studying the masters!" Kourtney had exclaimed with reverence and shaking with excitement.

Leaving the academy, he was grateful he'd have time alone during the short train ride back to Boston. He had so many questions to explore. So many messy thoughts and concerns to make sense of. Even his relationship with Malcolm, the one thing that had been rock solid around Christmastime had shifted. The feelings were the same, but they felt a lot more complicated. Patch certainly couldn't stomach another round of pickleball with the old men at the club.

But he felt confident that he'd figure things out with Malcolm. They had gone through rough things before, so they'd do it again. He found his seat on the train and pulled out his tablet. Out of habit, his eye went directly to the mapping app. He touched the icon to open it and instantly scanned over it until he found a certain geotag. The one that brought him a slight boost of hope and excitement every time he found it still activated. Gwendolyn Reynolds was still alive, and maybe they'd meet again sometime. He had thought about calling her so many times throughout the school year. He'd watched her geotag move so abruptly from D.C. to a random spot south and then to the middle of nowhere after that. Gwen must be busy trying to change the world. He didn't want to distract her from that, but he committed to reaching out to her once things settled down a bit on her end. He had a thousand questions about her group's revolution now that some things had become clearer for him, lighting his path forward.

As the train pulled into the Boston station, Patch pulled down his duffel bag and stuffed his tablet inside his backpack. He took the path he knew so well from the Cambridge terminal to the main entrance where he could count on Malcolm to be leaning against the front of his car, waving a friendly greeting and smiling.

Those are all very good things, Patch decided. He could figure things out from there.

Epilogue

The farm glistened in the late-afternoon warmth of the approaching summer. Trees were bursting with newly grown leafy canopies and the year's crop of vegetables had been planted deep in Gerty's special mulch mix. A cacophony of birdsong reverberated throughout the valley, and the walnuts on Gwen's secret hideout tree were wearing their thick green coats.

The first night they returned from their long trip to Kansas, no preparations for the party happened. Everybody went straight to bed. The next morning, however, the entire farm buzzed with anticipation and excitement. Meals at Gerty's farm were good under regular circumstances, but this feast was expected to be one to remember.

Gwen helped set up tables and chairs and then moved over to counting and sorting silverware, but once the actual cooking started, she escaped to her tree, knowing she would botch even the simplest recipe. She struggled with making proper toast, let alone a feast worth eating, especially since cooking brought back memories she'd rather avoid.

That morning, the view was particularly spectacular from her tree. Looking out from the comfortable perch on the thick tree branch, with her legs tucked in, she had a hard time believing that what she saw was real. A morning sheen of humid mist hung in the valley's bottom. There was an uninterrupted sea of green treetops that swayed ever so slightly in breezes far away from her.

Gwen heard a river flowing nearby that she hadn't realized was there. She was excited to explore that, but right then, she sat and thought and enjoyed the warm sunlight. Eventually, the sun would become oppressive as the full impact of the steamy, late-spring weather bore down on the farm. But, right then, she was grateful for the warmth.

She took off her jacket and let it fall to the ground, letting her exposed arms and legs soak in the morning sunlight. Only then did she allow herself to go back to the scene. Frantic flashes of the facility came back like a wave of nausea.

The smell of soybeans crashing down around her. The shrieking of thousands of soybeans striking one another rang in her ears. The suffocating dust. The visceral horror running through her as she realized that with the onslaught of falling soybeans, her strength wasn't enough to pull Alex free. Leaving him behind.

They're both fine. Alex and Cecily are here, and they're both healthy and alive. Somehow, that knowledge didn't transfer from her mind to her aching anxiety.

You saved them. You did your job. You did well. The thoughts hovered in her mind, but they weren't true. Stan had saved them. Sure, she might have been responsible for saving Cecily, but Gwen and Alex would both be dead if Stan hadn't stayed in that van. If Stan hadn't died.

Gwen had no idea how to even begin to pay forward a debt like that. She had seen plenty of death in her short life—far too much. But this was the first time someone she really cared about had died. At least, since her parents died. This was worse though because she had been so young then and she didn't have to live with the fact that her actions had led to their deaths. Because they hadn't. But they had led to Stan's.

If I had only called for the teams to abandon their packs and run sooner, or if I had been stronger, or if I had insisted on gathering more intel . . . There were countless things she could have done differently that would have led to a different outcome. But she had to face reality. Stan was gone.

Gwen took in a long breath and held it for ten seconds, then let it out explosively, letting the breath drift off into the clammy air. Despite all the misgivings and doubts circling within her mind like a black vapor, one thing was perfectly clear—she couldn't go back to Kansas and the way things were at Jefferson's home until she had finished what they'd started.

From all accounts, they had struck quite the victory. Food markets would be shaken and completely taken off guard. If people's food supplies didn't wake them up, she didn't know what would. And then they'd capitalize on that chaos to call for change. She didn't understand all of the particulars about their next step, but it was enough to know that Jefferson did.

Gwen now realized that, in losing Stan, all the relationships that were tied to him changed. Not necessarily in a bad way, but in a real and clear way. It was like waking up one morning around people she had known for years, only to have to jog her memory of how she knew them and then generate the familiar feeling of connection. It was easier to get back to a good place with Jefferson than with the others, though her relationship with him had shifted too. Thankfully, they were still close. In fact, in some ways, she felt closer to him, but things were complicated by the fact that it had been Jefferson's plan that led to Stan's death. She knew logically that Stan was a part of their movement for his own reasons, and she would never hold his death against Jefferson, but the inkling of resentment was hard to push out entirely.

And she didn't know how things would play out with Alex either. He and his crew would return to their market-building headquarters in D.C. in a couple of days, anyway. She and Gerty had encouraged them to stay and join Gerty's operation, but she and Gwen knew Alex's mind was made up. He was probably as eager as Gwen was for some sense of normalcy after the last few crazy weeks. She was pleased, at least, that he would be taking a large shipment of good potting soil and a load of seeds home for those planter boxes. And when he left, she was quite certain it would be with a hug and not a kiss. She still cared about Alex, but like with Jefferson, she hadn't found a pathway past the nagging thought that if he hadn't needed saving, Stan would still be alive and that the night's upcoming celebration would have a different feeling entirely.

Gwen climbed down from her tree, picked up her jacket, and brushed off a collection of moist, brown leaves. She had so much to sort through, but that could wait until later. It was time that she got back to the feast preparations.

Gerty had thought about every detail—candles for every table; volunteers to serve food and drinks so the group could focus on celebrating rather than waiting in line, buffet style; soft music wafting over the clearing; and good-smelling incense that mysteriously kept bugs away too.

When everybody was seated, Gerty stood and the crowd hushed the chatter to an excited murmur.

"I find it fitting that we're sitting and celebrating our success and those who made it possible in the very spot where it all started. It was just about a year ago that a headstrong young woman came with her trusty sidekick . . ." Gerty paused for the goodhearted chuckles to subside before she continued. "Yes, Stan was there too. It's a miracle I didn't kill him on the spot after how he'd snubbed me in college. But I can honestly say that, despite the messiness and disruption this year has brought my relatively safe and calm existence here at the farm, I'm glad I listened to you, Gwen." Gerty nodded in Gwen's direction, and the people around her leaned in and put their arms on Gwen's shoulder or squeezed her hand.

"Tonight, we all have reason to feel some hard and painful things. We will bear that weight for some time. But tonight, let's celebrate each other and the relationships that bond us to one another. Let's also remember the sacrifice and courage of those we've lost along the way."

Gerty raised her glass high, and the entire crowd did the same.

"Here's to friends with us tonight and those we still hold in our hearts," Gerty said resolutely.

There was a natural silence after the group sipped their drinks.

"Now, bring on the feast!" Gerty shouted, clapping her hands twice.

Fast guitar music kicked on instantly, and servers materialized from behind tents, bearing trays with the first course.

Gwen nearly went into sensory overload the moment the first course of roasted pear salad with candied pecans touched her tongue. So much good conversation, mingled with hearty bites of course after course. She didn't even know the names of the foods she was eagerly consuming—the meat that practically melted in her mouth with subtle sauces, the sautéed vegetables, the endless loaves of bread, all culminating in the dessert course of bread pudding in a banana sauce with freshly made vanilla ice cream.

Gwen had to admit—the night was fun. So much so that she almost forgot her worries and pain. Almost. She tried her best to freeze-frame that night in her mind so that no matter what challenges or future losses she might face, she could always recall it.

"It looks like you had a good night," Jefferson said from behind Gwen.

She turned and saw Jefferson's long silver hair that almost glowed in the bright moonlight.

"Yeah, way too much food. I'm sure I'll pay for it tomorrow," Gwen said, falling into step with Jefferson, both heading to the operations building.

"Wait until you get older. There are tons of new painful experiences in the world of indigestion for you to discover," Jefferson said.

"Great. Another thing to look forward to."

Both walked in silence with only the sound of their shoes squelching on the gravel and the call of an owl somewhere in the distant trees. Just before they reached their building, Gwen stopped. Jefferson stopped, too, with a curious look on his face. "What's up?"

"We did it, didn't we?"

"Yes. I think we finally have a clear win. Come fall, there will be some pretty major changes to business as usual in the food market economy."

"That's good," she said thoughtfully. She looked up at Jefferson. "You're sure it'll all be worth it?"

Jefferson took a long time answering, but eventually, he clasped Gwen's hands in his. "I don't know for sure, but I hope so. There's still a lot of work to do, but, yes, I think it'll be worth it."

Gwen nodded, and she and Jefferson walked into the warm pool of light inviting them into the building.

the end

About the Author

Chris Bentley is a District Ranger for the U.S. Forest Service. He received his Master's Degree from Indiana University's O'Neill School of Public and Environmental Affairs. Chris has written three books to date--*Running on Merit, Moments of Joy: Fifty-Two Ideas to Nurture Greater Meaning from Life*, and now *Soybean Revolution*. He lives in a small town in the mountains of Southern Idaho where he loves hiking and biking among the beautiful peaks and trees.

Start a conversation or ask a question on his website: www.chrisbentleyinc.com or email: connect@chrisbentleyinc.com. You can also connect with Chris through social media:

Facebook: @cbentley1160
Instagram: @christoph.w.bentley
X/Twitter: @chris1bentley2